BABAN

A ROUGHER TASK

DJG PALMER

CRANTHORPE
MILLNER
PUBLISHERS

This book is a work of fiction. Names, characters, places and incidents are either products of the author's imagination or are used fictitiously. Any resemblance to actual events or locales or persons, living or dead, is entirely coincidental.

First published by Cranthorpe Millner Publishers (2024)

ISBN 978-1-80378-197-6 (Paperback)

www.cranthorpemillner.com

Cranthorpe Millner Publishers

Printed and bound by CPI Group (UK) Ltd
Croydon, CR0 4YY

To Bob,

With best wishes,

Every war spawns heroes and villains, fame and infamy,
legends and stories. Some are true; some are the ingenious
blend of truth and fiction; many the wounded remembrances
of men who were there, clouded by the fog of war, the passage
of time, distorted in relation by those who were not.
This is merely another one.

From your 'neighbour'
DJG Palmer

XXIV

Dedicated to the memory of Major General AGC Jones CB MC “Uncle Tony” aka “Papa”. A promise to his late widow, surviving daughters, and granddaughter – kept.

Chapter One
England 1878

The morning was a fair one, it had to be said. Certainly lighter and a little dryer than it had been of late, yet far from seasonal, and anything but festive. For this was London in the grip of winter, and there was little or nothing of Victorian postcard ideology to suggest that the chilly streets, icy winds, and frozen puddles merited experiencing the cruel climate first-hand. The cold, grey heaviness of the last days of the year had fallen upon the unfortunate citizens without distinction, ruthlessly punishing exposed limbs, faces and toes; relentlessly compelling those who had doors to retire within them, and was characteristically merciless to those who did not.

For some, the privations of the season were easier to bear than others, although one would likely be hard pressed to have it admitted by folk in that soaking wet metropolis, as they bustled about with their hands in pockets and their chins in scarves. Some faces emerged to blow on frozen fingers, fewer to fumble about for money for the endless trickle of urchins and orphans rising out of dark, damp and murky corners like mucus from the nose of a frostbitten child. Admittedly, most of those poor wretches seemed to encounter less of the spirit of generosity than one might have expected from philanthropic Victorian society.

Despite the time of year, it seemed as though pity was for those who had time for it, and for the rest it was merely a pity.

The winter, having been harder in the city than usual, was felt by observers to have lowered the level of humanity amongst its less fortunate inhabitants.

There, a cry would sound from the bustling market street of the busy borough as a peeler or indignant trader set off in pursuit of some poor wretched child who, having swiped what they couldn't beg, now ran the gauntlet of offended justice. There, ladies in fine hats steered markedly clear of some old Chinese apothecary peddling potions, or some misfortunate old gin soak, calling out steps of her basement hovel, alternately pleading with the world for its understanding, or the value of a "medicinal" libation.

The black brickwork seemed to marry ill with the cumbersome silks and the pallid complexions of those preoccupied matrons, slipping and tiptoeing here and there, studiously avoiding the puddles of dirty water, the streaks of grime on the rusty iron railings. A black pall hung over the narrow streets, made narrower still by the abundance of stalls and barrows, while skirts trailed in water and the bottoms of trousers grew black from the spray thrown up from their heels.

Governess's led by the hand small children in pretty frocks or impractical white sailor suits that simply shone amid the drab greys and browns of the tenement street. Each one dawdled lazily behind their mentors, or struggled to get a proper look at the hustle and bustle of the rough and raucous market wherein the mongers cried out, and horses clopped hurriedly by, while bruised or damaged fruit and vegetables lay rotting in the gutters.

Just as one such neatly combed and costumed little child of a conservative five years was being hauled up along by the toes of his shoes, another boy of about the same age, dressed in ancestral hand-me-downs, clogs and an oversized cap, caught his eye.

They paused for a moment and smiled at one another. Wide brown eyes met blue ones, dark curls under the blue and white sailor's hat contrasting with the greasy, lank blond hair, the rings around the eyes and the dirt around the chin. The boy's governess, aghast even at so momentary a transcendence of the necessary gulf between such persons, physically hauled the small boy from the scene without a moment's pause for protest.

Such was this world, and through the smoky, smoggy cold and dampness of that drizzly scene – which the approaching season of Christmas seemed completely to have forgotten – the emergence of a decidedly different figure.

Dressed in a three-piece suit, with gloves, overcoat, hat, and cane, walked a young man, somewhere in his early twenties. He had a fine, handsome bearing, standing approximately five feet nine inches from his immaculately polished shoes to the smooth curls of collar-length bronze hair under the grey top hat. A broad pair of shoulders supported the elegant cloth of the expensive winter coat, and from the black velvet collar to the squared edge of the jawbone, a straight and noble neck; a sharp, well-trimmed, razor-sharp moustache beneath his perfect nose. He was to all appearances a fish very much out of water among the seedy, dingy tenements and the grim, weathered shopfronts and market stalls of the miserable area of the Capital. Yet his presence was significant, as his steady, dignified approach of the cluttered and shabby pawnbroker's shop on the corner of the street was about to make evident. With a last pause to ascertain and affirm the young man's fancy that he had not been observed – at least not by anyone of note – he took a deep breath and entered the establishment.

There was a rank, dusty and foreboding smell as he stepped gingerly through the door. Painted a dark brown on the outside, the place was no less dark and dismal within. There were bars on the windows, high shelves the length and breadth of the dirty floorboards, and from top to bottom the shop was crammed with the sobering relics of human desperation. Here stood an old clock, or hung some wretched garment, evidently the Sunday best of some poor man who could no longer put his Sunday repast on the table. There were piles of crisp white linen, which some sorry housewife must have scrubbed hard to buy and wept even harder to have had to pawn. Up above the counter hung yet more second-hand garments: articles of ephemeral, religious items of little or no worth, family silverware, and the various odds and ends of human misery, only parted from their owners by the direst of financial circumstance. Behind a desk sat a mean, wretched, little old man with a yellowing shirt collar, an eyeglass too small for his eye. He had a cruel squint, evidently the result of many years spent in his profession and the examination of the trinkets and valuables of the utterly desperate. Roused by the sound of shoes on the floorboards rather than boots or the bare feet to which he was accustomed, the old man looked up, squinted at the late arrival, and gave a gap-toothed leer of anticipation.

'Good morning to *you*, dear sir,' he crooned, with obsequious deference as he watched his prey approach the desk with considerable trepidation. Whether this boy was another toff shopping lowbrow for some cheap mistress, or some careless swell with a debt to settle and new to the business of credit without the remotest grasp on the values of commodities, he cared little. For either the smile, or sneer, was the same.

The young man offered no response, merely nodded his head once and removed, with his gloved hand, a small silken pouch, which the pawnbroker eyed with considerable interest.

Amongst the rubbish, faux pearls and paste gemstones in the cabinet sat one or two finer items. An amethyst set in a silver brooch sat beside a gold cross and chain. One further item caught the eye in the cabinet, however: a gold, half hunter, gentleman's pocket watch. There was no chain – the timepiece itself being attached to a silk tassel – yet demonstrating to the wary young man that this errand had not been in vain, and that the contents of his silk purse would not be unacceptable for the purpose of securing funds.

The old pawnbroker emptied the content of the pouch into his hand with a self-satisfied and decidedly sickening level of interest. A watch, this time a full hunter and of considerably purer gold than that of the pawnbroker's inventory, slipped shyly from its purple shroud. The pawnbroker leered. When the posh pawned, most valued discretion, even over price. At length, he looked up at the young man. Then he began to read aloud the inscription on the case. This irritated the young gentleman to no small degree, especially since the item in question had once been, as its sentiments declared, presented to him as a gift.

'To our son Albert on his twenty-first birthday, your ever-loving parents.'

Again, the young man nodded in grim acknowledgement, and the old man began to dislike his silence, which he took for aloofness.

'Inscription takes the value down,' the old man snapped. 'Mind you,' he added, recognising the insensibility of adding insult to injury to too great a degree, 'it's solid gold, and it ticks well.'

'Ticks well?' the young man repeated incredulously, adding more respectfully, 'Why then, my man, how much would you be disposed to offer for it? Rather,' he added with restraint, 'how much might you place against it?' The young gentleman was clearly nervous, disgusted by the whole business and probably quite unaware of the item's actual value in gold.

'Five pounds,' the old pawnbroker announced sharply. 'And if that's not enough, I must bid you good day, for it's all I have at present. Folks all... *placing*, never buying.'

The gentleman thought for a moment. Yet his apparent need for capital seemed to stifle his initial instinct to turn on his heel and depart, with his dignity intact. At length, his face fell, and he nodded in silent capitulation. 'Very well, man,' he replied quietly. 'Five pounds will be acceptable.'

'You know the terms?' the old man called after him, as he grimly pocketed the cash and made gloomily for the door. It was useless, for the young man had completely vanished.

The truth was, of course, that he knew from the finality of the young gentleman's miserable expression that he would not be returning to secure its release.

Albert Hugo Bond had, as the old man had observed, absolutely no intention of returning for his possession, one until this time in his life hardly treasured nor prized, but one among many fine and valuable items of property. Yet despite its price far exceeding the five pounds placed against it, and despite its sentimental value as a gift from his late parents, cash was cash, and both silver and brass watches both readily available.

Twenty-three years old, Albert was the only son of Sir Bertram Bond – owner of numerous textile mills and equipment manufacturers connected with the cotton industry

– and a recently commissioned lieutenant in the Corps of Royal Engineers. His father had inherited a thriving chain of businesses built up by his own father, Sir Albert Josiah Bond, prior to and during the Industrial Revolution of the previous century. Consequently, the Bonds had been a very rich family indeed, and one at the apex among the newer money of the county set of Yorkshire.

Educated to the highest affordable standard by his doting parents, Albert had left school and accepted a place at a good university, from whence – despite an apparent aptitude for literature and history – he had soon departed, leaving home to pursue other interests. Still heavily reliant on the generous allowance provided by his family fortune, Albert was nearly twenty by the time his father's decline in health found him obliged to request his son's return to Leeds, with a view to assuming the administration of the family mills.

Despite a lack of business knowledge and absolutely no experience of the textile industry, he managed to pick up reasonably quickly what the trade required of him, and even succeeded in applying some of his own ideas to practicality. Even so, the rapid decline in Sir Bertram's health had meant that no precautions had been taken for his indisposition, and consequently his son was forced to turn to the aid of a selection of highly dubious managers to provide the support he needed to run the business. This proved catastrophic for the firm's prestige and, despite the bravest efforts on Albert's part, the factories were forced to close, resulting in the failure of the firm to honour some of its commitments to some of its oldest established clients. Litigation followed soon after, and Bond found himself obliged to both lay off workers in the mills and consider the company's wider position in Yorkshire commerce.

All this took a terrible toll on the health of Sir Bertram, and in late September of that year, took to his bed with a respiratory complaint. He died a month later.

The following year was scarcely better. The death of so old and respected a figure caused even greater damage to the company's credentials, and Albert's relative youth and inexperience began to gain him a less than warranted reputation among his father's commercial circles. In November, Albert's mother, no doubt driven into a severe decline by the death of her husband of fifty years, and the slow cancerous destruction of the business which the Bonds had built over two generations, drove her to her own illness. The doctor diagnosed bronchitis and gave Mrs Bond a month to live. As it was, this was to prove optimistic, for she too died less than two weeks after taking to her bed.

Albert, bereft, alone, and increasingly mistrusting of counsel from those around him, became far too preoccupied by the loss of both parents to turn his full attentions to his litigant creditors, puzzling instead over the solicitors' gloomy summations that inexplicably left him the sole heir and beneficiary of loans secured against insurances, stock, and other intangible assets. The family's houses, as it transpired, were leased, and even personal and domestic expenses met through a business account.

Little could he have imagined it at the time, but more grief was just around the corner. In January 1876 the company's solicitors advised Albert to settle out of court with suppliers, to compensate clients awaiting unfulfilled orders and to carefully consider viability thereafter. The family houses were closed up, many of the paintings and carriages were sold and all but the most necessary employees received notice of their positions and, sadly, their tenancies. By the end of that, he was left with one remaining mill, no men to work the machinery, and little hope of a long-term future for the business.

Reluctantly, Albert was also obliged to relinquish the bricks and mortar, selling the equipment separately through a vending agent.

That was the final insult for a man who, despite his grandfather's humble beginnings as a clerk of works, had been educated in the finest traditions of the county society, and enjoyed all the luxury, comfort and indeed idleness that his family's former commercial success had afforded him. He had to give up riding, shooting, hunting and all other societal activities pursued by a young man of his class. The stables had to go, bloodstock sold on, and links with more than one notable and reputed family severed irrevocably. His friends also fell from him like leaves in autumn.

The sudden and catastrophic loss of his financial and social standing, married with the underlying stigma of his grandfather's Yorkshire origins, which had dogged him since his schooldays, finally came to the boil. Gossips gossiped; all but one of his tailors regretfully cancelled his account, and his club quietly requested that he resign, leaving him bereft of all but the mews house in which he lived, and one hundred pounds a week (that remained of the family's fortunes) with which to console himself.

One other thing in Bond's life which had been previously constant – his relationship and subsequent courtship of Miss Clara Vayne, daughter of the recently retired Colonel Anthony Vayne – inevitably suffered also. Although sufficiently satisfied by Bond's looks, cultivated class status and his family's former position in county society, both the colonel and his wife suddenly developed a disconcerting trepidation, no doubt fuelled by rumours and prejudice concerning the short-term lineage of the family Bond, and the courtship faltered for a time. Clara's girlish admiration, however, was not in decline. Blonde, pretty, sweet-natured and attentive, Clara was an intelligent conversationalist belying a hopeless romantic. She was utterly in love with Bond who, being handsome and seemingly worldly, represented the perfect potential husband. At nineteen years old, she was also one of the most remarkable beauties of her class and of northern England. Slim, elegant, and painted in nature's most pleasing manner, Clara had pale creamy skin, soft cheeks of the palest pink, the smallest, tidiest snub nose and the huge blue eyes of a china doll. Her hair was of a thick, golden blonde silk, and her lips were full, rounded and the gentlest shade of fuchsia. When she smiled, the whole of the room smiled with her, and her voice when she spoke was as gentle and mild as the quiet trickle of a crystal-clear stream as it flowed over pebbles. It had, in fact, been her suggestion that Bond enlist for the army, although the real reason for the advent of such a concept had more to do with bridging the growing gap between her father and her companion than any great desire to become a soldier's beau.

Even so, the pertinence of such a suggestion from one such as Clara could hardly be called into question, offering Bond the two things he now required of life: a secure and reliable profession in which to prosper and, most of all, the key to appeasing the colonel.

It would also be an advantage at this point to touch upon Bond's aunt.

Having no remaining family to speak of, and furthermore having always possessed a fondness for her sister's only son, Lady Agnes McGonagle set aside her trepidation concerning young Albert's subsequent choice of career and agreed to provide him with five hundred pounds for the meeting of his bills. This was fortuitous indeed and, although it was still insufficient to allow Albert to join a fashionable or prestigious regiment, he was able to enrol in the Royal Military Academy or RMA Woolwich, the college for officers entering Royal Artillery and Corps of Royal Engineers, known to students and professors alike as "The Shop".

Despite his lack of success with the lamented family firm, something in the Bond genetic make-up must have lent itself to the practical aspects of engineering. He prospered well, developing a distinct aptitude for all areas of the sapper's lot, as well as a good grasp on the merits and employment of artillery, fortification and construction, and the fervent desire to take up soldiering as a profession.

Thus, in September 1878 did Albert Bond pass out of the RMA among the top tier, enabling him to accept a graduate's first lieutenancy with the Corps of Royal Engineers, stationed at Brompton Barracks in the maritime town of Chatham in Kent.

Chapter Two

One might wonder why a gentleman on an officer's salary, with a property in London and a benevolent aunt, required indebting so personal and valuable an item in so furtive and humiliating a fashion.

The truth was, of course, that although the values of those portable commodities went some way to address the greater expenses, the small bills continued to mount. In fact, taking his third cab of the day from outside the George IV public house on Winkle Street to the slightly more auspicious destination of the gentlemans' tailors, he could not help but reflect upon how the fog and gloom of London reflected his own state of mind.

For years he had neglected that little place, owned by a bespectacled Yorkshireman who had made clothes for his father and grandfather; whose card had been pressed upon Albert when he took rooms in London, and whom he had subsequently thrown over for more fashionable, and expensive, tailors; the same tailors that had closed his accounts. Now, since officers were required to supply their own articles of uniform, and since the allowance provided towards the cost of equipping oneself by the army did not specify the supplier, Bond had cheerfully resolved to overlook the necessity of the excursion and turn the outing into a jaunt.

So, when he stepped in out of the drizzle, shook the rain from his coat and hat, and allowed the tailor's apprentice to remove his wet outerwear, Bond strolled smartly up to the counter and awaited the attendance of his old friend, like the proverbial prodigal son.

Upon seeing so familiar and previously extravagant customer of long standing, if lapsed loyalty, the tailor beamed approval over the top of his half-moon spectacles. 'Mr Albert, glad I am to see you lookin' so well. How you bin?'

'I have been well, thank you,' Bond replied politely. 'Although things have changed just a little since last we met.'

Here, the old tailor merely nodded, indicating to Bond that he knew all too well the problems lately besetting so good a customer. Waving away the attendance of the awkward young apprentice, he leaned over the counter in an air of assumed intimacy, and looked demurely at the damp and dispirited Bond amid the dark patches of rainwater he had trodden onto the rug. 'Words are funny things, lad. People say all sorts without being proper placed to do so.'

'I won't pretend, you know,' Bond sighed candidly. 'It's all gone, all of it. Mother and Father too. And the only thing left to me is the reason which brings me here today.'

'Oh indeed, Mr Albert,' sighed the tailor. 'I was right sorry to hear of your poor father. Talk of the county back home, so they write me. In Leeds too. Folk regarded him.' The old man smiled sadly. 'People just... forget, that's all. There's nowt personal in it. And he were a hard act to follow for a man of your youth. You've got to know where you are before you can properly begin in life.'

'I do indeed, and thank you,' Bond sighed.

He liked the sound of the old tailor's voice. The years of experience married all too well with the little round bespectacled face, and the sound of that honest accent was as comforting as sweet tea gurgling from the spout of a warmed brown pot on a cold winter's morning.

'Now the army's all I've got to hang my hopes on. If I don't do this...'

'Come now, you mustn't think that way,' the tailor remonstrated with him, as he unwrapped and presented to the young lieutenant his recently completed scarlet tunic, with handsome gold braid around the cuffs and collar and finished off in midnight blue silk velvet. 'If your poor father could only see you today, he'd be that proud of you, standing there in that uniform. You must know it?'

Bond hummed agreement, catching a glimpse of himself in the full-length mirror, set against the backdrop of oak panelling and the heavy rust drapes of the old established shop in which his grandfather had bought his very first tailcoat some fifty years earlier. 'These buttons... gold, or merely polished up as such?' Bond stammered in alarm. 'I mean, it's not that I can't afford... It's just that, well, the fashion is for silver.'

'Pinchbeck, Mr Albert,' the old man whispered tactfully. 'Read nothin' into it. We can expend a bit more on your captain's coat when it comes, eh?'

'Thank you,' Bond sighed in relief. 'I am trying my best, you know.'

'You'll be the smartest gentleman on the barracks, if I know you, Mr Albert.' The tailor chuckled blithely, as if their last conversation had not occurred.

Gold buttons they might not have been, but there was still the considerable cost attached to the remaining garments, boots, and denotations of rank to be considered.

These, when added to the costs defrayed by the army, and subtracted from the total to which he had added the value of his watch, left him in two minds whether to walk to the railway station. It would be an unpardonable indignity to have to enquire after credit, still further if he was to be refused, having admitted that his funds would only stretch to something more modest. Even so, he reflected, to return later for anything else he might have required was preferable to being visibly out of funds for the moment.

'Ah, I see you have an eye for those riding boots, Mr Albert.'

Bond thought for a moment, then the tailor seemed to read his thoughts, for he removed one boot from the cabinet, carefully removed the pinned label, and proffered the item for the officer to try.

'They're just my size,' the young officer observed.

'Do they fit?' asked the tailor.

'Well, yes.'

'Then they're yours for the same price as the mess shoes.'

'Please. It would hardly be fitting for me to accept.'

'Mr Albert,' gasped the tailor, raising both hands in a gesture of exasperation, 'please do not be offended. They were made for a gentleman adventurer who used to come in here on and off for a while. He was on his way to China and said that he needed a good set of boots to see him up and down those terrible high mountains over there. Destined for great things, those boots were.'

'As was I,' Bond replied morosely. 'Why then did he not collect them?'

The old tailor shrugged in response. 'Fell off a mountain, I suppose.' He sighed, adding, 'You wear them well, Mr Albert. You'll make us all proud someday, when I'll be able to look with pride at the *Gazette* and say to my boys that young captain bought his boots off of me all those years ago. Go on, take 'em, and I wish you the best to wear 'em with. Nice coat, young sir,' he added pointedly. 'I don't *think* that's one o' mine?'

Bond could only mumble his repeated thanks as the apprentice helped him back into the said garment, indeed from some more illustrious outlet in his heady, spendthrift days.

Even so, he paid for his remaining purchases, managed a tight smile followed by a bow, and sauntered off into the drizzly blackness of the dreary city from where he took a cab to Victoria, then a train to Rochester via Chatham.

So it was that a little after ten thirty that very night Lieutenant Albert Bond was to find himself walking up to the gates of Brompton Barracks complete with bag and baggage to be received with a courteous escort to his quarters, followed by the officers' mess. However superficially, his military career had begun.

Chapter Three

Barrack life did not always suit itself to some officers, especially those used to better, or at least since school days. Conditions were cramped, even at the engineers' depot in Chatham, and even though sappers were, like their officers, drawn from a better class of man, accommodation for both officers and men was best described as functional and rudimentary.

Even so, the British Army was entering yet another phase of reforms. Although greeted with some considerable distaste by the conservative high command, those measures seemed to have brought about a new military order in which the legendary scum-led-by-gentry of Wellington's time had been replaced by a more carefully structured, functional, and professional army.

Men were better fed, better trained and, for the most part, more literate than in previous years. Soldiers served a shorter period under the colours, and the system of throwing convicted felons into the ranks had also been recently abandoned. Officers too were cut from a more practical sort of cloth.

Edward Cardwell's army reforms had, after the disasters of the Crimea, resulted in the abolition of purchased commissions and, in turn, resulted in a more competent and less socially motivated caste of officer entering the army. Though it was still true to say that a private income was necessary to support an officer of any discipline, and despite the changes since the Iron Duke's time, much of the institutional social hierarchy still existed among the patrons of the mess, handed down in balanced measures of unconscious bias and learned behaviour among the officer corps.

Lieutenant Bond, in his first week at Chatham, managed to settle in quite well. There were the initial ceremonies and inductions to undergo, including the formalities of introductory drinks in the mess with field officers, company commanders, accompanied by the altogether more frivolous and bewildering – but no less expensive – riotous horseplay with the junior subalterns, all of whom exceeded him in seniority, according to the army lists.

Somewhat more sobering was the introduction to the non-commissioned officers, men, and operations of the company to which he was attached and his own troop within it. This included a truly bewildering immersion in the equipment, processes, and abundance of administrative paperwork that accompanied even the most minor daily task, action, or duty.

The barracks themselves were much like any other: grimy black brickwork, industrial casement windows and long, dark corridors, leading to cold, basic rooms. All in all, the place seemed a drab grey little world of mould and whitewash, where hard stone floors and communal washing troughs replaced washstand ablutions with a uniformity, utility, and a grimly invigorating hygiene. Soldiers slept seventeen to a dormitory, and the ever-present risk of boredom held at bay by a rigorous timetable of gymnasium, school room, chapel, and sports, not entirely dissimilar to Bond's own elementary education as a border.

It rained most of the time, and Bond, to his disappointment, found a notable dearth of interesting work. There were few inspections, even fewer parades. No one bothered to bring anything to his attention, and almost all but his direct contemporaries seemed to forget all about him after about a week as the new boy. In fact, the only person of commissioned rank he seemed to spend any real time with outside the mess during those early days , was his new friend and company commander, Captain Westgate.

Warren Hyde Westgate was a sapper officer in his late thirties, considerably older than Bond, and a professional military engineer of relative anonymity. Even so, he loved to talk about riding, shooting, and all the things that he had not the time to do, and for which Bond had not the money. In consequence, the two officers got on extremely well together. An Irishman by birth and early upbringing, Westgate did not regard Bond with the same unconscious caution and even awkwardness of some of his RMA contemporaries, having worked his way up as an educated lower middle-class professional. Consequently, the two men spent considerable periods of time talking together, and Bond began to form the opinion that Westgate was the man of whom to ask things.

One morning, he managed to catch up with the captain between rain showers. The thick black clouds had rolled away, revealing a remarkably blue sky. Bond, who could see the officer inspecting a chestnut mare from his tiny office across the courtyard, took occasion to leave his desk and seek a consultation.

The rain still glistened on the red roof tiles of the stable block, while the puddles on the cobbled floor of the courtyard reflected the pale winter sun. A chilly breeze swayed the trees behind the barrack buildings.

Westgate greeted him with jovial cordiality. 'Albert!' he beamed upon seeing him. 'Have you seen this horse? Arrived just now.'

Bond feigned interest for a moment. 'Absolutely.' There followed an uncomfortably long pause before simple embarrassment necessitated the resumption of Lieutenant Bond's uneasy monologue. 'Look, Warren,' he resumed, still a little gingerly. 'I've been doing company paperwork since I arrived and, since I'm getting to grips with it, I feel the clerks are taking more time showing me than I am doing it and... well, I was wondering if there was any other useful occupation that I might turn my hand to?'

'Anything else?' Westgate thought for a moment. 'D'you know, Albert, I don't think there is. Why, fed up with inventories, are you?'

'Well, to be truthful, yes.'

'Why not go home, then?'

'Warren?'

'Go home!' Westgate repeated cheerfully, with such heartiness that Bond mistook his candour for sarcasm.

To his surprise, however, the captain proved to be quite sincere.

'What about that young girl in town I heard you mention when you got here? Don't you see anything of her anymore?'

'Well, we've written but...'

'There you are, then,' Westgate told him gently. 'Take yourself off for a couple of days and visit her at home. There's plenty for you to do when you get back.'

'Warren!' Bond persisted, as the company commander smiled, and resumed his tactile wrestling match with one of the horse's fetlocks.

'Do you mean to say that it is quite in order for me to simply come and go, just like that?'

'Why ever not?' smiled back the captain. 'It's not as though we're at war or anything, although since we're on the subject, and before you disappear for the day, d'you think you might fetch the sergeant over here? I need this wretched mare shoeing properly before she's fit to ride, and I can find neither corporal nor sergeant anywhere!'

Bond nodded in stunned silence, then set off for the direction of the barrack block within which he knew the troop sergeant to be billeted. This was to represent the first proper meeting between Bond and the senior Non-Commissioned Officer – NCO, the highest ranking enlisted soldier to be under his command, though very much his own senior in years and service, and one that would formulate and underwrite his subsequent career.

The sergeant in question was in fact one Ludo Erasmus Friday. The son of a soldier, and he the son of yet another soldier, Friday had the thin red line running through his veins like the muddy waters of the mighty river Medway. In the same way as some aristocratic families produced dynastic sailors, soldiers and explorers, Friday's lineage produced sergeants. There had been a Friday in the British Army for as long as there had been a Friday in the week, he was fond of saying. Friday was in fact the tenth in a line of non-commissioned officers to bear the name and the third to serve amid the ranks of the Royal Engineers.

A bald-headed, yet heavily moustached and whiskered sapper of indistinguishable middle age, Friday was alarmingly prone to eccentricities, episodes of mania, and even attacks of outright insanity which only his rank and status forgave.

He would often walk about in parade order and patrol the streets for drunken sappers, whom he would march back to barracks to drill until the small hours of the morning. This, as well as being well known as a man who did not hold with liquor, the music halls, or the public house, gained Friday a reputation among successive batches of interns as something of an erratic disciplinarian, and a man not to be trifled with. He was also a noted authority on the men themselves, being able to ascertain within a moment of meeting a man if he was to be trusted; how well he would lend himself to his duties and even, it was rumoured, how brave in battle a man might be. It was on this basis, and in such circumstances as those already set forth, that Lieutenant Bond happened to wander into the elongated main barrack room of the sapper's accommodation block, just as Friday was giving very short shrift to a handful of recently passed-out recruits.

Watching the proceedings with silent fascination, Bond remained for some moments in the doorway to observe for himself the merits of this so much talked about non-commissioned officer.

Friday was just in the process of inspecting a particularly well-constructed young sapper, when a quiet tap of Bond's shoe on the floorboards alerted the scrupulous sergeant to the proximity of his new officer. Bringing the men to attention, the stalwart NCO proceeded to undo, in the blink of an eye and with a mere few words, all the respect and admiration Bond had previously held for him. For Sergeant Friday had a significant problem, a blight on his progress through the senior ranks of his profession, and one which must have made him so hard amid the slums of Chatham as to send him understandably mad.

An abnormal defect of his vocal cords (of which he seemed blissfully unaware) leaving him with a shrill, and decidedly emasculating high-pitched voice might, were it not for his stalwart reputation, have reduced all above and below him in the ranks to a state of helpless hilarity.

Bond, who had already been reduced to a state of severe discomfort by this terrible shrill squeak, was now faced with the unenviable task of retaining his composure long enough to address his sergeant in front of all the men.

With an effort, he managed to squeeze out that he needed to speak with him in private, and that the men were to be excused for the present.

'Very good, sir,' Friday replied, executing a smart about-turn and dismissing the contingent of sappers, who were either too canny or too scared to exhibit mirth at the unusually high tone of his voice.

Just as they were filing respectfully past him in the doorway, Bond's eyes met with the young soldier whom the sergeant had been scrutinising. They looked at each other for a moment, then the lad looked away again, as if checking himself in the presence of an officer. Bond turned back to Friday.

'Sergeant, Captain Westgate needs a couple of men to help him with his horse. See that he is obliged, will you?'

'Yes, sir, right away, sir,' he replied, catching hold of the last two departing recruits. 'Smith and Farrier, report to company commander... at the double!'

The two soldiers snapped to attention, saluted, and took off across the rain-soaked parade square.

'Sergeant, we haven't been introduced.'

'No, sir,' Friday replied abruptly.

Bond groaned inwardly. That voice would be the death of him. 'I'm Albert Bond. I came down from Woolwich last week,' he explained.

'I know, sir,' the sergeant replied. 'Fourth place at the RMA. Congratulations. Ludo Erasmus Friday, at your service,' he added, followed by a sharp salute.

'Ludo?' Bond found himself repeating.

'Ludo,' Friday nodded .

Oh dear, Bond thought grimly. *This enterprise will not be an easy one.* 'Oh, Sergeant,' he added as an afterthought, 'Captain advises I shall require a batman.'

Friday simply nodded once again.

Not exactly lyrical, Bond reflected, but maybe that was a good thing, under the circumstances. 'Oh, help me, Sergeant, do!' he groaned at last, after a short and even more painful silence had passed between the two of them. 'You see, I'm not at all familiar with these things. I don't know how to get a batman; I don't know how much I'll be expected to pay him. I don't even know what exactly it is he's supposed to do for me, beyond the usual domestic fatigues, I mean.'

Again, the sergeant simply nodded, and Bond had to be satisfied with the assumption that his request had not fallen on deaf ears. As events were soon to prove, he was not to be disappointed.

The following day, when Bond finally thought he had got the ringing out of his ears and returned to his normal state of sanity, he was once more sitting in his cramped little office when there came a knock at the door. Not being in any way a born clerk, and having only just finished fiddling about with the hook and eye fastenings on the front of his navy patrol jacket, Bond was almost thrown into panic by the sound of *that* voice, somewhere in the corridor outside. Almost spilling the ink in his pot, the young lieutenant scrabbled about to make his desk look officious, and his work look as engrossing as possible, before summoning his visitors to enter.

'Good morning, Sergeant Friday,' he observed, praying that it might not be necessary for the NCO to respond verbally.

On this occasion, and to his surprise, however, Friday entirely obliged him. Silently, he saluted, shifted into a credible left turn within the tiny space betwixt door and wall, and motioned for another without to enter and present himself. To Bond's surprise, it was the young sapper with whom he had exchanged brief glances in the barrack room.

He was indeed a very different sort of article from the thin, pallid juvenile, the meagre services of which he had expected his pittance would buy him.

The lad stood five feet six off the ground. A strong, broad pair of shoulders supported a short neck; a youthful, angelic face, clean-shaven, with a button nose and sparkling blue eyes that creased at the corners when he smiled. Any tiny traces of adolescent disruption had rapidly given way to the buttermilk smooth skin and the emergence of shaving stubble on the lower jawline, which was keen. The flawless forehead curved up under the silky curtain of smooth, straight blond hair, a strand of which seemed to have escaped from the band of his navy cap. This, he removed, and bowed his head slightly, affording Bond a view of the left side parting in his hair, and those plaintive eyes as they peered searchingly through his fringe.

'Sapper Coleman, sir!' Friday's shrill pitch announced perfunctorily.

To Bond's renewed surprise, the young soldier then gave one of the most warm, endearing smiles he had ever seen in his life before, his thick lashes curling as his face lit up with the greeting. It was rather as if it had broken out involuntarily, and the officer at once found himself disarmed and fascinated.

Privately, he was rather relieved that Friday was looking at *him* the whole time, as he was sure the lad would have received a rollicking for such unsolicited familiarity in the presence of an officer. He found himself smiling back, albeit momentarily, until he remembered himself and hastily sought to assume an air of benevolent formality.

Clearly unafraid of the mad staring eyes of the looming NCO, the young soldier seemed nevertheless to take the cue. The clear, sparkling blue eyes just seemed to shine back at him across the desk as the boy checked himself, resumed "eyes front" and the face settled into a calm placidity.

Without even speaking, the smiling face just seemed to radiate humanity and endearment, seeming to Bond almost to overlook the setting of the encounter, at once transcending the rank of the officer. The boy's subservience was undeniable and his posture rigid, yet the inner warmth and ease was somehow at odds with martial discipline.

It was a smile that looked as if it couldn't help but happen, sweeping across the whole of the boy's face, candid, genuine and utterly captivating.

'Sapper, dis-miss!' With that, Friday's second shrill interjection utterly shattering the momentary silence of their strange meeting, Bond and Coleman could only look and one another, staring into each other's eyes so fixedly, so as not to end up laughing. Sergeant Friday, presumably convinced that the young sapper's presence had affected the officer's temper, sharply gestured for him to leave the room, and closed the door behind him.

'Boy suitable, sir?' asked the sergeant, clearly pleased with his selection of candidate.

Bond, who was still completely overwhelmed by this new and alarmingly distracting visitation, could find no words with which to answer. As it was, the bewildered sergeant became so concerned for the officer's state of mind that he almost left the room in search of the barrack chaplain, before Bond was able to recover his composure and return to the matter under discussion.

'I'm sorry, Sergeant. Please continue your appraisal. I shall be extremely glad to listen.'

Here, Friday peered at him for a moment, and then nodded confidentially. 'Friday's eye, Mr Albert, sir. Friday knows what's best for his officers.'

'Yes, I am quite sure of it,' Bond replied. 'He has quite the most engaging personality. How old is he?'

'Strapping lad of eighteen, sir,' Friday replied. 'Caught the eye of his corporal first day of training, he did. Ten weeks' training. He was a favourite of the barracks. Best of the older boy recruits I've seen, sir.'

That was something indeed, although Bond was still of the opinion that such a promising intern would be more likely to go to a more senior officer than a newly qualified subaltern, especially one who was short of money. 'How is he as a sapper?' Bond enquired. 'Physically able, is he?'

'Best sapper in the batch, sir,' Friday continued. 'Strong, healthy boy, and bright with it. He's honest, with a good eye for his work, and a smart, healthy, promising lad, sir. God fearing, too.' Friday added the last aside with a confidential murmur, accompanied by a knowing nod which implied that he thought the officer would understand the nuance entirely.

'Excuse me?'

'Lad's popular,' Friday elaborated. 'Eye-catching in his uniform and about town. Don't matter. Boy's firm in his abstinence. Rejects temptations – harlots.'

'Harlots?' Bond found himself parroting.

'Yes, sir. Maids, shop girls... hussies. Lad resists all of them.'

Bond, himself not as worldly as he would like to have appeared either, nonetheless detected the subtlety and acknowledged the NCO's appraisal. Whether the boy's described virtue might be better attributed to Christian principles, or more realistically exhaustive army duties around Brompton, he certainly had the chapel-going sergeant singing his praises and believing in his piety and forbearance by whatever means.

'Now tell me, Sergeant, what was his occupation previously? And quite how did the army come to obtain him?' Bond continued.

'Pot boy, blacksmith's apprentice and labourer,' Friday replied, adding quietly, 'Fell out of work about a year ago. Very down when I found him, he was. Attended a chapel school 'n all. Knows his letters, sir, and his bible. Very willing to work.'

'Found him?' Bond exclaimed. 'Where exactly did you find him, Sergeant?'

'Gutter, sir.' A short silence ensued. Friday appeared to muse, recalling the boy's antecedence. 'Run over by a carriage, he was,' the sergeant resumed after an agonising pause.

'Really?' Bond replied airily, but his head was most definitely elsewhere. It was the voice that was doing it, he decided. It *had* to be. 'Odd way to recruit, Sergeant.'

'Sir?'

'From the hospital?'

'No, sir, from a lad,' Friday explained, even more slowly.

'My apologies, Sergeant, but the accident, or the enlistment?'

'Yes, sir.'

'Which?'

'Both.'

'Pardon me?'

Friday looked pained. 'Friday working back, sir,' he explained, seemingly to his own mind with patient restraint, despite what he clearly regarded as his officer's obtuseness. 'Chapel school when he was out of work... on account of the soup. Accident when he was little.'

'Well, he certainly isn't little now,' Bond observed, still trying to dispel the remarkable influence of the young sapper's presence on his oddly conflicted sense of anticipation.

As a graduate at Woolwich, he had been schooled to look out for a wise, time-served old sweat to serve as a batman, a commodity that might have proven quite as valuable in terms of insight into the ways and means of home service, as a good NCO in the field. Yet Bond habitually valued smart, pretty things over functional ones. This had been borne out in his tastes in clothing, lodgings, and furnishings. Even his entry into the military had, notwithstanding the academic and physical rigors of the academy, been principally about dressing in a gold laced tunic with a socially respectable facing colour on the cuffs and collar and redeeming his standing in society. He would ride back to Clara – or perhaps equally, or even more so, to her father the colonel – on a good-looking horse and with a young, good-looking batman in his thrall. If the boy could polish the odd boot and stitch the odd button, not to mention mend and maintain kit on a budget that would do, too.

RMA cadets were trained much harder than infantry entrants, and for longer, the payoff being a commission at full lieutenant in the engineers. Yet somehow Bond had come out of the process craving validity as a soldier as well as the status of an officer. From this one meeting, something about the boy had exuded just such a soldierly quality, despite his youth, status or his angelic looks.

'I fancy I might pass a word more with the lad, Sarn't. What was his name again?'

Chapter Four

As it turned out, and as Lieutenant Bond was to remark on many a subsequent occasion, the credit by which Sergeant Friday had come to deserve his reputation was well and truly borne out by his selection of Coleman to serve as his batman.

It was true indeed that at a mere four years of age, John Jacob Coleman – Jack as his mother had always called him – had been knocked down and almost killed by a coach and four. Even so, and despite the thrift doctor's predictions of a life of weakness and ailment, young Jack grew to be a healthy, industrious, and extremely fit adolescent.

Having been forced to abandon his rudimentary Christian education to pursue work in the slums of the maritime town of Chatham, Jack had, as Sergeant Friday was able to inform Lieutenant Bond, seen service as both a pot boy and a blacksmith's apprentice. At the age of fifteen, Jack had been forced to leave the already severely impoverished home, which he shared with his mother, and seek work in and around the naval dockyard, upon which the Medway towns depended for commerce.

This, despite being an environment noted for poor conditions, long hours and horrific industrial accidents, afforded the youth an opportunity to entertain thoughts of travel, adventure, and fortune overseas.

Consequently, when the work as a labourer finally ran out and left him both jobless and destitute, bright young Jack began to wonder about a life on the ocean wave.

Then, having been roughed up by some sailors outside a public house, Jack was saved from charges of affray by the strange, wide-eyed, bald sapper sergeant, who fed him without liquor, and entered in his mind the notion of enlisting. Friday, who had always possessed a sixth sense for what made good soldiers, and in particular good sappers, took care to point out to Coleman the danger and tedium of seafaring; suggesting that he join the army instead.

The army was still the last resort for those too poor or desperate to find any alternative employment, but Jack found himself drawn by the strange soldier's combination of flattery and storytelling, and in due course was passed fit for training at the corps' depot, right there in Chatham.

For the first few weeks, officer and man learned everything together. Indeed, it was true to say that Bond, with his two years at officer training school, was possessed of a little more aptitude for military engineering than his enthusiastic young batman, but Coleman was a sapper after all. Shifting, trenching, digging, and looking after Bond were his duties, and for his part, Coleman got on excellently with all of them. He cleaned Bond's only set of riding boots, polished his pinchbeck buttons so that they gleamed like the gold they were not, and generally looked after things to such a degree that both officer and man began to get noticed as a very promising pair.

Lieutenant Bond was left free to deal with the unreasonable mountain of paperwork provided by officers with a more colourful social lifestyle than his own, and Coleman benefited from the officer's generosity, albeit severely tempered by his financial situation.

Jack seemed to understand this, and whenever Bond was late in paying him, whenever an article of his apparel had either to be repaired or replaced, the young soldier always took care to see that his officer's purse was spared as far as possible through discretion and instantaneous loyalty. Perhaps an upbringing of renting rooms by the night and meals on tally by the week had instilled this forbearance, but who could say?

In return, Bond saw to it that Jack was taken care of, removed from the crowded barrack block that he shared with seventeen others, and located in a smaller, more convenient billet, nearer to the officers' quarters.

Porridge, bread, and bully beef was the principal mess of other ranks, but Jack seemed to do well on this, and Bond did his best to see that the separation in their respective stations was not so great as to isolate them from one another socially.

On one of the increasingly rare evenings when Bond found himself disposed to enjoy the amenities of the officers' mess, he was sitting at the bay window overlooking the garden and engaged in conversation with his friend and brother officer, Lieutenant Gideon Knight.

Promotion for officers in the Corps was a slow and trying business, being achieved on attainment of seniority on the army lists rather than the merit of the individual.

Though commissioned at full lieutenant, a sapper might expect to wait up to twelve years for promotion and, in some cases, even though some officers were recognisably brilliant, many never saw the rank of captain until early middle age, if at all.

Despite this, at the age of thirty, Gideon Knight had succeeded to the position of senior lieutenant, and company adjutant. A handsome, amiable young man with dark hair swept off either side of his forehead in a centre parting, a fashionably curled moustache and deep, quizzical brown eyes, Knight had earned the admiration and respect of his contemporaries at the RMA by coming second in his class. The grandson of a peer, a good oar and member of the corps' eleven, Knight was a classic example of a Victorian subaltern, wearing his dark, wiry sideburns and the gold crowns on his Prussian blue collar with equal and deserved satisfaction. He smiled at Bond and sipped his port wine with the educated palate of yet another son of the Emerald Isle and who, like his company commander, viewed his brother lieutenant without the customary class consciousness of Sandhurst graduates.

'Papers are still full of Africa,' he observed, idly folding his newspaper with a smart crease, and handing it to the waiting Bond. 'It looks as if the new high commissioner's appointment has brought matters to something of a head over there. Oh, Albert, perhaps I'm being short-sighted in saying so, but the scuttlebutt does seem to be making rather a lot of a tiny corner of the Empire, which is to my mind insignificant, and of no real value whatsoever.'

'I don't know about that, Gid,' Bond observed in response. 'It says here there are diamonds in the disputed territories, and the Boer trekkers seemed keen enough to settle the area than simple grazing land would imply.'

'Well, it's going to take a lot more than one battalion of a county regiment to make confederation a plausibility,' Knight added, sipping his wine, and accepting the returned journal from Bond's outstretched hand. 'If you ask me, they'll need transport systems, proper roads, pools of ethnic workforces and a good deal of proper technical application to make South Africa a workable Imperial asset. They'll call for the corps soon enough, Albert. You may have no fears about that.'

'Absolutely, and the sooner the better,' Bond smiled wryly. 'A minor altercation on the other side of the world is exactly what I could do with at the moment.'

'D'you hope to get a brevet?' Knight enquired politely.

'Not before you, Gideon,' Bond chuckled amiably. 'If anyone's likely to come back from Africa a captain, it's you.'

'I don't know,' the other mused stoically. 'Seems like very little to do for a star to go with my crowns. A warlike little tribe with a kingdom only a few generations old making the odd border raid and unsettling the colonials, I should liken to attacking a city militia.'

'We'd have more work before us in Afghanistan, Bond observed in reply.

'The Zulu kingdom is something of an unsettling influence in an otherwise stable South Africa. Always remember, Albert, our presence out there was not the result of direct invasion, nor was it brought about entirely by the Boer and his complete refusal to accept the reasonable constraints of modern society concerning slavery, confederation, and so on. No, Albert, we have only the foothold in Africa that the various peoples who populate her coastal regions permit us, be they British, European, or even African. Once they see and welcome the progress we offer, the further in we go.'

'I doubt whether the African would concur with that abridged precis,' Bond replied argumentatively, though he didn't altogether know why.

'Never forget,' Knight resumed in a placating manner, 'that it is those very same peoples indigenous to the areas surrounding Natal who find the ever-present threat of hostile brother Zulu almost as entirely unsettling as the white colonials. The Zulu king must allow his warriors to wash their spears, be that in their blood, the blood of their near neighbours, or any other poor devil who arouses their indignation. If you were the king of the Zulu, Albert, which do you suppose would be your chosen target?'

Bond thought for a moment and shrugged. 'The weakest link in the chain, I suppose!' he replied stoically. 'There's Warren Westgate. Why don't we ask him?'

'Well,' Knight called across to the captain, as if he had been privy to the conversation they had already passed, 'what do you have to say to all this business, Warren?'

'What, Africa?' Westgate replied, raising an eyebrow, and scratching his neatly combed and parted blond hair for a moment. 'Too little room for too many interested parties to quarrel over. A lot of long, hard work and a career move of little prospect.'

'You think it inappropriate, then, that we be sent out to reinforce the colony?' Knight retorted in surprise. 'I'm mildly put out by you, Warren.'

'Not so, my dear chap, you quite misunderstand me.' The captain gave a curt smile. 'On the contrary, I should say that a second field company being sent out to remedy those terrible colonial roads and to try to impose some sort of structured transport system would be utterly beneficial.'

'Who to? Us or them?' Bond enquired.

'Both, I should say,' Westgate concluded. 'Someone will have to look to it sooner or later, so it might just as well be us fellows. Now, as you both well know I subscribe to a liberal conservatism. As well as the moderation of Christianity, we do not conquer to enslave, but to enlighten, to refine. King Shaka's empire – the Zulu nation we know to hover on the borders of Natal and annoy its citizenry – never built a road, or laid a railway to my knowledge, so we have that to our credit, at least!'

Bond and Knight assented heartily, and Warren Westgate poured himself a measure and settling down in his accustomed chair by the marble fireside. 'I must say, I admire your tailor, Albert,' Westgate suddenly announced, as Lieutenant Bond rose to his feet in search of a stopper for the brandy decanter. 'Where were you measured for that delightful mess frock?'

'Oh, a chap in town,' Bond coughed in embarrassment, not liking the subjects of clothes or their cost when trying to relax of an evening. 'Dressed my father.'

On full dress uniform, both Knight and Bond wore the universal devices of rank on both cuffs and collar, the former being denoted by lengths of gold braid, formed into an Austrian knot embellishment for officers with the rank of lieutenant. On the other hand, a captain's rank, such as Westgate's, was signified by a similar device, while a field officer such as a major or colonel was denoted by further embellishment.

For this reason, officers engaged upon daily duties in the more practical undress regulation, tended to wear their rank about their wrists rather than their necks.

Denuded of the appropriate amount of braid, but not the crowns, Bond's coat had formerly been the property of a now retired lieutenant-colonel, hence its quality.

'I have told you before, Albert,' Knight chided, 'one only wears one's symbols of rank on dress frock order, not on the patrol jacket, nor on a knee-length mess coat. Suppose someone were to mistake you for the colonel?'

'Fine chance, the state of my things,' Bond retorted.

'It's all very well for those of us who have several sets of uniform for work and ceremony, and who've been here so long as to be recognised by the troops, clerks, townsfolk...'

'Gentlemen, gentlemen!' Captain Westgate intoned. 'Please remember, Gideon, that this is all quite new to Albert.'

'Thank you,' Bond interrupted, earning himself an irritated look from Knight, and a reproachful cough from the ever-patient Westgate.

'One also has to remember,' Westgate added, in mock severity, 'that certain members of this mess have been here a sight longer than some others, and that junior officers should sit back, hold their tongues still a while and accept the advice of senior prefects.'

'Such as?' Bond rejoined, this time with a little circumspection.

'Pour the brandy,' Knight suggested jovially. 'That's enough scorn for poor Albert this evening, and quite enough lectures from you, Warren.'

Westgate feigned a look of martyrdom. 'Even my wife disobeys me,' he lamented with a ghost of a smile. 'So how can I expect to maintain the behaviour of my subalterns?'

'Drink,' Knight replied. 'Grog us into anything, eh, Albert?'

'Sounds fine to me,' Bond replied.

Then, changing the subject very neatly back to war with the Zulu king, Bond asked Captain Westgate if he believed they would be mobilising soon.

'Well, the lieutenant-general's forces are in a pretty dire state out there,' he mused, striking a match and lighting his pipe. 'From what we know of Zululand, the roads are in a worse state than those in Ireland. There are rivers aplenty that will of course be in full swell at this time of year. They will need to construct forts.'

'Seventh Field Company is out there already, isn't it?' Knight asked Westgate, as the two of them shared a match.

The captain nodded assent. 'They were deployed to build gun batteries on Table Bay to keep the Russians out,' Westgate explained. 'Word is that a war's expected at any time now, and

Her Majesty's Government has already undertaken to send reinforcements, despite there being far more to worry about in other parts of the Empire.'

'Well, then?' Bond persisted. 'Do you think we'll get to go?'

'In an answer, yes,' Westgate replied. 'Now, I suppose one of us had better sign for the bottle.'

Bond froze and contrived to look distracted. Luckily, Knight acknowledged, and summoned the mess steward before their new brother officer's reluctance to accrue debt became self-evident. Thus the weeks rumbled on, and eventually, in late November, the word came through that they were to sail for Africa.

Bond, Knight, and Westgate were understandably excited, and not remotely nervous.

For a professional soldier fast approaching middle age as was Westgate, the prospect of taking command and having the responsibility of a field company in enemy territory, even if it was only Zululand, presented a path for opportunity and advancement.

Having been married several years, he secretly hoped to return to England with a brevet majority, maybe even a confirmed one, and see himself well placed in his long-term career. In either circumstance, no one ascended by remaining in barracks the entire time, especially those already halfway through their service careers.

Gideon Knight also held out hopes for brevet promotion, aiming to secure a captaincy and the first foothold on the ladder to the eventual division that Westgate had generously and enthusiastically predicted for him when first he had taken command of the company.

For Bond, however, the need was much simpler. He wished only to serve a short stint in a minor foreign conflict, return home in one piece, and marry Clara with a service career behind him. True to say, the possibility of a promotion had not failed to occur to him, although in truth, all he really wanted was to prove himself.

Whether to his father, his mother, Clara, her father, or even just to himself, he wasn't sure. Even so, he knew there was nothing else.

Chapter Five

On one of the more reasonable mornings in November the rain seemed to be holding off, and Bond was preparing himself for an inspection of the men by Captain Westgate, when there came a knock at the door.

'Morning, Mr Albert, sir!'

It was Sapper Coleman, complete with steaming hot tea in one hand, and a letter in the other. He proffered both at Bond, who was in the process of grappling frustratingly at arm's length with his boots, while trying to shave himself *and* see over the top of his buttoned-up dress frock. He seemed to be going a rather bright shade of crimson, which clashed most unfortunately with the cloth of his coat.

Coleman immediately got down on his knees, exchanged the shaving tin in Bond's hand for the tea, and rather haphazardly attempted to help the officer get his boots on. 'Not my place to say so, sir, but shouldn't you have put your coat on last, maybe?'

Bond looked even more embarrassed for a moment, and then he just smiled. 'If you breathe a word of this you'll be mucking out for a month.'

Coleman looked at him, utterly nonplussed.

'I didn't mean to do it, but I was trying the jacket on for size. The trouble is, it's so damned new and stiff that I couldn't get the buttons undone again. Would you believe it, I've still got my nightshirt on under this wretched garment!'

Coleman looked plaintively through his fine blond fringe for a moment, eyes fixed. Their noses were only inches away from each other now, and both seemed clearly to see what the other was thinking by the depth of colour in their brilliant blue eyes. Only when Bond started laughing again did Coleman allow a smile to creep across his own lips, creasing up his bright blue eyes in the corners.

'Oh yeah, I've a letter for you here, sir,' Coleman added, disengaging from what he was doing and neatly changing the subject by handing his officer the envelope.

'Really? And did you write it yourself, Jack?' Bond inquired.

'No, Mr Albert. Someone else must have.'

'Oh, I see,' Bond replied. 'But your writing is still coming along, is it?'

'Yes, sir,' the young soldier beamed proudly. 'I've written three pages since last time you helped me. I'm going to keep a diary now, I am,' he added, blushing slightly.

'That's nothing to be embarrassed about, soldier. You're improving all the time, and if you're good enough to eventually start keeping a diary there are so many things that might become open to you when you leave the army.' *That was tactless*, Bond thought suddenly.

The truth was that Coleman, having only just obtained his education certificate and passed from basic training to a real working troop with mates and a gymnasium, was in no hurry for retirement or discharge.

As if to compensate, Bond suggested that Jack read the letter he had brought. Knowing it wasn't from Clara by the writing on the envelope, he wasn't unduly bothered who it was from, or so he thought. Besides which, there was very little that he kept from Coleman anyhow, and it couldn't be anything terribly serious, otherwise it would have arrived by telegram.

When Jack's fingers had broken the seal, however, and the first line of the correspondence was read out to him, Bond let out a gasp of horror and snatched away the paper as if it were on fire.

Jack, sufficiently taken aback by the ferocity of Bond's change of humour to physically recoil, returned just as suddenly to his normal, unflappable self.

There was a short, painfully silent interlude before Bond invited Coleman to resume assisting him with his preparations.

It was not until much later that day, when Bond was on duty checking the sentry detail that the young soldier broached the subject again.

'Mr Albert,' he said cautiously, 'I know it's none of my business, but did I do wrong by reading that letter to you?'

Bond thought for a moment before replying. He did not particularly wish to share the story, but then again, Jack was always so good at making him see things in a different light by looking at them from his unique, untainted point of view. *Too good sometimes*, he reflected. 'When I was at the academy,' Bond began, 'I received a letter from my uncle in the Ninety-first Regiment, just as he sailed for the Cape.'

'Ninety-first? The Highlanders?' Coleman beamed, clearly pleased with his guess.

'Oh yes, it is indeed the Highlanders,' Bond sighed, the stress of a thousand jibes still resting heavily on his brow from his time at the RMA.

In fact, even as they spoke, Bond's uncle was already established in-country.

Captain Alec Wilbur McGonagle was a staff officer and questionable war poet, whose period of service in the Indian Army had been instrumental in blighting his career and leaving him effectively marooned in the Imperial Army and at the same rank he had held at the age of thirty. Now past sixty, McGonagle had to be content with being discontent at his lack of progress in life, and as if to compensate had taken to writing a series of critical pamphlets on the military establishment, which he published under his own name. This, perhaps understandably, drew acidic backlash from the higher echelons of the army, and meant that, if his promotion prospects had not already been very firmly capped with a lead turban, they most certainly were by the time the most scathing of his papers had been published. Censure and rejection only served as further provocation to McGonagle, who drew heavily on his experiences in India, which he believed held key implications for all aspects of colonial warfare around the Empire and refused doggedly to be quieted in his outspoken and increasingly rebellious opinions. He published theories and hypotheses relating to the wearing of khaki uniforms, which had been adopted in India, and during the Abyssinian expedition, but still considered quite improper for universal introduction. In addition to this, he argued constantly with his superiors and even wrote open letters to newspapers, criticising the short-sightedness of the high command and attacking continuing influence of the late Duke of Wellington on the army's evolution. This was the final insult and considered quite beyond the pale by many at Horse Guards. There were widespread calls for McGonagle to be cashiered and dishonourably retired, though some among the press and in radical politics supported his views. Many called for his resignation, and in 1877, one of his pamphlets was burned outside the Royal Academy at Woolwich, the same academy at which his nephew was a junior cadet.

While Albert might have wished to keep his association with the McGonagle family a secret, he had regrettably shown one of his uncle's letters to another student some months before the Iron Duke article had appeared in the newspaper. Before he knew it, Bond found himself the butt of the dormitory, and there were even dark murmurings about his future career being affected. This was the last straw for a young man who had almost lost everything anyway and, in July of that year, Bond abandoned his loyalties and wrote to the principle of the RMA distancing himself from the captain and condemning his pamphleteering. His familial disloyalty nonetheless purchased his reprieve, and respite from the dogma for long enough to engage with, and immerse himself in, his studies.

It was not until he had passed out of Woolwich, securing a good place and consequently a place in Engineers' lists that he even took to reading the letters that McGonagle had continued to send him since their public disagreement some months earlier. Even so, the indignity heaped upon him due to the old Scot's ramblings meant that it was not until November 1878 that Bond even entertained the prospect of reconciliation. As it was, he had waited until Sapper Coleman was well out of the way on errands for Sergeant Friday before he sat down in a quiet corner of the mess and read his uncle's letter. The points contained in the correspondence were, in fact, most useful to a junior subaltern in his position yet Bond, who could still see red over the academy business, hurled the letter out of the window after skim-reading the contents. It was only when he made the mistake of telling Coleman, who subsequently ferreted the flowerbeds and braved the mud (not to mention

Bond's chagrin) for the letter, that he actually took the trouble to read it over in full.

The contents reflected McGonagle's knowledge of Africa with suggestions on precautions to be taken to ensure the health and wellbeing of his men; justifiable warnings concerning scorpions, and points relating to sanitation, water sources and soldiers' diet.

It was also true to say that, despite the old captain's very public fall from grace, he was still an officer with considerable experience overseas, and thereby privy to important intelligence and information bandied about between his many fellow veterans of India.

Whether he was passing on this information to prove his ascendancy beyond his modest rank, whether it was an act of deliberate belligerence on McGonagle's own part, or whether he just didn't care, Bond was in no position to tell. All he knew was, at that point in time, the last thing he needed was the embarrassment of his associations with the man dubbed "that damned Indian" by his colonel becoming widespread public knowledge.

The storms in this part of Africa are sudden, unpredictable and tumultuous, his uncle's letter told him. Fords, it seemed, might be impossible to cross for weeks on end. Mountain streams were liable to overflow and flood both roads and crossing points. Engineer officers would, it appeared, be obliged to go on ahead of a column to ensure that it was possible to cross rivers, no doubt getting shot up and murdered before the infantry had turned so much as a hair behind them. Same old story, he reflected wryly, albeit with the wisdom of inherited prejudicial insight.

Captain McGonagle's letter went on to illustrate in graphic detail how, if he wished to earn the respect of his men and the skill of his profession, Bond would be obliged to get stuck in when engaged upon anything menial, which Bond knew well already. *This from an old school, purchased-in infantry officer*, he thought.

The letter continued with much more of the same, recommending the various ways in which an engineer officer should tackle his duties, approach his men, and generally conduct himself when in a foreign country. This Bond deemed to be quite unnecessary, and in fact highly offensive to one such as he who had been bred and educated in the respectable middle-class traditions of the English church. For a Scot to be giving him advice on conduct, Bond found disagreeable, but for an officer who had bought his captaincy thirty years earlier to be lecturing a qualified, professional RMA graduate such as himself seemed really to be the very height of farce.

Indignant, Bond decided to share his feelings with the only person whom he knew would not make judgements: Coleman. Bond confided in the young sapper one night as the two of them were wandering round the stable block, checking on the horses.

'It's so difficult to talk to anyone else, Jack,' Bond grumbled. 'The old boy is my uncle, but he's so old he can't possibly know better than the professors at the academy.'

'He is a captain, Mr Albert, sir,' Coleman ventured cautiously. 'And he is very old.'

'Yes, very old... to be a captain thirty years later,' Bond carped back at him. 'I mean, it's not as if he's exactly advanced himself beyond the promise of his youth or anything. Warren Westgate was thirty-three when they captained him, you know, and that was without purchase!'

'Maybe he just wants to help you, Mr Albert,' Coleman suggested, with even more trepidation than that with which he had made his last suggestion, for he knew Bond was in a mood.

'No, Jack, it will not stand. It's unconscionable!' Bond continued, with such ferocity that he even made one or two of the horses jump back in alarm as he trailed his baton along the painted iron railings, as the two of them ambled down the long, repetitive avenue of stabling berths under the twinkling November starlight.

Pausing for a moment, Bond searched out a small cigar from the pocket of his voluminous greatcoat, and asked Coleman to light it for him. 'Do you smoke, Sapper?' he asked, as Jack clumsily struck the match, fumbled about with the lighted cigar, then let out a belch of choking blue smoke as the tobacco successfully ignited between his lips.

'No, sir!' the poor lad gasped, coughing, and spitting as the vile taste of the rolled leaves lingered on his pink tongue and robbed him frustratingly of speech for some time.

'No taste for it?' Bond queried, blowing a satisfactory ring of smoke over the blond head of the convulsing young soldier, still bent double with the exhalations of his heaving lungs.

'No, it's not that, sir,' Coleman continued to bark disjointedly, although it was obviously not the taste that agreed with him. 'It's just that I never had spare for anything other than eating before I joined up.'

'Carry on being my batman, you'll soon acquire the taste,' Bond smiled generously. 'It's like brandy, or liquor. You'll either develop a palate for one or the other. You might even prefer to smoke a pipe.'

'Yes, sir,' Coleman coughed agreeably. Privately, he was utterly resolved that the only smoke he ever wanted to taste again in his life was from the breech of a rifle. Yet he was also very aware that Bond was, in every way his superior, and he wanted greatly to learn from him the graces of the socially advantaged. He smiled, thanked his officer kindly, and waited until he had turned away before blowing the appallingly noxious weed in the direction of the tethered horses, who seemed to like the smell even less than he did.

The two of them passed the remainder of that night in the usual way, wandering among about the sentry boxes, examining the store buildings and supply depots to ensure that all was well, before retiring to Bond's quarters just outside the barrack block for an evening beverage and a final farewell until morning.

That night, however, they were joined on their lonely vigil by Sergeant Friday who, being unable to sleep, and having observed with some satisfaction the fruits of his careful husbandry of both officer and man, decided to accompany them for the remainder of their patrol.

'Evening, Sarn't,' Coleman smiled, snapping his heels together as the familiar bald head glowed back at him through the lantern light.

'Evening, Mr Albert, sir,' saluted Friday, turning to acknowledge Coleman only after dutiful obeisance had first been observed.

It was a well-suited practice, Bond decided. He had his brother officers for company: necessary shoptalk and estimable company by day, and the more permanent, subordinate company, council and, on some occasions, consolation of his sergeant and his brilliant boy batman by night.

In fact, the more night duty Bond was given by Captain Westgate, the less he seemed to mind missing sleep and patrolling around the dark, gloomy, and decidedly spooky corners of the edifices of the brick barrack buildings. The gas lanterns gave very little in the way of either heat or light, and Bond was not so empowered by his new uniform and status not to hold a healthy reservation for the uncertainties of night and darkness.

Even so, he reflected, *what a fine set we must make walking up and down in that deserted parade square, I wrapped up in my voluminous greatcoat; Sergeant Friday beside me in his elevated status as senior NCO, red sash across his chest and a heavy stick under his arm; young Coleman, dressed in a serge jacket, with the neat little sapper cap perched on the top of his straight blond hair, transformed to an ashen white in the ghostly winter moonlight*. For just that moment, as the three of them walked along, sedately approaching the gates and the sentry box, they might all three of them have been generals, lone commanders of some silent, spectral army, seen only by their mind's eye, and never to be heard by others.

They said their goodnights at the gate. Sergeant Friday paused to inspect and relieve the sentries at their posts, while his officer and star recruit marched quietly off into the absorbing, inky blackness, far away from the mischievous flame of the flickering lantern light, left behind to play its relentless game of cat and mouse with the shadows beneath.

The next morning saw Bond woken decidedly earlier than usual – not by Coleman with his usual mug of tea and hot shaving water, but by the excited and decidedly animated spectacle of Bond's friend, lieutenant and adjutant Gideon Knight. Bond greeted him with an enthusiasm that he considered appropriate to the hour.

'Not so many oaths from you, Albert!' Knight bantered cheerfully. 'Second lieutenants should be seen and certainly not heard swearing at their friends.'

'Bunkum!' Bond responded scathingly. 'There is no such thing as a second lieutenancy in this corps, or what did I study for two years for if not a crown instead of a pip? Anyway, what on earth can you possibly want at this hour, Gid?'

'It's marvellous, Albert. They're talking about nothing else all over Chatham.'

'What are you talking about, Gideon? And where on earth is Jack with my shaving kit?'

'That is *just* what I am trying to tell you, my dear ignorant Albert!' cried Knight, adrenaline and enthusiasm clearly getting the better of his patrician upbringing. 'Westgate got his orders in the early hours of this morning. We are to proceed to the camp at Shorncliffe. It's Africa, Albert. They're sending us to the Cape!'

'By all things... Jack!' cried Bond, leaping out of bed, furiously sweeping his smooth bronze locks behind his ears with his fingers, and checking his appearance in the gentleman's glass on his dressing table. 'Where are you, boy?'

'Haven't you been listening, Albert?' Knight laughed uproariously. 'They chucked him out of bed about an hour and a half ago. The whole company's being mobilized for the move to the transit camp. Beards will be permissible by the time your boyish fur starts to show, my friend, for we're off, Albert. We're going to play our little part in a little war on the other side of the world! Isn't it just the best news?'

Bond gazed vacantly at the image in the looking glass and laughed mechanically. 'We're off to war,' he repeated to himself. 'You, me, and everything we've learned! Gideon,' he added, as the beaming officer assisted him with his preparations by whipping up lather on his shaving soap, despite their discussion of beards, 'Do you think it would be quite proper for me to go about unshaven?'

'My dear chap, it's the done thing on foreign service, and Warren and I shall do so.'

Bond smiled amusedly. 'Then I might just do it, too. Come on, Gid, there's just time for me to order myself an Adams from the gunsmiths if we hurry. They can send it on to Shorncliffe if they've a run of orders. It's about time I thought about going prepared.'

'Shouldn't think you'll need it, old boy,' Knight chuckled in response. 'One look at those bags under those evil red eyes of yours and the Zulu will be off like a shot!'

Chapter Six

From that moment on, there was precious little time to sit and worry about the implications of their impending active service.

Bond, as one of two junior lieutenants in the company, was absolutely snowed under with the paperwork, stock checks and itinerary that such a transit necessitated.

Stocks and stores had to be checked and packed away, rail travel had to be organized, and there were any numbers of preparations to be made for the horses, troops, and equipment to be got safely on and off the ship at either end. Queen's regulations concerning livestock were almost as rigorous as those concerning the welfare of the men themselves. Specifications stated that a horse was to be given an area of no less than one hundred and twenty-five feet on board ship, while officers should expect a cabin allowance of one hundred and seventy-five cubic feet. In the case of officers sharing, such as Bond and Lieutenant Knight, the cabin space was required not to fall short of two hundred and seventy-five cubic feet, while a sapper or private soldier could expect a less generous allowance of fifty cubic feet when billeted on board ship.

Coleman of course was not apt to complain about privations, but there were many grumbles and murmurs from other 'old sweats' in the company who believed that they were observing a return to the dark days of the Crimea and feared being loaded onto the ships like cattle into crates.

Even so, they seemed to manage tolerably, and Bond even succeeded in dumping a good deal of his work on an academic brother lieutenant who, lacking Bond's personality and good looks, seemed to compensate with a very high boredom threshold.

Consequently, when Bond decided it was time to take a cab into Chatham to collect his revolver from the local gunsmiths, it did not take him and Gideon Knight very long at all to persuade the aptly named Earnest Penfold to complete the bulk of the paperwork in their absence.

Since Warren Westgate had been given only one day's notice to report to Shorncliffe Barracks in Hythe, speed was very much of the essence.

Fortunately, he had two well qualified young officers in Knight and Bond, the former being adjutant and excellent at his job; a stalwart sergeant in Ludo Friday, and a complement of reliable NCOs and a few experienced sappers to keep an eye on the new recruits. As it turned out, Captain Westgate need not have worried. By ten thirty that morning, Sergeant Friday was able to report to Lieutenant Knight that all was ready for the off, and that the men were fallen in for the short march to the railway station from which they were to embark.

It was a wet, miserable, and urbanised vista which met the eyes of the younger men and their officers as they marched off for the first time to embark upon a journey to a strange new land with all the promise of adventure, peril, and uncertainty.

The weather had kept most people who might have turned out to see them off under normal circumstances, well and truly indoors. A few old mothers in their tatty working clothes, a few old widows in their black shawls, and a handful of old men in medal ribbons crowded into the lea of the great bridge which straddled the banks of the river, but most remained at home.

The year 1878 had not been one of great or spectacular change on the banks of the Medway. The busy naval dockyard was still the main provider of employment and related commerce in the maritime town. Soldiers and sailors still pursued that love-hate relationship shared between society and the bully-boy elements of rank-and-file, who drank hard and swore even harder, yet never failed to turn up week after week and spend their wages in the public houses.

The truth was of course that the town itself was reliant upon their own 'scum of the earth', be they land or sea-going, to provide the merchants, peddlers, and liquor stores with a steady trade during the winter months. There were always dark murmurings among the folk of a garrison town, although the sapper could hardly be tarred with the same brush, considered as they were to be cut from a better sort of red cloth to their infantry brethren. It was also well known among the Chatham folk that the senior barrack sergeant was a man of strict Christian views concerning liberal entertainments, with a reputation for keeping both indiscipline and vice very firmly at bay. The local borough constables were more in awe of Sergeant Friday than of their own police sergeants, and prostitutes who would heckle and argue with coppers betook themselves to the shadows when the bald sapper NCO marched past the flop houses and brothels. The Christian man was not above raising a hand to any woman.

As they trooped down the cobbles of the cluttered streets from which cellar windows peeped at angles from beneath the stone steps of the sloping gutters, the sappers could feel nothing if not a little sense of pride in that town; the town that had been home to so many of them for so long, some for as many years as they had served, and for many as long as they had lived.

In Coleman certainly, this sense of pride in ownership pervaded strongest. For he was a Chatham boy, born and bred, and the very life blood of the mighty Medway flowed through his veins like the fresh river air that tinted his glowing cheeks and blew about his smooth blond hair. As a boy he would stand and watch the river for hours. He stood upon her banks and gazed with half imagined notions of glory and adventure into the great and tantalizing unknown. For him the adventure was surely to begin as soon as he embarked upon that ship for so distant and wondrous a land, too far flung in a corner of the Empire for the imagination of a poor lad from the backstreets even to dream of, let alone travel to.

Yet he really was to go... just as soon as they boarded that ship.

From then on, the whole town just seemed to fall away beneath their feet – rambling, ramshackle and whitewashed shambles of weatherboard terraces still burning gas lanterns, and swathes of washing crammed into backyards and side alleys, which groaned and staggered its way towards the very source of its existence: the mighty River Medway.

Cradled in the geographical epicentre of a community that relied solely upon it for wealth and prosperity, the great river stretched below the town, spread across the landscape like a giant silver serpent, either bank apparently teeming with the various activities associated with so vital a commercial highway. Chatham had been a maritime town since time immemorial, even before the Corps itself had existed, and Coleman knew it would remain that way long after he was dead.

The truth was of course that Chatham had not been

nearly so good to young Coleman, or indeed to any of them as nostalgia would have had them suppose.

The fights, the drunken brawls of a Saturday night, and the stink of vomit in the blocked gutters of the fearful slums seemed almost forgotten as they said their unspoken farewells to the town that had, in whatever way, made them the men they were. For if only by poverty, desperation, and hunger, it had made them into soldiers for their queen, and by hook or by crook, the rhythmical tramp of boots on the cobbles was their strange, indirect means of offering their thanks.

For the officers as much as for their men, the feeling of adventure and excitement pervaded, especially for Lieutenants Knight and Bond. For Earnest Penfold, or indeed Warren Westgate, some might well have wondered. Yet for the most part, their image was one of might and anticipation; a red-coated procession of youth, strength and readiness; a time that all ranks felt surely must see them triumph and prosper in their new and thrilling careers, the coming of the time of their lives.

It was with mixed emotions of sorrow, pain, and yet somehow great relief that Coleman recognized his mother to be absent from the company of well-wishers and spectators sporadically lining the route to Chatham station. What he did not know (indeed could not have known) was that the poor woman had had every intention of seeing off her first born. Indeed, she had been there well in advance for the first of them.

Even so, the sudden sight of Warren Westgate and Gideon Knight rounding the corner on their splendid horses suddenly sent a thrill of anxiety up the poor woman's spine. Did he really want her there? Could it be that her presence might make him wish his very mother away... or worse?

The reason for her uncertainty was simple, for as the column of sappers tramped steadily on, past the calling children, the clattering horses and carts and the seedy tenement blocks, they had inadvertently wandered past the King's Head. The public house had acquired something of a reputation among the people of Kent, and indeed of England, as a house of some ill fame and notorious repute.

For Coleman, that place was an anathema to his strangely concrete and deep-rooted convictions. He hated the thought of women, especially his own mother, selling themselves to soldiers, sailors and dock workers for money, and the thought that one such villain as those might well have been his own father was enough to make him wretch.

Friday also let out a hiss of derision and disgust, fuelled by rumours of the grim and sordid establishment. Yet in no way could he have known the truth behind the stony expression of the normally cheerful boy who now marched beside him.

It was a truth that hurt, a truth that could not be washed, polished or beaten from the smooth skin or firm muscles of the young sapper. Back in 1858, just after her father had been committed to St Mary's Prison on the banks of the Medway, seventeen-year-old Gladys Coleman had changed her name to Joy and took to working that very house. This, the poor young soldier knew, and this he tried so hard to forget as he marched steadily past, teeth clenched and grinding, fighting to erase the notion through pain. He also knew that by 1860, when that house and all its sights were disposed of for ever, Joy Coleman had a small place as a singer on the music hall bill and a baby son watched over in turn by friends, or anyone else she could conscript while she earned. Yet, when Jack had been born, so great was the happiness of the mother at the cheerful little scrap of blond hair, blue eyes, and magical smiles that the poor woman knew there was something left to her of the handsome sailor who made him.

It was those eyes, so wistful and jaded, that searched the streets and pavements for sight of the woman who bore him, and the woman who, despite the shame and scandal surrounding his birth, he still knew had suffered hardship and degradation to raise him.

Yet Joy Coleman *had* been out to wave him off, although she had only learned that they were to embark for Africa from gossip in the local shops. Maybe it had been the sight of those red jackets, the black boots, and the snorting and stamping of the horses' hooves that served to remind her painfully of the lace garters, black stockings, and stale sweat of the King's Head in her past. Whether it was those sights and sounds, a glimpse of someone she recognised from those terrible days, or that she simply could not face saying goodbye to the one thing she knew had kept her sane all those years, she did not know. To her, Africa meant lions, snakes, and all the dangers and uncertainties that her little boy would have to face, alone and without her; her little boy, now in the army, who would come back a man, and likely as not learn to be just the same as all the others she had known. *Not him*, she thought, *not my Jack*.

For a moment, she thought of the handsome sailor who had just come off the boats: a fine young man of twenty with straight blond hair, who had blushed when she took off her dress and promised to pay her, then broke down and spoke to her of his unrequited love for his crewmate. She remembered the strong, broad back, the kindly spoken words, and the unusual gentleness of that strange seafaring youth, so unlike his contemporaries, and the reflection of those wonderful eyes in the proud, handsome features of her only son. *Why*, she wondered sadly, *must the only good thing ever to come of my wretched life be taken away from me so soon*?

With scarcely more than a backward glance, she fled back down the alley.

Chapter Seven

For Bond too, the notion of having no one there to see him off was made yet worse by the apparent abundance of wives and children flocking to the station, pressing into the arms of their fathers, and husbands' words of endearment and tokens of affection, the tears of parting flowing as freely as wine at a table.

Somewhere in the throng of the bustling platform, looking past the rows of red coats, shabby hats and bonnets and the rhythmical chuff of the approaching train, Bond noticed Coleman standing alone and forlorn amid the baggage. For a moment, he thought of walking over to him, but was prevented from doing so by the fond farewells pressed upon him by both Annie Westgate and Flora Knight, the wives of his two closest friends.

'Oh, do take care, Albert,' Mrs Westgate implored him. 'Don't let my husband be goin' and doin' all sorts now. D'you hear me?'

'Look after yourself, Mrs Westgate,' Bond smiled back weakly. 'You too, Flora,' he added, turning to receive a dainty peck on the cheek from his best friend's wife as she stood beside him in the pretty blue gown Gideon had bought her only the week before. It matched her sparkling eyes beautifully, and the curls of golden blonde hair that fell beneath the brim of her wide blue hat reminded Bond of the absence of Clara from the throng, at which, if truth be told, he felt something more akin to self-consciousness than sorrow.

'Don't you look well in your uniform, Albert!' Mrs Westgate enthused. 'Quite the picture,' she added, before taking him in her arms and hugging him goodbye.

Bond liked Annie Westgate. She was a decent, plump, and cheerful Irishwoman of around thirty-five, with big, red rosy cheeks and a large cloud of dark brown hair under her pink bonnet, which she wore to please her husband, who had often said that the colour suited her. As the elder of the company officers' wives, she was invariably charged with the task of running here and there after the younger women, often acting as unofficial welfare officer to the wives of the other ranks, many of whom were weeping uncontrollably on the platform at that moment. Bold and maternal, if not a little bossy, Mrs Westgate was typical of the mettle of woman required to marry an officer above the rank of lieutenant. While it was accepted army lore that captains were permitted to marry, marriages by subalterns below those ranks were positively frowned upon.

Although not yet in middle age herself, Annie Westgate was already in the process of grooming the much younger, slightly more emotionally fragile Flora Knight in preparation for her inevitable position as future company commander's wife.

In accordance with Westgate's predictions of high rank for his star subaltern, it was also an accepted fact that Flora Knight would be as instrumental in her husband's future career prosperity as his own success in this his first campaign. Consequently, she would need to be fitted for the extreme social and political demands that army life would be likely to make upon her and, in such a field, Annie Westgate was a most suitable mentor.

Besides which, it did the officers as much good as their wives to know that their other halves – in the case of Warren Westgate, the mother of his children – should have someone else to lean on for support during the coming months of separation.

Suddenly, from somewhere deep within the steam-covered platform, there appeared yet another, somewhat less obvious figure of an officer's wife, searching high and low for her departing husband in the crowd.

Henry Earnest Penfold was another subaltern who seemed to have broken the accepted convention of not marrying before attaining the rank of captain.

In his early twenties, quiet and introspective, yet not at all disagreeable, the officer who aptly went by his middle name, Earnest, was very much the stranger of the mess. Just under five-foot five, with blond hair in a thick fringe and a flat, wide nose, the little subaltern rarely smiled on account of his slightly crooked teeth, spoke mostly when spoken to, and attended social functions only when absolutely obliged. Penfold was the accepted last post for most of the unwanted clerical duties, shirked by such officers who were more possessed of a social life than him. Not best describable as popular, he was still well appreciated by his brother officers, and could always be found doing something on someone else's behalf, generally fagging for Lieutenants Knight and Bond. Assuming his introspection and appearance to have rendered him a long-term bachelor, Bond was therefore rather surprised to see a tiny, skittish-looking woman of similar age and stature dash up to the young lieutenant on the platform. They spoke a few words together, she briefly kissed him on the mouth and pressed into his hand some small trinket or keepsake, before running off again down the platform in floods of tears.

'Ah, that'll be poor, dear little Mrs Penfold,' sighed Annie Westgate sympathetically. 'Sure, I'll go after her and see if she's all right.'

Then, as she smiled warmly at her husband, taking both his hands in hers and looking deeply into his eyes, and as Flora Knight clung bravely to her Gideon, determined not to cry as she clamped her arms around his broad, scarlet shoulders, Bond felt like weeping. Then he took another look down the platform at the lone figure of young Sapper Jack Coleman and reflected for a moment on whether a single officer might give comfort to a young, single enlisted man while neither one had a parent, spouse, or beau to see them off. At that moment Jack looked up. Their eyes met, then the whistle blew for embarkation. Still the boy smiled disarmingly, a gesture to which his officer responded, and broke off, with a cursory nod.

During the train journey Bond shared a seat with Gideon Knight, while Warren Westgate sat opposite and endeavoured to complete the mountain of company paperwork, which their sudden and early start had necessitated.

After about an hour, the landscape all began to look the same, the throws of late autumn having rendered even the golds, russets and oranges of October a drab collection of greys and browns amid the stripped bare, iron-hard skeletal framework of the formerly glorious English countryside.

Bond, who had neither the interest to read nor the desire to say anything, looked sideways at Lieutenant Knight and found him busily engaged in scribbling down notes with a very short pencil in a dark red, velvet-covered pocketbook. The edges of the little book were trimmed in gold, and a small brass lock was fitted onto a thin brass clasp, attached to the book from one side to the other. Bond could just make out some tiny handwriting on the ornately decorated flyleaf.

When he queried what the officer was doing, Knight smiled back sadly and told him that Flora had begged him to keep a diary of the things that took place while he was away. 'She thinks that if I come back all introspective and cowed, there might be something in it she can learn from and console me by it. My darling dear, she seems to think this whole damned Zulu business is anything at all to worry about. I tried to explain to her that they were untrained heathens for the most part, but it seemed to make the poor thing even worse.'

'Sensitive of you, Gideon,' Westgate remarked casually, momentarily glancing up from his paperwork.

'She will be worried by these things though, Albert,' Knight continued, replacing the pencil in the spine of the pocketbook, and sweeping his dark hair back over his ears as he spoke. 'You know I love her to bits, Warren, but I can't help but envy Albert with him having no one back here to worry for or be worrying for him while he's away.'

'I can't say I share your view, Gideon,' Westgate replied, peering over the rim of his gold-rimmed reading glasses and studying the young lieutenant with cautious curiosity. 'Bedrock of my life has been having Annie and the children waiting for me when I came back from Salisbury, or Dublin on the occasions I've been to see Mother back home. Best feeling after a field day or exercise, one's own hearth and home.'

'Oh, I don't deny it for a moment, please don't misunderstand me,' Knight continued. 'All that I'm saying is that it must be nice to be spared the grief of leaving a loved one on such an occasion as this. Don't *you* agree, Earnest, old chap?'

Somewhat preoccupied by his own thoughts, and clearly somewhat taken aback at having been suddenly involved in conversation by the exclusive officer threesome, Lieutenant Penfold merely nodded in assent and returned to his book.

'Lest we forget about Albert's young lady, now, Gideon,' Westgate remonstrated with him. 'After all, she's— Where's Albert going?'

'Albert!' they called after him, but it was useless.

Bond, murmuring something about a quick check on the men, soon found himself out of the officers' car and making for the carriage in which he knew the other ranks to be passing an even less comfortable, though no more miserable, journey than his own.

Sergeant Friday, who had little use or affection for railways, was singularly unamused at having to attempt to stand the men to attention on board what amounted to little more than a very wobbly cattle truck. He succeeded in moments, but very nearly ruined the whole spectacle by almost poking Coleman's eye out as he tried to replace his baton under his left arm for the salute, then fell victim to the movements of the train and landed up in a pile of disgruntled sappers on the floorboards. In the end, Bond told his sergeant to let the poor wretches resume their benches, as he had a few words to pass with his batman.

Coleman's delight at receiving a special visit from his officer, who clearly wanted nothing more officious than a friendly chat, found himself in an agony of embarrassment when, as the train went round a sudden bend in the rails, both were thrown to the floor. As it was, the poor young sapper could only blush in horror as he and the bewildered lieutenant found themselves in the middle of a pile of baggage, with Coleman sprawled flat on top.

Not that it served to ease his own discomfort one little bit, but Coleman was suddenly aware that, above the noise of the train's whistle – or perhaps Sergeant Friday's falsetto shriek – Bond was, in fact, laughing uncontrollably.

Little did they know it, but Coleman's feelings of hurt and abandonment at the absence of his mother were not unlike those of the prostrate officer, and for what it was worth, equally unfounded. For no sooner had the massive engine hauled its martial load out of the grimy, frenzied activity of the busy station, a young woman dressed in a white dress came shuffling onto the platform in her impractical shoes, agonising over her failure to catch the departing train, while her matronly companion stood by, poker-faced, a few paces back from the turnstile.

Turning desperately to the weathered old porter on the platform, she begged for him to tell her where the train was going.

'That's the army train, miss,' he explained with a roguish leer. 'Them's off to the wossit camp, you know, down Dover way where the nice folk have their holidays. At least, beggin' your pardon.'

'Yes, yes. I understand,' she smiled anxiously. 'You mean Folkestone. But can you tell me if there's a telegram office anywhere locally?'

'Oh, you want the post office for that, you do, miss,' explained the guard. 'But it's a cab ride away for the likes of a young lady like you,' he observed, adding, 'Especially in them shoes.'

'Oh dear!' wailed the poor girl in frustration. 'What on earth can I do?'

‘What is it you was looking for exactly, miss?’ asked the porter more kindly as he contemplated the coin in her silk gloved hand while her lady’s companion, a spinster, rolled her eyes in the background.

‘Oh, an officer,’ she sighed forlornly. ‘One Lieutenant Bond of the Corps of Engineers. The man I hope one day to marry!’

Chapter Eight

Captain Westgate's company arrived at Shorncliffe Barracks in time to see the setting sun vanish over the English Channel.

Bond, Knight, Penfold, and Friday, who were just as exhausted as their captain, had little else to do on arrival but subside wearily in their newly erected bell tents and catch what sleep they might in preparation for the punishing schedule of the following day. They enjoyed, if such a word was appropriate in the wake of so recent a parting, a quiet dinner in the improvised mess tent that also doubled as the depot for all the stores requiring cataloguing for transit, general offices, chaplaincy, and clinic. In fact, the whole place was so full up that no more chairs could be excavated from the chaos, resulting in both Lieutenant Bond and Penfold, being forced to improvise by sitting on drums.

After a plain repast and a glass of red wine, Bond was just on his way back to the tent, which he shared with Lieutenant Knight, when he came across Coleman on sentry duty. Pleased to see a friendly face and less constrained by the propriety of rank by the wine, he decided to stop for a smoke and a talk.

Coleman, who had come to regard his officer's choice of tobacco with a healthy and definitive terror, began flapping about with small talk at a rate of knots that might have made a warship proud.

'You needn't worry,' Bond commented at last. 'I'm not about to force anything in your mouth, you know. Not if you don't care for the taste.'

'I'm sorry I didn't like the one you gave me last time, sir,' he mumbled apologetically. 'It's just that I ain't used to shag,' adding, 'Tell truth, sir, I hoped you hadn't noticed.'

'I think it might have been when you turned green that gave it away,' Bond remarked carelessly, amused by the young sapper's embarrassment, and relief that he wasn't going to be forced to smoke another cigar.

Coleman looked at him in silence for a moment, and then a broad smile broke across his face with that familiar expression that narrowed his blue eyes to slits. 'I should have just said no thank you, shouldn't I? I'm sorry I didn't, sir.'

'On the contrary, you did *exactly* the right thing by me,' Bond explained kindly. 'It's good manners to refuse something when in company, certainly to start with, though not if it may give offence to the person who's offering it to you.'

'I see, sir,' Coleman nodded, though he very obviously did not.

'It's very simple, you see,' Bond continued. 'Manners rely not upon what you believe or disbelieve, rather more what other people assume or expect of you.'

'I'm sorry, sir,' Coleman sighed, shaking his head in bewilderment. 'I ain't smart or proper enough to follow them things. Just as well they ain't for me, anyhow.'

'Not at all!' Bond exclaimed. He was quite put out by the idea that his musings had made his batman feel inferior, though for why he was by no means so sure. 'You are the most thoughtful young man I think I have ever met. You work tirelessly, you're cheerful, and you never complain about anything, ever. Granted, you might not know which fork to use at a dinner table, but you've got heart, and that's what really counts, believe me,' he added, thinking gloomily of his 'proper' friends in London who had flocked from his side as the money evaporated as quickly as they had flocked towards it in the first place. They *certainly* knew which fork to use at a dinner table. 'I'm going to turn in, Sapper,' Bond smiled at last, as the dwindling light of the campfire began to crackle and fizzle to just the ghosts of embers. 'Inform Sergeant Friday that I said he's to relieve you from your post. I need you to be fresh for tomorrow, after all. Our work will be cut out for us, and I'm not going to have time for toecaps, brass polish, and buttons.'

Jack nodded obediently and saluted.

As Bond turned to go, he called after him. 'Night, Mr Albert, sir.'

'Goodnight,' Bond responded, murmuring, 'God bless,' almost surreptitiously.

Chapter Nine

The following day passed pretty much as it had ended, beginning early, and ending excruciatingly late for the officers and men of Warren Westgate's Royal Engineer Field Company.

Coleman was kicked out of his blankets at sunrise and dispatched by Sergeant Friday to instruct the bugler to sound reveille. By 6:30 a.m. the men had been given their breakfast of porridge, tea, and bread; by 7:00 they were packed and ready; tents were struck down and at 7:15 they were marched out of Shorncliffe for the equipment laden tramp to the railway station for transfer and embarkation.

As a consequence of the punishing winter weather, the march was a very messy and muddy affair. Captain Westgate and Lieutenant Knight were mounted on their own horses, but Bond and Penfold (who were obliged by costs to wait until they arrived in Durban before purchasing mounts) were forced to bring up the rear on foot with the men.

Bond, who had already earmarked a pair of buff riding cords, was unable to wear them prior to embarkation on account of the strict dress regulations for home service. Even so, the field company still retained a decidedly commanding, imperious presence as they tramped through the muddy quagmires which passed for rural byways.

Indeed, Bond thought he heard a remark passed by one of his corporals, a man named Denham, about the English countryside being all "mud, shit and horses," but decided to let the sentiments pass unchecked, chiefly because he agreed with them entirely.

The town, when they arrived in it, was not a great deal better than the march from the transit camp. Cold, foggy, and smelly, with all the usual smoke, soot, fog, and an absence of the affordable amenities of the Medway towns to which they were used, added to the cheerlessness of a coastal resort in winter. The brickwork of the houses, factories and viaducts was black and grimy, splattered with seagull excrement and running with moisture where the gutters had fallen into disrepair. The height and seeming endlessness of the buildings, crammed, and packed one on top of the other made the officers and their men almost wistful for the open and windswept fields and highroads they had just abandoned. The charmless rusty iron railings, the endless black and filthy windows, the tiny cellar-like arches below the steps of the wretched houses, and the endless puddles which filled his boots still further made Coleman ache inwardly and wish desperately for sunshine.

The men were wet; their shoulders ached from carrying their equipment on their backs all day long. Feet were sore, and Bond for one was miserable enough with his lack of a horse and bringing up the rear in his now saturated uniform, without the endless clatter, clink-clank, and tramp of the company in motion resounding relentlessly in his ears all day.

At one point, a decidedly shabby mongrel ran out from one of the tenements. Wet, boisterous and, Bond thought, quite likely flea-ridden, it ran straight up to Sapper Coleman and, flinging itself at him with a bark of delight and endearment, nearly succeeded in knocking him off his feet. It was indeed a ghastly-looking beast, with shabby brown fur, wet and blackened at the ends from the dirt and the damp, with muddy paws which left their prints well and truly stamped on the poor soldier's jacket.

Sergeant Friday, who was sharp enough to see that his prize recruit was in some grave difficulty, without turning round, called out to Coleman to fall out of the file. This he did, almost tripping and falling with the weight of his equipment, and the wobbly, white Foreign Service helmet on his head; the agonising lacerations in his shoulders from the cruel valise straps. With an oath of irritation and impatience, he was just about to kick the mongrel into the gutters when a small girl, approximately three or four years old appeared from the same doorway and rushed up to him. She had big, sombre brown eyes, filthy black hair, and soot all around her face. The mongrel was evidently hers, and she was evidently distressed by its sudden escape through the open door while she and her mother had watched the troop movement. Swallowing his curses and forgetting the mud on his uniform, Jack smiled warmly down at the child, gathered the dog up in both arms, and presented it to her, kneeling in the water as he did so. It was a full size bigger than the girl, but she flung her arms around its neck, kissing and remonstrating with it over its unwarranted disappearance. For a moment, she looked back at the handsome boy soldier, and then she smiled as well.

'Sapper, get back in line or you'll get left behind!' shrieked Friday. 'Don't get on a charge for a street mongrel!'

Jack smiled, winked at the girl then dashed after the departing column to resume his place in the ranks, pain almost forgotten.

Bond, who had subtly dithered so as not to allow Jack to fall behind too far, felt a pang. *Thank God there were no goodbyes left*, he thought. *I just couldn't do it.*

They arrived on board the steam ship *Dover Castle* at one

thirty in the afternoon, to be played on board by the band of the first battalion, The West Rutlands, who were also being shipped to the Cape.

Firstly, the horses were fed and watered, and the necessary arrangements were made by Captain Westgate and Lieutenant Knight to see them shepherded on board before any of the men or supplies commenced embarkation. Having brought their own private mounts, Westgate and Knight were fairly concerned as to the effect such a voyage, which was expected to run for around a month, might have on the health of the beasts.

Dover Castle was part of a line of steam ships, owned by a wealthy local shipping family, and employed during peacetime as both passenger ships and conveyance for the Royal Mail to the colony of Natal. Consequently the voyage, at least for the officers, did not look to be as basic and uncomfortable an affair as many of them had originally fancied. The cabins were reasonable generous, allowing for Queen's regulations governing the living space of both officers and men, and the moderate luxuries of a passenger vessel looked to make the arduous weeks at sea slightly more bearable.

There was little or nothing in the way of entertainment on board ship. The officers were kept busy with administrational duties, and on December third, the ship embarked from its berth bound for Durban docks, via Madeira and Cape Town.

On the fourth day, however, as *Dover Castle* lay anchored off Sheerness to take on fuel and supplies, the first calamity of the excursion struck.

Earnest Penfold, who had been feeling decidedly under the weather since their long and arduous march from Shorncliffe in the pouring rain, fell ill with a bowel complaint and was forced to take to his bunk in the infirmary.

Surgeon-Major Lamb diagnosed diarrhoea and prescribed arrowroot and confinement to bed. That was a severe blow indeed and resulted in double the amount of paperwork for the already beleaguered subalterns in the company.

Warren Westgate watched Penfold's progress anxiously over the following few days, but the poorly officer seemed to show very little sign of improvement.

Bond detailed Sapper Coleman to keep a vigil by his bunk and, by the time the ship docked at Madeira on December eighth, Westgate was seriously minded toward issuing Penfold with his dispensation papers and send him back to Chatham Barracks on the first available boat. However, poor Penfold begged not to be left behind, and as soon as the crew had finished coaling, he managed, with help from Coleman, to resume his duties. For once, this involved Bond and Knight pulling together to help *him* for a change. After a few days he was almost back to his old self, if a little slower than before, and after another week of considerable badgering from the two lieutenants, Westgate recanted on his decision not to allow Penfold to continue with the voyage.

The following fortnight removed any spring that Bond might have had in his step when they left Chatham. For the first short journey up the estuary, all had been going along quite well. Then, as the complement of military personnel on board the ship had doubled – due to an additional company of troops that boarded the boat at Sheerness – the shared experiences of sickness, diarrhoea, lice and despondency became rife among all ranks.

Bond, who had previously been accustomed only to direct command of a handful of men under the expert guidance and interpretation of the ever-invaluable Sergeant Friday, suddenly found himself well and truly confronted with thoroughly unpleasant aspects of command. These included the detection of drunkenness amongst the men, the clamping down upon any hint of indiscipline and, in some cases, handing out appropriate punishments. This was not an easy task for Lieutenant Bond, who regarded his men as very much his own, and preferred to leave all matters connected with discipline and correction in the more experienced hands of Friday.

The infantry verged on mutinous; after a few weeks the conditions were beginning to resemble those of an Elizabethan warship. The sailors were rude, abrupt, and deferred only to the ascendancy of their own officers when it came to supplies, messing and sleeping arrangements (and pretty much anything else on board).

Gradually, as the weather began to get hotter and the temperature below decks began to rise, the most even-tempered individuals began to develop serious mood swings. Gideon Knight retired further into his diary and letter-writing to Flora; Bond began to think that Sergeant Friday was putting on the unfortunate voice simply to get on his nerves, and even Warren Westgate was less like his usual amenable self as the voyage around the Cape wore on. Pain was passed down the ranks.

Even so, this did not seem to affect the mild temperament of the ever-dependable Coleman who, with all and sundry dropping around him like flies, turned his hand more and more to looking after the sick, miserable, and plain irritable. This included Bond who, ever since Christmas Eve, had been suffering with most uncomfortable complaints associated with the bowels. Hard as he tried to continue in his activities, the privations of his condition soon forced the gallant officer into the position so lately occupied by Lieutenant Penfold. Despite the intimacy and, on occasions, vulgarity of his affliction,

Coleman was never far from his side the whole duration. He often covered for the orderlies, changing Bond's sweaty sheets, using his charm to wangle extra blankets off the most scrupulous quartermaster, and even dealt with the necessities of his officer's chamber pot. This act alone established beyond doubt that Friday's nomination was to pay dividends in the months to come, and firmly planted in Bond's mind the conviction that his batman was of a very special material indeed.

On some days, Bond would be a little better and could be seen up and about. Others, however, would find him once more returned to the sickbed and in considerable need of chicken broth, bread, and arrowroot.

Coleman would also, on some occasions, take him up on deck to take in the fresh and bracing sea air. The evenings, although still a little cooler than their geographical situation might suggest, were still colourful, magical, and highly medicinal affairs.

Bond would often ask to be placed on a chair near to the prow of the ship, and seemed to take some considerable restorative pleasure from sitting and watching the massive white breakers part in front of him, while the irate sailors were forced to conduct their business around him.

Gradually, as Christmas approached, and the climate above decks became more conducive to recovery, Bond took advantage to recuperate his health and strength. Coleman helped him get up and about, dressed him, aided him with his toilet, and went so far as to secretly sacrifice some of his own rations so that his officer might be fit and well enough to alight at Cape Town.

They arrived at the old colonial port late on December twenty-seventh, not actually docking the ship until around

11:40 p.m. All heavy baggage, including those wives and children who had been allowed to accompany the troops, were ordered to disembark. Leisure equipment including polo mallets, tennis rackets, croquet mallets and non-military issue firearms, were set ashore, and the contingent from the Corps of Royal Engineers found it slightly easier to breathe, move about and concentrate on the impending invasion of Zululand. Rumours were rife and talk of a Zulu war medal to follow the campaign seemed to inspire the officers to untold deeds of courage and frustrate them by the notion that their work in the colony might well be limited to that of a collective civil engineer.

'The fly in the ointment may prove to be the qualification,' Westgate observed to Knight one evening. 'Assuming our work were to be confined to the border, we may not even make it into an active theatre, bar the odd incursion or raiding party from the Zulu banks. That being the case, depending on how long it takes to settle the thing, we many of us may return as we came: bereft of ribbons and still of the same rank.'

'That might send old Friday over the edge completely,' Knight replied glumly. 'I often worry about the chap's sanity, and quite what malady is brewing under that bald pate and behind those mad, darting eyes of his. The man must be fifty if he's a day, and the only medal on his breast is for long service.'

'*Peacetime* service at that,' Westgate interjected, to which Knight assented knowingly.

'He's been there every day I have, and that's some now. He may never see staff sergeant, let alone sergeant major,' Knight concluded. 'To retire without a shot fired beyond field days, Warren.'

'The lot of some sappers,' Westgate retorted. 'Best hope not ours, eh, Gideon.'

Chapter Ten

By Monday December thirtieth 1878, they had almost completed their journey up the coast to the key port of Durban.

Then on thirty-first, Bond's stomach began to play him up again. There was a thrill of panic amongst the subalterns that Bond might be forced to remain in Natal, should Captain Westgate discover yet another case of sickness in one of his officers.

Consequently, and with the ship making excellent time for a landing the following day, a hasty conference of Friday, Knight and Coleman saw the diligent young sapper re-billeted in Bond's cabin, much to his own discomfort, for the purpose of aiding a speedy recovery, and to monitor his progress.

Bond, having been moved from his double cabin that he shared with Gideon Knight, now remained there. As a result, no provision was available for Coleman's accommodation and in a rather absurd performance the officer's campaign furniture, which had taken the form of two folding garden chairs, had to be modified to fulfil the office of a camp bed. A space was duly cleared in Bond's cabin and the two chairs of the canvass-backed, twin-armed variety, were arranged one in front of the other, with Coleman forced to squeeze his ample shoulders between the arms while curling his legs up under a greatcoat. Even so, the young soldier did this without the slightest hint of complaint, and Bond's remaining journey was much the pleasanter for having his batman on hand.

In the end, the ship docked at the port of Durban, named after Sir Benjamin D'Urban, Wellington's governor, and comparably the Chatham of Natal Colony.

They staggered ashore on the third day of January 1879, with Bond very much recovered, and great excitement among both officers and men of the company. For the British ultimatum, which the high commissioner had made the king of the Zulu nation, had expired, and with no word from either the monarch or his ministers, the invasion of Zululand was set to begin.

It was only when they disembarked, and the small landing vessel containing Bond, Coleman, Friday, and the stores, shoved off from the massive steam ship and swayed alarmingly into the harbour itself, did they finally realise their presence in South Africa.

For Friday, the experience of being flung fore and aft in the keel of a boat was no more or less than the experience of the same sensations on board the train from Chatham some several weeks before. Perhaps not surprisingly, the sergeant's narrow view of the world in which he lived owed about as little to boats as it did to trains.

Bond, on the other hand, was quite unperturbed by the short trip from the ship to the landing stage at the end of the jetty. The reason for this was that, despite his grandfather's humble background, Bond's enjoyment of all the pursuits of an English gentleman had not been in any way dampened during the time between public school, university and the untimely sale of his bloodstock.

Rowing for one's school and river punting during the season were yet further examples of the versatility that was expected to prepare young men of the correct background for life as an officer. Presumed to have been born to lead, by both merit of character and early chapel doctrine, Bond had been endowed with the usual sense of duty and expectance of greatness as his contemporaries at the Royal Military Academy. Whether the loss of both his parents made this duty prevalent in his already racing mind, he did not know. In fact, about the only thing of which Lieutenant Bond was acutely aware on that little boat was the fact the cruel sun on the back of his neck, which after so long under hatches, was becoming almost infernal.

For Friday too, the heat of the African sun was beginning to act in the manner of a kiln, baking his unprotected bald head with the same effect as a boiling pot had upon a newly caught lobster.

In fact, soon the whole of the top of his head had become a rather terrible shade of radish pink, as had his nose, the tops of his ears and the back of his neck, which was also quite absent of hair.

Only Coleman seemed to be enjoying the experience. Maybe it was the sea in his blood, the excitement of seeing so strange and wonderful a land for the first time, or all that Pacific calm and sparkling blue serenity, seducing his senses like nothing before.

The harbour walls seemed to have their own microclimate; the shifting grey-green of the ocean seemed almost lost amid the tranquil turquoise waves of water breaking beneath the bows of the boat and parting in a white foamy trail, as far back as the distant troopship.

Glancing from Friday, who seemed to be making strange guttural noises as the boat rose and fell, Bond noticed Coleman, his left hand trailing in the foamy surf, smiling meditatively at the seemingly endless stretch of ocean within the harbour walls.

Something about the massive ships in the docks at Chatham, and now the long, grey, seemingly endless expanse spread all around him gave Jack the strangest feeling of minority, and even insignificance. Straining to look up, he felt himself go almost dizzy with the rippling water all around him, the shimmering reflection on the water below the boat, and the blazing sun directly overhead.

Coleman looked back at his officer, smiled, and was just about to say something when the boat seemed to hit a sudden change in the current. The hitherto calm and placid temperament was suddenly replaced by an almost storm-like tumult, causing the little boat to bob up and down in an alarmingly violent fashion. Sergeant Friday let out an uncharacteristic yelp; Coleman had to restrain his white Foreign Service helmet as it tried to fall into the harbour, and Bond was just about to order abandon ship with every man for himself, when the boat suddenly struck something solid.

There was a loud thud, followed by a crash as Coleman toppled off the side of the boat and landed, for the second time, on top of his now prostrate officer.

Friday let out a squeal, grabbed his helmet and made a giant leap for the nearby jetty.

For a moment, all was a shambles of noise and confusion. Then, above the sound of the waves lapping gently and relentlessly against the stone steps of the harbour wall in great foamy torrents, Bond suddenly became aware of Gideon Knight and Warren Westgate. They were only a few feet away from him, and apparently laughing uproariously. Bond muttered a few dark and subdued words of comment on the hilarity of his brother officers at his unfortunate predicament.

Then, as he noticed the furiously blushing face of poor Sapper Coleman, he thought better of it and reluctantly feigned collusion with the merriment taking place on the quayside. It was only after a minute or so that he realised that they weren't laughing at *him* at all.

Bond could hear the water slapping relentlessly against the side of the stone steps below the jetty, the endless barrage of great green waves as they broke and crashed over the lower and foremost of those, running off again in torrents of white foam and seaweed. He could see that they were currently bobbing up and down amid a flotilla of other landing craft, piloted by sailors from the ship and apparently waiting for Bond's compliment to disembark. In fact, it was only when Coleman tactfully pointed out the absence of his troop sergeant from the vessel that the hitherto bewildered officer was made aware of a pair of boots, apparently dangling from the lowermost beams of the wooden jetty above.

'Oh dear,' Bond groaned in agony. 'Why must it be one of *my* men?'

'Shall I get him down, sir?' asked Coleman quietly. He was also extremely conscious of the growing chorus of derision, mixed with hilarity, from the men in the boats behind them. He was also aware that, having sprung in blind panic from the boat in a desperate bid to affect a premature landing, the screaming Sergeant Friday was now in some danger of losing his grip altogether.

'Better had, Jack,' Bond replied with a sigh. After all, the last thing he wanted was his troop sergeant to be fished out of the drink with a boat hook, he reasoned.

Even so, the very act of salvation began to cause additional problems when, having safely secured Friday's kicking legs and amid great assurances that it was safe to let go, Coleman suddenly lost his footing. The boat began to lunge from side to side. The sailor at the rudder sprang up onto the wooden jetty and poor Coleman was just given time to retain his balance while his officer alighted with his dignity broadly intact, before gravity got the better of him. Bond landed feet first on the landing stage just in time to see his batman release his grip of the legs of the now apoplectic Sergeant Friday, and a mop of blond hair vanish below the water in amid a massive pool of foam, and a very loud splash.

'Get him out of there, damn it!' roared Bond, as a cry of delight went up from the assembled companies around the dockside who had flocked to the locality to witness the spectacle of a young sapper, fresh from home, getting dunked in the "oggin".

There was none too healthy a rivalry between sapper and ordinary infantrymen. Sappers were paid considerably more as a rule and tended to regard themselves as a cut above their line regiment counterparts. Even so, Coleman could hardly have been described either as conceited or even mildly above himself, and the catcalls and cheers at the poor young soldier's plight was absolutely infuriating to the already humiliated subaltern. Either way, Bond needn't have worried. For practically as soon as he had entered the water, Coleman had dog-paddled back to the capsized vessel, mercifully unburdened by his equipment, which had already been landed.

'Marvellous!' Knight laughed heartily, as Bond and the somewhat disgruntled pilot hauled the bedraggled Coleman out of the water and set him down on the flagstones. 'Put that man on a charge or buy him a brandy, you think?' he continued.

Westgate, who was so overtaken with mirth that the tears were beginning to stream from his eyes, could only nod in assent at one or other of Knight's suggestions.

Bond, who was furious at the whole spectacle, was made even more irate that Coleman seemed to bear the humiliation with laddish sportsmanship, laughing along with the mockery despite the work and discomfort getting utterly wet through would engender.

'Are you sure you're not hurt?' Bond whispered through gritted teeth and blazing red cheeks.

Coleman nodded forlornly through his drooping fringe of wet hair, and subsided into quiet circumspection as the reflected ignominy of the spectacle dawned upon him.

'It wasn't your fault,' Bond found himself assuring him gently. Then, as if to reaffirm his sense of authority, he added, 'Someone get Sergeant Friday up off that damned pontoon!'

'Albert, language!' Knight remonstrated lightly, before resuming the chuckles.

'I'm sorry if I let you down, sir,' Coleman mumbled, as Bond helped the still awkward soldier up the steps to the waiting assembly of men.

'I told you, it wasn't your fault,' Bond repeated. 'Now, for God's sake get your kit out of the tiller and go and get dried off, or this will go on all day.'

It was a hollow remark, they both knew it. However, Coleman managed to smile at his officer, and that in turn served to quell the boiling sense of indignation and embarrassment that they both knew Bond to be feeling at the spectacle.

Friday, by contrast, had remained uncharacteristically silent and introspective.

Despite the false start, which was of course to make Coleman and Friday the butt of every joke and ditty for several weeks to come, their march from Durban to the colonial capital, Pietermaritzburg, was none too harsh an affair.

The drought, which had held the colony in a vicelike grip for the last few months, had suddenly broken. Yet after a few days, the early nostalgia of rain amid the arid dryness of the dusty roads was soon to be replaced by severe discomfort. Wagons became bogged down in the mud and oxen seemed to fall like flies around them, leaving the unsightly spectacle of rotting carcasses on either side of the road.

Further problems were created on the march for Lieutenant Knight and Captain Westgate who, having brought their own mounts at great personal expense from home, were faced with the alarming revelation that they would not eat the local grasses. Hurried provision was made for them in the form of several hundred pounds of bagged forage which, although sufficient to see the beasts fed on the short trip up the coast, also succeeded in adding yet another wagon to the already growing train. This was a severe blow for morale, involving as it did yet another several ton weight to be pushed, pulled or, as in some cases, physically hauled free of the mud on the dreadful roads.

If confederation was to be achieved through transport systems, Bond observed to Penfold, they were going to be in Africa for a very long time.

The wagons themselves were flatbed, plank affairs of long wheelbase design, topped off by canvas on wooden frames, and required considerable strength to pull along. Spans of sixteen oxen, arranged in eight pairs, were the accepted amount required to pull a wagon. Even so, there were instances on the muddy and poorly constructed colonial roads when double teams were required. In such conditions the wagons, while quite capable of carrying a payload of some eight thousand pounds on a good road, were hard pressed to drag even two or three thousand through the mud and mires of the Natal roads.

This proved to be yet another headache for Warren Westgate who, frustrated at the amount of stops for grazing (especially when his own horse wouldn't eat) was beginning to lose patience, both in the ability of his own men to control and maintain the stubborn animals, and that of the civilian drivers, also known as "voorloopers", whom he considered to be an extreme waste of money.

Chapter Eleven

By the time the column arrived in the old border town of Oscaarsberg, Westgate, Bond and the rest of the men were already beginning to look like seasoned campaigners.

Bond's tidy little beard now covered half his lower jaw. Although it had to be said the aspect certainly suited his defined features, Bond greatly lamented the disruption of his hitherto neatly combed and cultivated moustache. Facial adornments were once more highly fashionable among gentlemen, although the transformation of the sapper company seemed to have taken the form of a decidedly unkempt, not to say downright scruffy, body of men.

Sergeant Friday, whose baldness did not seem to have affected his curling brown whiskers, now had an equally curly beard of almost chest length to add to it. A bushy blond beard had also joined Westgate's thick, yard-broom moustache, and Gideon Knight had begun to look decidedly foreign amid a new emergence of black whiskers. Only Coleman seemed to have retained his youthfulness, although Bond was even able to discern a distinct line of blond stubble around his otherwise fresh features.

The capital itself was a pleasing ramble. The houses, being mostly whitewashed weatherboard, were highly reminiscent of the ones they had passed by in Chatham only a month before. The gardens, with the exemption of aloes, palmettos, cacti, and other indigenous shrubbery, could almost have been mistaken for that of an English municipal park in high summer. White picket fences ran in tidy little rows along the front of the handsome civil servants' residences, and the painted verandas that ran along the front of those were simply bedecked with hanging baskets, comfortable-looking garden furniture, and presided over by proud, if rather harmless-looking domestic dogs.

The rain, having mercifully held off for the last few days, afforded the drenched and wearied company a little respite from the punishing slog through the mud of the bad Natal roads.

Coleman, whose short muscular legs had been aching for days at having to carry what seemed to him to be several pounds of thick, red brown clay on his boots, now breathed a deep sigh of contentment as the hot sun caressed his smooth skin. The warm rays of the afternoon stroked the back of his neck, and the vivid colours of the plants and the bright green of the well-kept lawns so recently revitalised by the heavy rain of the last few months, seemed so cheerful and inviting after so many weeks on board ship.

The girls gazed at him, so did the lads, though probably out of resentment, he assumed.

Bond too was enjoying his first glimpses of that which the colonial capital had to offer. His interest was in shops rather than scenery, and a pair of buff cord riding trousers in the window of a nearby livery store could not help but catch his eye.

Gideon Knight seemed immediately to pick up on this and delighted in goading him. 'Shopping again, Albert?' he asked. 'I bet you'll be glad when we've finished this war, and you can go and set up accounts with the best Durban tailors!'

'Needs must, Gid,' Bond grumbled back at him. 'It's all very well for you. Earnest and I haven't even bought a horse between the two of us yet, never mind any riding breeches.'

'I don't see why you don't borrow my spare mount, Albert,' Captain Westgate intoned, cheerfully nodding at the chestnut mare being ridden by the officer's groom. 'I didn't bring two horses out here to ride both at once, you know.'

'It's awfully kind of you, Warren, but I don't really know where I am on someone else's horse. Thank you all the same,' Bond replied evasively.

Westgate seemed to read his mind, adding in a slightly lower voice, 'It's all right, Albert. I'm thinking of a gentleman's agreement. I don't want to sell you the beast, you know.'

'Albert's afraid he'll fall off, aren't you, Albert?' teased Gideon Knight mercilessly. 'Still, all the same, you can have my other nag if you don't want to borrow off Warren.'

'Thanks very much, both of you,' Bond mumbled, while doing his best to effect amiability through embarrassment. 'But I'll sort a horse out as soon as we've found our billets at headquarters.'

'Better not leave it too long, though,' Westgate added paternally. 'Nor you neither, Earnest,' he added, turning to address the quiet little officer over his right shoulder, as he brought up the rear of the column, adding, 'It can't be long, now.'

It was a sentiment echoed by all of them. Surely in the next few days they must receive their orders for the off.

The British military headquarters at Oscaarsberg was yet another pleasant situation for the tired party of soldiers. The main buildings housing the offices and quarters were largely occupied already, with new arrivals, company commanders and subalterns being billeted in tents all around the huge expanse of ground outside.

It was a fine, sunlit sight that met their eyes as they rode up to headquarters to present themselves and report for duty.

Row upon row of white bell tents, mounted troops exercising their horses in the shade of the trees, and the fine stirring sounds of the regimental band of the One Hundred and Tenth Regiment of Foot played them into their camp with the sound of a popular tune.

Even so, as soon as the sappers had been dismissed by Friday, one of the more mischievous among their number afforded himself the chance to sneak over to the podium on which the band was playing.

Coleman, who had just begun sorting and arranging Lieutenant Bond's belongings in one of the officers' tents, was suddenly struck with a wave of horror.

'What's wrong?' Bond asked, as Coleman went very red, screwing up his eyes and adopting an expression of thunder.

'It's that song, Mr Albert, sir,' he explained at length. 'I can't stand it.'

'What song?' Bond listened intently but was unable to discern the melody without lyrics. It was only when a couple of sappers wandered past, giving it their best flat chorus, that he knew the song for that standard of the Medway music halls which Coleman's mother had apparently made so popular prior to their embarkation. 'I can't say I dislike it *that* much, Jack,' Bond observed although from what he could see from Coleman's expression, what he thought of it clearly didn't help one jot. They were interrupted from further critiques by a familiar voice outside the tent. 'Come in, Sergeant Friday.' Bond sighed slowly, sitting up in one of the folding chairs that had served his batman inadequately as a bed on board *Dover Castle*.

Sure enough, Friday's navy blue-capped, bald head popped in around the tent flap, his straggly beard dangling from his chin like the tumble of some muddy, russet waterfall. Coleman had to look away and suppress a smile.

'Captain Westgate's respects, Mr Albert. He's been asked for you to join him and some company commanders at headquarters, sir.'

'It's all right, Sergeant, I'll be there in a minute,' Bond sighed.

'Isn't that—' began Coleman in a whisper. 'I mean, won't that mean—'

'My uncle. That's right,' Bond replied grimly. 'And there's no need to whisper. If anyone doesn't know we're related, they very soon will.'

'What do you mean, sir?' asked Coleman innocently.

'What I mean, Jack, is that the old buffer will probably set about ruining my career before it's even started by parading me around the mess and insisting on introducing me to everyone at the same time,' Bond snapped back, adding, 'I'm sorry, I didn't mean to snap at you.'

Coleman smiled reassuringly, once again transcending the barriers of rank in the way he so often did when the two of them were alone. 'I know, sir,' he added sympathetically, as he thought of all the nights spent cringing with humiliation, surrounded by fire-eaters and ventriloquists, with his mother centre stage in her feathers and garters. 'I know how it is, believe me.'

The officers' mess was one of the many luxuries of domestic military life that had necessarily gone by the board in Natal. The army was poised to move, and the lieutenant general's

Number Six Column, to which Westgate's company was to be attached, had no such amenities as an actual building in which to house their officers' social gatherings. Consequently, the necessary rituals, and perhaps more importantly dining arrangements, were housed in two large medical tents lashed together and suspended centrally by a series of ropes to simulate the dimensions of a mess hall.

Perhaps not surprisingly, Bond's mind was racing as he made his way past the ranks upon ranks of bell tents, past two impressive-looking seven-pound Armstrong guns, and a battery of newly greased rocket troughs. To him, the whole army seemed to consist of brother officers, most of whom were senior to him, and nearly all of whom would probably be in the mess that night to witness the spectacle of his reunion with his uncle. When he entered the tent, was saluted, and admitted by a somewhat too knowing-looking Indian sepoy, Bond initially went very red. Then, taking the trouble to look around, he realised that the mess was less than half full.

A few officers of the infantry regiment whose contingent formed the backbone of the proposed column, sat smoking or chatting in one corner, interspersed with service corps.

A poorly turned out and slightly mean-looking subaltern sat in his blue patrol jacket in another corner, shooting suspicious grimaces over a newspaper now and then.

Then, as Bond's eye moved steadily around the tent, there right in the middle of the place, in full view of everyone, sat his uncle. He was sitting at the bare dining table, apparently ignorant of a sea of papers to the left of his elbow, preferring to apply his focus to some absorbing item of work on his blotter instead. He did not look up as Bond entered the tent, although the young lieutenant sitting in the corner appeared curious, in a most unfriendly way, at the arrival of a new officer. He looked at Bond unsmilingly for several seconds. Then, as if he had weighed up the new addition and apparently seen enough, the subaltern returned to his broadsheet.

Unheralded and still unnoticed, Bond picked his way awkwardly across the grassy floor of the tent, placing himself directly in front of the desk at which his uncle was seated. This position afforded him a better view of the man whom he had come to regard with so many contradictory feelings, and Bond took some time over surmising his appearance.

Captain McGonagle was a short, rotund Scotsman in his early sixties. Passed over time and again for promotion pursuant to his Indian career, his face had taken on something of a grim weariness despite its rounded features. His hair, which he wore short, was plastered down with hair oil, and of a decidedly grey appearance. The beast, in this case, did *not* have horns, and the overall appearance was one of venerable, even benign geniality.

'Uncle— I mean, Captain McGonagle.' It was a clumsy start, and Bond knew it. Yet the old officer never looked up from the subject of his preoccupation, grunting shortly that the "damn bastard" was in his natural light, and to get out of the way. Here, Bond went perfectly crimson, blushing furiously as he tried hard to ignore the amused, and *he* felt, slightly malicious look from the scruffy officer whom he had originally noticed when first he had entered the mess tent.

After a short time, chiefly spent in an agony of silence, the old man looked up. This afforded Bond an opportunity to stand and further regard the man and myth with whom he had so long been at odds, and who had caused such unique and unforgettable difficulties during his time at the academy. Now, with the sun shining through the tent flaps and into the eyes of the elderly captain, Bond was able to observe the slightly aquiline nose, the tanned complexion (no doubt the result of so many years in the sub-continent, followed by a period under the African sun) and the furrow of the troubled brow. He wore a scarlet coatee, rather than the undress frock or black braided blue patrol of his companion officers in the mess. His pinchbeck buttons denoted a dour frugality, and the crown and star denotations on his collar spoke, with the single red and white silk ribbon on the left breast, of a man whose entire career had been cut frustratingly short by what most regarded as a minor mutiny, or a tinker who had laid all his wares out at once. His yellow collar and buttoned, gauntlet cuffs spoke of his Highland lineage, and the tartan of Campbell of Cawdor on his worsted trews when he rose to shake hands confirmed the captain to be of the Ninety-First Regiment of Foot, the Princess Louise's Argyllshire's.

Apparently quite ignorant of his initial scathing rebuff, McGonagle shook Bond's right hand with solemnity, but then apparently returning to his offhand disposition, ordered his nephew to move into a position where the sun wasn't behind him. 'How am I meant to look at you if you're right in my eyes like a gas lamp?' he demanded shortly, his lilting Celtic twang contrasting ill with his apparent irritability. 'Now, let's have a proper look at you. Aye, you're fine enough for a man, aren't you?'

It was true. Even since Bond had grown his beard, there was no mistaking the officer's bearing in his dashing appearance. He wore the navy patrol jacket of his corps, fastened across the front by rows of black braid, with a row of three netted olivettes on each, and the sumptuous silk velvet trimmed his cuffs and collar. His pistol was slung beneath his left arm on a brown leather shoulder strap, and his black adventurer's riding boots gleamed on the end of his navy trousers with all the lustre of Coleman's hard work.

'Your mother's eyes,' McGonagle commented wistfully. 'She had beautiful eyes. You'll not be sorry to have inherited them when you go looking for a lass.'

'I already have one, Uncle. Sorry, I mean Captain,' Bond stammered clumsily.

'Uncle, captain, sir – all's well enough if you use them separately,' the old man chuckled, clearly enjoying a private joke to which company was not to be admitted. 'After all, what's in a name, eh, Albert?'

Bond nodded mutely. He was just about to utter some weak reply, when the captain's attention was drawn to the suspicious little officer in the corner of the tent, now alternately glancing up at them and back at his paper any time either of them looked in his direction.

'Come on, Lieutenant.' McGonagle grunted, affability thinly veiling his apparent desire to cause the officer shame. 'Stop reading your paper upside down, stir your stumps and come and meet ma nephew.'

Sulkily, sullenly, and clearly highly chagrined at having been so deliberately humiliated in front of a stranger, the officer dumped what he was reading and tramped across to the desk where the two kinsmen stood.

'Albert, I have the duty to present my lieutenant, Mr Simonides.'

Bond, for all his feelings of apprehension towards the other, could not help but feel slightly sorry for him. Close up he was a mean, drawn-looking little man of roughly twenty, with straggly brown hair and the beadiest pair of ghostly grey eyes Bond thought he had ever seen. He leaned forward, almost at a stoop, and Bond found himself naturally retiring slightly so as not to get too close to him. Even so, the way in which McGonagle had introduced him had implied clearly that knowing Mr Simonides was a chore rather than a pleasure, and he began to feel rather ashamed of the uncharitable way in which his uncle had introduced the subaltern.

'Simonides here is on holiday from the Ninety-Ninth, aren't you, laddie?' McGonagle continued, despite the undisguised resentment on the face of his subordinate. 'For the present, my only junior officer, as I'm under strength.'

'An honour,' Bond smiled with an effort. 'I'm glad to know you, Simonides.'

The young officer merely scowled again and began twiddling with the single row of olivette buttons down the front of his own jacket. This was indeed very poorly cut, and the drop loops of braid fell away with the small, bony shoulders at either end. This, when added to the ill-fitting trousers and rather old boots, gave Simonides even more of a look of monetary depravation than Bond even believed himself to betray.

Moving matter on in a manner that suggested the climax of their meeting, McGonagle turned to pick up the scrap of paper on which he had lately written some considerable amount. Failing through his inexperience to sense the change in atmosphere, Bond was just about to comment on the sudden departure of virtually everyone in the mess – bar himself and the unfortunate Simonides – when the reason for the evacuation made itself apparent. The notes upon the desktop were evidently the beginning of a poem, and the captain was evidently bent on reading it.

'In Africa there are no trees,' he began, to the incredulity and shared horror of both remaining men. 'So, search I, instead, for the green of me—' Suddenly, he stopped, grunted, and resumed his seat at the desk.

Salvation had arrived, mercifully in the form of Warren Westgate, Gideon Knight, and several of the officers, including the commander of the second battalion of the Hundred and Tenth Regiment of Foot, whose infantry complement was to form the major invasion force of his lordship's centre right striking arm.

McGonagle, who clearly resented the presence of anyone senior to him by rank, or at any rate preferred the company of his juniors when reciting his poetry, replaced his spectacles and sullenly returned to his company's books. It was a lucky icebreaker, both for Bond and Simonides, yet one they knew would not keep them from one another's paths indefinitely, nor that of Captain AW McGonagle.

Chapter Twelve

The Hundred and Tenth of Foot, or 'The West Rutlands' were in fact something of a misnomer, raised as they had been in Huntingdon during the Civil War, and based under the new system of regimental affiliation at a depot on the border between Rutland and Northamptonshire. The founder of the regiment itself had been a no less strange and formidable figure than its present colonel, one Peter Henry Roystone.

In fact, Sir Algenon Fenrick had been a senior colonel in the army of King Charles but had defected to Cromwell before the end of the war and had consequently been charged with the task of raising a regiment of good loyal men as part of the New Model Army. There were dark murmurings among those ordinary people still loyal to the Crown after the war of this sinister and wolverine leader of the militia. Indeed, some even suggested that Fenrick might have been descended from that ancient and fearsome breed of werewolves who had terrorised the coast of England during the Dark Ages. Whatever his nature, or however terrible his lineage, the symbolism of this tough and tenacious colonel remained strong, well into the nineteenth century. Indeed, The West Rutlands were also nicknamed 'The Wolves', wearing the dark grey of their fabled heritage on both cuffs of their red serge jackets, and the brass wolf surmounting a scroll with the regiment's name formed the insignia on their dark grey collar tabs.

It was both battalions of The West Rutlands that were to form the basis for the centre-right column of the army invading Zululand, alongside two rocket troughs of the Royal Artillery under the command of Captain the Honourable David 'Snooker' Collingwood, with additional support of the two Armstrong guns previously observed by Lieutenant Bond.

Two additional battalions of the so-called Natal Native Contingent, comprised of local African tribesmen, as well as a large squadron of the recently raised Flambard's Horse, comprising of irregulars – white European settlers and colonials, would also support the column, led by their commandant Gillespie Flambard.

The column would fall under the overall command of Colonel Peter Henry 'Harry' Roystone VC, a ruddy-faced, heavily moustached bulldog hero of the Crimean War, by this time well into his middle years.

It was the first battalion of The West Rutlands to which Captain Westgate's sapper company was to attach itself. Serving in their capacity as engineers, their job was to support the principal companies of the regular infantry by constructing pontoons, shoring up the terrible roads and establishing lines of communication for supplying the column.

The first battalion fell under the command of Lieutenant Colonel Arthur Jackson McEnry. A slight, quiet, unassuming man in his forties, McEnry was turned prematurely grey by the loss of his wife, and a veteran of both the Indian and Abyssinian campaigns.

As he looked up and down the mess table, Bond thought how much each of the more senior officers resembled their individual commands. McEnry, with his silver hair swept back off his ears, his neat slightly artistic grey beard, and his well-cut scarlet undress frock with its crowns of rank on the completely grey collar seemed so aptly reflecting his lonely status.

So too, Captain Collingwood, whose hawk-like eyes, keenly pointed moustache and aquiline nose seemed to resemble the Hale rockets under his direction as commander of the battery.

Then Bond's eye fell upon his uncle, sat at the far end of the table in some sort of offended gaggle with Lieutenant Simonides. Like sulky guests at a party to which they had not been invited, the two of them muttered away with all the muted derision of two people who clearly disliked one another but were forced to get along by their neurotic uneasiness in the company of others. Breathing a deep sigh, Bond put on his best brave face and waited for the disaster of his relationship with McGonagle to overtake him, as he felt it surely must before too long.

The Wolves put on a good spread, and the sapper officers were considerably better received than their subordinates amid the rows and rows of tents in the transit camp outside general headquarters.

Several times in the night, Sergeant Friday would be roused by one of his corporals to restore order and avert brawls between his own men and the private soldiers of The West Rutlands, who had been there for several weeks already, and very much resented their clean uniforms, equipment and perceived superiority accompanying specialist troops quartered alongside infantry.

For Coleman too, the bully-boy instincts of the ruffians among The Wolves were to prove most problematic. Quick to seize, not only on his blond hair and youthful appearance, but also his status as the soldier who had fallen into the docks with his sergeant, they soon managed to work out a strategy of provocation. Coleman reacted with all the scorned pride expected of a lad of his age from the tough slums of Chatham, and Friday had to fight hard to quell his burning loyalty and thus restrain him from the inevitable punishments that such aggression would necessitate.

'You mustn't let the devil get the better of you,' he told Coleman, as the two of them sat in Friday's tent, with the former nursing a black eye by the aid of a poultice. 'Pride. Devil's tool. Comes before a—'

'Fall, Sarn't?' Coleman mumbled gloomily, his pride still stinging from the ignominy of being overwhelmed by two buglers and a second corporal. 'I don't want to let Mr... I mean, the lieutenant, down. He ain't lived down being made a fool out of myself by us, I mean, by *me* getting dunked in the 'arbour.'

Friday looked as though he wanted to say something encouraging, but Coleman was sharp enough to see he was also still smarting from a humiliation that was of his own making, though too proud – despite his doctrine – and too threatened by their new situation to admit as much. In Chatham, at Brompton, even at Fort Amhurst and his chosen chapel, Friday was king. The unmarried, respectable solider for life. Back home, the rough diamond yet angelic Coleman had been his to polish. To father, even.

Now, mobilized, embarked abroad and in the field among infanteers and NCOs younger in years yet equal or even senior in rank, he felt small, backward... rustic. Even so, he had to maintain his status. Accordingly, he patted Coleman stoically on the shoulder and, turning the lad out of his tent with a sharp warning about being too loyal for his own good, reminded him that his officer would require him immediately the next morning.

Even as he nursed his black eye in the cold, Coleman felt a wave of pride wash over him as he lay under his blanket. He knew perfectly well that Friday had been pleased with him despite the remonstration, and he felt quite sure he could make his Mr Albert equally proud, if only he were to be given the opportunity.

The following days brought little variety. Stores had to be arranged, two hundred-pound mealy sacks had to be sorted in not too backbreaking an order, and on account of the massive demand for Natal oxen to draw the wagons, Captain Westgate reluctantly informed his officers that they would have to make do with mules.

This was to prove no mean feat, especially for the increasingly erratic and irritable Sergeant Friday. The heat was getting to him; boils had begun to form under his arms, on his chest and anywhere else that there was hair of any sort. He was fed up with the annoying, insensible African pioneers, who had alarmingly been placed under little Earnest Penfold as auxiliaries to the existing strength of the sapper field company.

Even so, the two lieutenants were on good terms with the local Natal Africans and were soon well on the road to securing the procurement of a reasonable number of mules for their wagons. Consequently, a few hours later, Bond and Penfold sat on a fence with a crowd of African children, laughing uproariously as Friday, Coleman and the hired pioneers, now known as Earnest's earners, attempted to secure, hold down and, even worse, load the cantankerous and aggressive animals.

'Watch out, Jack!' Bond called out helpfully from the safety of the barrier as yet another mule decided to take yet another bite at Coleman's backside. 'Don't let the beggars see you're not watching, or they'll have it away with those panniers!'

'Sounds like you mean my men,' Penfold commented quietly.

'But I *was* talking about your men, Earnest,' Bond laughed back. 'Why, did you mean the mules?'

'Try taking your tunic off, Sarn't,' Coleman suggested, as Friday became hopelessly enmeshed with a nearby picket fence while trying to hang onto the legs of a braying mule and secure the panniers at the same time.

The children rippled with laughter, and Coleman smiled back, shirtsleeves rolled up above the elbow and his blond hair hanging over his face. The boiling hot sun, which seemed to be turning Sergeant Friday into a red billiard ball, was beginning to tan Coleman up to a very pleasing golden brown. Despite his fair hair, he seemed to be coping well with the temperature, and that wretched black eye seemed to be vanishing amid his darkening skin.

'That's another matter entirely,' Bond reflected grimly.

'What is, Albert?' Penfold asked in response.

'Oh, Coleman's eye,' Bond began. As it transpired, he was saved from the embarrassing confession that he had failed to report an altercation, by a horse, surmounted by a cloud of dry red dust on the Pietermaritzburg road. The African children scattered at the sight of the horse, and Bond was just about to return to his conversation with Penfold when Warren Westgate rode into view.

'What the deuce is going on here, Albert?' asked the captain, never offering to dismount from his horse, or to join the two subalterns at the fence.

'Friday, Coleman, and Earnest's African lads were just trying to yoke those damn mules, Warren,' Bond replied, letting out a bellow of laughter as Coleman succeeded in mounting one of the mules, only to come rolling off again in a cloud of dust. 'Are you all right though, Jack?'

Coleman nodded amiably, but Bond was brought up sharply by Westgate, who demanded they cease this pantomime at once and try to borrow some oxen off another company instead.

'What on earth is wrong with Warren?' Bond muttered to Penfold, as the captain rode off again in a cloud of dust, and the two subalterns were left to deal with the mumbles and grumbles of the sappers as they were informed that their pains had largely been for nothing. 'Still, it gave us a jaunt,' Bond smiled, ruffling Coleman's tousled blond hair as they walked back towards the Capital, Africans forlornly trailing a handful of vanquished beasts in their wake.

'I do hope we're not in trouble,' sighed Penfold, scratching his blond beard in deep thought. 'I wonder what's upset the captain.'

The truth was in fact that Westgate, having only just taken command of the field company, was deeply concerned by a rumour that suggested that a lack of white pioneers might see him forced to give up one of his subalterns by permanent arrangement.

His lordship's Number Two Column consisted chiefly of African troops, Basuthos allies and irregular units, and the thought of surrendering either Bond, Penfold, or worse still, Gideon Knight, did not bear thinking about.

There was also a scuttlebutt amid the middle ranks of the officers in Number Six column that at least one non-infantry captain was likely to be appointed acting major, or even breveted on account of the colonel's distaste for an unnecessarily large complement of retaining officers permanent on his staff.

This he desperately wanted, and this was beginning to rob him of both his sleep and his normally even temper to the extent that when the news went round that Flambard's Horse were riding into town that very night, all he could do was complain about the loss of space. For everyone else, however, the reception could hardly have been as tumultuous were Queen Victoria herself to have arrived in Pietermaritzburg with the band of the Grenadier Guards.

At fifty-seven, Commandant Gillespie Flambard was the dynamic magistrate for the border town, who's tough, irregular volunteer unit had scored almost as highly with the colonial press, and lieutenant general, as the tenacious officer had himself. Flambard was a big, bold, strong and confident man. To those around him it seemed that the older he grew, the stronger his body became; the firmer his certainty, and more daring in his already legendary courage.

He ate well, slept heavily, and threw himself into his duties to the colonial administration with the ardour of a junior officer. Rarely would he force an opinion on a matter, but when he spoke his words were the sound evidence of many years experience. When he gave an order, he expected it to be obeyed, and when pressed for his advice, expected it to be taken. He was also an imposing figure to behold, with a shock of completely white hair, formidably huge white whiskers, and thick, bushy eyebrows above his watery blue eyes. These were bruised and turned down in the corners with the kindly, grandfatherly glow about them, surrounded as they were by a thousand crows' feet and the lines of a million smiles. The deep, dark reddish brown of a face weathered beyond its years and scarred by any number of conflicts, told of a man who enjoyed food, wine, and the outdoor life with equal and confirmed enthusiasm, while his abundance of silk ribbons stood testament to a lifetime of soldiering.

A veteran of the Ninth Cape Frontier War, the Maori Wars in New Zealand and more than one Indian campaign, Flambard also had a keen eye for all matters concerning the Zulus' warlike disposition. Indeed, Oscaarsberg had suffered at the hands of one of the early raiding parties whose actions had necessitated the ultimatum by the British high commissioner, and Flambard was as keen to see their threat diminished as anyone who lived on the Natal border. Even so, to say the commandant was either a racist or a fool would have been a gross miscalculation of the truth. Flambard was, in fact, quietly opposed to the war. He, like most landed colonials, saw annexation as a necessity for the future stability of the region but feared the process of rushing in too quickly. Flambard was all too aware of the threat posed by marching in blindly, or worse still, allowing the Zulu impi to simply circumnavigate the columns and attack Natal.

These worries weighed on his mind as he and his men thundered through the streets of the town, receiving cheers and shouts of adulation from the colonial citizens, and a rattle of applause from the officers and men of The Wolves, who recognised Flambard's presence as invaluable.

Mounted on a huge and formidable mare, Flambard shifted all fifteen stone of himself as lightly in the saddle as if he were an African scout.

He wore well for his age, the massive presence of his formidably large frame and the wide-brimmed hat trimmed with a red puggaree giving the air of a conquering general as he rode triumphantly into the tumultuous reception. Dismounting at the head of his party, Flambard strode across to the equally formidable Colonel Roystone, shaking hands warmly and publicly, to another cheer from the assembled soldiers, and some frantic scribbling by both home correspondents and the already awestruck Natal press. By stages, Flambard was introduced to the assemblies of Imperial officers. It had been decided beforehand that one of his subalterns would be designated to each of the column's companies, in order that every captain should have at his disposal at least one officer who spoke the local tongue and knew the topography, and the temper, of the nearby Zulu border.

One such subaltern was Lieutenant the Honourable Claremont Faunce-Whittington, a larger-than-life and highly imposing character, whose huge waxed moustache, high ruby cheeks and narrow glinting eyes apparently succeeded in unsettling all but the indefatigable Flambard, almost into a discomfiture. The only son of Lord and Lady Faunce-Whittington, Claremont had tried some years earlier to pass through training for a commission in the Royal Navy. Not even Flambard, who had become something of a surrogate father to the much-misunderstood young man, knew exactly what had happened during his studies. All the papers knew to reveal was that the Honourable Faunce-Whittington would take to a farming venture in Cape Colony and had no plans to return to London society. Perhaps unsurprisingly, supposition and gossip did not fail to circulate, but no real details ever came to light.

Now, at the age of thirty, Faunce-Whittington had been drafted onto Flambard's Horse when his own irregular small unit, chiefly comprising gentlemen socialites, had been refused government subsidy to fund their official status.

'Heavens above,' muttered Bond, as Flambard's procession of officers similarly dressed to the formidable commandant and the large lieutenant, seemed to shrink further and further, as each one peeling off to meet and greet the company to which he was to be attached. Somewhere at the back of his mind, he could not help but imagine the doggerel if this large, colonial butterfly who seemed to be flapping about in the background were to be dumped on their party.

Gideon Knight was similarly disposed. 'D'you reckon much on the large chappie to his rear?' he asked Bond.

'Look at the size of him. He's almost a head bigger than the old commandant, and that takes some! Sort of queer chap you got at school. Always loitering, despite their size. Oh God, I think they're coming over here,' Bond simmered through gritted teeth. 'They are, too. Look, Gid, we're going to land up with an elephant!'

'Stop that, both of you!' hissed Westgate in an agony of suppressed hilarity. 'If you two rascals keep that up, you'll have me at it as well!'

'Captain Warren Westgate, Royal Engineers,' Colonel Roystone announced, by way of an introduction.

'Splendid. Superb. Excellent!' beamed Flambard. 'May I have the pleasure of presenting to you gentlemen the Honourable Faunce-Whittington? Faunce, come over 'ere and introduce yourself.'

For his size, the officer seemed at first to be slightly bashful. He blushed, looked at his feet and smiled shyly, like a young girl on her first night of the season. Yet as his eye moved from Captain Westgate to Bond and Gideon Knight, and then past the fixed, staring eyes of the horrified Sergeant Friday, he seemed to begin to resume something of that overwhelming character which had been so apparent before. Then, his beady green eye fell on Coleman, and to their dying day, all who lived to do so would swear that he heard an audible sigh as the officer paused to inspect the file in which the young sapper was stationed.

Unsettled by the man in a way he was quite unable to fathom, Coleman almost stepped back a pace, when Flambard placed a heavy hand on the officer's right shoulder. 'Come on, Faunce,' he boomed warningly. 'Let's go and meet the other officers.'

The whole business was done with mercifully quickly. The Natal Africans, which included Earnest's earners, some irregular Africans from Faunce-Whittington's farmstead and a small group of Basutho mounted riflemen, were placed under the command of Captain Westgate, with the former acting as Zulu speaking adjutant to the Africans.

The following morning they received their orders, with Lieutenant Knight acting as overall second-in-command to Westgate, Bond detailed to all pioneering duties and therefore responsible with Lieutenant Penfold for the Africans, and Faunce-Whittington to accompany the sapper company as a guide.

The following evening, Friday and Coleman, who had moved past their divergent approaches to matters of unit pride, and The Wolves, who in turn had grudgingly come to terms with Coleman, sat drinking around the campfire. Piquet duty was not at that point necessary, but it had been suggested by Friday as a means of keeping the men on their toes and, if necessary, preparing them for an immediate state of readiness for the advance.

That night the two sappers were joined by two NCOs of the Hundred and Tenth, one corporal and two privates of McGonagle's company, and a few local traders.

‘I suppose you make a killing, all the same, though?’ Friday asked innocently, as he filled the beaker of one of the traders yet fuller with army issue rum.

‘Nothing like a war to boost sales,’ the trader laughed garrulously. ‘Stupid idiots come all the way from the old country—’

‘The mother country!’ Jack cut in proudly.

‘As you like, son,’ replied the trader rudely. ‘Then,’ he continued, ‘them officers expect special favours off us that’s left all that behind to begin with.’

Friday nodded, feigning assent, but had to place a restraining hand on the arm of a simmering Coleman.

The truth was of course that the bald sergeant was by no means as silly as people – especially drunken ones – came to assume. He was in fact subtly plying those unscrupulous hawkers with the might of British army liquor to establish which of them might or might not be likely to attempt to defraud his officers when they came to buy their horses. It was a deception with which Coleman was wholeheartedly in favour, his loyalty to Bond necessitating his co-operation with such a scheme.

Gradually, after some time had elapsed and nearly all but Coleman and Friday had drunk themselves into a state of complete and utter transparency, they seemed to have a good idea of which ones were trustworthy and which ones were not. A few very small sums of money changed hands; a few salutary words of warning were passed between soldiers and salesmen in the form of veiled threats and guarded warnings on the part of Sergeant Friday.

Consequently, when the following day came and Bond and Penfold had spent a fruitless morning in Oscaarsberg in search of suitable horses to purchase, Friday was able to report that a Dutch colonial by the name of Piet had been identified as being an apparently trustworthy source. Arrangements were duly made, and the two lieutenants were soon making their way towards an improvised kraal consisting of a couple of rickety-looking wagons and a pair of rather flimsy wattle fences.

'I hope this is worth the effort,' Bond complained to Penfold, as the two of them tramped through the red dust in the heat of the midday sun. 'Much more hoofing it in these kinds of conditions and my feet aren't going to be fit to carry me back to my tent, never mind lead a party into Zululand.'

'I've only got forty pounds until my next banker's draft arrives,' Penfold muttered gloomily. 'If we buy these horses, Albert, it looks as if we'll have to eat grass for the next few days, at any rate.'

Bond was no longer listening. For there, grazing happily within the confines of the improvised kraal, were two of the most magnificent beasts either officer had ever seen in their time as horsemen. The coats gleamed, the tack hung from the wagons in a brilliant parade of polished brass and lustrous black leather, while the contented snorts and neighing as they grazed calmly on the Natal grass was almost nostalgic to Bond.

'Fine pair of handsomes,' commented the Dutchman, who had clearly been awaiting their arrival for some time. He was dressed in a brown cord Norfolk jacket, buff cord riding trousers and a brown felt hat. He wore a collar, necktie and carried a British Webley revolver in a brown leather holster. He beamed at Bond. 'Fine a morning as the pair of gentlemen you are, *captains*,' he added, affecting the imposing pretension of a music hall playbill in his deliberate elevation of the two men.

Penfold was about to correct him when Bond tapped him on the arm.

Sapper officers wore no badges of rank below that of major and rarely in undress uniform. Still, heavily bearded and dressed in the navy patrol and red serge jacket respectively, Bond and Penfold could quite easily have passed for Warren Westgates, especially to the untrained eye of some Boer peasant, and the notion of respect due to a rank above his own rather appealed to Bond. After all, he and Penfold had been forced to endure being bottom of the officer pile in both the mess at Chatham and there in Pietermaritzburg, and the notion of exploiting rank for the sake of closing a deal seemed like a divine opportunity.

'How much do you want for the two?' Bond enquired in his best authoritative voice.

'Hundred pound the pair, your honour,' replied the trader quickly.

It didn't sound quite so bad when you said it so fast, and the idea of walking away with those two magnificent steeds for less than the price of a week's shooting seemed almost too ridiculous to be feasible. Even so, the canny Boer seemed to know far more about horses than they did, and Bond was just beginning to wish that they hadn't allowed flattery to overwhelm them and had brought Gideon Knight or even Captain Westgate along for a second opinion. *Come to that*, thought Bond, as they rode back towards the transit camp on their two new acquisitions, *any of my Irish sappers should have been able to tell a good horse from a bad one*. 'If only we'd ignored the flattery, we might have got the damn things cheaper,' he grumbled, as they rode past the tack shop in the high street, and Bond was forced to gaze wistfully at the tack, clothing, and equipment, which he was now unable to afford.

Penfold had wanted to point out that it was neither his idea nor his intention to keep up the fraud of pretending to be captains, simply on the strength of one Boer's flattering remarks, but thought better of it. He knew Bond when he was 'right' about something and, in any case he, like so many of his caste, looked up to Bond with an awe and admiration which often took first place over common sense. He would sooner have been wrong with Bond than argue against him, and that philosophy was to undergo its greatest test very shortly after they returned to camp.

'Hi, what do you think of these, boys?' Bond called out, as he and Penfold cantered across the grassy field of the parade square where Coleman and Friday were overseeing the loading of some of the mules they had successfully tamed the day before.

'Oh, be-Jesus!' muttered one of the Irish sappers.

'Damn it to hell,' mumbled another.

'Oh dear, what have them bastards been sellin' our officers, Sarn't?' murmured another.

'Why?' shrieked Friday. 'What is it, Paddy? What's the matter with them?'

'Albert! I say, what *have* you two got there?' It was Gideon Knight, thundering across the green on his own horse, and apparently in dire earnest about something or other.

'Horses, Gideon,' Bond replied lightly. 'After all, you chaps have been telling old Penfold and me to get mounted up since almost the day we got here.'

Knight said nothing, dismounted and examined the gleaming equines. He hummed and whistled a good deal but persisted in saying absolutely nothing.

Bond took this as a sign of admiration, and still further when he proudly announced to the assembled company that he and Earnest had managed to swing the deal for a mere hundred pounds, not including the tack.

'That's a lifetime,' sighed Coleman.

'That's two lifetimes,' corrected Friday.

'Hmm, that's a pity,' added Gideon Knight, like a cloud across the midday sun.

'Why?' Bond and Penfold demanded in unison.

'Because I've just been chatting to two of the officers from The Rutlands,' Knight replied grimly. 'Apparently Horace Fenton and William Glazebrook bought a couple of red and black nags off some plausible Dutch tinker, and he vanished with their money three days before the damn things keeled over with twisted guts.'

'Don't tell me,' Bond simmered, 'this trader took them for a captain and a major, respectively?'

'Took them for a ride, that's for sure,' chuckled Gideon Knight. 'Still, I'm glad you two didn't go near the fellow. Now, where did you say you bought those chaps?'

Chapter Thirteen

The territory surrounding the British colony of Natal had long been a contentious issue. In the years prior to the British arrival and settlement in 1805, the various indigenous African peoples who populated the area had already been hotly contesting its ownership. Untroubled by the tsetse fly, and covered in a bed of lush sweet and sour grasses that the hot wet summers and the cool dry winters had made lush and abundant, the area came to be regarded as prime grazing ground. This was soon to be contested by the various tribes of the Zulu people who had been ruthlessly moulded into a single nation by a series of bloody battles, during a time known as 'The Crushing'.

Not so for Bond's joyous and handsome mount, so like its owner in looks and breeding, yet utterly repugnant towards the grasses of the area.

All had otherwise been well for the first few stages of advance. The band had played them out of the capital, and Bond's sapper detail had marched out behind him and his new horse to the tune of the song made so popular around Chatham by Coleman's mother. Then, after they had travelled about five miles along the road, Bond's horse suddenly started to shy, slacken pace, and sometimes stopped all together. Bond, who was more used to stable boys and grooms dealing with the caprices of beasts that he deemed to be no more than quadrupedal transport, irritably demanded to know what was wrong.

'Has the nag eaten anything, Albert?' Gideon Knight enquired, as the steady tramp of the column began to overtake the bewildered lieutenant.

'I'll try him on the grass,' Bond shouted after him. 'Thanks, Gid.'

Sadly, it was not to be.

Coleman, who had suddenly fallen into a state of shock horror as his officer, who usually rode beside him, was doing his best to look behind him for signs of Bond, when he was almost flattened by the horse in front of him. The horse in question belonged to Earnest Penfold who, having also neglected to consider anything but pasture, came to a sudden and untimely halt, almost flattening Coleman and the party of African pioneers at the same time. Rearing, backing, and snorting contemptuously, the beast forced its way out of the line of the column, planting itself firmly by the side of the road and refusing to move.

'Damned bloody horses!' cried Bond, as the irate Warren Westgate broke off with Faunce-Whittington to see what was happening to his officers.

'For goodness sake, you two!' barked the captain, as the two cringing lieutenants watched their mounts tuck happily into a bag of forage provided by the company farrier. 'I thought you said they were grazing when you first saw them?'

'Nuts,' put in Faunce-Whittington airily. 'Those beastly traders scatter grape-nuts in the grass around the kraal so that you think they're eating pasture. Trouble is they can be *so* convincing,' he sighed, wistfully.

'Right, thank you, Faunce, but I think you can go now!' barked Westgate. 'Bert, Earnest, you see these nags are properly fed, then catch up with the column when you've finished. And use your spurs!' he called back at them. 'I don't want you lagging too far behind. We're none too far from The Buffalo River as it is, and there might be Zulu raiding parties about.'

'So what if there are?' Bond mumbled subversively to Penfold. 'We must have at least twelve shots between us in our revolvers, alone. Shouldn't think they'd stand, would you?'

'Probably be frightened off by the horses,' commented Penfold. 'I don't suppose they've seen a horse before, do you, Albert?'

'Tally-ho, chaps! What's the hold up?'

Turning in recognition, Bond and Penfold realised to their horror that the voice in their ears was that of Captain Collingwood, and that they were in grave danger of even being passed by the Royal Artillery.

'Don't fancy giving us a lift on one of those African carriages do you, Snooker?' Bond called lightly after him. He was determined that it should not appear as if he and Penfold were experiencing even the slightest difficulty, especially since Bond was gravely conscious that it had been he who had instigated the purchases in the first place.

When the two officers did finally catch up with the rest of their company, it was well and truly after dark, and the column was already camped on the outskirts of the town of Oscaarsberg, just a mile and a half from the mighty Buffalo River.

There was much hilarity as they rode into the camp, and the subsequent comments and funny remarks of their brother officers were almost sufficient to eclipse those made upon Coleman and Friday by their contemporaries at Durban.

Consequently, when Bond and Penfold galloped through the ranks of white bell tents to the area designated for their own troops, they were greeted by a scornful Gideon Knight, and an utterly unsympathetic Warren Westgate.

'What in God's name did you pair mean by allowing yourselves to be so royally defrauded by a bloody Dutchman?' Westgate demanded. 'For goodness sake, you two, you're supposed to be officers, not idiots. As it was, I had to leave your men in the charge of Mr Faunce-Whittington, Earnest. And as for you, Albert, your poor batman is presently on loan to half the officers of The Hundred and Tenth as *your* punishment for holding everybody up today!'

'Nobody told us we were buying mules,' Bond complained bitterly. 'Really, Gideon, you might at least stick up for us, mate.'

'Not me, Albert!' chuckled Gideon Knight. 'I told you to be careful whom you bought off. As it was, I understand even the combined efforts of your sergeant and batman weren't sufficient to stop you walking into a swizz.'

'Anyway, you're expected in the mess,' Westgate intoned heavily. 'We're expected to give a dinner for The Wolves this time, and you chaps had better show a little willing after today.'

As it was, the two subalterns could only nod mutely as Westgate and Knight wandered back in the direction of the mess tent, so well-lit and already vibrating to the sounds of raucous laughter and merriment.

'Bet I can guess what they're laughing at, too,' Bond added grimly. 'Come on, Earnest, what say we volunteer for duty officers tonight instead?'

'No, better go,' the quiet little officer replied wearily.

Bond snorted in contempt. 'Come on, Earnest, I know there must be some spirit behind that cowardly face of yours, so why must you just fall in all the time?'

'Because that's what we're here to do, in case you had forgotten,' Penfold replied shortly. 'And I don't know about you, Bert, but I want very much to stay in the army, so I'm jolly well going to do as I am told.' Then he added by way of a goodnight, 'and I suggest that you do the same!'

Poor Bond was left simply to groan in the darkness. He had always liked Captain Westgate, and Gideon Knight was supposed to be his best friend, but for Penfold to turn on him as well seemed quite unfair.

As a result, and partly due to the heavy impact of the recent major purchase on his income, Bond decided to snub everyone who had snubbed him, and deliberately neglected to attend the dinner.

The truth was of course that his finances were in an even worse state than Penfold's. The draft from his modest little bank had not yet arrived; his aunt had apparently failed to discern his lamentations of poverty in his last letter, and Coleman needed paying as well.

He hadn't even thought of writing to Clara, or indeed, much of her at all.

In fact, he was just plumping miserably down on the canvas chair in the corner of his tent and weighing up the obvious evils of remaining absent from the mess with those of financial embarrassment, when there came a sound of shuffling in the long grass outside.

Normally, common sense would have suggested he look to his revolver, but so depressed and sorry for himself was the young lieutenant that he merely nodded his head in the direction of the door as his visitor entered.

'Sorry, sir, I d-didn't realise you were here,' Coleman stammered in embarrassment. 'I thought you'd be at the big mess do with all those other officers.'

Bond was about to ask how he knew about it, when to his horror he realised that the poor boy had probably spent the last four hours cleaning boots and polishing buttons for the officers of The Hundred and Tenth.

'Oh, Jack, I am so sorry!' Bond moaned pitifully, as he took in for the first time the appearance of the young sapper.

Jack was, in fact, utterly wretched. The nails of his fingers were all clotted with boot polish and brass cleaner, his laughing blue eyes were red and sore and squinting from the poor lamplight in the tents, and his face was covered with grubby marks and spots of mud from the long day's march.

Coleman tried to look nonchalant as Bond lambasted himself on the fate of his batman on his own account, but soon his weariness began to show through, and tears began to gather behind the bloodshot blue eyes. Even so, he was too proud to cry openly, and there was no way he was going to let Mr Albert down by allowing him to feel even worse. Instead, he managed a tight smile before falling to his usual fatigues. 'Are you all right, Mr Albert, sir?' he asked quietly, as Bond subsided forlornly back down in his chair and began grimly circumcising a short cigar, which he then mechanically unravelled, the rolled tobacco falling to the floor like leaves.

'I'm in trouble, Jack,' Bond confided, rather selfishly under the circumstances. 'Captain Westgate's cross with me, Lieutenant Knight seems more worried about his next promotion than helping me out, and not even Penfold is speaking to me now. And all over those damned horses.'

'Yes, I'm sorry about that, sir,' Coleman mumbled feebly.

'Why? What do you mean?' asked Bond huffily.

'Well, sir, you can blame me, if you like,' the young soldier sighed, genuine guilt flooding into his pleading confession. 'Me and the Sarn't tried talking to them, Mr Albert, but it seems they conned you anyway. Mr Penfold, too,' he added miserably.

Bond starred at Coleman in silence for a second; shame and frustration simply falling on his from Heaven. There was this poor lad, blackened and sore from a whole night's thankless labour apparently in punishment for his officer's bad judgement, blaming himself. Suddenly, Bond recollected who was the elder and, for that matter, the officer. 'Jack, do you truthfully mean to say that you hold yourself and Sergeant Friday responsible for our stupid business dealings?' Bond asked incredulously. 'And what on earth are you doing in here at this hour, in any case?'

'Cleaning your kit, sir,' Coleman replied truthfully. 'I haven't had chance to do it yet, what with all the others and everything.'

'Oh, for goodness sake!' Bond moaned, burying his face in his two hands as he surveyed the results of his handiwork. 'You must accept that this situation is my fault, and no one else's. I made a silly mistake, and you've been punished for it. Now leave those wretched boots till the morning and get yourself a little bit of sleep.'

'You want me to go, Mr Albert?' Coleman asked. The officer was clearly tired, and he could not help feeling guilty for trying to save himself more work at the crack of dawn the following day by completing the job then and there.

'No, wait!' Bond added hastily. 'I mean, I'd rather have your company. I'm not going to get any sleep tonight, anyway.'

Coleman nodded obediently and settled himself down on the grassy floor of the tent. 'Might as well give these a wipe while you've got them on, Mr Albert, sir,' he suggested, gently taking up a cloth and vigorously, yet with almost soothing tactility, massaging both Bond's booted feet while he sat there.

‘I truly am sorry for everything you’ve had to go through on my behalf,’ Bond sighed as he gazed wearily at the fervent expression of dutiful dedication on the sapper’s young face as he worked. ‘Don’t think I don’t know why, either.’

‘Sir?’

‘It’s me, isn’t it?’ Bond continued, with the candid resignation of a man for whom confession had finally become a mercy. ‘It’s my affairs. They’ve noticed my thriftiness in the mess, the economies. It was the same back home when we had money, always being talked about. Now, even here in the army, it’s the same old story. Not quite up to par.’

‘I don’t understand, sir,’ Coleman replied, pausing, eyes widening in concern. ‘You’re an officer! A gent. Least, you are to me,’ he added carelessly, then blushed.

Fortunately, Bond laughed. Although it was undeniably an empty one, something in the lad’s total honesty, faith and downright kindness seemed incongruous, if welcomed.

‘I have my pay as an officer, but it’s negligible next to my social commitments. You see, we must fund our own provisions, uniforms, and sometimes we even must pick up our fellows’ tabs in our turn. The only way to keep out of the rounds is to keep out of the mess, and that’s frowned upon as much as shirking an obligation.’

‘Why?’ asked Coleman, accidentally omitting “sir” in his confusion.

‘Duty,’ Bond replied simply. ‘Obligation, expectation. Form!’

‘Like... paperwork?’ Coleman added, even more bewildered.

‘No! Well, partly, I suppose,’ Bond replied. ‘Oh look, it’s awfully difficult to explain to someone who isn’t.... I mean, who hasn’t...’

‘I’m sorry, sir,’ Coleman blushed, this time with hurt.

'No, don't be!' Bond retracted. 'You're just you, and you're fortunate by it.'

'I'm me,' Coleman repeated unguardedly. 'Well, I reckon that's true enough. If nothing else, life's simple enough when you're poor. Stuff you worry about is above my head and goes right over it 'n all! But I get that you're embarrassed, though you needn't be, sir.'

'That's just it!' Bond coloured, lowered his eyes then raised them once more. The class gulf seemed to be rapidly diluting, leaving two young men in a tent. Two friends, even.

'Getting stitched up over a bar tab ain't new, mind,' Coleman resumed. 'They used to hire in the pubs, see. You'd have to buy drinks for the foreman on a tab if he took you on. Then you got your grub and grog after, settled your tally, then you'd have nothing for the next day, and have to sleep on the floor to be in time for the next day's hiring. You'd owe for that then 'n all. It kind of went on after that. For days, sometimes.'

There was a long silent pause, and Bond was just beginning to wonder whether the boy would ever lower those twinkling blue eyes, which seemed fixed upon him, when there came the sound of further movement outside the tent.

The camp was now in the grip of total darkness. Only the faint glow of the burning oil lamp suspended from the dome-shaped canvas above them gave any light at all. There was a strange scent in the air that had been there since the sun went down, and the mist from off the river was just beginning to creep in and out among the tents.

Painfully aware that the sound they had heard while talking must have been *tattoo* – when all lights must be extinguished and all troops not on designated duties tucked up for the night – Bond hastily gestured for Coleman to hide under his own bed while he investigated the noise.

'You can't be found in here chatting to me like this, do you understand that, Jack?' Bond whispered frantically, as the clatter of sword on boot died away, and the officer became aware of someone standing directly outside. Coleman nodded obediently and slid underneath the blanket as Bond held it up. 'Don't move a muscle,' he murmured. 'If you do, they'll see you through the canvas.' Then, snatching up his revolver, Bond blew out the lamp and peered out of the tent flaps.

The mist was thick, and well in amongst the tents now. A heavy grey pall hung over the camp, and a damp wetness filled the air around them. Gazing through the gloom, Bond was just able to distinguish two figures in the heavy darkness. 'What is it?' he whispered, alternately feigning sleep and praying that they wouldn't notice his blue patrol jacket in place of his nightshirt.

'It's us, Albert – Earnest and Gideon,' answered a voice.

'What do you want?' Bond replied, all too aware of the perils of admitting them with poor Coleman still planted under the bed.

'Warren has a sore head with you for not turning up. It was remarked upon,' Penfold told him quietly. 'You'll owe a bottle or two tomorrow night to make up for it.'

'Well, can't this wait until then?' Bond demanded, anxious above all that the two subalterns should go away and leave him free to dismiss his impromptu bunkmate.

'Just warning you as a mate, not a senior,' Gideon Knight commented blithely. 'Come on, Earnest, Bert's obviously not for talking to this evening.'

With that, they vanished, and Bond was just about to collapse into bed when he realised that Sapper Coleman was still there, crumpled up against the wooden uprights of the frame like a sack of flour in a mill loft. 'Sorry, Jack, but you'll never make it out there,' he whispered. 'You'll just have to make do with one of my blankets for tonight and get back to your own tent before stand-to.'

'I can't take your blanket, Mr Albert,' Coleman protested quietly, yet he could see that there was nothing else for him to do but accept. He must start out first thing tomorrow, long before reveille if he was not to be spotted. 'Thank you.' He smiled through the dark, once again omitting the usual entitlements in an expression of gratitude. 'It's right odd, this is, but... kind... sir.'

You're too good for a soldier, Bond thought to himself, but had the good sense to realise that Jack would not take such an observation as a compliment.

Though by no means fat, Coleman found sleep like one of Shakespeare's "sleek-headed men", more likely as a result of a long day's work than the rudimentary overnight accommodation. Bond, on the other hand, sat and brooded with a "lean and hungry look", thinking far too much, though now about something very different and far removed from his own affairs and the pettiness of mess etiquette.

For now, he sat and starred at the sleeping sapper, the thick blond hair, the biceps folded across the ample chest. If they had been school fellows, the boy would doubtless have been an athlete, a good oar. Boys would have worshipped him as a strong, noble example. Yet he was a labourer, an enlisted man, a boy. Bond was an officer, a mature man of the world, or so he fancied, with his majority and two years, with a gulf in rank and class to temper a growing sense of friendship, kinship, even love, which he knew himself to be developing.

Chapter Fourteen

When he woke the following morning, Albert Bond could only feel a sense of gloom for all that the day would hold in store. He was depressed, had slept badly, and had been shaken by the most terrible dream of the most indescribable nature. Blinking as his eyes adjusted themselves to the harsh glare of the bright morning sunshine directly above his head, Bond leaned forward and scratched his leg. Then he ran his fingers through his thickening hair and rubbed his face, as if to exorcise the rough feeling of dereliction brought on by such terrible sleep, and looked around.

No Coleman to be seen.

Glancing blearily around, he noticed that his blue patrol jacket was slung across the back of his canvas chair, as was his shoulder holster and binocular case. His trousers were neatly folded up on the seat of the chair, and his gleaming black boots stood next to his Foreign Service helmet, now denuded of its shako plate, and darkened to a streaky brown with mimosa bark according to unofficial custom. *God bless that boy*, he thought wearily. *At least that's one less thing for me to worry about today*. In fact, two less, now that the young sapper was no longer in his tent.

It had to be admitted that during the last few days of their station on the Natal bank, Bond had become equally expert at dodging both the probing questions of his brother officers, and the undeniably taxing social obligations that his status as a subaltern entailed.

In fact, it was only after an absurd performance, during which Bond found himself slithering under the canvas of a bell tent while his men were all still inside it, to avoid an invite to a drinks party, that Coleman began to realise that something was up.

Friday, who had long been credited as a seasoned campaigner when it came to sniffing out furtive or erratic behaviour among the other ranks, was also quick to spot the changes in Lieutenant Bond's conduct of affairs.

Consequently, on the evening before the column moved off, Coleman's blond head suddenly popped around the flap of his sergeant's tent, with the very same concern in mind as that which had been troubling the NCO for most of the evening.

To his surprise, Coleman found Friday to be engrossed in performing what seemed to him to be the most bizarre ritual. Rubbing something looking suspiciously like saddle soap into the soles of his feet, Friday then began securing around the arch of each foot strips of impregnated bandage that he then tied off with another strip of the same, until both feet were mummified under his socks.

'Soap and liniment,' he declared, as if to answer the question that clearly betrayed itself on the young sapper's fresh face. 'You should do the same,' he added, nodding seriously.

'Sarn't?' For a moment Coleman's placid face contorted into a mask of bewilderment. Then, as if to check himself for questioning, he nodded obediently and removed both boots and socks. His feet were indeed in some poor condition. The heel, sole and fifth toe of each foot had been hardened to a yellow callous; the normally rough skin between his other toes was sore and scabby, and both heel and toe were beset with blisters from the march. Chatham street lads didn't have shoes, often until their late teens. *Even the cobbles were kinder to my feet than those rotten bloody army boots*, he thought wryly.

'Looks bad. Must learn to take more care,' Friday told him, wagging his finger reproachfully at the mess on Coleman's feet and passing him the liniment, together with a roll of bandage. 'Feet come first, lad, at least, after your belly!'

'Sorry, Sarn't,' the boy mumbled. 'It's just that I've been so preoccupied with Mr Albert to worry about my feet.'

'Pre— What did you say?' Friday repeated incredulously, dropping his poultice back in its bowl with a damp splat, and raising his wiry eyebrows.

'Pre-occu-pied,' Coleman repeated slowly, so that his startled sergeant might have more time to comprehend it. 'Mr Albert said I was too preoccupied with his problems, and that I ought to write a letter home to my ma rather than deal with him.'

'Oh, and have you?' Friday demanded, utterly nonplussed. The truth be told the bald sergeant was secretly rather pleased by the lad's loyalty, if not the implied familiarity. It had been a partnership that he had created after all, and even though he had thought to have been through it all before, never had he seen one so transcendent of the class barrier between officer and man without apparent break in discipline or protocol, at least as yet.

Even so, he did not hold with too high a standard of literacy among the lower ranks and attempted to mask his secret satisfaction by warning Jack not to get above himself by learning too many long words.

Slightly embarrassed by all this discussion of his own life, Coleman swiftly returned to the point of his visit: the increasing furtiveness of Lieutenant Bond.

'Officer business, I'm afraid,' Friday shrugged dispassionately. 'Can't be helping them with everything after all, too much work to be done,' he added, double fastening the bandage around his left foot, tucking in the ends to stop them trailing out of his boot on the march.

'Yes, but if Mr Albert's in trouble over money, wont he get in more trouble with the captain, Sarn't?' Coleman persisted doggedly.

Friday thought for a moment, the hairy eyebrows drawn in close above his staring green eyes as he pondered the predicament. He scratched his beard, and Coleman was almost beginning to imagine that he could just make out the noise of the sergeant's brain ticking, when the eyebrows suddenly lifted. An idea had come to mind, and for Ludo Friday this was a rarity indeed.

For he did not hold with ideas as such, and firmly believed that it was not the soldier's prerogative to be forever consumed by too much consideration. A thinking soldier was, to his mind, a non-conformist and individuality made for indiscipline among those who most needed it. Even so, he had never in his life met a soldier like Jack, and the young lad's obviously genuine concern for the plight of his officer stood as testament to his own skills as a professional judge of character. 'If the officer is short of money,' he declared at last, 'is our fault since we let him buy that wretched horse. So, we are obliged, Sapper, to help him with his difficulty. We took upon ourselves to investigate those traders, and to offer judgement to Lieutenant Bond, but our faith was misplaced. It falls to us then to see what we may do, as common men, to redress the slight to his dignity and, if necessary, his purse.'

'Chatham ain't the Cape,' Coleman replied, colouring deeply at the implication that his sergeant's name and standing might have diminished, and praying Friday hadn't caught the drift. 'He can have my pay, Sarn't!' Coleman suddenly added, well-meaning overmastering propriety for a moment. 'He needn't pay me for fagging for him, neither,' the young soldier added firmly.

'Sapper!' Friday snapped back at him. 'We do *not* go about giving our money to officers. It would be a slight to his dignity, if such a thing ever came out. Huh!'

'Yes, Sarn't. Sorry, Sarn't,' replied the crestfallen Jack. 'Mr Albert's a gent,' he added. 'I want to help him so much, but he'd probably go and shoot himself before he'd let me give him anything of mine. He told me, you know, Sarn't, gentlemen don't take help off of other people. He's so proud.'

'Keep your voice down, soldier!' squealed Friday, suddenly aware of the fact that there were other tents near his own, and that others might be listening in. 'You are loyal. That's good. But he ain't your mate. It don't do for folk to think you're familiar. Mark me, lad, both of you will lose by it!'

Coleman was just trying to recall something that Mr Albert had said to him once about pots and kettles, when they suddenly heard the alarm go off.

A shot had been fired, and the bugle called stand-to immediately the noise was heard. As it turned out, the incident was nothing more than a minor scare, and yet it heralded the first fatality of the campaign.

Several of Lieutenant Penfold's African pioneers had suddenly decided to leave the camp and wander down to the river to refill their water carriers, apparently either ignorant or unconcerned by the surgeons warnings about contaminated water sources. It was also quite probable that their white non-commissioned officer had not bothered to acquaint them with the dangers, but in the event, it was not the water that proved to be fatal. Venturing so near the Zulu border, one or two of them had decided to remove the twisted strip of red rag that denoted their loyalty to a British African contingent. It was for this reason that, when the Africans came running back from the river, shouting to one another brandishing spears, that disaster struck.

A young soldier in The Wolves, presumably posted on daylight sentry as some form of punishment for a minor transgression, suddenly saw some eight or ten African warriors come bounding up the track from the drift. Alarmed, he had shouted a challenge, but the local men, clearly unable to understand English, apparently took his oratory to be some sort of a lark, shouting back and making throwing gestures with their spears. Admittedly, they had still been larking around when they did this, but the grim reality of their impending action must have told heavily upon the young soldier's mind for he fired, killing one of the Africans. As the remainder had surged forward indignantly, stirred understandably into action by the apparent cold-blooded murder of a comrade, several white African NCOs jumped up from their breakfast and joined in the pandemonium. As it was, both the young soldier and several of the Africans were hauled up before Colonel Roystone, and were very nearly flogged as a result.

It was only the intervention of the much-respected Commandant Flambard, and the outrage of Lieutenant Penfold over the rough treatment of his men that successfully averted a mutiny among the African troops.

'Admittedly it wasn't entirely the Africans' fault,' Colonel McEnry remarked to Snooker Collingwood later. 'But these fellows are turned out more African local than soldier, so what are our poor chaps supposed to think?'

Even so, the men of the West Rutlands blamed the Africans, who in turn looked to their engineer officer for support, and the bad feeling between the sappers and The Wolves was not all together extinguished by the time the orders came to proceed to the drift.

Whatever Penfold's introspective disposition suggested, the little lieutenant was by no means blind to the effect of the incident upon his "earners", nor the events to which their disquiet might eventually lead. As it turned out, the events that were to follow would have even more profound an effect on their loyalty than even he could begin to imagine.

Chapter Fifteen

The day was in fact a good deal less sunny than it had been of late. The mist of last night still hung with thick density over the river crossing and made walking about in the early morning dew a rather chilly and unpleasant business.

The grass was sodden; the regular tracks to and from the kitchen tents had been turned to mud by the constant stream of tramping boots, and the clingy wetness of the cold, pale grey sunlight infiltrated even well covered limbs.

As Bond wandered past them, Collingwood's seven pounder guns were just being prepared for mobilization and limbered up for attachment to the horses.

The boxes were just being fitted to the saddle trees, and the horses being harnessed for riding, when he arrived. Looking up from the business of loading his rockets into their panniers, Collingwood called across to Bond. 'Hi, Albert! Sorry you missed last night's do. Gut cramp, wasn't it?'

'Eh? What's that? Oh yes, of course. Thank you, Snooker, I'm much better now,' Bond replied hurriedly, having only just cottoned on to what the officer was saying.

'Yes, Gideon Knight told us you'd been down with it since you got in last night. Damn shame, that. Missed a good one, you did.'

'Well, never mind. Perhaps another time, then,' Bond added hastily. 'I must go, Snooker, we have to move to the river before the rest of the column wakes up.'

In fact, any misgivings the young officer might have had as to the response of his contemporaries would prove to be unfounded. Orders had been received, and at 4:00 in the morning Captain Westgate had been asked by Colonel Roystone to assemble a heavy pont – a floating bridge designed to ferry troops across the river by way of a series of ropes – in preparation for the mass crossing by Number Six Column.

By the time stand-to was sounded after breakfast, Bond, Friday and his small contingent of sappers had successfully constructed, secured, and transported the pont some two hundred yards to the riverbank. Shortly afterwards, they were joined by Lieutenant Penfold's African pioneers, and the tricky, tedious business of hauling the pont on wooden runners was undertaken.

Bond, stripped to his shirtsleeves despite the mist, was now sitting exhaustedly on a stump of one of the trees so recently felled to make the runners. The sweat clung to his forehead, and his bronze hair hung in limp, soggy curtains over his rapidly tanning face.

Coleman, whose back had borne most of the responsibility for felling those same trees, now leaned on his axe with his sleeves rolled up, and his silky blond hair simply running wet with perspiration.

Friday mopped his brow; engineer's bun-tin cap still placed on top of his bald head to keep the sun off, and his long straggly beard hanging in a wet mass down the front of his grubby blue shirt.

All white collars had been turned black by the work, and bits of bark, sawdust and small twigs had been liberally mixed in hair, beards and down the back of necks, causing considerable irritation and discomfort. Every crease and contour of their bodies was cluttered with dirt from their work, and the muddy banks of the river clung to their boots and gaiters and, for Bond, simply made a mockery of all Coleman's efforts.

'Morning, Albert,' greeted Penfold cheerily. 'Although by rights I shouldn't even be speaking to you, I thought I'd bring my chaps down here to give you a hand.'

'Nice of you,' Bond retorted dryly. 'But I think you'll find all the hard work's been done now, eh, Jack?'

Coleman nodded, before upending his already half-empty bottle of water over his head and shaking the drips from his hair like a dog taking a bath.

'Sorry, Earnest,' Bond added apologetically. 'Of course we'd like some help. Tell your chaps to get either side of that pont and get it down to the water. Friday!'

'Yes, sir?'

'Get on top and make sure you don't fall off. I don't want those auxiliaries shoving the damn thing into the water before we've even had a chance to sling the ropes. Am I understood, Sergeant?'

'Yes, sir!' Friday repeated, before leaping bodily onto the back of the wooden construction and shouting some bizarre garble of slang, which he obviously meant for the auxiliaries to understand, and a brisk hand gesture denoting far better that he wanted them to move!

Penfold dismounted from his horse and, removing his helmet, proceeded to join Lieutenant Bond at his work.

It was only when they reached the banks of the river that the cultural challenges of Earnest's "earners" were to come readily apparent to their officers. For, having pushed and heaved the thing the few extra yards to the edge of the water, they suddenly stopped dead in their tracks.

Friday, who was straddled like the Colossus of Rhodes with one foot on either side of the pont, nearly fell into the water. As it was, the manic sergeant was only able to save himself from further humiliation by grabbing hold of the sides of the modified raft and involuntarily yelling something derogatory, which the high pitch of his voice mercifully disguised.

'Why won't they move on?' Bond demanded, jumping to his feet, and snatching up a shovel with the same menace as if he were about to use it on the diffident African auxiliaries.

'I can't understand it!' wailed Penfold in horror. 'They seemed so co-operative earlier.'

'Sergeant Friday, get these idiots moving. Now!' cried Bond, virtually reduced to apoplexy by the sudden decline in their productivity.

'Won't move, sir!' Friday replied. 'Friday don't understand a word they're saying.'

'Well, that's fairly understandable, Sergeant, seeing as they're Africans!' cried Lieutenant Penfold, leaping stubbornly to the defence of his "earners".

'Try being quiet for a moment, you lot!' intoned a fourth voice. Then, to their mixed astonishment, amazement, and awe, the two officers turned to look on the rugged features, massive bulk and huge white whiskers of Commandant Gillespie Flambard, commander of Flambard's Horse. He shouted something in African; riding a little way down towards the riverbank to glean the reason for the sudden disruption in the process of moving. Next, he exchanged some short words with the leader of the party before returning to the two lieutenants on the knoll above the crossing. 'They say they're scared of the

Zulus, and they don't want to cross the river until it's been blessed by their diviner.'

'Diviner?' Bond repeated incredulously. 'You mean a witchdoctor, Colonel?'

'It's their belief, which India teaches us that we dismiss at our peril!' Flambard reproved. 'It's no different to the superstitions of a Christian sailor or farmer, and no easier to shift! You'll not get them across without it!'

Bond and Penfold went into a huddle. They had to do something, lest the whole crossing would be felled at the first hurdle. Whether by magic or despite it, the pont *had* to be floated on time, and the padre wasn't available for a conversion, or a miracle.

'Sapper Coleman!' Bond called, an idea suddenly occurring to him. 'We don't need, or have time for a witchdoctor to sail a barge now, do we?'

'No, sir!' cried Coleman enthusiastically. 'You show 'em, sir!'

Bond looked at Coleman flexing his muscles under the ripped shirt, and damp blond fringe hanging over his face, which was simply lit up with the prospect of rising to their first real challenge, and his self-confidence soared. 'Sergeant Friday,' he yelled across Coleman.

'Yes, sir?' called back Friday, still straddling the grounded pont like a deserted child on a park swing.

'Get two good men and some even better rope,' Bond instructed. 'Coleman and I are going to get that pont across the river ourselves.'

'For God's sake, wait for some armed support, Albert!' squeaked Penfold in alarm. 'There could be Zulus waiting for you. You'll be killed.'

'For heaven's sake, stop being such an alarmist, Earnest!' Bond remonstrated lightly, unbuckling the shoulder strap from which his revolver holster was suspended and dashing with Coleman towards the edge of the river.

Dumbstruck, and probably slightly bemused at the erratic behaviour of the white *induna*, the auxiliaries fell back and observed.

'Grab a sapling or something, Jack,' Bond instructed. 'You are going to take me punting.'

'Punting, sir?' Coleman repeated excitedly.

'Ponting, I should more accurately have said,' Bond corrected. 'I'm going to stretch a rope across the river, and we are going to ferry it over on that pont. Once we get to the other side, you and I will dig in some stakes, and then we'll send the damn thing back for Friday and those blessed superstitious Africans. If Mr Penfold,' he added significantly, 'is too windy to come with us and would prefer to remain on the other side, then that is up to him.'

Turning away, Penfold remounted his horse and thundered back to the camp to raise the re-enforcements he felt sure would be necessary to such an undertaking. Taking the pioneering pont across the river was indeed a hazardous task but there was no other way to do it, in any case.

Bond was determined that he should not be left making excuses to Captain Westgate, and so resolved to ferry it across himself with the able aid of Sapper Coleman. 'At least we'll know if the thing floats or not,' he commented to Friday, as both he and Coleman snatched up dormant rifles, placed them on top of the pont and began the process of floating her on the river.

The drift itself was not an easy one to traverse by anything less than a horse or barge, being a wide, brown expanse of water, shrouded on the opposite sides by two large, craggy hills and a nek, a pass, between the two. The normally exposed sandbanks on either side had been engulfed by the post-drought rains of the previous few weeks and seemed to drop away about thirty feet from the river into a sort of muddy depression. This was shrouded by all sorts of aquatic foliage – bulrushes and weed – and might easily provide some measure of cover for any waiting enemy.

Even so, the two of them launched the pont into the water and were soon scrambling aboard. It went a few feet, rocked from side to side a bit, but overall maintained its stability. There was a cry of delight from Earnest's "earners", and Friday was just about to toss his cap in the air for sheer joy when Captain Westgate rode up, heading up the remainder of the company and followed by Faunce-Whittington with a large contingent of Flambard's Horse.

'Carry on, Sergeant,' Westgate saluted, as Friday snapped to attention and did what he could to arrange the "earners" into some semblance of military order. The trouble was of course that they all looked alike to someone like Friday. Indeed, were it not for the red rags twisted around their heads, the African pioneers he could well have taken for hostile Zulu raiders. To the unworldly sergeant they were numberless Africans, and so the last thing that he was likely to notice was when a group of them broke off from the main party and skirted a few hundred yards down the bank of the river, out of sight of the assembled company.

Penfold dismounted, took out his binoculars, and dashed across to the knoll, just above the point where the bank fell away, to watch the pont's progress.

Coleman had a strong right arm; in consequence, the improvised barge seemed to move very quickly across, as the fit young sapper wrestled with the prevailing current. At last, they managed to traverse the main body of the river itself and came gradually in on the spit of the bank.

Coleman plunged the improvised punt into the soft silt of the riverbed, and Bond gathered up the ropes and stakes before making a massive cat-leap for the shore. 'Come on, Jack!' he called up to the young sapper on the pont. 'I need your muscle down here to set these anchors fast.'

Coleman nodded in obedience, hopping lightly off the flat deck of the improvised barge and landing feet first in the rushes.

'If we work fast, we should be able to get the wretched thing back to the other side in time to get some deck down,' Bond informed Coleman, as they swiftly yet steadily hammered home the two wooden stakes in some solid earth a few feet from the bank.

The barge itself, having only just been constructed that morning, and still being only a prototype variation on the standard "floating bridge" of the Royal Engineers, still had no proper planking to support large numbers of infantry, and was essentially still a timber skeleton.

With an effort, despite the combined power of their well-toned physiques, the sapper and officer succeeded on stretching the ropes around in a pulley fashion, before gathering up the considerable remains and hurling them back onto the pont.

Westgate, watching through Penfold's binoculars from the opposite bank was, quietly, highly impressed with the efficiency of Bond's methods. Observing that the officer had completed his work on the other side and was now about to return to his side of the river, Westgate had just sent word to the column commander when the sound of horses' hooves, bits, axle trees and jangling harnesses came upon him. 'Hi,

Snooker,' Westgate called out to the arriving officer at the head of a convoy of artillery carriages. 'Don't tell me you're ready to get your guns across the river, because we haven't even completed our pont yet!'

'No matter. The colonel wanted you to have some cover over the opposite bank, anyway,' retorted the captain cheerily. 'We'll un-limber, the horses can have something to eat, and you chaps can finish messing about with your boats.'

Westgate laughed and returned to the task of assembling his sappers in groups along the edge of the bank.

They were still waiting on the necessary equipment to be sent from the ship when the sound of a single rifle shot penetrated the still keen morning air.

'Take cover!' Friday ordered, as he leaped down from his position on top of the log runners by the left side of the improvised drift, and the auxiliaries rolled underneath them as if the enemy were really upon them.

Bond and Coleman, meanwhile, had only just completed their work and were disengaging from the other side of the river when the shot rang out across the water. That was followed in short bursts by even more sporadic firing, and the sound of raised African voices in tones of high excitement, which carried across to their ears like the unmistakable peal of a church bell in winter.

At the first sound of shooting, the two of them literally stepped backwards, plunging with a loud splash into the dark water between the stabilising arms of the pont and vanishing below the surface of the river. They were under for several seconds before their two glossy heads emerged from the foam, hands grasping instinctively for the rifles on the planks of the barge, and eyes straining to see over their necessarily obscuring cover. Spitting out a large quantity of water, Bond reached across the foremost of those planks and, hauling himself up a little way, cast around to see what was going on. From his position, he could see really very little indeed.

There appeared to be some considerable commotion on the other side of the river. Several sappers were pushing and shoving some of the Africans, although this in itself was nothing out of the ordinary.

What Bond could not have seen from his position was how the confusion had been caused in the first place.

Several of the African pioneers, apparently highly disgruntled at being treated with such scorn over what they considered to be a legitimate fear of crocodiles, had broken off from the main party. Having wandered a little way downstream from the crossing, those Africans had proceeded to open fire on several logs they fancied to be crocodiles. This had caused great alarm, and their fellows had instinctively let off a volley as well. This cacophony of small arms activity had led Sergeant Friday to believe that they were indeed coming under attack from Zulu fire on the opposite side, and he had acted accordingly by raising the alarm.

Having ascertained either way that the threat was not on their side of the river, nor did it pose any risk to their security on the pont, Bond found himself glancing down at Coleman's glossy, wet blond head instead.

Being still up to his neck in the lapping water below, Coleman was subsequently treated to a considerable drenching and a further mouthful of water as Bond re-entered the river with a loud splash. Coleman cursed, spluttered, and shook out the drips.

Without thinking, and certainly without reflecting on the portents of such frivolities, Bond suddenly reached out and plunged Coleman's head under the water, remaining for several seconds before releasing him, and allowing him up for air.

Gasping, mouthing incredulities and utterly amazed by his officer's behaviour, he thrust out his hand as if to seize Bond's shoulder and reciprocate the prank. Then, as though suddenly mindful of the barrier between the two of them, he hesitated. His hand fell limply back under the water and though still making good-natured sport of his dunking, respectfully refrained from further horseplay, and waited for Bond to do likewise.

Still laughing, Bond looked back at Coleman as they bobbed up and down on the current. Then Coleman began to giggle; the relieved giggle of one acutely aware of a near over-reaction turned to relief by the false alarm. Yet oddly no embarrassment.

Then, as they looked searchingly into one another's eyes for a moment more, they finally realised that the gulf placed between their respective rank and upbringing was gradually beginning to disappear forever, replaced by a fraternity that only such circumstances could instil in two so very different people.

The smiling, not to say laughing, eyes of the face before him conveyed to Bond all that his exile from his London set had so long deprived him. Yet this was far more genuine, borne of a spirit so untainted by pretension and social self-consciousness that it allowed itself the freedom to shine from the boy's face. He was Bond's social and hierarchical inferior, yet he was confident, unvarnished, unapologetic. Boyish yet manly... beautiful, even.

With an effort belied by a casual remark about not letting the duckweed grow under their feet, the officer hauled himself onto the barge and, with outstretched hand, lifted Coleman's stocky frame from the tumultuous waters beneath. They were both upright now, and Bond was just beginning to wonder how on earth he was meant to redress the balance of propriety once more, when another shot rang out.

This time, however, it was neither panicking troops, nor the overzealous Sergeant Friday.

No sooner had Bond managed to secure a hand on his Martini-Henry, an actual hostile bullet whistled past his ear and splintered the wooden rail beside him.

With a cry of warning, Coleman swept Bond off his feet, spreading himself across the widely spaced timbers of the improvised deck, the officer firmly beneath him, and the full width of his back obscuring Bond's upper body, physically protecting him from fire.

Rounds were flying thick and fast now, and back on shore Collingwood was already bringing his guns into line to shell the crag from whence the Zulu rifles were sniping.

Another bullet plopped into the water, just inches away from Coleman's right ear. Terrified beyond his wits yet driven by an overwhelming urge to protect his officer, Coleman pressed his body still harder on that of the prostrate Bond.

Having hit his head as he fell, Bond had allowed his rifle to fall between the open timbers of the pont. In any case, they had brought no expense ammunition with them, Bond's hasty desire to complete their task completely overwhelming an officer's natural attention towards the finer precautions for personal safety.

Even so, as the blood seeped from his head and dripped into the murky waters below, Bond was spared the chilling sight that fell on Coleman's wide open eyes.

For there, just below their position on the river, a large flotilla of black and brown objects, with highly ridged backs and a long, disrupted line of scales had begun to make its way downstream, and Coleman, in his fear, knew exactly what they were.

Having been terrified, like most new recruits of his age on their first Foreign Service, Coleman was acutely aware of the reputed ferocity of all types of African wildlife. He checked his blankets nightly for scorpions, examined his boots thoroughly for snakes and spiders, and regularly scanned the horizon for sight of the swarms of killer bees that his mind's eye – with aid from scuttlebutt – had repeatedly conjured in him.

As soon, therefore, as the presence of the carnivorous reptiles had flitted into view, he was scrabbling frantically with the two or three rounds that he had in his expense pouch.

As the weeks of training at Chatham slowly worked their way back into his racing mind, he carefully called to mind the screeched instructions of his troop NCOs. Slotting one brass cartridge containing one lead slug carefully into the breach of his rifle and snapping block with the lever arm behind the trigger guard, Coleman lifted the sight arm above the chamber and carefully took aim at the advancing crocodiles. Then, utterly disregarding the rounds still whizzing overhead, he lifted the muzzle of his Martini-Henry and fired.

The brave young sapper's actions were suddenly rewarded by a quantity of blood in the dark, murky waters further down the river, as one of the fearful creatures rolled helplessly over in the water like the hulk of a capsized fishing boat. Then, as suddenly as the firing had started, the heavy burst of one of the seven-pound Armstrong guns being fired off on the opposite bank broke into the confused wall of sound already thrown up by the commotion. That was followed almost immediately by the loud, deafening whistle of a shell flying directly overhead, and a cataclysmic blast as it burst upon its target on the further side of the river. Huge clouds of smoke and dust bellowed from within the crag, and much of the sniping ceased all together, and yet much of it seemed to continue from isolated pockets along the Zulu bank.

Preparing his second gun, Snooker Collingwood studiously redirected his line of fire on a small clump of aloes, just to the left of the base of the escarpment, from whence much of the remaining rifle smoke seemed most prevalent.

Bringing the field gun about, the gunners set about training its muzzle on the already decimated landscape of the sandy embankment. Satisfied that his salvo would hit home, Collingwood gave the order for number two gun to fire.

Yet another deafening boom echoed across the rippling water and burst on the other side in a massive cloud of dust, sand, and uprooted foliage. For many on the Natal bank, the mangled, disfigured glimpses of lifeless limbs on the farther side were their first real ones of the Zulu people. Several had bits missing; bent arms and legs were twisted into peculiar shapes, and from somewhere in the shattered canopy of the rock face, the mournful groan of an injured warrior could be heard, droning his lamentations until death finally overwhelmed his body.

A loud cheer went up from the assembled companies on the Natal bank and, as soon as the pont was within reach from the shallows, Commandant Flambard raised his right arm and ordered his irregular horsemen into the river.

As soon as one of the sappers entered the water, however, yet another shot ricocheted off the wooden sides of the pont, striking him square in the face and causing him to pitch into the water. The engineers had suffered their first fatality, and it was not for several minutes that another party of men could be persuaded to emerge from their cover behind one of the wagons and attempt to bring in the floated target, still containing the incapacitated Bond and the heroic Sapper Coleman.

This they finally did achieve, however, and the pont was hauled in and anchored to the Natal bank, while Sergeant Friday and Lieutenant Knight dashed bravely down to the water's edge and grappled with the two survivors to bring them ashore.

Coleman was conscious but had hurt his knee rather badly through falling so heavily on Bond and had consequently to be lifted off the engineer officer so that both could be removed to a position of cover.

Commandant Flambard, meanwhile, was the first to gain the opposite side of the river, after wrestling fearfully with the current and urging his exhausted horse up the steep embankment. As soon as he was across, however, several Zulus broke cover, and throwing down their rifles took up an assault on the advancing magistrate.

As soon as his horse had gained a footing, the dynamic commandant had already loaded and fired his short barrel Swinburne-Henry carbine, bringing down the first of the attacking warriors with a single bullet. Then, aware that to load the rifle a second time would mean certain death, the ferocious Flambard spurred his horse and galloped straight for the remaining dozen, who were alternately throwing their spears and attempting to charge him down with their broad bladed assegais.

Drawing his revolver as the fearsome warriors converged upon him, Flambard succeeded in hitting several of them at close range, and in different parts of the body, before one of the lightweight throwing spears met its target, the head embedding itself in his burley shoulder, and unhorsing him. With a roar of indignation as he crashed to the ground, Commandant Flambard continued to fire on his assailants, killing two of them only feet away from his position of prostration on the sandy bank. As one of only four remaining warriors pressed home his attack, sharpened assegai raised menacingly overhead, and Flambard could clearly see the whites of his eyes, the pulsating of his chest and the long row of teeth on the amulet about his throat, another shot rang out.

Faunce-Whittington, who had succeeded in gaining the bank only a few seconds after the commandant, upon seeing the predicament in which his commanding officer had been placed, had immediately produced his revolver, and shot the warrior dead.

As it was, the formidable magistrate seemed to be utterly dismissive of his wound, using the mighty muscles of his powerful thighs to physically repel his second attacker, before pulling the spear from its entanglement in his own body and stabbing it into his assailant. Then, before his loyal lieutenant had time to fire a second round, Flambard had the fourth man between his knees, had him disarmed, and his throat between his fingers, furiously throttling the breath from his body. The white whiskers and yellow teeth glared against the magistrate's ruddy face as he killed, his enemy of more than a generation slowly asphyxiated by the mighty fingers of his bloodied hands. Once the breath had been expelled, Flambard regarded his noble adversary and prayed.

The remaining Zulus were soon cleared from the hillside by Flambard's irregulars under Lieutenant Faunce-Whittington, and a handful of spears, shields, knobkerries and obscure firearms brought back for auction among the officers who had not been in on the kill.

The commandant himself however was, despite his protestations, deemed by the surgeon to be too severely wounded to continue to accompany the invasion.

'For goodness sake stop fussing!' he bellowed at the terrified orderlies, as they attempted to carefully remove the bloody mess of the ripped patrol jacket from his massive bulk. 'And now look, I've got blood all over me wretched medal ribbons.'

'I really do think it would be better for you to stay here, Colonel,' Faunce-Whittington persisted in earnest. 'That wound could be sloughing, and you have no idea what they might have tipped the head with.'

'Oh, do stop flapping, Faunce!' Flambard barked impatiently.

'You really ought to consider yourself a little more,' the surgeon remonstrated with him severely. 'That little spearhead might well have penetrated your chest, had the warrior thrown a little further. As it is the wound is quite likely to suppurate, and you have lost a lot of blood.'

'Mrs Flambard never nagged like this in twenty years of marriage,' the commandant barked in response. 'And I had far worse than this to deal with during the last war with the Xhosa. I'm perfectly all right, I tell you. So will you chaps please see to more urgent matters and leave me in peace!'

Nonetheless, Lieutenant-Colonel McEnry decided that the magistrate's wounds were too likely to cause him discomfort, and that he should not be allowed to proceed into Zululand. As a concession, and largely since they did not want to lose his valuable irregular battalions, the decision was made to place Flambard in command of a large, combined garrison of irregular volunteers.

Having been ordered by Colonel Roystone to guard the massive zinc sheds and recently constructed supply depot on the Natal side of the drift, Flambard felt very much as if he had been pensioned off, and grumpily resigned himself to spending the war as a glorified quartermaster. This was a major blow, not least to Warren Westgate's Field Company, who had subsequently to do without much of the valuable support and assistance of a seasoned colonial war veteran. Even so, there was much joviality in the air already, as the news of Bond and Coleman's heroism under fire began to make its way down the ranks of Number Six Column. Recriminations over Bond's failure to attend the dinner were forgotten, and there were even rumours of a brevet majority in the air for Westgate.

This was one bit of good news for which the sapper captain had been praying since the news of a war first broke at home. Now fast approaching forty, Westgate was troubled with the notion of remaining too long at the same rank and perhaps failing all together in his career ambitions, and those of his loving wife. Still further perhaps had this sense of the necessity for self-advancement come about as a result of finally meeting the mythical AW McGonagle.

This grumpy, defensive, derided old Scot had instilled in Warren Westgate upon their very first meeting an almost pathological fear of stagnation, a dread of failure and an even keener sense of awareness for the social implications for Annie and the children if he failed to successfully achieve promotion.

Linked to this was the almost contemptuous regard in which Captain McGonagle was held by most of the officers in the column. Naturally objectionably and in apparent spite of his time in India, even openly opposed to annexation, Bond's uncle let it be known that he believed the use of Natal Africans as auxiliaries would ultimately lead to the trouble. McGonagle widely proclaimed that too many British officers were like those of the "John Company" who had been massacred with their families when sepoys of the Indian soldiers had run amok while they were in church one Sunday morning.

This caused much derision, and opened old wounds for Bond, who was just getting past the idea of his uncle as some heretical buffoon. As it was, the old captain's tirade pervaded all ranks, sparking several fist fights between the men of the Ninety First, and those of the West Rutlands who had seen service fighting in India.

It also had the result of relegating Bond, hitherto the hero of the hour, to the far less coveted status of being the nephew of the man dubbed "That damned Indian". Fortunately, serious disaster was averted the following day when the column received orders to cross the river, and from then on everything was secondary to that.

Bond was far too preoccupied by his duties as pont master general, while Friday and Coleman busied themselves with the arduous task of helping Gideon Knight to throw up an earthwork on the Natal side of the river. Those elements of the West Rutlands who might have given them further earache on account of Lieutenant Bond's uncle were, in turn, far too busy with the march into enemy territory. This was no mean feat, since it entailed moving several hundred head of cattle across the lowest point of the drift, along with tools, equipment, and the now lately stuck tents from the camp, not to mention their supplies, ammunition, weapons, and medical equipment.

Wagons were dragged, levered, pushed and pulled through the muddy river and up the bank on the farther side, while Snooker Collingwood's artillery were obliged to wait until both battalions of infantry, most of the African pioneers, and the remaining sappers had been ferried across. Once this had been done, they were able to dismantle their precious Armstrong guns, haul them onto the now empty pont and then charged with the further task of hauling everything connected with their trade across the river before the horses could be driven across.

The meat had to walk for itself, but rum, beer, wine, tinned preserves, and mealie bags had also to be ferried or carted from bank to bank in the several hundred wagons necessary to a column of their size.

As the day drew to a close, Colonel Roystone sat mounted on his horse on the opposite side, watching his army move by stages into Zululand. He had been highly pleased with the operations so far, not least the success of shelling several Zulus before they had even crossed the river. He was also highly relieved that the worth of the venerated Commandant Flambard had proved his contingent of horsemen to be as well worthy of his own reputation by clearing the Zulu scouts from the immediate areas local to the drift. To his own mind, Roystone was convinced that a swift, lightening series of attacks on the neighbouring homesteads of the influential Zulu chiefs who populated the areas would soon quell the impi into submission. A great believer in the merits of modern ordinance, Roystone was also quietly ambitious that the use of both field gun and rocket trough would have such a profound effect on the "unsophisticated tribesmen" that their traditional attack strategy would prove ineffectual and crumble under the first few salvos.

Snooker Collingwood was very definitely his boy and, he hoped, would provide a series of victories so straightforward and abrupt that the ten-to-one man ratio expected of Anglo-Zulu engagements should see the enemy utterly wiped out by superior firepower.

'It's all very well, old man,' grumbled Flambard to McEnry, as the remaining troops trickled across the moonlit river that night, 'but you have to realise that these people are not going to simply run away the instant you produce a rocket or unlimber a gun.'

'Are you saying you don't think artillery is an effective deterrent, Commandant?' McEnry enquired, somewhat incredulously.

'Not as a deterrent, no,' replied the magistrate wearily. 'Don't you see what I'm telling you, Arthur, The Zulu impi aren't just about to peel off in the face of artillery or a few horses. They're a warrior people; people who resent our coming into their country in the way we have. Don't get me wrong, old man, I fear the Zulus as much as any man on the border, but you must not make the mistake of assuming they are stupid... cos they ain't!'

'Even so,' replied McEnry, tossing his cigar butt idly into the rushing stream of brown water below, 'the Afghans, the Pandis and the Xhosa haven't managed to get the better of us yet. Damn it, in Abyssinia we wiped out most of King Theodore's army with our advanced guard. Are you trying to tell me the Zulus are so very different, Gillespie?'

'All that I am saying is, if we can do that to a standing army with ordinance, how hard can a relatively small national force be to subdue?'

'That is exactly what I am trying to tell you, Arthur!' moaned Flambard. 'If it weren't for this bloody scratch, for which you lot say I must remain behind, I'd come with you and show you! The Zulus have firearms of their own, many more than you or Harry Roystone realise. I know because I've spent the last ten years trying to control the gangs who supply them, but there is only so much one provincial beak can do about anything so determined, and I'm nowhere near as young as you are.'

'Nonsense, Gillespie!' McEnry protested lightly. 'You know full well you'll outlive us all, in spite of all your moaning. I expect you'll still be knocking back Cape Mist when I'm cold in the ground,' he added, waving a cheery goodnight to the magistrate as he left to join his battalion.

'Yes, and that is *exactly* what I am afraid of,' Flambard sighed. 'For God's sake take care, Arthur' he called ominously after the departing McEnry. 'Believe me, I mean that for all of you.'

The day had by no means been an easy one for Bond either. By all accounts, the sapper officers and their men had worked as hard as any throughout that long and arduous crossing.

It was with some reluctance that Bond had watched the last of his baggage and personal belongings being bundled into the back of one of the wagons, and began the process of coaxing his troublesome horse across the wide stretch of river to the point where the rest were waiting. The water was deep; it rushed just inches below the toes of his boots, and the mist, which seemed to have lifted earlier on in the day, returned with a vengeance to chill the limbs and lock the hands around the reigns in a grip of ice.

Both Westgate and Knight had crossed well in advance of the main column of infantry to be in a position to oversee the progress of the pont from the other side. Bond, Friday and Penfold remained for some time on the Natal bank, helping with the final work on the earthworks, and overseeing the disbanding of Earnest's "earners" who had been ignominiously demoted after the two river debacles, and dumped on the now grounded Commandant Flambard.

Had Penfold been a stronger character, he might well have kicked dreadfully against such a move, but as it was, he allowed the decision of his superiors to overmaster his sensibilities and did his best to see his men disarmed and settled with the minimum of fuss and bother. Consequently, the two officers and their sergeant crossed the river with the last of The Wolves, followed only by Snooker Collingwood's champing artillery battery, and made the Zulu bank just in time to latch onto the remainder of their company as it tramped off into the night.

Chapter Sixteen

Long after the last of the column had vanished behind the cover of the hills on the opposite side, and the pale moon had been mercilessly engulfed by a disconcerting mass of black cloud, Flambard and Faunce-Whittington dug in for the night. They had chosen to billet in an old hut that used to form part of an original mission station long before the outbreak of hostilities.

By the time they had finished inspecting the piquets outside and Faunce had put the horses under cover, it was very nearly midnight.

'Don't like the sound of that at all,' Flambard commended dryly, as the heavy patter of rain began gradually to be replaced by the torrential downpour of a full-scale storm as it hammered upon the corrugated iron roof above their heads. 'Poor buggers out there in this won't be too happy.'

'I wonder how they're doing, the boys,' sighed the lieutenant wistfully.

'They can cope,' Flambard replied shortly. 'They're regular soldiers after all, and we aren't, so don't feel too badly about being indoors tonight eh, Faunce, there's a good fellow.'

'Don't you wish you were going, though?' Faunce-Whittington continued.

'Not a bit,' Flambard replied. 'Oh, very well, that's not true at all... but I don't see why you're so keen to go off and be shot at and stabbed at, likely as they are.'

'Oh, not me,' replied the lieutenant hurriedly. 'The sooner this terrible business is all over, and we're all safely back in Oscaarsberg, the better I'll like it. More port, Colonel?' he added with a flourish, jumping to his feet on the dusty boards of the mission hut and wandering across to an improvised sideboard in the shape of a stack of boxes.

'Don't mind if I do,' Flambard replied, adding, 'Good God, what the devil was that?' as a curious noise fell upon his left ear, somewhere to the south of their position.

'I don't hear anything, sir,' clucked the other officer, cocking his head on one side and listening with an intensity that almost caused his waxed moustache to curl at the ends. 'Oh, my word, now I do!' he corrected, eyes popping open like those of a startled hare.

The commandant, struggling out of his chair with an effort, beckoned for Faunce to do likewise and listen, which they did intently for several moments longer. Then a wistful smile began to play beneath the commandant's grey whiskers. '*Hark when the night is falling*, Faunce,' he observed.

'I don't follow,' the officer replied, perplexed.

'Pipes, laddie!' Flambard explained, in his best worst assumption of an accent. 'That's a piper of a Scottish regiment, or I'm no judge. By damn, I haven't heard the bagpipes in the field for very nearly thirty years.' He suddenly trailed off, as if preoccupied by something other than the sound of music.

'Well, I heard some in the town last week, actually,' Faunce-Whittington informed him. 'They were playing with that company of the Ninety First under old what's his name? You know, the old orator from the mess tent. The Scot who fancies himself to have the gift of poetry. Indian chap?'

'McGonagle,' Flambard murmured coolly. 'I knew it had to happen,' he sighed, adding, 'You'd better go on out, Faunce.

I'll be in here, should he happen to want to come inside.'

'Yes, I think I'd better had!' the officer replied, snatching up his wide-brimmed suede hat, plopping it neatly on his head at a protective angle, and calling, 'Don't drink all my wine, Colonel!' before picking his way through the mud outside.

Surely enough, it had been the sound of the approaching piper that had raised the sentries from their sheltered positions long before the clatter, tramp and squelch of the small Highland company advancing on them through the drizzle.

From his position on the covered veranda of the mission hut, Faunce-Whittington could just about make out the distant forms of some several wagons, with a medieval-looking procession of approximately eighty men, proceeded by an officer on a cantering horse.

The rain was becoming torrential by that time, and both black and white irregulars on piquet duty peered on through the downpour as the steady stream of wagons, muddy horses and weary, bedraggled and highly dispirited soldiers plodded towards them through the darkness. The rain ran off their beards in rivulets, and the officer who rode ahead of the convoy was very nearly upon them by the time Faunce-Whittington had staggered out into the quagmire of the earthwork for a better look at the visitor. 'Dear God, not that miserable little piker,' he moaned to himself, as recognition caught up with the galloping horseman.

Indeed, the tatty blue patrol jacket had been moulded onto the unmistakable physique of McGonagle's junior officer by the relentless rain, and the forced grimace could clearly be seen flashing briefly beneath the rain-soaked helmet as the horse got closer. Lieutenant Simonides rode up to Faunce-Whittington, nodded briefly and curtly informed him that Captain AW McGonagle's Ninety First Highland Company were approaching their position, having been given orders to take up a station at the drift in readiness for further instruction.

A decidedly bedraggled Faunce-Whittington returned some moments later, the water dripping off the wide brim of his hat like the torrent from a broken cistern. When he relayed his information to Flambard, the magistrates response was less than enthusiastic.

'Simon who, did you say?' Flambard demanded. 'Oh, Simonides. I see. So it is McGonagle, after all,' he sighed, almost sombre for a moment. 'Ah well,' he added, more blithely as he remembered his company, 'the peace was nice while it lasted.'

Faunce looked heavenwards as the sound of wagon wheels began to catch up with the sound of McGonagle's piper, and the dreary patter of rain was soon augmented by the wet slap of boots in the mud outside.

It was indeed the Scottish captain, battling with his own deafness in the roar of the downpour; barking orders this way and that from the cover of the wagon in which he rode and trying his best to ascertain the responses when they came flying back to him. Repeating himself and growing more irritable as the rain soaked into his rheumatic bones, McGonagle finally barked at his sergeant to, 'sort the lazy bastards out, damn it!' and alighted from the wagon in a large splash of mud, with all the grace of a wounded hippopotamus. Then, hammering on the already half open door of the now fully occupied mission hut, the elderly poet finally stomped in and presented himself.

Flambard and Faunce-Whittington could only look on in horror as McGonagle and his mean little lieutenant had their baggage dumped down on one side of the room, and took up strategic positions on either side of (and obscuring) the small fire they had so lately and so exclusively enjoyed.

They had clearly been riding for some days, and the journey

had certainly taken its toll on the appearance of McGonagle. In addition to his sideburns, the elderly captain now also sported a huge and decidedly bushy salt-and-pepper beard, which ran from his chin to the third button down on his coatee. This he wore with neither denotation of rank, nor any other distinguishing features. The yellow collar was obscured down the front by his beard, and the little that remained at the back was blackened and greasy from rubbing his hair, which had lately been cut short in readiness for his posting. The serge cloth of his jacket seemed to accentuate still further the pronounced line of his belly, and his tartan trews were tucked into a pair of muddy old riding boots. His sword trailed a long trickle of foul-smelling mud on the floor, while his pistol he wore slung from a shoulder belt, as did Simonides.

Eyeing the two with the same distaste as had his men, Flambard made a courteous, if facile, suggestion that the officers might be tired after their ride.

'Oh, absolutely!' groaned McGonagle, promptly taking the commandant's inquiry as a cue to break into chapter and verse on the shortcomings of his men, the idiosyncrasies of the commissariat department, and an all-out attack on the hierarchy's handling of the war so far.

Sensing that this was not to be an easy affair, Flambard then suggested that perhaps the two newcomers might like to join them.

It seemed an empty offer, since apparently both the newcomers had already decided to invade the comfortable hut, whether they liked it or not. Even so, it was one that the magistrate would regret making, for no sooner had he done so that McGonagle subsided in the commandant's own chair, barking something to Simonides about fetching him a drink, declaring that they would, 'Just 'ave to bunk down in 'ere for the night.'

Barely concealing his horror at the prospect, Faunce-Whittington found himself obliged to make awkward small talk with his mean and withdrawn brother lieutenant, while Flambard held, or rather engaged in, a singularly one-sided conversation with the irritable McGonagle.

Several glasses of port later, Faunce-Whittington was nearly fit for the madhouse after hours grudging of monosyllables from Simonides, while Flambard had been virtually driven to murder by the endless moaning of the increasingly inebriated Scotsman. Only when the two intruders finally decided to retire to bed, did Flambard remove the plugs from his ears, pour himself another large drink, and settle down to his book over an oil lamp.

By that time, it was roughly midnight, and the Number Six Column had already made excellent progress into Zululand.

Before he left, Warren Westgate had received some highly welcome and long-awaited news from the colonel. As soon as they had pitched camp, and the captain found himself well under canvas, he took out his writing paper and scribbled a note to his wife.

Almost as soon as he had written his letter, Westgate blew out the lantern in the six-foot by four-foot tented wagon in which he slept and whispered a grim goodnight to the strange new country, laying his head on the pillow to rest.

It had to be said that he had found the better location, for not more than a few yards from the foot of his wagon, Bond was experiencing some very different conditions.

The rain, since leaving sight of the river, had been utterly relentless. It soaked through most forms of covering, ran through seams in the tent canvas and seemed to simply bubble up through the saturated grass, causing the feet of his camp bed to sink despairingly into the mud. At one point, Bond even thought that the rain was going to start forming into droplets on the inside, so intense and endless was the barrage of freezing cold water on the thin canopy above him.

It was worse still for the soldiers, who only had their greatcoats and a rolled-up blanket on which to sleep. In fact, it was at that point in the night that Coleman began to wish, for the first time since leaving Chatham, that his fortunes had not led him to take the Queen's shilling. Never had he felt so bitterly cold, despondent and, although he would never ever complain about it, so utterly bereft and dispirited.

For the loyal young sapper, war so far had been about one man: Albert Bond. Even though he did not expect to be recognised for all he had done, alone, in the dark and the damp, with seven other men snoring, grumbling, and breaking wind around him, he could not help but wish for some scrap of comfort in the long, lonely night. 'Dear God, look after my officer,' he whispered. 'He's been good to me and, if you're willing, when we eventually face those Zulus, I'll do whatever it takes to protect him, make him proud... make him want me to stay close.'

'You missin' a mother, boy?' mumbled an older sapper kindly from somewhere in the darkness beside him.

'A lass, more like it... or they're missing him!' another quipped, less so.

'Yeah,' Jack sighed miserably. 'But no more than I ever did.' There was a loud snore in response, and not for the first time, he knew that no one was listening.

Chapter Seventeen

A wood pigeon was calling out from its perch on top of the chimneypot.

Outside the white latticed window, the sky was a brilliant blue. A slight cooling breeze was all that disturbed the peaceful note of the English countryside in mid-July, flowing gently through the long grasses of the meadow and tenderly caressing the branches of the old willow tree by the stream. Every so often, however, a grey cloud could be seen here and there. The birds flitted past the open window like the second hand on the old gold pocket watch; bees and butterflies took off across the darkening sky for the cover of the gables, and the summer atmosphere seemed to trickle away like the dark waters of the river, flowing irrespective of so tender a moment. Then again, the clouds came over, the greyness began to replace the blue, the birdsong ceased, and the world was once again troubled by darkness and rain. The tree begun to sway too much and, as with all things put to too great an extreme, rock violently backwards and forwards, shaking off its leaves until the iron hard, skeletal vision of the cold grey winter once more affirmed its authority.

'Such is the truth,' said a voice, 'and you know it for what it is.' Then a bough snaps on the great tree, and the grey limb rips itself from the trunk, crashing down among the thorns and brambles, shaken and tormented by the rain and the gale, like the mocking laughter of some latent devil.

With a gasp and a cry of horror, Bond suddenly awoke. Sitting bolt upright in his camp bed, he suddenly began, by stages, to realise where he was. The damp smell of the soggy canvas roof, the wet flapping panels of the bell tent, and the persistent slapping noise of the ropes on the loose canopy above reminded him well and truly that he was in Zululand. His initial reaction was to try to look at his watch. Even after all those months, he could not quite get used to being without it.

Wiping the sweat from his brow, and once again pushing his soaking wet hair back off his face, Bond struggled for his water bottle. He took a long gulp from the neck, pouring what was left into his cupped hands and frantically washing his face, and dashing the sleep from his eyes.

Then a shadow began to grow on the brilliantly illuminated canvas above him, and a head suddenly popped in round the flap.

'Jack?' Bond breathed in relief, closing his eyes and taking a deep sigh.

'No, old man, it's me, Will.'

'Oh sorry, mate.' Bond, now fully awake, recognised, with some considerable shame, the smiling face of the young officer whom he and Gideon Knight had befriended in The Wolves' mess on their first evening with the column.

Reserved, well-spoken and good-looking, Lieutenant William Glazebrook was a junior subaltern under the command of Colonel McEnry. At twenty-two, with soft fair brown hair, hazel eyes, and a chiselled jaw, young Glazebrook was an amiable, conscientious, and considerate officer with many friends in all the various officer complements that made up the column. 'You were making quite a bit of noise, old fellow,' he remarked casually. 'Just thought I'd look in and make sure a scorpion hadn't got hold of your toes, or some other ghastlier appendage.'

'No, no. I'm fine thanks,' Bond replied quietly. 'Look, Will, I don't suppose you've seen Gideon Knight or Warren Westgate anywhere on your travels, have you? I need rather badly to talk to one of them.'

'Not so far as I'm aware,' Glazebrook replied honestly. 'Mind you, I did hear one of the chaps say they saw him riding off with the colonel and old McEnry in the direction of those hills to the north of the camp. Probably plotting the advance, I should say. Expect trouble, do you, Albert?'

'Only having to get you lot across another river,' Bond replied miserably, kicking off the blankets and resignedly swinging his limbs out of bed. 'I saw that one looming up before us on the map yesterday. Another short foot slog and we should be right on top of it.'

'Dare say,' Glazebrook replied. 'Anyway, I should stir my stumps if I were you, here comes that lad of yours. Good fellow, is he?'

'Marvellous,' Bond replied. 'Simply couldn't afford to be without him... especially as I don't pay him,' he added grimly, as Glazebrook departed to make way for the ever-cheerful Sapper Coleman. 'Morning, Jack,' Bond greeted, gratefully accepting the proffered mug of hot tea, which the young soldier had probably gone out of his way to bring him. 'Did you sleep well?'

'Yes thanks, Mr Albert, sir,' Coleman lied. 'What about you?'

'Not much,' Bond replied quite truthfully. 'I kept dreaming about home in summertime.'

'Ain't much appealing about my home, to tell truth Sir, at any time of year.' Coleman muttered gloomily. 'The river stinks in the summer, and we go cold in the winter. I loved the docks, mind. Them big ships steamin'... I s'pose to places like this.'

'In my dream it kept turning to winter,' Bond mused. 'Sorry, Jack, I don't suppose you dreamed at all, did you?' he added as an afterthought.

This was in fact a decidedly pragmatic remark, and rather hurtful to the young sapper. All too aware of the differences in their class, he somehow did not care to be thought of as some Jack-the-lad who drunk himself to sleep and never held a lengthily thought to anything. To him, Bond's thinking way was the proper way, and the affection with which he toiled so ceaselessly was to win approval. Admittedly, it was the Methodists who had taught him to write back home in the slums as a child, but Bond had taken an interest, and Coleman wanted to impress. Bond had taught him to think, and that was something else again.

'How is it coming along... your writing, I mean?' Bond enquired, interrupting Coleman's thought pattern.

'Better than it was, Mr Albert, thanks to you,' Jack replied, smiling blue eyes glittering with all the promise of his eagerness to improve. 'I even taught the Sarn't that thing you taught me about double negatives.'

'What about the other men?' Bond asked, amused.

'No,' Coleman shook his head. 'Last time I tried to tell them all that stuff, one of them hit me.'

'They're just ignorant,' Bond told him categorically. 'Just because sappers can already read and write, they think that they don't need to learn anymore. That's why the army has an education programme, right, Jack?'

'Yes, sir,' Coleman replied. 'Still, I have been keeping a journal, like you told me to do. I've even been writing a letter.'

'To your mother?' Bond suggested innocently.

There was a considerable pause. For no sooner had the words passed the officer's lips, Coleman's smile suddenly fell from his face, only to be replaced by a look of thunder. It was not a look that Bond enjoyed. Not because Jack was his subordinate, but because he held an especially great affection for the young sapper, and for some reason, unconsciously sought his approval in return.

Sitting up and tugging his breeches over the shirt he had had on for three days and nights, Bond took occasion to move slightly closer. Looking carefully up under the thick blond hair, hanging over the face like a protective curtain over a stage, Bond could see the normally sparkling blue eyes misted with frustrated emotion.

All too aware of the time, and aware too that the column was scheduled to move before 6:00 a.m., Bond placed a consolatory hand on the broad shoulder of Jack's rough scarlet jacket. 'I'm sorry if I upset you,' he whispered. 'Now, is anything troubling you?'

For a moment it seemed as if Coleman did not know where to put himself. He looked up at Bond, eyes wide open, clearly trying to make what he could of so frank and honest an inquiry after him – Jack – personally. 'You're an officer, sir. It ain't my place to talk out of turn, nor yours hearin' it.'

'That's just the point: it is my place and my decision. I'm not captain or adjutant. I'm a junior subaltern. It's the same for me in the mess as it is for you in the barrack block of an evening, in many ways.' He smiled kindly, fondly massaging the muscles in the sapper's shoulder between thumb and fingers. Admittedly at that moment Bond had no idea at all where the smile came from, or indeed the comforting rhetoric, for he was feeling miserable himself, and in need of some consolation.

'I never thought of it like that, sir.' Privately he thought otherwise and was certain his officer wouldn't care to make the swap to find out when they got back to Brompton.

'I prefer it when you call me Mr Albert,' Bond replied, colouring slightly.

'Do you, really?' Jack replied, blond fringe lifting slightly and allowing the officer a glimpse at the long, thick lashes and those mystifying blue sapphires in his once more smiling eyes.

'Yes, I do,' Bond repeated, hesitating as he added, 'You've become very... important to me, Jack. I'd be lost without you out here in this wilderness.'

Coleman smiled again and appeared just on the point of adding something when the bugle sounded stand-to, and he knew he must return to the task of helping to strike tents with the others.

'Back to the grind,' Bond remarked lightly, as if to dismiss that indefinable sense of intimacy which seemed increasingly to pervade their private moments. It was a hollow attempt though, for as Coleman rose to leave, Bond found himself adding, 'Take care today.'

Coleman nodded. 'I'll be right beside you, sir, the whole time.' He added suddenly, 'Even if whatever happens means, well, something bad, I'll take it all on if you're there with me.'

Bond was rendered utterly speechless and could only nod in acknowledgment as the young sapper left the tent and wandered out into the sunlight.

Chapter Eighteen

By sunrise, the column was once again ready for the off. The tents had been struck, packed away and made ready for their use at the next camping place. Flambard's Horse, under the temporary command of one Captain Robert Toteaux, peacetime commander of Flambard's border police, was sent off to head the column, with a handful of mounted infantry from The Wolves.

The wagons were lined up in single file, with Collingwood's guns towed behind – under the guard of a squadron of mounted troops, while the rocket battery, under Lieutenant Glazebrook, went ahead for more rapid deployment and use, should Snooker's party be held up at the crossing.

Lieutenant Bond's sappers, accompanied by the now acting major, Warren Westgate, set off in advance of the main column, well behind the videttes but quite some way ahead of the main column's infantry and artillery protection. It was not an undertaking to which Bond was looking forward with any great notions of enthusiasm. The terrain was rough, thorn bushes and aloes clogged the countryside, and the high grasses seemed to be able to provide cover for any number of the half-imagined enemy, while a profusion of flies seemingly conjured up by the tormenting heat of the sun drove them near to distraction.

By 9:00 a.m. the heat had become almost unbearable. Topi

helmets filled with moisture like a sealed greenhouse on a summer's afternoon; boots began to bake and boil the already tortured soles of those on foot, while the smell of the mud from the previous night's rainfall as it churned up under the wagon wheels became quite sickening.

By about 10:45 a.m. Westgate called the party to a halt beside a narrow donga, a deep drainage gully cut into the face of the landscape by rainwater escaping from the mountaintops. The course itself was dried up; by the bed was a quagmire of mud, choked up with foliage, and a nightmare to traverse either by foot or on horseback.

'Albert, I reckon on us having to clear that bit to get the infantry past these hummocks on either side of the wagons,' Westgate announced, as he and Bond dismounted. and clambered to the top of one of the grassy slopes, which dominated the narrow track on either side.

'I can get a party in there and clearing, if you like,' Bond suggested helpfully. 'Sergeant Friday!' he called across. 'Can you put a detail on that mess down there in that donga, please?'

'Yes, sir, right away, sir!' squawked Friday, throwing off his equipment and selecting a party of several men to aid him in his work.

'Sapper Coleman, organise picks and shovels. Corporal Denham, see to it that every man clears at least half his own height in brambles. Now! We'd better chop some of this earth away too, Warren,' Bond observed, running a casual eye over the grassy hummock to the left of the track. 'Otherwise the wheels might start to mount the camber, and we really don't want the wagons turning over up here.'

'Good thinking, Albert,' Westgate replied. 'And see that every man has a rifle fairly close at hand. We don't want to get caught napping if the mounted chaps come across anything in the hills now, do we?'

'Absolutely not,' Bond assented. Turning his attention to the donga in which his men were working, he asked, 'Are you all right down there, Jack?'.

'Fine, Mr Albert, sir,' Coleman replied, beaming away as he bodily ripped yet another tangled root out from the bed of the watercourse.

'Let me see that,' Bond persisted, waving a finger at a large tear on the left shoulder of Coleman's serge.

Coleman obediently laid down his pick and approached the officer, and not without some considerable discomfort. He adored working for his officer and the privileges and kindness that being his batman entailed, but that did not mean he wanted to be singled out for special treatment in front of the others.

'This looks bad,' Bond remarked again, examining at close quarters the lacerations on the boy's hands, and the deep cut in his right shoulder, now exposing to view a profusion of blood under the sticky flannelette shirt.

'Really, sir, I'm no worse than the other lads, thank you,' Coleman insisted politely, seemingly quite keen to resume his punishing work rather than be made a fuss of.

'Permission to speak, sir?' interrupted Friday.

Bond turned to face his sergeant. He too had been reduced to a state of some wretchedness by the work in question. Thorns had got caught up in his beard, the mud was thick up to the knees of his navy trousers, and the yellow worsted of the sergeant's chevrons on his right sleeve had been pulled to pieces and shredded up by the brambles. Arching his neck a little, he motioned for Bond to step aside with him for a moment, out of earshot of the other sappers, and Major Westgate.

'Mr Albert, sir, this is tricky, this is,' he began quietly, showing no sign whatsoever of having taken in Coleman's lesson on the use of double negatives. 'Coleman good, very good. Very bright, special boy, he is.'

'What are you trying to say to me, Sergeant?' Bond enquired, more than a little curtly. He did not care for being brought up by Friday, and he knew it was partly his own fault, which only made it worse.

'N-not to single out, sir,' Friday stammered awkwardly. 'Difficult for Friday to say but, well... don't look good, Mr Albert.'

'Oh, for heaven's sake, Sergeant, I was only asking after his injuries,' Bond replied airily. 'It's not as if I'm trying to obstruct him from working or anything, is it?'

'Officer known his business,' Friday answered briefly. 'Not Friday's place to say nothing. Apologies,' he added, snapping to attention, and saluting sharply before dismissing himself and returning to his labour.

Bond was left thinking for some time. Did he really show an overt favouritism towards Coleman? If he did, it wasn't intended, although he had rather assumed that Friday did the same thing. He was an incredibly popular lad after all, and no one would really put anything by it... would they?

In a quandary, deeply embarrassed and heavily insulted by such a notion, Bond irritably pulled off his patrol jacket, helmet, and pistol belt, before grabbing a shovel and joining his men in the ditch, well away from Sergeant Friday, and at least a dozen men down from Sapper Coleman.

The sappers' efforts with the donga continued right the way through the remainder of the morning, and well into the afternoon. The only respite from the arduous slog was when Major Westgate called stand easy, and they paused to eat a hurried lunch of beef stew and hard tack, which Sergeant Friday and Corporal Denham managed to prepare on an open area of the grassy hillside. It seemed to Bond that, the harder they worked, the harder their work became. The sweat ran off them in torrents and more than once they thought that Friday was going to collapse through heat exhaustion on account of his baldness.

Several, including both Bond and Coleman, had removed their shirts for some relief, and been royally burned as a result. Water was strictly rationed, and only by the end of the afternoon were the sappers finally able to lay down their tools and rest, just as the advanced guard of the main column crested the hill.

It was an awesome sight, even in such glaring sunshine and unbearable heat. Row upon row of tented wagons; scores of different coloured oxen all pulling and heaving in teams, jangling along amid the rhythmical tramp of boots and the crack of the drivers' whips. Lines of red-coated infantry followed in perfectly straight ranks, flanked on either side by the African contingent, their spears glinting and the black and white of their skin shields contrasting sharply with the red earth of the dusty veldt.

Behind them rode yet more irregular troops, white colonials, and Africans both, dressed in khaki uniforms and armed with short Swinburne carbines.

Behind the irregulars rode the headquarters staff, Colonel Roystone clearly visible in his scarlet frock, steel scabbard of his great sword gleaming by his side.

To the left of him rode Colonel McEnry and Henderson, flanked by Captain Fenton and Collingwood, with Lieutenant Glazebrook, Masters and Knight bringing up the rear. More wagons and infantry companies followed one upon the other, and to the rear of this steady stream of human traffic the two Armstrong guns of the Royal Artillery could just about be seen, clambering up the adverse camber of the steadily sloping track.

'Bloody something, isn't it, Sarn't!' Coleman sighed in youthful admiration.

'Watch the bloodies!' Friday quipped back at him. 'Don't want to end up on a charge, and end up digging latrines, do you?'

The heat was beginning to tell on him dreadfully, and the white-hot sun on his red-hot neck seemed gradually to be burning away his cordiality, if he had any to begin with.

'Take one hell of an army to trifle with that, though, wouldn't it?' Bond remarked to Westgate. 'And look, the old man even had the colours unfurled for the occasion, too.'

'Bloody infantry,' growled Corporal Denham to Sergeant Friday in disgust. 'Waving the dusters about. I ask you.'

'You mind your business, Corp,' Friday snapped back, aghast at such a lack of respect for the West Rutlands' regimental pride. 'Took two hundred of them to beat off two thousand of the Pandies in India, it did. My father was there.'

'Here we go, Friday history,' one sapper mumbled subversively and earning himself a kick in the shins from Coleman, whom Friday had as good as adopted, and who in consequence felt very protective towards him. In any case, Jack had loved listening to Friday's tales about his family during those long, cold nights spent cooped up at the Chatham depot.

Somehow Sergeant Filo Friday, hero of the Peninsular, Sergeant Cosmo Friday, who blew up the Taku Forts, and all the other apparently bald, endless senior NCOs in the colourful soldier's equally colourful past, seemed to inspire something wonderful in the boy's adventurous spirit. Not mentioned

Sergeant Elmo and Fido Friday, twin brothers killed at Aiden, nor Sergeant Major Magnus Friday, Ludo's father, who allegedly beat off an assault by about a hundred and twenty Maori warriors in New Zealand, winning him the Victoria Cross, by rolling logs down a hillside. Whether or not this had been just another case of overzealous storytelling on the part of the present Sergeant Friday, Coleman had never known. Either way, he did not care for the aspersions of others on his NCO any more than he cared for gossip about Lieutenant Bond's financial hardships, and reacted accordingly to both.

Yet as the column gradually proceeded to drag its massive convoy of bulk through the mud, and the leading vedette of mounted soldiers began to approach their position, Coleman forgot all about past campaigns and began excitedly to wonder when they would come up against some Zulus.

As it was, Westgate was just giving a cheery greeting to the major in charge of the mounted infantry party, when the sounds of loud cries and repeated shots came rebounding off the surrounding hillside.

Sergeant Friday replaced his helmet and immediately called stand-to, while several sappers under Lieutenant Bond grabbed their rifles and dashed up onto the grassy ridge to investigate.

The sun blazed relentlessly down from above.

Coleman, who was still only dressed in his blue trousers, and with his rifle in one hand and his ammunition pouches in the other, jumped up on top of a rock and gazed in wonderment at the valley below.

Corporal Denham was next up, sweat clinging to his sodden flannelette shirt as he struggled to see through the arch glare of the blinding sunlight.

Bond too was soon up there beside them. His broad back was now tanned to a reddish-brown colour, and freckles were beginning to appear all over his shoulders and about his upper arms. Breathing a sigh of astonishment equal to those of the other two before him, he turned to look at Sapper Coleman, and found that he was laughing.

Bond gazed at him for a moment longer, rows of clean white teeth flashing, and the clear blue eyes creased to slits in the hot afternoon glare.

Then he began to smile too. He wiped the sweat off his hair, face, and beard, and then he too began to laugh like Coleman. For there, stretched out below them lay the lush, green, and abundant valley of the river they were soon to cross. It was their first real glimpse of the other side of the kingdom they had found themselves invading, and the scene before them made all that had gone before a well worthy undertaking.

Shrouded in the lea of the great, craggy mountainous hills, with deep, dark mealie fields, right in the middle of long grasses and sweet meadowland lay a small collection of dome-shaped huts. Their first Zulu homestead.

The huts were arranged in a sort of circular formation, with the outermost of them serving to mark the perimeter, and yet more wattle fences between each building in the shape of a rudimentary kraal.

Further, they could clearly see the silvery shimmer of the river itself standing guard over by the massive rocky escarpment, which stretched all the way from a sandy spit on the riverbank to a high shoulder of the mountainous hillside beyond. Cattle grazed on the nek below the ridge, and even more livestock was visible, both in and around the kraals themselves. Nothing stirred, and apart from a solitary wisp of blue smoke that rose like a puff of tobacco from a fine cigar, all was still.

Bond cupped his hand over his eyes and scanned to the furthest horizon.

The noises they had heard must have been made by the mounted infantry who, having been sent to scout ahead by the colonel, had clearly spotted fruitful valley and the lonely little homestead on their second skirt for home.

'Warren, will you come up and look at this!' Bond called back down the slope to his commanding officer, who had paused in his conversation with his fellow major until the source of the disturbance had been identified.

Scrambling up the ridge, his patrol jacket and brown topi helmet in stark contrast with the tanned, half-naked torsos of his men and brother officer, Westgate also breathed a sigh. 'It's beautiful,' he breathed, almost moved beyond speech by the majestic calm of the tranquil setting.

'Never in my life,' Coleman purred in wonder, apparently forgetting the presence of more than one commissioned officer in his amazement, 'could I have imagined I'd ever stand in a place like this. Like... like a picture bin painted.'

'Nor I,' Bond replied placidly, also equally unaware of his company, and forgetting to address anyone in particular.

They needn't have worried, though. For Westgate was far too spellbound, too awestruck and affected by the scenery to even notice Bond and Coleman, let alone what they were or were not wearing.

'I left my tunic in the ditch,' mumbled Corporal Denham, drifting mindlessly back down the slope.

Utterly oblivious, Westgate stepped forward a couple of paces until he was standing on the foremost and uppermost of the rocks that dotted the sloping hillside above the valley itself.

Unthinking, and utterly swept away by the drama of the moment and the spectacular panorama beyond, Bond placed a hand on Coleman's hot back.

He was stood directly behind and slightly to the left of

the young soldier, so that even if Westgate had been able to notice anything, he would never have spotted the gesture from his position on the rock. The sweat still clung to Coleman's broad shoulders, and the skin was hot and glistening with moisture. Bond himself could only watch in silent fascination as it trickled down the young soldier's back, soaking into the rough waistband of his irritatingly rough navy trousers, and ending in a dark patch around the keenly defined line of the firm pair of buttocks. Coleman never turned to look at him, but Bond could tell from the creases in his cheeks that the boy was smiling.

Looking away as if suddenly checking himself, Bond removed his hand and whipped round, glancing sharply back at his men on the road with a sharp intake of breath.

They were all far too taken up with the steady progress of the advancing column, stretched as it was out over a mile and a half of the rough countryside and disappearing behind the hills in the distance, as mere specks on the vast landscape.

At length, Colonel Roystone and the mounted colour party came abreast of the engineers' position on the crest of the grassy slope. Hailing Major Westgate, he enquired after what exactly it was that was so diverting their attention, and whether the sapper officer had seen anything of the enemy so far.

Westgate replied in the negative, but explained that the object of the vedettes' curiosity appeared to take the form of a deserted homestead and that, apart from a trail of smoke from the firing rifles, there had been no sign visible of anything whatever. 'I can take my company down and investigate, if that's your wish, Colonel,' Westgate added, glancing about for the means of a safe path to traverse.

Roystone shook his head. 'Good of you, Warren, but there's no knowing what's down there until you're in amongst it all and then, well... You don't need me to tell you that it's far too late.'

'May I take men down there, Colonel?' asked the major in charge of the advanced guard, who had paused to speak to Westgate some half an hour earlier.

'I think not just yet,' Roystone replied thoughtfully. 'I suggest we move to the other side of this bank, which Warren and his men have so kindly widened for us, and take advantage of that flat grassy bit just the other side of here.'

The area to which the colonel referred was a spot where the enclosed roadway opened out into a gentler camber, and the grasses were less strewn with such boulders, as might trip or foul the horses' hooves.

'Looks like the picture's about to change somewhat,' Bond remarked to Coleman, as Roystone and the two lieutenant colonels stood for some time in quiet consultation, before calling up both Captain Toteaux and the officer in charge of the now returned patrol, who had first discovered the abandoned kraal.

Coleman looked at Bond for a moment. Stripped to the waist and literally dripping with perspiration, he might arguably have passed for a common soldier. Bond must have recognised something of what seemed to be passing through his mind, because he casually passed a remark about them being all the same, really. Then, as if to goad fate just a little more, he asked what *exactly* Jack had expected to see under his dress shirt and patrol jacket.

'The same,' Coleman replied quietly, smiling as he gazed on Lieutenant Bond, his hair blown about by the ghost of a breeze, and the rays of the afternoon sunlight bathing his freckled back and turning it still deeper into brown.

'Not quite the same, though,' Bond smiled back, looking

properly for the first time at the young soldier's smooth body – fit, toned and now tanned beyond its burns, bathed in the golden sunlight. 'I think you have the edge over me. So, tell me, is it boxing, the gymnasium?'

'Nah, just working,' Coleman replied, suppressing a smirk.

They were almost at a point where the dialogue graduated into something of far too deep a nature to be entertained on such a location, when yet another shot echoed on the lately emerging breeze. Suddenly aware of their position, and the fact that neither of them was wearing any article of uniform before the commander of their column, Bond and Coleman dashed back down the bank where the remaining sappers were waiting.

Surveying the scene from his position on a grassy knoll, which was arguably a strange tranquillity of almost total desertion, Roystone was able to command a view of the entirety of the valley. The homestead had an air of hurried abandonment about it, as if the inhabitants had quite simply got up one morning and decided summarily to leave, taking nothing but their immediate belongings with them.

The shot in question had, it later transpired, been fired off by a party of Flambard's Horse who, having been dispatched on a looting spree in recognition of their first blood at the river several days earlier, had apparently stumbled across something in one of the huts. Having no real logistical value as a base, not being suited to a supply depot, and having been condemned by Major Westgate as about the worst possible potential fortification sight anywhere around, Roystone had dispatched Captain Toteaux to round up the stray cattle in the kraals. This herd was undoubtedly the property of the local chieftan, one of the important Zulu officials whom the lord lieutenant general had instructed the colonel to pacify and which, if captured, could serve as a major propaganda coup. Even though the turning of some of the more minor Zulu clans had not been in his brief, Roystone was by no means slow to recognise the potential value in the support of any local families too wary to openly oppose the British invasion. Therefore, when reports of a Zulu shooting came back from the kraal, the colonel himself was incandescent with rage.

As it turned out, the perpetrator had been none other than Captain Toteaux who, having dismounted and entered one of the huts, discovered within an old Zulu woman of roughly eighty years of age. As soon as the officer had entered the hut, followed closely by his sergeant and a corporal of the mounted infantry, the old woman had launched into a tirade of chanting, followed by considerable waving of a small wooden artefact and a great deal of spit and bile. According to the imperial corporal, Toteaux listened grimly to the abuse for some moments, presumably comprehending the tongue in which it was uttered, followed by his calmly raising his right arm and shooting the woman dead with his revolver. Toteaux would later defend this act of superfluous murder by claiming that the old woman threatened him, but his justification fell on deaf ears, and Colonel McEnry was instructed to place him under arrest.

This episode undoubtedly placed a stain on the otherwise easy success of their first conquest, and there were many rumours the following night of strange howling in the dark and odd shapes seen flitting to and fro on the tent canvases after lights out. Much of this was attributed to bats, however, and the overall feeling was certainly one of success and positive progress for the rest of the campaign.

Chapter Nineteen

'Been arrested? You can't be serious,' cried Faunce-Whittington in alarm.

Having been interrogating the miserable, exhausted African NCO for the last hour and a half, the large lieutenant was beginning even to lose that remarkable cordiality he possessed, and which endeared him so entirely to the skittish and temperamental among the colonial high society.

Commandant Flambard sat in his usual bow chair, studiously retaken from Captain McGonagle over a period of several evenings and quite a quantity of soaping with Scotch whisky. He said nothing, merely glancing with grim severity at both the NCO and his own officer, a dark red colour about his normally ruddy complexion as he quietly combed his silvery whiskers in the lamplight.

'He can't mean it, surely!' Faunce-Whittington persisted. 'Bob Toteaux is inspector of police, isn't that right, Colonel?'

'Do be quiet a moment, Faunce,' boomed Flambard, a chilling calm overtaking his usual heavy oratory while he pondered. 'All right,' he added, turning to the uncomfortable African solider and addressing him in his own tongue. 'You may go, but be ready to come back if we call you.'

He nodded quickly and fled from the hut.

'But he never told us anything, Colonel!' wailed Faunce-Whittington. 'Captain Toteaux might be in real trouble. He might need us to help him. You're the magistrate after all, and Bob is the chief of police.'

'I know, damn it!' barked back Flambard. 'Dear God, man, you know as well as I do we can't afford to alienate the few friendly chiefs who aren't loyal to the Zulu Crown by killing their isangoma and defiling their beliefs. And now some silly idiot's gone and shot a civilian. Bob Toteaux might be a decent enough captain, but he's a bully, and he drinks!'

'That's gossip, and I ought to know!' quipped back Faunce-Whittington. 'That's why you had to reinstate him as chief of police.'

'I would never have done so, had he not been chief before I arrived,' Flambard replied angrily. 'You know damn well I'm a fair man, Faunce, but I had to bow to pressure from the lieutenant governor and keep the peace. I didn't want him back. And now he's shot a civilian.'

'Yes, an isangoma... a witch,' the lieutenant exclaimed. 'I thought witchcraft was illegal, you know.'

'A healer you mean and be it witchcraft or otherwise, outlawed in our colony only!' cried Flambard indignantly. 'But not in the Kingdom of Zululand which, until it has been pacified, is an independent state. The reason for the war was the fact that the Zulu king rejected the ultimatum in the first place! Can't you see – can't any man among our society? Are we all too blind to realise the harm we will do by trying to force these people to live the way we live?'

'Colonel?'

'Oh, for goodness sake, Faunce, it's the Zulu army we are supposed to be fighting, not the Zulu people. If we go about messing with them the way we messed with the Sikhs in India we'll all come unstuck. Haven't you heard enough of old Wilb's stories to realise that yet?'

‘Oh! Did I hear someone mention India?’ intoned a familiar voice.

‘Untimely, Captain, I fear,’ muttered Flambard, as the well-known figure of McGonagle came tramping into the hut, furiously shaking the dust off his tunic, and kicking off his boots.

‘I was there, you know,’ the old man continued, pointedly stabbing with his finger at the red and white silk ribbon on the left breast of his tatty undress frock.

‘I *know*,’ the commandant replied – to Faunce’s mind a little solemnly – as he seized his patrol jacket brandishing the rows of silk decorations above the pocket, all stained a dark blood-red from his wound at the river.

‘Oh, ho!’ laughed McGonagle, his hilarity being even more alarming than his usual curmudgeonly behaviour. ‘Then you know of what I speak, right enough!’

‘Only too well,’ Flambard replied darkly. ‘As you may come to remember.’

By the time the sun began to fall behind the mountains, the column had caught up with itself and, coming to a sedate halt on a gentle camber the other side of the rocky hills, had begun to prepare for the wagons to be laagered and for the entrenchment of the camp. This had to be done before nightfall and before any movements towards eating or sleeping arrangements could be made for the troops.

Trenches were dug around the outside of the perimeter, and the wagons themselves were run in one against the other, forming a huge circular fortification that was then barricaded with boxes of provisions, and piled high between each one with soil from the earthwork. Bottles and general refuse were idly lobbed across the defences to act as a sort of mantrap and, with any luck, foul the feet of any Zulu scout foolish enough to venture within five hundred yards of British firepower, or somehow creep past the piquets. The trenches themselves, as with the overall fortification, was planned and theoretically overseen by the senior engineer officer, Warren Westgate. Despite this, it was ultimately Bond and his sappers who ended up overseeing and, in some cases, physically executing the excavation of the camp perimeter.

As a result, they remained later into the evening, when the sun had disappeared well and truly behind the hills, and a dreadfully cold mist had sprung up to envelop them. This pervading mist chilled the bones, soaked through the flimsy serge cloth of their jackets, and gradually began to seep in between thumb and fingers, almost freezing red raw hands to the tools of their trade. Toiling was the only way in which to keep warm, but it was not something that could be done without the means of sustenance.

Barking irritably that his men had worked quite hard enough for one day, Bond, who was himself waist high in mud and digging with the rest, yelled across to a sergeant of The Wolves to get a party of men together and set to digging the last section of trench. This task was not greeted cheerily by the men of the Hundred and Tenth, who resented this young lieutenant, with his velvet cuff and collar facings, ordering them away from their dinners. Worse still was the fact that, despite the only engineer NCO available being a mere corporal, Bond insisted on placing his newly conscripted pioneers under the direction of Gideon Knight's men, who had all been fed immediately after they had made camp. Ignoring their muffled protests, and casually remarking that it would only be their lookout if the Zulus decided to creep up in the dark and stab them all in their beds, Bond instructed Friday to stand the men down for the remainder of the evening.

'Come on,' he whispered gently to Coleman. 'Let's get something hot into you.'

'I'll see about fetching yours first though, Mr Albert,' Coleman protested weakly, for the lack of food and hours of sustained marching, followed by such active bursts of manual labour, had begun to take a considerable toll on the fit young sapper, and the want of food literally reduced his muscular strivings to mere feeble gestures.

'I'll see about fetching the officer's grub, soldier,' Friday grunted, trying desperately to ignore the furious and highly undignified grumbling of his stomach. 'You get off and see to your own.'

'I'd rather stay up with you, sir,' Coleman whispered to Bond.

'It's all right,' Bond smiled back. 'You do what the sergeant says and fall in with your fellows.'

'Yes, Mr Albert,' Coleman nodded obediently, but he was damned if he felt it.

Back in the headquarters tent, which had been erected almost before the wagons had stopped coming in, the colonels were deeply involved in a state of conference over the movements of the following day. At least two of them were certainly conferring, but one was notably absent.

An experienced soldier of some thirty years, Henry Roystone had seen service in several of the Empire's "native" campaigns, before assuming command of the Hundred and

Tenth. A purchased major at the age of thirty-nine, Roystone had retained both that rank and the rank of lieutenant colonel, during which time he commanded both battalions of the regiment, until breveted at the age of forty-six.

When the war with the Zulu had become something of a certainty, Roystone had appealed to the secretary of state for an active command. Having such experience himself, and commanding a regiment made up largely of 'old sweats' recruited under the pre-Cardwell system, it was decided that Roystone be appointed full colonel and embark for Cape Colony with immediate effect.

Now, with the sun well and truly over the yard arm, and a pair of brass desk lamps lighting the rickety old campaign table on which were spread the maps, general orders and detailed intelligence reports on the land and its inhabitants, the mighty colonel stood and smoked his cigar.

'Coastal column moves to the right of us,' Roystone informed the commander of the second battalion. 'And His Lordship's own moves to find camp at Isandula directly after crossing Rorke's Drift.'

'Is there any word of Matabyana himself, Harry?' Lieutenant Colonel Henderson enquired.

'Old bugger's probably hiding out in the hills, waiting for us to move,' sighed Roystone. 'My fear,' he added, 'as shared by his lordship the lieutenant general, is that the damned impi will wait for us to move well into the country, then outflank us on either side and counterattack Natal.'

'What of the other chief, that fellow... Blacker, or something?'

'Imnyamana, or some such, you mean,' grunted Roystone. 'Means darkness or the like. Chap's supposed to be a bit of a bounder, all told. Led some of the raiding parties into Flambard's magistracy and killed a load of farmers.'

'Black or white? Oh well, it wouldn't make any difference to old Flambard,' chuckled the commander of the second battalion dismissively. 'Man's a radical!'

Roystone said nothing at this, yet his eyes narrowed.

When it came to controversy, Brevet Lieutenant Colonel Francis Henderson was something of a veteran. Having served a period with the Queen's 'other army', the then Major Henderson had been fiercely criticised for executing some thirty-odd sepoy deserters during a regional amnesty, following the mutiny of '57, incurring the wrath of several notable war correspondents, including Mr Russell of *The Times*. At the time, it was widely held that the actions had cost him any chance of a future colonelcy.

It had taken his old friend and advocate Harry Roystone, who had served with him in India to advocate for Henderson and reinvigorate the officer's stalled career. It was in the face of some opposition from the colonial administration, and the ever-vocal Captain McGonagle in his correspondence with the papers, that Henderson was appointed temporary commander of his old battalion.

'Sorry I'm late, gentlemen,' put in a third voice, albeit belatedly.

'Arthur , where on earth have you been? I had expected you coming up on an hour since!"

'My apologies, Colonel,' McEnry replied awkwardly, fumbling about with the papers in his portmanteaux. 'You see, it's my youngest, Colonel,' he added, by way of explanation. 'Since I left, she's been inconsolable. I promised I would write to her daily. I'm sorry if I've caused an inconvenience.'

'Think nothing of it, man,' Roystone replied quietly. Privately, he could not have cared less how or why the delay in his comrade's arrival, but he was a compassionate man and a father himself, and he knew the circumstances of his battalion commander's domestic situation. Indeed, Roystone himself had been McEnry's battalion commander when that officer's wife had died so suddenly and so tragically while in labour. The child survived but had grown into a weak, paranoid adolescent – of marriageable age but childishly needy – and always a distraction to her bereaved and sometimes professionally conflicted father.

Moreover, both he and Roystone were only too aware that, were it not for McEnry's seniority and higher level of experience, Henderson would by no means have been so cordial about his brother colonel's preoccupations.

As it was, Henderson could only growl quietly that they really ought to return to their plan of campaign, if they intended to go forth and meet either the local chieftan or any of his lesser chieftains the following day.

'Quite right,' Roystone assented, stubbing out his cigar in an improvised field ashtray and replacing his eyeglass. 'We should all be very familiar with the geography of the region into which we are to advance with our troops. Gentlemen,' he added, throwing open yet another large map on the table in front of them, 'this is our conquest.'

The route by which they were to take the column was to be one that would see the entire complement of soldiers, horses, wagons, and artillery trains advancing across country, traversing two rivers, and crossing a steep mountain range before coming into some several hundred miles of open veldt. They might expect attacks at any time, and since their intelligence sources had been confined to a handful of African families sympathetic to the colonial administration, the element of second-guessing was going to be a vital tool in the war against a so far invisible enemy.

The weather had already shown itself to be at best manic, and at worst downright biblical in its turbidity. It rained both morning and night; the mists fell upon the hapless soldiers just when discipline relied on them being bright and alert, and the sun when it did emerge was torturous to literally anything that moved.

With these factors in mind, and with the health and wellbeing of his troops a paramount consideration in a swift and effective campaign, Roystone leaned forward over the table, and grimly began plotting his course of action.

Henderson had taken McEnry to one side and was just on the point of raising a quibble about supplies, when a heavy patter, followed by a positively thunderous deluge of raindrops began to fall on the canvas canopy above their heads.

Roystone paused, removed his monocle, and briefly looked up. Then, with a brusque comment about getting down to it, the three colonels returned to the matter in hand.

The campfire built by the men of Warren Westgate's sapper company had, like those of the West Rutlands, suffered immeasurably as a result of the sudden downpour, causing Friday and several others to abandon their efforts at mess and decamp in search of shelter. Even though they had pitched their position in the lea of one of the massive, covered wagons that formed part of the laager perimeter, the relentless rain somehow managed to become a complete sheet of water, thrashing across the already reddened faces of those who remained outside.

Gradually, as the rain grew heavier and conversation devolved into mere spitting matches, the junior officers' concern for the welfare of their men began to escalate.

Several made provision for men of their company in the wagons themselves, and Earnest Penfold even made over half the space in his tent to both his batman, the company bugler, and a senior NCO from The Wolves.

Gideon Knight, who shared a tented wagon with Warren Westgate, looked grimly out through the rivers of water that fell from the canvas canopy. 'Won't do morale any good, this stuff,' he remarked.

'I concur entirely, Gideon, but what the devil are we to do about it?' Westgate sighed resignedly. 'I mean, we can't very well do ourselves out of a tent and cram the entire field company in here instead, can we?'

'Admittedly not,' Knight replied. 'Although I really do think we ought to have made some provision for this sort of thing beforehand.'

'How?' Westgate shrugged. 'Matters connected with the commissariat are down to battalion commanders of the West Rutlands. Arthur McEnry did his best to accommodate us, but his priority must be his own men – the infantry.'

'What do you say, Albert?' Knight turned to Bond, who was sitting at the other end of the wagon, sipping brandy, and gazing thoughtfully out into the gloom. His own tent was about five hundred yards across the camp. In such circumstances the slog through the mud and rain to his own damp quarters seemed hardly to compete with a nice dry wagon, up off the ground and well away from the rapidly rising drainage gullies.

'The conditions are terrible,' Bond replied grimly. 'The men are already having to put up with long treks in the mist, followed by boiling sunshine when the mist clears of a morning. They're still on whatever rations we can wangle off The Wolves, and they have had no real provision made for them as far as sleeping arrangements are concerned.'

'Thank you for that comprehensive precis, Albert,' Westgate replied, a note of impatience pervading his normally measured accents. 'What we want is suggestions, rather than a protracted complaint on behalf of the deprived of the company.'

Bond was no longer listening. There, somewhere just within his field of vision, he had spotted the miserable, bedraggled cluster of his own men, who were now huddling under the flatbed of one of the wagons, the flank of which fell within the camp confines. One of those was unmistakably young Coleman. 'You want ideas, Major?' Bond replied curtly, as soon as a sharp cough had drawn his attention away from his sappers and back to his company commander. 'I recommend that all officers take their own batman and at least one other into their respective billets, yourself and Gideon excluded. Naturally, I volunteer to take Coleman and Friday.'

Then, without waiting for a reply, and with a brief but polite snap about the brandy, the young lieutenant threw his greatcoat over his head and squeezed past the two officers, plopping down in the sodden grass, and squelching off in search of his men.

'What do you suppose that was all about, Gideon?' Westgate gasped, perplexed. 'He's never called me captain before, let alone major.'

'Formality, in deference to your promotion?' Knight suggested, albeit with a vague hint of a twinkle in his eye.

'Acting promotion, damn it,' muttered Westgate gloomily. 'It's only a promotion when I've got the stars to go with it. Until the brevet, I'm paid as a captain, just with more paperwork!'

'Is that why you haven't written to Annie lately?' the younger officer enquired cautiously. 'Don't be offended, Warren, but I couldn't help but notice.'

'I shall turn seven and thirty next week,' Westgate sighed, lighting a cigar and dragging heavily on it for emphasis. 'I don't want to get her and the children excited until I'm confirmed. You've served long enough, Gideon. You know as well as I do that won't happen until we get home and the colonel reshuffles the commands,' he replied. 'Worse still, knowing the army, my brevet might be followed by another order replacing me with a substantive major after all! I suppose you'll be captain, Gideon,' he added, a vague smile beginning at last to appear under the bushy blond beard as he spoke.

'A medal for this lot would do me just fine for now, Warren,' Knight replied, modesty forbidding further reference to his own ambitions. At thirty, he had everything he could want and far more. He was married to a beautiful woman, his property in Ireland that his father had made over to him was turning a profit, and he was at last engaged upon a military campaign, which could only serve to accelerate his already healthy promotion prospects.

'Colonel at forty, general at fifty,' Westgate slurred, as the effects of the alcohol began gradually to take hold of his already melancholy feelings. You'll be a general, my boy,' he continued, echoing sentiments oft directed at Knight. 'And I'll be a very old captain, just like bloody McGonagle!'

Chapter Twenty

When Bond did at last come across the straggling remnants of his company, they were all huddled together underneath an improvised tarpaulin lash-up, with the rainwater gathering ominously in the middle, and running off in great torrents by way of huge depressions on either side. Under the cover of this pioneering dormitory lay about twenty-two men, all crammed together in full kit, with their blankets and greatcoats wrapped around them like beggars under a railway arch.

The water poured down around them, and just outside the cover of the awning, the last embers of their campfire spat and smouldered gradually to death, finally dwindling to its ultimate demise amid a sizzle of blue smoke and steam.

'Hang this for a baked potato!' Friday cried at last, idly tossing the singed remnants of his otherwise stone-cold supper he was trying to cook back into the asphyxiated fire and dashing for cover beneath a nearby wagon.

Everything was utterly wretched. Their clothes were wet, their things were wet, and the little food they had was either eaten uncooked or had simply to be thrown away.

Coleman had made the mistake of trying to cook some vile-tasting mealie porridge over the early stages of the fire. He had just about brought the solid lump of gruel-like oats and water to the boil when the rains had suddenly begun to fall. The porridge was ruined, and the poor young soldier had to make do with some cold tea and a couple of hard tack biscuits, which were nothing if not slow to consume.

Friday's trick was to place one or two in his boots, or even under his armpit on the march, by which means once they found camp, the terrible titbits might at last be of a reasonable standard to attempt to force one's teeth into.

When they caught sight of the soaking wet subaltern approaching, both let out a groan. Friday's was undeniably a groan of despair. Officers when on the walkabout usually ended up scrounging cigarettes or sometimes even booze off their men. Friday's tobacco was limited, and he certainly didn't possess any alcohol.

For Coleman, the alarm was that his officer should still be up and about in the mud and rain so long after he was supposed to have retired, and because he knew deep inside that the reason for Lieutenant Bond's insomnia was probably closely akin to his own.

Even so, both men saluted as the drenched officer slid with a pulpy squelch under the bed of the wagon. He looked terrible, too. The fingers of his hands were red raw with cold; the rain had soaked right the way through his greatcoat and deep into the knees of his trousers. Coleman could see that the collar of his now filthy white shirt, just sticking up above the saturated velvet of the patrol jacket collar, was turned almost a dark grey by the heavy rain.

'Officer ought to be under cover, sir,' Friday muttered briefly. 'Doesn't do to be mucking around in the mud with the other ranks, it doesn't. Officers need their sleep, sir.'

'Yes, that's all very well, Sergeant Friday,' Bond replied quickly. 'But under standing orders from Major Westgate, I am to take at least two of you under the cover of my tent tonight, so grab what you can, and we'll all three of us make a dash for it, all right?'

Things were definitely *not* all right. To Friday, nothing could have been worse than removing himself to the cover of an officer's quarters, even if it *was* under emergency orders. To him, the prospect of such a flagrant breech of propriety was anathema not to be entertained by an NCO of his seniority, and he for one would much rather have remained out in the elements than go under canvas with a subaltern, however junior he might have been. 'Friday keeps the watch,' he muttered briefly to Coleman. 'Friday stays put.'

Coleman, who was already halfway out from under the wagon in his eagerness to get under cover, was suddenly brought up short by the bland finality of his sergeant's statement. His blond hair hanging in a wet curtain over his face, and his feet up to the ankles in mud, Coleman looked forlornly back at Friday, nodded obediently and slunk back into his former position. Yet to his complete surprise, as he looked at Friday for approval, he saw that he was shaking his head.

'Coleman gets dry. Lad goes with his officer.'

'I can't, Sarn't, not while you're—'

'Not to argue with Friday!' he snapped suddenly.

'No, Sarn't.'

'Do as Friday tells you! Friday knows best!'

'Yes, Sarn't!' poor Coleman replied, perplexed, and bemused a little by this sudden outburst, yet elated. He didn't need any second telling. Without another word, he took off at the double like a jack rabbit, slipping, sliding and stumbling in his frantic pelt in the direction of the officers' tents.

Tripping on a rope, falling flat on his face in the mud on several occasions, virtually blinded by the driving torrent, the young soldier finally found the one he was after. With a deep sigh, he spat out a quantity of water and ducked under the canopy.

'Hello, Jack,' Bond greeted cheerily, as he rubbed his wet hair. 'Sergeant Friday with you?'

'No, sir,' Coleman replied apologetically. Clumsily dragging his aching limbs to attention in the presence of his officer, the poor lad suddenly realised that he wasn't wearing his hat, and so could not salute properly. Hardly pausing to think, and not having his cap to hand, Jack fumbled clumsily with his helmet, and succeeded in dislodging some half a pint of water from inside over his already soaking wet head and shoulders. With a groan of humiliation, he quickly looked the other way, the sopping wet blanket and greatcoat trailing behind him like a comforter. He looked so helpless.

No longer able maintain a straight face, Bond decided that enough was enough. Ending the pantomime by instructing Coleman to get his things off and make a space for himself on the dry floor of the tent, Bond handed his young guest the remaining half bottle of brandy, which he had liberated from the increasingly inebriated Knight and Westgate upon leaving their wagon.

'I don't drink, sir, thank you,' Coleman replied hurriedly.

Bond looked at him quietly for a moment. 'Sergeant Friday is not here, Sapper,' he told Coleman slowly. 'You are wet through, you've hardly had anything to eat, and more than anything you need a good night's sleep. Here,' he repeated, proffering the bottle like the barrel of a loaded revolver, 'take it.'

Coleman nodded obediently, took a quick gulp from the neck of the bottle, then screwed his eyes up in pain as the hot sting of the strong liquor burned the lining of his throat, warming his stomach and putting his nerves back in touch with his chilled extremities.

Seeing that the brandy had, in part, effected the cure that he had sought, Bond reached under the bed and produced a half-opened tin of bully beef, some biscuits and a small jar of preserves.

Coleman shook his head. 'I can't take that, Mr Albert,' he protested.

'You'll do as you're told,' Bond smiled mischievously. 'Here,' he added, unravelling one of the blankets from the mass on his camp bed. 'You're to take this, instead of that sodden rag you've been sleeping in.'

'Th-this is—' Coleman stammered.

'Yours,' Bond interrupted.

'But it's so soft, sir. It's too good for me,' he protested.

'Lamb's wool,' Bond informed him, dismissing all arguments with a wave of his hand. 'Keep you warm as toast that will. Now try to get some sleep. And for goodness sake,' he added quietly, 'you needn't worry about taking your clothes off in here. The damn things are soaking through.'

Coleman smiled and nodded. 'Besides,' he added, as the officer blew out his lamp beside the bed, 'it's nothing you ain't seen before... right, Mr Albert?'

The following morning was pretty much the same as all those so far on the campaign, bar one significant difference. On most mornings, the chilled mist that hung over the camp until sunrise usually burned off by about breakfast, just about in time to prepare and drill before the march, which was as unpleasant and oppressive as possible.

On this occasion, however, when the mist did clear it revealed yet another magical image, ten times as serene and becalming than the one upon which Bond and his men had been so fortunate as to gaze the afternoon before.

Consequently, Bond awoke from his slumber to find Coleman gone a second time. Scrambling out of bed, he enacted his pre-breakfast ritual of checking that his revolver was loaded, cleaning the lenses of his binoculars, and setting about arranging his plate, mug, and cutlery for taking his morning repast.

He was just in the process of replacing the revolver in its tan leather holster, when the shadow of his late sleeping companion began to descend on his tent with a speed that seemed to defy stopping.

Popping his head around the flap, Coleman, who was clearly puffed out from such excitement, beamed endearingly at Bond, and respectfully pestered him to come and look.

'What on earth is it this time? More lost valleys?' Bond laughed incredulously. 'Or have we suddenly come up against an army?' he added, slightly less so.

'Neither, Mr Albert,' Coleman replied buoyantly. 'But you must come while it's still so fresh and there's no one else about.'

Grudgingly casting aside his personal effects, Bond could only pause to snatch up his brown and tatty helmet, before dashing after Coleman across the still squelchy grass of the soaking wet laager.

A collection of soldiers, both officers and men, had congregated on and around the wagons to the north-east of their position, and were all pointing and staring, furiously chatting away to each other in great excitement.

'What's all this, Snooker?' Bond enquired of Captain Collingwood, who had necessarily been up even earlier than most for the sake of the horses.

'It's the big pond, old man,' the artillery officer replied. 'That's your river, Albert, and the primary border with Matabyana's own territory.'

'It's all very well, this spectacle,' Warren Westgate grumbled to Gideon Knight, both of whom were nursing terrible hangovers from the night before. 'But what they don't realise is that we still have to get across the wretched thing.'

'Quite possibly under fire from the other side,' Lieutenant Knight concurred grimly. 'Personally, Warren, I am *not* looking forward to today.'

Nevertheless, and despite the engineers' misgivings, there was no denying the natural beauty of the panorama. The river itself was not too wide, running at a majestic curve around the foot of high and rocky hills, about a mile and a half to the north-east of their position. Underneath the foremost of the craggy outcrops, the river tapered in slightly on either side, running into a sort of natural sandbank, and cut into the lower foothills were a series of dongas and dried up rainwater gullies, leading directly from the hilltops to the river itself.

It was this natural embrasure in the topography of the area that Colonel Roystone examined most carefully. Seated on his ferocious black charger, Dante, the formidable commander could be seen a little way outside the laager, with a small personal guard of Flambard's Horse, and the charmingly named Major Turnpenny, together with a squadron of mounted infantry. A dense and imposing black beard, emblazoned with great white flashes from the tips of his moustache to the fourth button down on his scarlet jacket, had now joined his normally thick and curly hair, and the colonel's overall appearance was one of awesome power and superiority.

Lieutenant Colonel McEnry was seated to the left of him, mounted on a dappled grey charger and dressed similarly to Roystone in the field uniform of the West Rutlands, although the wispy line of silver grey that adorned his own chin seemed, to all appearances, pale and shadowy.

'If anyone is going to see off the Zulus and see us all glorified, it's Colonel Roystone, right, Mr Penfold?' one of the sappers asked of his officer.

'He's a big man, and no mistake,' Penfold replied quietly. 'I just hope he's not being too brave, sitting out there in full view of the whole countryside.'

'Oh, for goodness sake, Earnest, stop being so depressive,' Bond complained. 'You should try to be positive, otherwise we'll never get the men across.'

'Yes,' Penfold muttered mournfully. 'It's just that I remember the last time we crossed a river together. It's always the same – engineers across first.'

'It's what we signed on to do!' Bond quipped aggressively. Then, realising that the little officer's reticence was more than mere banter, he drew Penfold to one side and asked him what the matter really was.

'It's my wife, Hen,' Penfold explained miserably. 'I do miss her terribly, and I promised that I'd be very careful.'

'Are you afraid, Earnest?' Bond asked quietly.

Penfold bowed his head, arms folded, with one hand aimlessly caressing the end of his beard while the other fiddled about with a loose thread on his scarlet frock jacket. 'Not afraid, Albert, but I am sad.'

'Sad? Why ever should you be sad?' Bond persisted, quite perplexed by his comrade's sudden loss of spirits.

'I'm sad because I know I shall die,' Penfold replied honestly. 'And I don't mind that so much – it's what we do, after all – but Hen will be so lonely without me.'

'Really, old man!' Bond whispered, gently drawing Penfold even further away from the eyes and ears of the assembled company still gathered on and around the wagons. 'What on earth has brought this on, Earnest?'

Penfold shook his head and smiled. 'Don't ask me to explain it, Albert,' he sighed placidly. 'I just feel something is coming, that's all. We shall all of us have to see to ourselves when the time comes, but as I said, it's Hen who I'm worried about.'

'God forbid that I should make matters worse by encouraging you in this pessimistic fancy of yours,' Bond began carefully, 'but if anything should happen, you know I shall do what I can.'

'You would do that, for Hen, I mean?' Penfold pressed him seriously.

'Of course,' Bond found himself promising. 'That is, if I'm spared.'

The mists lifted in due course and, true to form, the sun baked down on them without distinction. The rain had held off for the most part of the morning, meaning that they had not yet been forced to march during a downpour, but the roads were like quagmires. The arid African sun-baked crusts on the thick, slippery mud on the road surface, caused a queer crunching sound on every occasion it was marched upon by either boot or hoof. The smell, too, was utterly revolting.

The heavy rainfall the previous night had raised the level of the drains and, worse still, the latrines, while mealie bags and biscuit boxes had suffered from considerable seepage and been utterly ruined as a result. Several of the oxen had died during the night, and their corpses were left to lie where they fell.

After they had been marching a few hours, a calm breeze akin to the one that had sprung up so suddenly that magical afternoon when they had discovered the Zulu homestead arose to caress and soothe hot limbs, sore feet, and sunburned skin. It played through the long yellow grasses of the open veldt, and here and there some wonderful exotic bird could be heard calling out, a song sweet and sonorous compared to the endless clanking and squelching of Colonel Roystone's army on the move through Africa.

They moved briskly, despite the oppressive nature of the day, the weight of their equipment, and the heat of their irritating coats and smothering helmets. The sun blazed down on everyone and everything.

Bond, Coleman, and especially Friday had learned a hard lesson through having been badly sunburned on both face and neck while still in Natal, and their excursion into the mountains a couple of days earlier had left them positively red as lobsters after so long with their shirts off.

As it was, the clumsy, sweaty Foreign Service helmet was still highly preferable to the severe cases of sunburn sustained to exposed areas as a result of not wearing one at all, and the oceans of sweat, which poured from their foreheads, had simply to be put up with.

By mid-morning, the abuses of the perilous heat were beginning to make themselves apparent on all ranks, blazing down with such scorching ferocity that both men and animals perspired freely. Several horses died on the road, and here and there officers of one company or another could be seen walking beside their men in their riding boots or hitching lifts on wagons that were not too overloaded to take them.

Such an extreme temperature after so many nights of rain and fog oppressed and ground down the weary troops. Men and animals sweated profusely, to the extent that a large swarm of flies began to gather in a ghastly mass, hovering above the heads of the marching soldiers, and hounding the horses without respite.

'It's a plague!' Bond complained to Gideon Knight, as the two officers thrashed wildly with their riding crops, trying desperately to fend off some of the masses of swarming insects. 'If the Zulus are half as bad as these damned flies, then I'm for home straight away!'

'I don't know about your nag, Albert, but my horse can't stand much more of this blistering heat,' Knight replied, removing his shoulder belt, and whirling it above his head like a voorlooper's whip.

'You should have bought an African,' Bond quipped back at him. 'This one doesn't seem to mind the heat too badly, in spite of the false start.'

'Mr Albert, sir!' A cry from behind them had drawn Bond's attention momentarily away from the flies. Turning his horse and side-stepping off the road so as not to hold up the advancing column, he turned his attention to the source of his calling. It was Coleman, and he and Corporal Denham were gathered in a small group to one side of the road, cradling between the two of them an exhausted, overwhelmed and almost fitting Sergeant Friday.

'How long has he been like this?' Bond called in earnest, dropping from the saddle, and handing the horse's reigns to the corporal.

'Hour or more, Mr Albert,' Coleman replied. 'We wanted to get you sooner, sir, but the Sarn't wouldn't have it.'

'Said he didn't want to hold up the company, sir,' put in Corporal Denham.

'The heat is having a profound effect on all the troops,' Colonel Henderson opined to Colonel McEnry, with whom he was having an argument. 'It does not do to try and fit them all onto wagons, Arthur.'

'Be that as it may,' McEnry replied. 'But we cannot permit officers and NCOs to simply pass out in front of the men on the march. Morale will suffer immeasurably if soldiers see their superiors peeling off all around them, while they are still on the go.'

'Quite!' Henderson continued. 'And it is for precisely that reason that we cannot allow men to simply jump off the road and onto the supply transport as they see fit to do. Subalterns are our eyes and ears, Arthur . They need to be seen in amongst the other ranks at times like this, or how else do we maintain order and discipline?'

'Certainly not by shooting them at random,' McEnry muttered subversively. 'And I'll thank you to address me by my proper title in front of the men,' he added pettishly. 'I am a confirmed colonel, after all, Henderson.'

Dealing McEnry a look of pure venom, Colonel Henderson merely snorted, and turned back on his horse to chivvy up his companies.

'I appreciate that the two of you have differences of opinion on many things, Arthur ,' Roystone intoned quietly. 'But while I appreciate that fact, I don't really approve of pulling rank on a brother colonel, whatever the state of his appointment.'

'I'm sorry, Harry,' McEnry replied ashamedly. 'But you know how he gets at me. Thinks that I spend too much time worrying about my daughter's health, and not enough time worrying about the battalion. Is that fair, do you think?'

'Have I ever made pronouncements on your life or your ability to command the battalion?'

'Well, no. I suppose not,' McEnry admitted.

'In that case, you may rest assured that my judgement is sober, and that I have made the right choice in *both* my lieutenant colonelcy appointments.'

McEnry nodded in agreement, disarmed as usual by the sobriety of his old friend's counsel.

'One more thing Arthur , and far be it from me to presume I know better, but the bastard is right, you know,' Roystone added grimly.

'About Africans?' McEnry replied, the incredulity crumpling his already troubled features.

'No, I meant about your daughter at home. He's right, I'm afraid. You should send her to live away before it becomes too late, and she hasn't even you to hang on to. I can see from your expression how painful it must be to hear this from me, but what future must she have as a spinster daughter, forever awaiting her papa's return?

'Henderson hasn't even got children!' McEnry snapped back in annoyance. 'He never even married. Do you really think that I should take advice from a man who's never loved anything more than the crowns on his collar tabs?'

'Believe me, Arthur , I'm not saying this because I think you want to hear it. I can see that you don't. But I am a father of two myself, and I know how hard it can be to let go.'

'You have no complaints with my command, Colonel?' McEnry repeated coldly.

'You know I haven't.'

'Then do not presume to comment on my fatherhood, Harry. A VC doesn't entitle you to know any better than the rest of us... in that respect, at least!'

'If only it did,' Roystone sighed to himself, 'I shouldn't be so worried right now.'

By the time the afternoon was upon them, and the column had halted for a hurried meal of beef, potatoes and yet more wretched hard tack, Bond and his collection of exhausted men lay sprawled on the grass in the lea of their tented supply wagon.

Regardless of the lessons of the previous occasion, all three officers and most of the men had stripped off their top halves, the only exception being Lieutenant Penfold who felt it inappropriate to expose his pale and modest physique to open regard as well as possible sunstroke. At length, stand-to was sounded and the column prepared for the off once more.

Sergeant Friday, having been well fed, watered, and set back on his feet with Coleman only a few yards away at all times, was now feeling well enough again to yell very loudly at some African pioneers, who appeared to be straggling behind.

They made good time and were almost level with the previously distant cluster of hills to the north-east, when Coleman thought he spotted something far off in the distance, and well to the left.

'Did you think you could see what it was?' Bond enquired, albeit a little lightly, for he was fairly convinced that the sun was playing tricks with every shadow.

'Well, sir, it was something like a load of flies,' the young sapper replied straightforwardly. 'I couldn't quite see, but something was there, over that way, sir.'

'Better mention this to the colonel,' put in Gideon Knight, scratching at the line of thick black growth that now beset his normally clean jaw.

'Better not, old chap,' Bond whispered hurriedly. 'After all, if it is a false alarm, we'll never hear the end of it. I don't want Coleman taking the blame for something that's been happening to us all on and off the whole time.'

'What? You mean you've been seeing things as well?' Knight demanded sternly. 'Why on earth didn't you say something before, Albert?' he added, turning back to Coleman for a more detailed account as to what he thought he saw.

'Sentries' ghosts!' Bond protested. 'Common enough, even *you* might be susceptible!'

'Well, sir, it's like I said before,' Coleman began again. 'Something like a load of flies, glinting now and then and catching my eye up there on the hillside. I *was* 'eyes front', sir,' he pleaded, unconsciously turning to Bond for support.

'That's all right, Jack. Now go on,' Bond encouraged him. He was by now thoroughly nervous and beginning to think that indeed he should have acted sooner. Such things placed a terrible strain on his overheated mind, and the ghosts of a hundred wrong decisions over his father's businesses seemed to throb and murmur beneath his topi.

'They were black things, I thought,' Coleman resumed. 'But then they looked like they were white things all the time. Then they seemed to be both, like them.' The two officers looked while Coleman pointed, and saw from his right hand that the gesture had been directed at a grizzly swarm of flies, which were just beginning to mass around the fresh carcass of a dead ox. As they looked, they could see that the silvered wings were held open on either side of their thin black bodies and dotted around the dusty red skin of the animal they were set about devouring like rows of little matchsticks when lined up on a gaming table.

'Flies?' Bond repeated quietly.

'Best hope so,' Knight muttered in response. 'Otherwise, who knows?'

Chapter Twenty-One

Even as the two lieutenants had been perusing the countryside and weighing up the possible risks in a false alarm, the party at the head of the column some half a mile further on had been left in no doubt whatsoever of the presence of their hitherto illusive enemy.

Trooper Bonnerville of Flambard's Horse had been the first to genuinely believe that he saw something. By no means as conscious of raising a panic and being left looking like an alarmist in front of the infantry, Bonnerville had reported the matter to his commander immediately. He, having sent a message some five hundred yards back down the line, was presently joined by Colonel Roystone and Henderson, flanked by a large squadron of the mounted infantry under Major Turnpenny.

At first it did look indeed like a load of matchsticks, as row upon row of black, white and tan objects began to make themselves apparent on the raised ground just the other side of the river.

'Damned odd,' growled Henderson. 'Do you suppose it's cattle, Harry?'

'No, I do not suppose anything of the kind,' Roystone replied, searching out his binoculars and raising them to the level of his bushy eyebrows as he scanned the veldt with the eyes of a hawk. 'Ah yes, now we have them,' he muttered to himself. 'Not matchsticks after all, but war shields. Look for yourself, Theo,' he added, passing the glasses across from the saddle to the hands of the excited Major Turnpenny. 'The little sliver glints you will find are their spears,' Roystone informed him coolly. 'Gentlemen, we have engagement.'

An electric thrill of fear and excitement went up around the three colonels, and somehow the buzz began to communicate itself to both troops and horses from one end of the line to the next.

'I volunteer to lead the attack, Harry,' piped up Henderson. 'I can take two companies of infantry and—'

'They'll be gone before you get there,' Roystone interrupted. 'Don't be silly, man. Major, will you take your men across at the safest point and see if you can flush them out of those hills?'

'My pleasure, Colonel,' Turnpenny replied, huge grey whiskers curling at the ends as a smile of anticipation played across his weathered face. 'Hundred and Tenth, advance!'

The first Bond and his men knew of the impending engagement was when Snooker Collingwood's two Armstrong guns went thundering past their position in the line, boxes rattling on the back and two bombardiers clinging to the flimsy canvas seats on each gun for dear life. Collingwood himself rode to the fore, directing his battery to set up on an area of flat grassland to the right of Colonel Roystone's position.

'Captain, I require you and your artillery to prepare a salvo immediately. Hurl a couple of shells in amongst all those boulders and see if you can flush them out into Turnpenny's path.'

'Very good, sir,' Collingwood replied. 'Bombardier Smith, bring number two gun about and direct fire at the north-eastern side of the escarpment, would you?

'What's happening, Warren?' Knight called out, as Westgate's horse came charging down the column at speed.

'They're forming up on the other side of the river,' Westgate replied. 'Colonel Roystone has ordered us in behind the irregulars so that we can prepare a crossing down river from the nek. Gideon, I want you to take Bert Bond, Sergeant Friday, and a handful of sappers down there now and start getting the men across. Is that clear?'

'Yes, Major,' Knight beamed in response. 'Albert, stand the men to and follow me!'

'Is this what really happens now, Mr Albert?' Coleman panted, as he and a collection of sappers under Sergeant Friday dashed towards the riverbank.

Bond and Knight had ridden down on horseback and had assumed a commanding position beneath a tree on a grassy knoll by the edge of the potential crossing.

All was quite calm as they watched the long line of mounted infantry, black and white African irregulars, and a handful of Africans fording the river some distance upstream.

Suddenly, a loud bang shook the earth beneath their feet, momentarily startling the horses and making both Bond and Coleman jump right out of their skin.

'That must be Collingwood and his artillery,' Knight remarked to Bond, as a loud whistling noise followed by a cataclysmic explosion sounded on the other side. There was a huge cloud of smoke and dust, and scarcely had this blown away before yet another shell had traced its course, this time landing right in the middle of a crease in the rocks above the river.

More explosions followed, and the sight of white balls of smoke and a heavy yet ill directed gunfire bellowed forth from the rocks and boulders that strew the hillside.

Gaining the opposite bank, the red-coated infantry spurred up the sandy ground, horses' hooves throwing up clouts of wet mud and debris behind them as they cut the hundred yards or so before them and began carefully to negotiate the rocky spur.

Here and there, the part-clad form of warriors popped up from behind cover, firing in a fog of gun smoke and retiring once again behind their positions.

The sound of musketry echoed across the river, and from his position on the other side, Roystone watched with some relief as Major Turnpenny's party began gradually to climb the hillside, firing their carbines from the saddle.

'I'd say from the sound that old Matabyana's men are using old smooth bores,' McEnry remarked to Roystone, as the huge clouds of blue smoke drifted up above the hilltop and floated off across the veldt.

'I just hope we can get enough men up there to push them out,' Henderson added before turning to the colonel. 'Sir, shall I take a company of infantry, throw them out on either side of the irregulars and take the enemy with anything that comes down on either side of Turnpenny's advance?'

'That sounds feasible,' Roystone replied. 'You have my permission, Colonel.'

Then, as the rocky ascent became more hazardous to the horses, and the debris and scrub caused them to have to struggle with their footing, Turnpenny ordered his men to dismount and advance on foot up the hillside, flushing out the enemy as they proceeded.

There followed a confusion of noise and smoke, with men running a few yards, crouching to fire their carbines, trigger hands yanking back levers to expel used cartridges from the breech of the gun so that a fresh round could be inserted.

Here and there, Zulu snipers would pop up again from behind their rocks to fire on the advancing soldiers, or to throw down their rifles and attack with their assegais when the enemy got near enough to stab at.

One young soldier of The Wolves was halfway up the slope when he was attacked. Having advanced at a half jog, firing all the way, he had paused momentarily to reload his rifle when a Zulu warrior had jumped up out of the thickets, only inches away from his nose. Stunned, the young soldier could do nothing as the huge warrior took a furious stab at him, plunging the broad blade of his assegai into his forearm, causing him to fall back in pain and shock. Before the Zulu could remove his spear and finish off the young soldier there was a shot close at hand, and the warrior fell dead, killed by Turnpenny himself.

All around them the Zulus were breaking cover. Warriors jumped up out of nowhere, either to shoot or be shot by the advancing infantry. Here and there, bitter hand-to-hand fighting had broken out, and half-clad African warriors could be seen grappling with the red-faced, red-coated troops, spears flashing, rifles firing amid the sickening stink of gun smoke, the ripping of flesh and the flash of cold steel.

Major Turnpenny dismounted at the base of a large rock, pausing only to fire a few rounds from his revolver. A warrior popped up from the crag above, aiming to shoot the major. They both fired at once, both missing, and the warrior fumbled to reload his antiquated musket. Turnpenny, however, was possessed of two more rounds, which he fired, killing the warrior, and causing him to drop noiselessly from his position up on high. Then, drawing his sword, the major turned back to his men and calling, 'Forward men, from here on in it's the metal!' he led them up the rocky embankment. Just as he turned to advance, however, a seasoned Zulu warrior of about thirty summers sprang up from the aloes a few feet away. He fired, hitting the courageous major in the chest and causing him to tumble helplessly back into the dense shrubbery on the ground below.

Major Turnpenny died before he could be moved, surrounded by his officers, his sergeant and a handful of Flambard's Horse, who had already joined in the pursuit of the surviving Zulus.

'Mixed fortunes gentlemen,' Roystone told his officers gravely. 'A fair mornings work purchased at an unfair and tragic price. However, we must not permit ourselves to fall idle, either in victory, or in grief. Captain Collingwood, you may limber up now, but make sure that you have cover from your rocket battery before the guns are removed.'

'Yes, Colonel.'

'Major Westgate, you are to be responsible for negotiating the crossing of the river. I want it done as quickly as possible'.

'Yes, sir, although Lieutenant Bond and Knight are downstream digging in stakes for the ponts as we speak.'

'Well, bring them back up here immediately,' Roystone instructed the engineer. 'Oh, and Westgate.'

'Yes, sir?'

'Let Flambard's Horse and the mounted men scout well ahead of you before your men even think of crossing. I don't want you getting shot up before you've even slung the hawser.'

Saluting, Westgate turned his horse and rode back down the line to acquaint his officers with their orders.

While all was being done according to his detailed instructions, Roystone decided to ride across the river himself and inspect the landscape they had to traverse.

As soon as he arrived on the other side of the river, Colonel Roystone began to reflect upon Major Turnpenny's death.

'Dear God, what a waste,' he muttered grimly, as himself and two of his officers stood and watched the body be removed to a place of burial. 'Poor old Theo.'

The red blood had clotted on the front of his scarlet frock jacket and around the silver whiskers above his top lip, while the medal ribbons above the wound spoke mournfully of the officer's long and distinguished career.

'He will be missed, Colonel,' Captain Fenton remarked sadly. 'Officers of his pluck don't seem to come about more than once in a while.'

'He was a very brave and courageous man,' agreed McEnry. 'He saved my life more than once in India and arranged for my passage when my wife died.'

'I'm sorry to interrupt you, colonels,' intoned a fourth personality, 'but there is something which you ought to see on the other side of the ridge, sir.'

'Not another lost valley, Lieutenant, surely?' Roystone demanded, echoing Bond's sentiments of earlier in the day.

'No, sir. It looks like there's a path through the mountains, coming out just below the crag, sir.'

Sure enough, the young officer's surmise had been correct for there, spread out before the colonel as he looked out over the valley from the top of the rocky summit was a winding, hilly and very narrow road, curling and twisting between the rocky escarpments.

'I must consult with the map,' Roystone informed McEnry on returning from the summit. 'But if my nose is correct, we may have found ourselves a way through the heights, rather than around them.'

From that moment on, everything moved quite briskly. Westgate and his sappers set to preparing a crossing by carving out a ford in the bank, opposite the point where the hills opened out and the dongas emptied their contents into the river during the rains. The column was stood-to again and prepared for the off, while a large detachment of mounted troops dispatched to piquet well in advance of the column itself. This, in addition to the two rocket troughs under the command of Lieutenant Glazebrook of The Wolves, and the full strength of the sapper company, was set up to ensure that there would be no danger of a repetition of the incident at the drift.

Having also been instructed to throw up a small stone fort as an answer to a temporary supply depot, Westgate detailed the hitherto unemployed Lieutenant Penfold to oversee the work of a handful of Africans, based on his former command of the African pioneers. The construction went well, and at the end of which, Roystone was delighted to see a small stone and sandbag fortification, entrenched all the way around apart from a small plank bridge, and cut with loopholes facing the escarpment on the opposite bank.

'It's absolutely marvellous stuff, given the time you had to build it in, Earnest,' Gideon Knight enthused, as the three sapper officers stood admiring the fruits of Penfold's handiwork.

'It certainly is remarkable. You've done brilliantly, old chap,' Bond added generously. In truth, he had never really rated Penfold as anything more than an accessory before, as he had never had the chance to. Presuming that his quiet little friend's talents lay only in the interpretation of other people's orders and clearly defined textbook strategies, Bond had to admit to himself that he felt quietly exceedingly jealous of little Earnest Penfold.

'It's all down to Coleman, I have to confess,' Penfold replied modestly. 'He just seemed to keep their interest going somehow. I don't know how. African pioneers are normally so mismanaged and act up occasionally, but if you give them what your young batman and I seem to have given them today, then there is no reason why you shouldn't get the best out of them, after all.'

Bond looked at him sideways for a moment, then smiled. 'You really aren't as silly as you look, are you, old chum?' he laughed warmly. 'And as for your remarks about my likely lad over there,' he added, winking at Coleman, who was revelling in the praise of his officer and beamed adoringly back at him, 'God certainly made a rare one when he made young Jack.'

'Wouldn't be worth my making you an offer, I suppose?' Penfold suggested with gloomy futility. Bond simply shook his head. 'You'd never consider sharing him either, I take it?' Penfold ventured, this time quite seriously. 'My batman's gone down with stomach cramps, poor lad.'

'Who, Fletcher?' asked Bond in alarm. 'Is your man's the first case, Earnest?'

'As far as I know he's the first of our lot to fall bad,' Penfold replied. 'Although The Wolves have been through the mill with it of late. Horace Fenton seems to have lost half his corporals through one thing or another.'

'This is terrible,' Bond mumbled thoughtfully. 'Do they know what's to blame yet?'

'Surgeon Lamb thinks it's the water sources,' intoned Gideon Knight. 'He blames the men using rainwater puddles and little trickles in the bottom of dongas to serve their immediate thirst on the march. He's published a pamphlet on the subject, as a matter of fact.'

'Don't talk to me about pamphlets,' Bond replied grumpily. 'Remember whose nephew I am, after all.'

'I don't think old Lamb-cutlet would take too kindly to being likened to Old Wilb, dear boy,' Knight chuckled heartily, as the two of them left for their work on the crossing.

Surgeon Major Alfred Lamb "Cutlet" was in fact a highly esteemed and greatly respected military surgeon. A confirmed modernist who did not believe in simply hacking off the limbs of wounded soldiers left right and centre, Lamb had been singularly misnamed by the men in his care, who realising little of his noted research into waterborne diseases, apparently took him for just another sawbones. Now, with the fruits of the late Major Turnpenny's fatal engagement to deal with, he stood in his shirtsleeves under an erected canvas awning, quickly effecting treatments of the multiple stab and gunshot wounds that came before him.

While the main body of the invading column was busily engaged in crossing the river, Surgeon Lamb was making the best of an improvised nursing station, constructed from a large square of canvas slung between two wagons.

His first patient was, as it turned out, the young soldier who had been stabbed on his advance up the hill.

'Nice little wound you have here,' he remarked, casually peeling back the bloody garments around the forearm. 'Well, I'm afraid I have some bad news for you. I shall have to enlarge this wound a little, so as to ascertain the exact vessels that are causing blood loss. Once I've done that, we should be in a position to—' but the young soldier had fainted in his arms. 'Orderly!' cried Lamb. 'Help me clean out this clot. His pulse is weak, but if we can pressurise the limb, we might be able to locate the source of the bleeding.'

As it turned out, the young soldier recovered after the wound had been bound. Surgeon Lamb was mightily relieved. 'You gave us quite a scare, young man,' he informed the soldier kindly. 'Sergeant Major, see to it that this young man is on the detail left behind to guard the supply depot, would you? We need to rest the limb more than anything else. Throwing darts aren't so bad,' he remarked to the orderly. 'At least when its trajectory is tempered by either the wind or some item of clothing, the blade has less chance of hitting an artery or severing a nerve or tendon. But those assegais, mark my words, lad, would be the death of us all if, those warriors ever get near enough to use them on us a second time.'

Chapter Twenty-Two

While Colonel Roystone's column was picking its way across the river, things back at fort Flambard had taken a strange and rather unexpected turn for the worse.

Commandant Flambard, having just taken his early morning ablutions and was by then alternately trimming his whiskers and settling down to a pot of tea, was suddenly burst in upon by Lieutenant Faunce-Whittington.

Excited and flapping like a large goose, Faunce spent the next few minutes gabbling about wagons and orders and bagpipes, until Flambard almost choked on his tea and rather irritably ordered him to stop it. 'For goodness sake control yourself, Faunce,' Flambard complained bitterly. 'Sit down, have some tea, and try to explain things in a clear and coherent manner.'

'Sorry, Colonel, but I thought you simply *had* to know,' Faunce continued breathlessly, furiously wiping the beads of perspiration off his flushed face. 'A dispatch arrived at about 4:00 this morning,' he continued, 'bringing orders in a sealed envelope from Oscaarsberg.'

'Were you there when they came? Where are they now?' demanded Flambard crossly. 'Come on, Faunce, I must know. Give them to me if you have them!'

'That's just it, I don't,' replied the large lieutenant simply. 'They came through for McGonagle, not us.'

'Came through for McGonagle?' Flambard repeated incredulously. 'Why?'

'Well, I'm damned if I know, Colonel,' Faunce replied airily.

'Never mind that, Faunce.' Flambard growled impatiently. 'What happened next?'

'Well,' Faunce continued, settling down in a chair and pouring himself a tin beaker of tea, 'that mean-looking chap on detachment, Simo-thingy, you know.' Flambard merely nodded. 'Well, he tells me they're off, and that the captain has received orders to move to resume command of something or other.'

'*Resume* command! What of?' Flambard persisted. 'In that condition he couldn't command an audience in a poetry recital! What on earth can they be placing him in charge of now?'

'Probably just wanted him as far away from headquarters as possible,' Faunce quipped lightly. 'I expect they'll run plop onto the Zulus!' he added, deftly dropping a teaspoon into his beaker, as if to illustrate the point.

'That's exactly what worries me,' Flambard replied grimly. 'I suppose we shall just have to wait and see what our masters wish us to do about it.'

'Fret not, Colonel, it's not good for you,' Faunce remarked casually. 'Here, let's open a tin of something!'

It was not until much later in the day that the true severity of Captain McGonagle's early morning flight had been fully recognised by the officers of the African contingent. Flambard, having taken his early morning ride and inspected a newly raised company of local irregulars – nostalgically named the Lyndhurst Mounted Rifles, was busily engaged in catching up on his backlog of paperwork, when the door of his hut burst open.

'Oh, for heaven's sake, Faunce, what is it this time?' Flambard demanded. 'Can't you see I'm working, man?'

'Yes, yes. Sorry, Colonel, it's just that something else has happened.'

'Well, spit it out, man!' Flambard sighed heavily, removing his spectacles, and placing them resignedly on the blotter before him.

'That Simonides, you know—'

'Yes, I know. Please get to the point, man!' put in Flambard.

'Yes!' Faunce-Whittington assented in compliance. 'You know I said there was something he wasn't telling me?'

'Yes?' Flambard responded. 'So unless you intend to imitate him, bally well get on and tell me!'

'Well, I know what it is now.' Here, Faunce paused momentarily for extra effect. 'They've taken the African sappers as well!' he announced dramatically.

'What?' Commandant Flambard's roar could be heard as far away as Durban. 'The so-called Earnest's "earners"? Small wonder he was grinning like a—'

'Cheshire cat?' suggested Faunce.

'Hyena!' Flambard exploded. 'Wretched little man and his wretched old captain! Damn pair should have been packed away safe where they can't do any harm. It's lucky the Lyndhurst men hadn't arrived, or old Wilb might have nicked them as well!' Gulping his tea like a large slug of brandy, the commandant was only calmed down by the assurance that Earnest's "earners" were awaiting disbanding in any case, and that no major threat had been posed to the garrison strength by McGonagle's coup. 'Oh well, I suppose it's good riddance to them both,' Flambard sighed stoically. 'One hopes we can at least look forward to a little peace and quiet.'

'Yes,' Faunce-Whittington assented. 'I think I know all I need to about India by now, considering I'll never go there.'

'You don't have to tell me,' Flambard added, meandering briefly into his own thoughts until a dry cough caused him to resume. 'Anyway, it's jolly well good riddance to the whole sorry lot of 'em!' Flambard's temper suddenly cooled and, just for a moment, his mind began to wander back to another time all together.

Later that day, the sad news arrived by mounted dispatch that Major Turnpenny had been killed. His death was a shock, even to the tough, pragmatic Flambard, who regarded his passing as a sign of his own age and mortality.

'You shouldn't be upset, Colonel,' Faunce assured him, patting the commandant gently on the arm as they took their afternoon tea.

'He was killed in action, after all, sir,' put in one of the border officers, posted to the drift only a few days before. 'At least he went doing what he did best.'

'Bravado,' sighed Flambard. 'It's been the end of many a good friend of mine in the past, and Theodore Turnpenny was one of the most valiant soldiers ever to sit on a horse. Charged the rebels at Barrackpore, you know.'

'Oh, Colonel, you sounded just like old Wilb!' Faunce laughed lightly.

'No damn wonder, is it?' Flambard replied, with a remarkable lack of chagrin.

They had just completed an afternoon's work, and were now sitting down to yet more tea, when the border officer suddenly spotted riders in the lea of the nearby escarpment.

'Oh, for goodness sake, what now?' Flambard demanded irritably 'Ride out before they get here, Faunce, there's a decent fellow, and see if you can stop them from coming back here and interrupting us for the sake of a wretched message.'

'Yes, Colonel!' the large lieutenant replied, hauling his bulky frame out of his chair, and slinging it across the back of his waiting yellow charger, before setting off at a gallop across the open country.

'Might it not be important, sir?' enquired the other officer nervously. He had seen Flambard in action and did not wish to be blasted off his feet with yet more of the magistrate's thunder.

'If it's only a message Faunce can bring it back,' Flambard told him curtly. 'If those two come here, it will simply mean less cake all round. So, with any luck, the poor chaps will be so afraid of old Faunce, that they'll turn round and ride back to Oscaarsberg faster than a change in the weather.'

The commandant was wrong, however, for no sooner had the two converging parties met some nine hundred yards away from the outermost piquet, both were seen thundering hell for leather in the direction of their post.

'Oh, drat!' Flambard cursed, as a sheepish Faunce-Whittington rode up to him, this time with two more guests in tow. 'I thought I told you to get rid of them, Faunce?'

'I know you did, Colonel, but I really think you need to hear this.'

'Oh fine,' Flambard replied sulkily. 'But they're not getting any cake!' Yet such was the severity in his young officer's normally light-hearted accents that it made Flambard sit up and listen in a decidedly troubled silence, as the reason for the message was alarmingly laid before him. 'Damn and blast it!' he roared, as Faunce and the two dispatch riders cowered in the corner of the hut, rendered utterly speechless by the shouts and oaths from the enraged magistrate.

'This fellow here,' Flambard bellowed, jabbing maniacally with his finger at one of the riders, 'brings a message for the commander of the garrison to send two of his wagons to supply the mounted troops who left yesterday. *What* mounted troops?'

'I don't understand, Colonel, we haven't got any wagons!' Faunce wailed in anguish. 'At least, we don't have any supply ones, at any rate.'

'Precisely!' roared he commandant indignantly. 'This order,' he continued, calming his enraged monologue, and speaking with a chilling slowness, 'is supposed to be for an imperial officer of the Ninety First.'

'Colonel?'

'It's for McGonagle!' bellowed Flambard, his blood pressure soaring to the brick red of his contorted face. 'That old buzzard must have intercepted my orders – *my* orders, Faunce – and run off with them into Zululand instead of reading them properly!'

'How can this have happened?' Faunce was very nearly apoplectic by now, and Flambard was fit to explode.

'A lack of spectacles, or the want of new ones for all I know! The worst of it all,' he groaned, as the ferocity of his outburst suddenly began to drain him of his energy, 'is with Bob Toteaux gone, and now poor old Turnpenny gone and killed, command of my irregulars will probably fall to that native-killer Colonel Henderson. He'll probably use them as spear fodder, then complain when the survivors desert. I told you what he did in India, didn't I?'

Fortunately, Faunce was able to recognise that this was neither the time for stories nor the usual pretence that he hadn't heard them all before.

Removing the commandant's mug, and replacing it with a full beaker of brandy, the large lieutenant quietly dismissed the messengers, now more afraid of Flambard than they were of the Zulu, and sat down beside his commanding officer. 'You must think of your health, Colonel,' he told him gently.

'There's nothing to think about, Faunce,' Flambard replied simply, his bushy silver eyebrows raised above his staring grey eyes as he spoke. 'Lieutenant!' he called across to the border officer, who had been taking tea with them when the storm broke. 'You shall be in command for now, until re-enforcements can be sent from Oscaarsberg in support of your company.'

'What are you proposing to do, Colonel?'

'The only thing we may do under the circumstances,' Flambard replied grimly.

'Brew up another pot?' Faunce-Whittington suggested hopefully.

'No, Faunce,' Flambard reproved him sternly. 'We must make ourselves ready. That poor misguided old fool has stolen nearly twelve hours march on us, and I intend to catch up with him before his ludicrous antics can place anyone else in danger. So come on, Faunce, there's a good fellow, and tell the men to saddle up and ride!'

'Commandant, surely!' wailed Faunce imploringly. 'We could be riding to our deaths!'

'That, my dear boy, is what we all agreed to do,' Flambard continued, unperturbed. 'Men,' he told his assembled force of over five hundred black and white colonial troops over an hour and a half later. 'We shall be fighting for our homes, our farms, and our families on the border. If they kill the whole of the army, so long as they don't avoid contact, all shall be well. Remember, if they can circumvent our force, our homes are their prize, and I need not tell you of the consequences. Men, we fly to fight!'

A massive cheer went up as the old magistrate addressed his troops. Huge, formidable, and whiskered, mounted on an equally massive grey, and smothered in a full-length fur coat, Commandant Flambard stirred up every passion of pride, courage, and inspiration in both black and white troops, willing them to win. Hardly pausing for goodbye to his African contingents, many of whom being on foot had had to be left behind, Flambard spurred his champing warhorse, and took off at the head of a deafening thunder of hooves, bits, and carbines. 'Come on, Faunce!' he cried, as the roar of his lightening army began to drown out the rushing river before them. 'For good or ill, our part in this story begins!'

Chapter Twenty-Three

During the time it had taken for Commandant Flambard to realise what had happened, Captain AW McGonagle's dangerously small expedition was making a slow yet steady progress across country. Having forded the river at the drift, McGonagle now decided to cut across country and, rather than follow a road that he deemed to be both out of their way and exposed to enemy attacks, cut straight across the open veldt instead.

Born in Perthshire, Alec Wilbur McGonagle was the fourth son of a poor and unsuccessful Scottish peer. Having virtually broken his finances by sending his two eldest boys to vastly expensive schools, his father, Lord Willie McGonagle, had been forced to recognise that there was virtually nothing left of his estate to give his youngest son, Alec. With only the money from the sale of several family heirlooms, Lord McGonagle had purchased his son a commission in the 'John' Company of East India and packed him off with just enough money to see him through his obligations as a subaltern.

The young McGonagle had been bitter with frustration. His eldest brother Archie had died as an undergraduate, while his older brothers Angus and William had both gone on to careers in the law and the navy respectively. Then, in 1840, Lord McGonagle, wracked with remorse and desolate at the slow cancer that was eating up his family name, took a boat out on the loch and shot himself with his flintlock pistol.

Wracked with grief, Angus became Lord McGonagle, William became the Honourable Willie McGonagle, and Alec McGonagle had to be content with a small annuity and the purchase price of a captaincy in the Queen's "other" army of India.

Passionate about the great works of history and literature, and himself the son of a poet, McGonagle longed to turn his experiences in India into immortal verse for future generations. A lover of words, which only served to defeat and humiliate him, McGonagle fought a desperate battle with writing, composing and publishing prose until in '57 his career was interrupted by the Great Rebellion, or mutiny, as the British would have it.

By then out of his twenties, McGonagle saw in the mutiny the first real opportunity to make something of his life in the army. Armed with his theories, which were at that time just beginning to grow into the outspoken and radical innovations that were to be so damning to his reputation by the time he ended up in South Africa, McGonagle fell back on his firm faith in the men of his company. What he had not bargained for, however, was the introduction of the Enfield rifle and, more significantly, the cartridges greased in pig fat to which his men objected with the entire religious fervour to be expected of their high caste. The catalyst for mutiny was present and very swiftly those who wished to see the fuse lit had their cause. Dissent rampaged through the ranks of Indian troops, and European officers and NCOs almost ceased to communicate with their men.

One morning, so the story went, some of his enraged sepoys began to run amok. McGonagle intervened, and the rampaging soldiers fell upon him with their knives. McGonagle was stabbed several times, and nearly bled to death as a result. As it was, his whole company turned on the wives and families of his officers and NCOs, and the whole congregation of the barrack chapel was brutally hacked to pieces.

This feasible yarn was one of the many scuttlebutts and rumours bandied about the unfortunate officer's early career; a hard luck story to explain away the eccentricities, with Indian troops as the villains of the piece. He survived only by a miracle, but whatever the truth of that fateful day, his career was never to recover. Blamed for losing control over his troops and costing the lives of civilians, McGonagle sank into a bitter and resentful obscurity, grounded at the rank of captain, and apparently doomed to sit out the rest of his life falling out with superiors until he ran out of friends.

Yet it had been in India where he met the man who was later to become the lieutenant general commanding British forces in South Africa. He had liked McGonagle and felt rather sorry for his misfortune, for which he compensated by offering the then fifty-year-old captain an appointment to his staff. McGonagle, on the other hand, soon began to feel even more bitter and resentful that a man of fourteen years his junior should have succeeded to so high an appointment. Trouble followed, and a period began that saw the start of the old captain's career as a pamphleteer. Public disagreements soon overtook, and the general was forced to remove so embarrassing and controversial a figure from his staff all together, shunting him off to what he hoped would be a short stint before retirement in the Princess Louise's Argyllshires. McGonagle, however, refused to be pushed, and to the general's horror was eventually to appear on the lists as one of the officers shipped out to the Cape with the Ninety First Highlanders.

Even as the hot sun played on the topi helmets of his exhausted soldiers, Captain AW McGonagle wiped the sweat from his brow with the back of his hand and fanned his face with the brim of his straw hat. 'What are you staring at, laddie?' he barked at Simonides, who had just ridden up alongside the wagon on which McGonagle was now travelling.

'Nothing, Mr McGonagle,' Simonides hissed in reply.

'That's captain to you, you wee piker,' snapped the elderly officer irritably. He did not care for Simonides and knew that the younger officer resented him for not treating him with proper regard. McGonagle did not like officers who had been foisted upon him and it suited him to regard them in his lengthening age and suspicion as officious academy trained spies. 'Look at you!' he sneered, never offering to lower his tone in front of the men in Simonides's platoon. 'Your bony little arse on that great big horse, and your shoulders poking through the top of that blue coat of yours. You ought to build up a wee bit of muscle, like that nephew of mine in the engineers.'

And if you weren't so fat, thought Simonides spitefully, *you might be able to ride a horse instead of rattling around on that cart like some sort of overweight pig going to market*. Instead, he merely scowled, and spurred his horse on at a greater speed.

'You're a miserable whelp!' barked McGonagle, taking a huge slug from his hip flask of malt whisky. 'Piper!' he called, addressing a blue jacketed and kilt-wearing young corporal of his company. 'Let's have a tune, eh?'

'What would you be a hearing, sar?' barked the piper, his thick Scotch accent as deep and dark as the malt in the officer's belly.

'We'll have a bothy ballad,' McGonagle chirped, and then began humming his fancy in a rolling baritone, supported by some of his older troops, to even more scowls of disapproval from the musically disinclined Simonides. 'What are you away with, you killjoy?' McGonagle demanded cruelly. 'Go on and away with you, if you've no spirit for a good Highland song!'

You've missed your vocation, thought Simonides in bitter undertones. *At least if you tried to sing for a living, the rest of us might not have ended up in the middle of nowhere with even less hope of getting there.*

'I'll give ye all a poem, lads!' cried McGonagle above the pipes. 'Let me see now... *I remember how ma love and me walked along by the Dover sea.*'

'D'you reckon he's written the end of this one?' Sergeant Andrews muttered to Corporal Stewart somewhere to the back of the column. 'Or de ye think it'll just fade to mumbles, like that wee one about Africa... and trees?'

'*With the waves on the shore and the gulls in the sky,*' McGonagle slurred as the whisky got the better of him, '*I sit and watch as France goes by...*'

Sniggers and guffaws were suppressed as they rippled down the ranks.

Simonides, ruing his desperate attempt to advance by volunteering for special service assignment nobody else had wanted, simply stewed, brewed, and rode on ahead, upwind of McGonagle's oratory.

'What are we doing here, Colonel?' Faunce-Whittington groaned.

It was not the first time during their day's frantic scramble across country that Faunce had raised concerns as to their location, direction, safety, and wellbeing, but the commandant knew better than to pander to the question by responding in a similarly hopeless vein. 'Captain Tyler!' he barked instead, addressing the officer in charge of the Lyndhurst Mounted Rifles.

He was a man of about thirty-seven years, dressed in the elaborate and self-designed uniform of his irregular unit. Funded by colonial government, the Lyndhurst men were mounted on privately owned horses, but armed with short barrel Swinburne-Henry carbines, and rated under the same structure as the Imperial forces. The Lyndhurst men wore topi helmets, rather than the soft hat and red puggaree hat band denoting Flambard's volunteers, and nearly all carried some form of small arms in addition to their rifles.

Saluting Flambard, the officer brought his horse to a halt on the crest of a hill and awaited his orders.

'Looks like we still have very little to go on,' Flambard remarked gloomily.

'Have the Africans spotted any signs of a wagon train yet, Faunce?'

'Nothing so far, Colonel,' the latter replied, raising his binoculars to his eyes and scanning the distant horizon. 'It looks as if they've broken from the roads all together.'

'Oh well, we really can't expect to find them tonight,' Flambard concluded. 'I suppose we shall just have to make bivouac somewhere, set out tomorrow and, if we don't find anything more, branch off and join the main column.'

'Speaking of which, Commandant,' put in the captain of the Lyndhurst men apprehensively, 'dusk is beginning to gather on us, and my men have no particular cover or any special supplies.'

'Did all men draw two days' worth of rations as instructed?' Flambard enquired of him.

'Oh yes, sir,' the officer replied.

‘Then there should not be any need for “special supplies”, as you put it, Captain,’ the magistrate concluded. ‘The men can make do with preserved grub tonight, and we’ll see about something hot when we rejoin the main column tomorrow.’

‘Very good, sir,’ the captain replied, peeling off to rejoin his unit in quiet despair.

‘Have *we* anything hot to eat at all, Colonel?’ Faunce enquired, almost too lightly for Flambard’s humour.

‘Certainly not,’ he replied briskly. ‘I would not deny any solider the means of heat and sustenance, nor comfort for that matter, if it were within my gift or power. You should know that of me, Faunce.’

‘Yes, Colonel,’ seemed the only inevitable response.

In accordance with Commandant Flambard’s orders, the men were roused at an excruciating hour the following morning. That was followed by yet another punishing ride in the blazing African heat, and yet more increasingly desperate searching for signs of AW McGonagle’s company. During the time spent fruitlessly searching the hillsides for little more than a few springboks, a couple of dead cows and an irate secretary bird, Flambard had been missing out on the one thing that he had hoped most to see in Zululand. For, while he and Faunce had been hopelessly hunting the elusive McGonagle, Colonel Roystone had seen thorough his binoculars a far more disturbing sight.

The morning on which Flambard had set out with his army had been very much the same as usual for the men of Number Six Column.

They awoke from their tents at 4:00 a.m. to find the ground sodden, the mist from the river creeping in amongst their possessions and their bedclothes, and a deathly pall hanging over the entire encampment.

On that occasion, their closeness to the foothills of the mountains had placed much of the camp within the rough undergrowth and tall aloes that sporadically dotted the well-nourished riverbank.

Coleman, who had been secretly sleeping on his blanket under the somewhat more hospitable canvas of Lieutenant Bond's canopy on every occasion that circumstances afforded, woke to the smell of wet herbage and damp canvas after the heavy rain of the previous night. He had risen early to organise the officer's breakfast personally, and to get his own grub while it was still hot. Having put in an order for two steaming hot bowls of porridge and two cups of hot tea, he was now sitting outside the flaps of the tent, polishing Bond's boots, and taking in the morning air.

There was a none too displeasing herbaceous smell in the warmth of the air; the earth when he walked upon it was damp and squelchy, like the dark reddish brown leaves in a teapot. The lush, tangling grasses and shrubbery hung with lustrous dark and acid-green density, the tips of their leaves groaning and thick with buds, while the wild orchids radiated colour in pinks, whites and yellows from amid the saturated undergrowth.

When Coleman got up to move, the rain-soaked ground sang all around him, a buzz and a slurp of waterlogged earth as each booted footstep took him this way or that. It wasn't that he didn't like the earth in its new morning state, or that the ground so muddy and marshy that his kit would be caked in next to no time. It was just that the newness and freshness of it all reminded him so painfully of home. The damp grass of a spring morning, somewhere back in early childhood; walks amid the flowers in the park on a Sunday while all the nice people flocked from church.

Of course, he had been far too young then to realise why it was that he and his mother could not actually attend church, or that they hadn't the money for Sunday clothes. What did used to get to him, however, was the sharp and some might almost say judgmental looks from the passers-by as they headed for home, and doubtless, hot dinners. It was only when he was older that young Jack finally recognised that those disapproving looks from the clerks and shipyard foremen were largely the hypocritical guilt of those who had been his mother's audience on a Saturday and, as likely, her clients thereafter. He never wanted to go after that, anyway.

A voice broke his reverie. It was Bond, and from the way he was whistling, he was obviously in reasonably good spirits.

'Morning, Mr Albert,' Coleman smiled warmly at his officer, coming to attention, and saluting his arrival.

'At ease, for goodness sake,' Bond replied blithely. 'After all, you're not fallen in yet, and you haven't even got your tunic on, in any case.'

'My tunic... oh no!' Coleman gasped, looking down in horror at his soaking wet shirt, still clinging to his body with the same aspect as a dew-soaked petal on a cactus.

He smiled disarmingly, and Bond could only smile back. Then, chucking his dirty shaving water over a nearby aloe bush, the officer suggested that they take a walk through the bush to the water's edge, and wash in the river.

'Won't we get into trouble, sir?' Coleman asked in concern.

'Not if I'm with you,' Bond replied carelessly. 'We used to do it all the time at school, sneak out and bathe in the river, I mean.'

'Where was that, Mr Albert?'

'Near London, by a tributary of the Thames,' Bond replied nostalgically.

'Couldn't do it in the Medway,' Coleman sighed, equally nostalgically.

'Why, because of the current?'

'No, because of all the sh— Well, I mean on account of the cold, sir.'

Again, Bond smiled warmly at the young sapper's candour. He really liked this boy, even when he was blushing.

As they walked, their boots began to sink in the wet mud, so Bond suggested that they take them off all together. 'Doesn't it feel wonderful, Jack?' Bond sighed ecstatically, as the wet grass soaked in between his toes, 'I never thought I'd be glad to be cold and wet again, but after marching all that way in the sun.'

'On a horse?'

For a minute, Bond looked at Coleman impassively. The lines of his face and the narrow scrutiny of his misty-blue eyes made the young sapper draw breath in the horrid fancy that the officer might hit him. Until he winked. Then Bond just broke into another broad grin.

'I shouldn't have said that,' Coleman mumbled, glowing with embarrassment, and as utterly amazed by his own impish gesture as his officer had been. 'I'm sorry, Mr Albert.'

'To Gideon Knight you shouldn't, or Major Westgate, I agree,' Bond replied sharply. Then, his voice took on a softer tone. 'Me, on the other hand... I'm a different matter entirely.' As he spoke, he twitched his nose a little, and something seemed to twinkle deep in the officer's eye.

Coleman looked at Bond, then he looked again.

The light, so dull and grey at the onset of morning, was now beginning to filter through the thick herbage in a sort of eerie green glow. The rain, now silenced after a long night's work still fell occasionally in huge droplets from the overhanging foliage gathering above and then falling on their exposed heads, running off their sleek, wet hair and down the backs of their necks.

Coleman laughed as a huge cluster of raindrops suddenly poured off the end of a large banana leaf and showered down on him from above. The sun was well and truly up by now; the steam was rising from the saturated plant life as the thick mist humidified, and the warm rays began gradually to burn off the chill of the dawn from the bush.

Conscious of the time, the two of them threw off their trousers, shirts, and belts (although Bond took care to hang his revolver strap from a nearby branch) and flung themselves into the dark water.

Oblivious, perhaps a little too much so, of the potential presence of crocodiles, snakes, and even Zulu scouts, they splashed, swam, and played about.

Bond was physically fit, strong in both upper and lower body, with broad, defined biceps, triceps and pectorals, his thighs and calves toned from years on horseback. The colour of his tanned skin was a golden brown, and the freckles on his back had now spread across his shoulders, down his upper arms and even across his nose. His glistening bronze locks were pushed back off his face, and the soggy tendrils clung to back of his neck, dark brown curtains hanging over his smooth forehead. The water glistened in his beard, emphasising still further the contour of his jaw, set in stone like the statues Coleman had seen in the Guildhall in Rochester.

Yet for the officer, the picture was of Coleman: his toned upper body rising above the level of the water, blond hair gleaming like tarnished brass, thick and wet and seemingly held in place, just above his sparkling blue eyes. He was so fresh and young, yet so tough and so fit to have survived the slums of the maritime town in which he grew up. Boyish, yet masculine. Hardly naïve but open, frank yet sharpened by his upbringing... and the admiration, indeed the fascination he knew to be turning into something far, far stronger.

It was only when a shot rang out across the veldt beyond, and the two soldiers scrambled from the pool to dress themselves that the truth of their developing feelings made itself so readily apparent. They both knew that they feared it, that deep burning pain so far inside, which throttled back speech and asphyxiated the breath in their bodies. The silence was deafening, as the humid mist swirled around their glistening bodies. Hot, stripped back to their bare emotions in the beautiful, tranquil, and secret glade, lit only by the thin rays of pervading sunlight as it struggled in through the canopy, the only sound borne to their ears was the rhythmical hammering of their terrified, frantically beating hearts.

All life seemed somehow disconnected just then – the birds, the rustle and drip of the dense greenery, the seeping slurp and bubble of the saturated earth – seemed so isolated, so unreal to the two young soldiers, lost, captivated by each other, and so totally insulated from the unperceiving world. Then, as the tension increased, and the fear and longing they knew must either bind or destroy them for ever, they moved towards one another in silence. As if mindful all the time of the reality that awaited them outside their little haven, Bond reached out and placed both hands on Jack's shoulders. They were firm, and wet, and hot from the sun, now arching its way through the dense pocket of plants and grasses. Steam was boiling up from the ground beneath them now, and all around was lost up to waist height in a thick, swirling grey.

Studiously, yet transfixed by the depth of the sapphires that burned and shone and sparkled in the boy's eyes, Bond looked at Coleman. Then, as their arms found their way around one another, they dreamily closed the gap between them, closing their eyes and pressing together with a gasp of final abandonment. It seemed like for ever they held there. It should have been for ever, but they both knew it could not last a moment longer.

'What does it mean, sir?' Coleman breathed, as he buried his face in Bond's shoulder, breathing in the scent of his damp locks and clinging with feverish tenacity to the warm humidity of his naked body.

'It doesn't matter,' Bond murmured in his ear. 'All I know for sure is that I never want it to end.'

'Nor me, Mr Albert... But that gunshot?'

It was as if the mention of his name with the prefix of formality brought Bond back to his senses. He was a lieutenant in Her Majesty's army after all, and this conduct would be considered both unseemly and, he knew, injurious to himself, Clara's father and, worse still, for that beautiful boy now looking so tenderly back at him through the mist. With a tight smile and an effort at indifference, Bond wriggled back into his damp shirt, snatched up his shoulder strap and threw the revolver lanyard over his head. Then, with nothing beyond a gesture for Coleman to follow him, dashed back up the track to the camp.

Everything looked so forlorn now in the harsh and emerging heat of the day. The mud and foliage stank as the water dried, and the puddles on the boggy path seemed woefully to reflect their faces, distorted into shapes that reminded him so painfully that their little bit of paradise had been so cruelly short-lived.

Coleman trailed along behind the officer in a stunned silence, his feet dragging in the heavy mud. He didn't speak as they trudged back to camp. What was there to say? It seemed as if his world had turned upside down twice, and the end had left him desolate. *What am I to do now*? he wondered miserably.

Chapter Twenty-Four

By the time Bond and Coleman had dashed back to camp, and snatched up their weapons and kit, the whole thing had been and gone.

The flap had, it seemed, been created when one of Flambard's irregular mounted men – who presumably had the same idea about taking a bath in the river – had emerged naked from the water, and pausing only to snatch up his rifle, called out something in African. As bad luck would have it, only a few feet away were two men of the West Rutlands, doing their best at some laundry, seemingly ignorant as to the identity of their nearby African comrade. They challenged him, he challenged back, and shots were fired.

Fortunately, on this occasion neither party sustained more than a bruised ego and a dressing down from their respective sergeant majors. Yet another false alarm.

'It's too bad, these mixed contingents,' Colonel Henderson remarked to Surgeon Lamb later that morning. 'These men don't understand how to conduct themselves among regular servicemen. It's always the same when one allows local forces to taint the battalions.'

'Let's hope you're right, Colonel,' interrupted McEnry coldly. 'For if that is the case, the so-called local forces we've come here to fight should give us little trouble.'

'Either that, or we'll end up sorely and bitterly surprised,' grunted Lieutenant Cookins of Flambard's Horse, adding, 'I do wish the commandant was here.'

'We'll see,' Henderson retorted sulkily. 'For when we hoist the colours of the first battalion over the ashes of the king's kraal, you'll see if I was right or not.'

As it turned out, both Colonel Henderson's theories and Colonel Roystone's ambitions for the usefulness of the Royal Artillery were soon to be put to the test, for at around 8:30 that morning, the first shots were fired in anger.

The camp had been struck, and all baggage, stores, equipment, and ammunition had been loaded into the wagons in readiness for the off.

Colonel Roystone, having breakfasted early, rode up to the head of the column to brief the advance guard of the mounted infantry on their day's objectives.

Major Westgate, having assembled his officers and NCOs, now informed them that yet another, slightly smaller river bisected their route for the day, and that Lieutenant Bond, with the aid of Sergeant Friday and Corporal Denham, would be responsible for executing the crossing. Lieutenant Penfold was to be placed on general duties with the remaining sappers and a core of vagabonds from The Wolves, who had failed to distinguish themselves during a brawl the previous night and were consequently on fatigues for the rest of their lives.

Lieutenant Knight would, in the absence and due to the illness of Lieutenant Byrne, ride ahead to act as aid-de-camp to the three colonels. It was not a duty that excited Gideon Knight, although he knew full well that a certain amount of fagging for seniority was a natural prerequisite of the steady promotion that he hoped to achieve in the future. In view of this, he took a slightly sombre farewell of his brother subalterns and rode off ahead with Warren Westgate to supervise en route the teams of men freeing up the wagons and shoring up the tracks.

'That's bloody typical, that is, Sarn't,' Corporal Denham complained to Sergeant Friday, as the two of them picked their way across the pebble-strewn bed of their stretch of river. 'We have to go on foot, while his nibs and the brass cut across on horseback.'

'You watch your mouth, Corp, or I'll have them stripes!' Friday warned severely, pausing mid-stream to illustrate his point. 'Mr Knight is not his nibs, is that clear?'

'Sarn't.'

'And if I ever hear any member of this troop calling any officer a name again, I'll have *his* name, and you can be sure what Friday will do with it. Do I make myself clear?'

'Yes, Sarn't, it's just—' Before the NCO was able to finish his mitigation, yet more firing had broken out in front of them, the sound of which was now echoing around the foothills of the mountains like resounding tramp of boots on a cold parade square.

'Where the hell did that come from, Arthur?' cried Major Westgate as a bullet whizzed past his ear and only missed Colonel McEnry by a whisker.

As the column had approached the nek, just below the shoulder of the mountain, the advance guard comprising Flambard's Horse and the men of the mounted infantry had come under heavy, yet poorly directed rifle fire from all sides.

Captain Horace Fenton, having been largely asleep in the saddle during the moments leading up to the volley, was suddenly brought back down to earth by the heart-rending thump of bullet piercing flesh.

One of Fenton's lieutenants, who had been riding just to the left of his company commander, had suddenly screamed, fallen back off his horse and was now laid out at a ghastly angle, utterly soaking the surrounding area with his blood.

'Oh, for mercy, no!' cried Fenton in dismay.

The officer had taken a bullet in the head, and the remaining company could only watch in horror as half of their young subaltern's face seemed to come away with the force of the shot, his blood draining off the road like rain in a ditch. A heartbeat later, Fenton felt an agonising pain in his left shoulder. A shock and complete numbness of the limb followed this, so that he knew he too had been hit, and was forced to dismount and crawl to the side of the road for cover. The blood seemed to be everywhere, but that was not the worst of it. It seemed as if the lieutenant was still hanging on to life with both contorted hands, the red froth welling up from his mouth and nostrils like lava from a volcano, while his convulsing body writhed and fitted, arms and legs thrashing about in all directions. Half his head was shattered into a hideous mess, but the ghastly choking and gurgling still came bubbling to the surface, chilling the marrow of all around him as they watched, aghast.

'For God's sake someone, help him out!' cried Colonel McEnry, averting his eyes from the sickening scene before him. 'Horace, you have your revolver?'

'I can't, Arthur!' Fenton moaned in disbelief. 'I...I just can't!'

'Do something, sir!' moaned a young private, breaking the silence with his impassioned pleas. 'Can't you do it, Colonel?'

McEnry swallowed hard. He knew it had to be done – the boy was falling to bits on the road before them – but how on earth was one man to do that to another?

The horror was beginning to buzz up and down the line like the chill cry of a banshee by this time; the screams of agony and unearthly choking sounds causing more than one old sweat to gasp in terror. Was it to be them next?

With tears streaming down his twitching face at the horror and reality of the thing he knew he had to do, Fenton raised his quivering right hand until the muzzle of his revolver was near enough to the convulsing officer's blood-soaked temple.

With an audible whimper, Fenton looked into the young officer's eyes. To his dying day, the captain would swear that the subaltern was willing him on. There was a moment's evil pause, followed by a huge gout of blood as it erupted from the lieutenant's mouth. Fenton clamped his eyes shut and, with an effort, pulled the trigger.

Not a man in the company failed to wince as that shot rang out. Many moaned or sobbed, and McEnry had tears streaming from his eyes as he watched the body quietly cease its convulsions. The deed done, Horace Fenton collapsed in a sobbing pile on the ground, quite regardless of the bullets that were now whizzing home all around himself and his comrades.

Almost as soon as the column had been fired upon, Colonel Roystone had quit his inspection of Major Westgate's work and thundered up the narrow road to join his staff at the head of the column. From their position on a raised section of a grassy slope by the roadside, Roystone could clearly see the chaos breaking out among his infantry up ahead, and could just make out a long line of red and buff uniforms on horseback forming up in a depression below the nek.

Roystone was a big man who had seen action in several major conflicts before being posted to Zululand. Bullets, spears, and assegais held no fear for him, and he was quite happy to ride as near to the front line as required, irrespective of the heavy volume of fire being put down on them from the surrounding countryside. Dressed in his dark blue patrol jacket, and with his helmet dyed to a dark brown colour, the colonel did not present so clear a target as the red-coated infantrymen, and regarded his huge physical form as being almost impervious to the reputedly poor quality of Zulu marksmanship.

Even as the flak fell in about him, the colonel calmly instructed the buglers to sound, sending orders for Colonel McEnry to throw out his battalion in skirmish order. The instruction buzzed back and forth down the line like an electric charge. The men bristled with excitement at the prospect of their first real fight, and the officers charged up and down the road on horseback, desperate not to miss a moment of the drama as it unfolded before them.

Frantically, a messenger rode down the line with an order from Colonel McEnry. He came to a halt by Major Westgate's conscripted pioneers, instructing all men of the West Rutlands who were fit for duty to abandon their work and join the firing line up ahead.

'Colonel says you are to remove the wagons from the road, Major,' the young subaltern informed Warren Westgate. 'Colonel Roystone wants Captain Collingwood to have a clear run up the track with his artillery.'

'Gideon!' Westgate called after the departing Knight, now back among the throng after his temporary secondment to the Colonels' staff. 'Can you get these wagons off the road for us? Snooker needs to be able to get his guns up to the head of the column.'

'Yes, Warren!' Knight replied, frantically gesturing for his sappers to oversee the work.

'Earnest, I want you to ride to Bond. Tell him to be ready to assist Snooker in any way necessary with the transportation of his artillery.'

'Yes, Warren,' Penfold replied obediently.

'I just hope he's got them across the river by now,' Westgate added quietly, as the small sapper officer rode back the way they had come.

Topographically their position was an absolute nightmare. The mountains between which they had hoped to pass rode up on either side of them like malignant stalagmites, while the ground on either side of the narrow road dropped away after about two hundred yards on either side. The gullies and dongas through which the rainwater drained off the slopes of the mountain left the road in an isolated position and open all around to fire from the crag.

Fortunately for the British, the banks on either side of the road did afford a reasonable space for a wagon to be driven over to one side, allowing a narrow margin just sufficient for two-gun carriages to pass them on the right.

Further down towards the river crossing, Bond was busily engaged in a shouting match with an incandescent Surgeon Major Lamb. Lamb wanted the medical stores and equipment required by his department moved across the water first, but Bond was under orders, and could only yell back that his instructions were to get Captain Collingwood's artillery into position before any other crossings were to be undertaken.

Surgeon Lamb protested, shouted, and even tried to pull rank.

'I'm sorry, *Major*,' Bond emphasized pointedly. 'But my orders come from the colonel, and I have to see to the guns.'

'Damn it all for a hat, man. Don't you think my medical supplies are equally as important? It's vital I get to the front before the casualties have time to mount up on us.'

'I'm sorry,' Bond repeated. 'As soon as we have the guns across, you have my word that Sergeant Friday's troop will give your supplies their fullest attention. You'll have priority after the artillery,' Bond continued, hastily beating a retreat. 'But that really is the best I can do at the moment.'

By this time, Captain Fenton's company had been deployed in full skirmish order and were standing and kneeling in two ranks overlooking the left-hand slope of the mountain when a chilling sight suddenly made itself apparent on the brow of a nearby hill. At first, they looked indeed like Sapper Coleman's little imaginary matchsticks, or the flies on the corpse of an animal. The little black, white, and brown patches on the ruddy grassland were soon joined by the flashing of spearheads and the rhythmical banging of assegais on shields.

Fenton, who was now standing at the front of his men, his left arm bound up in a sling and his revolver balancing in his right hand, gave a low sigh of wonder. 'Let's hope we shoot better than they do,' he muttered grimly.

'Flambard's Horse, fall in with the mounted men!' cried Colonel Henderson, as the thundering hooves of the irregulars' mounts boomed forth across the open valley to the right of them. 'I want your men in two flanks, Sergeant Major,' he called out to the enlisted soldier in charge. 'Be ready to move the men across if gaps start to form in any part of the infantry's firing line. Is that understood?'

'Sa!' replied the Sergeant-Major.

'Come along now, quickly!' gasped Lieutenant Glazebrook, as he and a handful of his company scrambled up the grassy slope of the base of the hill, manhandling into position the two rocket troughs that would eventually be loaded with two seven-pound Hale rockets.

As officer on special duties with Snooker Collingwood's rocket battery, Glazebrook was charged with the unenviable task of riding towards the forefront of the enemy attack, to set up a barrage that would hold off the advancing warriors long enough to enable Collingwood to get into position. As he stood there, Glazebrook tried desperately to recall quite exactly what Snooker had told him to do.

First, he knew he must set up the metal tripods to the front and rear of the troughs, pulling the arm well out so that there was no danger of destabilising the weapon.

He was conscious too that both himself and his men, attired as they were in the distinctive red tunic of the regiment, served as particularly good targets for the marksmen among the rocks up above.

Even so, time was of the essence, and as soon as the rockets were in place and he had fumbled about for several precious moments with the lanyards that ignited their flight, Glazebrook nervously awaited the order to fire.

All around, the infantry was being deployed. The air was thick, not only with the sound and prolonged crackle of sniper fire from the smooth bore guns of the Zulu marksmen, but also the protracted and precise shouts and screams as the officers and NCOs conveyed their orders up and down the line.

As a bullet whistled past his ear, Colonel Roystone decided that it was time to quit the grassy bank and retreat to a point of better cover from whence he could direct the sequence of battle. Calling to McEnry that the rocket battery was to commence with the first salvo, he turned his horse and cantered back towards his staff, tucked away behind a rocky outcrop nearby.

Shouting was coming in from every direction now. A cry went up here; a shot ricocheted off a box or tore into a wagon canopy there. The volume of the banging on the hillside intensified, and the chilling yet ethereal rattle of spears on skin shields was soon joined by a low humming from the warriors themselves.

Watching with grim placidity, Roystone noted the deployment by the Zulu induna. Firstly, the vanguard fanned out across the horizon. That was joined almost immediately on both sides by the left and right horns, spread out in a voluminous mass across from the furthest point of the rocky hillside to the furthest point of the opposite end, seemingly limitless in their numbers, controlled with martial precision and matchless discipline.

As far as the eye could see, the crest of the hill, the nek and the shoulder of the mountain slopes were covered from end to end with Zulus. Ranks of ten, maybe even twenty deep could be seen to be preparing, all hammering away, almost frustrating in their uniformity, and not remotely ill-disciplined in deployment.

'Odds are on the others, I fear,' one private of the West Rutlands remarked gloomily to his colleague beside him. 'They drill even better than we do, and there sure as hell is more of 'em!'

'Colonel!' came a cry, forcing Roystone to abandon his reverie and return with a thump to the impending conflict. It was Lieutenant Masters, adjutant to the Second Battalion, riding with some speed and purpose towards the headquarters' position.

'Your report, Masters,' Roystone requested, the steely calm in his deep voice completely overwhelming the officer's excitement and fright as he came to a halt before his colonel.

'Colonel Henderson is h-hit, sir,' he stammered breathlessly. 'Major Verity is hit also and sends for orders.'

'How is our position, Lieutenant? Is the rocket battery in place?'

Yet before Masters could summon up the voice to answer through the swollen glands of his dehydrated throat, Roystone's question was greeted by a deafening screech and a terrifying *whoosh* somewhere up ahead.

Looking up towards the nek they saw a huge cloud of white smoke, proceeded by a shower of yellow sparks and the manic squeal of the Hale rocket.

It ripped into the Zulu ranks, turning, snaking, and swivelling to and fro, casting white hot sparks and a long grey vapour trail in its wake, before detonating amid the forefront of the Zulu left horn. A cry went up from the warriors on the hillside, and with a single chant of 'uSuthu!' they plunged down the grassy slopes.

'Colonel McEnry is stretched as far as he can go on that side,' Masters resumed, taking a huge slug of water from a proffered water carrier. 'Although there is an embrasure to the north of his position that might let in an attack from the left where he's had to give cover to Glazebrook's battery.'

Roystone thought for a moment. 'Bring up the African contingents,' he instructed. 'Have them climb the hill on the farther side and be ready to counter the left horn when it moves down from the crest. I want both companies of mounted infantry held in reserve until they are most needed. You may call Colonel Henderson back from the front.' He added as an afterthought, 'Is he badly wounded, Lieutenant?'

'Shoulder wound, sir,' Masters replied quickly. 'Can't move the limb at all, and the whole thing's swollen up so much we had to remove his patrol jacket, Colonel.'

Roystone nodded gravely. 'Warren!' he boomed, as Westgate rode up alongside with his handful of sappers. 'See what you can do about getting those guns up here, will you. And take what men you have left to plug the gap for Colonel McEnry, if you would.'

'Yes, Colonel,' Westgate replied. 'Earnest, will you ride back to Bond for me? Tell him he can't make passage for those guns quick enough, then come down and join us on the firing line.' It was only now that the broad Irish accent, which the officer had spent so many years anglicising and suppressing, came bubbling to the surface.

Penfold, his eyes wide with terror and adrenaline, merely nodded in obedience and rode back the way he had come.

'Front rank, present... Fire!' cried Captain Fenton, as the descending Zulu Left Horn came within the five-hundred-yard range of the men's sights.

The Martini-Henry carbine was a powerful, if idiosyncratic, article of weaponry, prone to overheating and occasionally jamming. Sighted to a thousand yards, but with a reach of about eight hundred in experienced hands, its limitations were known by its wielders.

The men of the West Rutlands were mostly old sweats who had seen plenty of service with their carbines, and the volleys of white smoke and lead bullets crashed into the advancing ranks of the Zulu impi with deadly accuracy, felling dozens in the first assault. As the infantry fired, stepped forward a pace, then knelt to reload, the kneeling rank in front stood up, presented, and fired. This system insured that neither rank was left passive for more than a few seconds. Then, as the Zulus thundered down the steep slope of the hillside, both ranks took to firing at once. Volley after volley ripped through their midst; white smoke blinded and choked the soldiers as they fired, and their efforts were rewarded with wave after wave of falling warriors, killed in their scores by the paper-cased lead slugs of the modern British rifles. Brass cartridge cases littered the ground for over a mile, falling in their hundreds amid the long grass and thorns of aloes about the feet of the men of the Hundred and Tenth Regiment, their blackened faces, singed beards and bruised right shoulders a testament to their courage.

For many, it was their first close encounter with the fabled Zulus. Many were struck by the fit, muscular limbs, now twisted and contorted into a knot of tangled flesh by their death falls. Glistening tips of stabbing spears, and the massive skin shields now riddled with bullet holes, presented themselves time after time, each to be cut down as the one before, chopped to pieces by the disciplined firepower of the red-coated volleys.

Yet even as Roystone watched, another massive cry went up from the opposite side of the mountains, and he knew the Zulu right horn was well on the way down. 'Where, oh where, is that wretched artillery?' he groaned in despair.

'Snooker, for God's sake get off your horse and help!' Bond called above the din.

Captain Collingwood's two Armstrong guns were, at that moment, struggling furiously with the dire pitch and muddy surface of a particularly steep embankment, hundreds of yards back from the position that they were supposed to have occupied just over half an hour before. The main column had been pushed, pulled, and generally shepherded across via a slightly shallower ford, followed by a slightly gentler camber further downstream. However, with time as pressing as it was, and the sound of volley fire so readily apparent to Bond and his sappers, the decision had been taken to opt for the altogether tougher yet mathematically nearer slope to the position of the road itself.

Lieutenant Bond, therefore, albeit with the aid of the more than capable Sergeant Friday, Corporal Denham, and several muscular sappers, which included Coleman, was faced with the challenge of a physical tug-of-war with the heavy guns, limbers, axles, and horses of the gun carriages.

'Come on, Chatham boys, put your backs into it!' Friday's shrill voice projected, as he and the others struggled furiously to lever the wheels of the carriage clear of the churning quagmire that was rapidly forming at the base of the slope.

Bond, his brow soaked in perspiration and his lacerated hands bleeding all down the front of his muddy cord trousers, was just about to pass a soothing remark to the fuming Captain Collingwood, when yet another deafening screech ripped across the valley. He winced at the high-pitched screaming sound and shuddered as the sound of an explosion echoed back and forth between the mountains.

'That'll be young Will with my damned rockets,' Snooker wailed in frustration. 'Albert, can't you get these damned nags up the hill any quicker for me?'

'For pity's sake, man, my boys are doing their best!' Bond snapped back at him.

'Mr Albert, she's going again!' came a cry from behind. A second later Bond's jacket was off again, and the young sapper officer was writhing in the mud and clay, wrestling to save young Coleman from being crushed by the wheel of the descending carriage. 'Hold the bastard still, damn you!' he screamed up at the furiously panting Friday, who had gone as red as his serge through clinging to the rope with all his strength and shouting orders at the same time. 'Push, push, push!' Bond screamed, as he, Coleman and the corporal struggled frantically with the gun, while Friday and several others lay flat on their backs and struggled for all their strength was worth with the long ropes.

Up above their heads, Bombardier Matthew Smith and the gunners of the Royal Artillery tugged furiously at the horses' bridles and did their best to drag the beasts up the slippery slope to the summit.

Friday let out a wail of agony as the rope cut and sliced through the exposed palm of his right hand and he propelled himself backwards up the muddy surface of the treacherous bank. Then the right wheel of the gun itself suddenly locked, jamming the axle and causing the whole thing to slip back several inches.

Bond, who was right in the path of the massive limber, was almost decapitated in the process.

'The damn thing won't budge!' Coleman wailed in desperation.

'Jack, be careful!' Bond screeched, as the young sapper let out another yelp of pain, trapping his fingers as the whole thing began to sink back towards the ground.

'Damn it!' cried Corporal Denham loudly.

'Language!' cried Friday, even more loudly.

'Oh, wrap up, Sergeant!' Bond snarled improperly, as he helplessly watched poor Coleman battle with tears of pain and frustration, still grappling with the locked wheel of the static carriage.

They cursed and whimpered in equal measure.

'Albert, really! How much longer are you going to keep us waiting down here?' Collingwood complained.

'If you weren't a captain...' Bond muttered subversively.

Coleman, who was now parallel with his officer in the struggle with the cumbersome cannon, nearly choked on a giggle. Bond smiled too, although he knew it owed as much to agony and frustration as it did to suppressed hilarity.

The horses were making one hell of a din. Their fear and fury at being so physically and ignominiously pulled and pushed about so adverse an obstacle began to manifest itself in the usual way for any enraged mammal.

The dung fell on and around the sappers like rain, and the steaming clouts of horse manure proved to be a stiff fight as they struggled with the already tiresome burden of the mud and the punishing weight.

'For heaven's sake, don't look up, Jack!' Bond yelled across to Coleman, as a large quantity of what could only be described as very fresh soil came tumbling past his own head by a whisker.

'Shit!' cried Coleman in alarm and was then convulsed with helpless laughter as the steam arose from the loathsome barrage around the brim of his already filthy topi helmet.

'Language, please, men!' Friday screamed apoplectically. 'There is no excuse for— Oh!' Even Friday had to suppress a curse, which he swallowed along with some horse dung.

Yet by degrees, and with much persistent pulling on the part of Snooker Collingwood's men, they finally did succeed in forcing the horses to struggle their way to the top.

Elated, the gunners remounted their steeds for the pull, and the wheels of the hitherto marooned carriages began slowly to churn up the mud once again.

'Bloody hell that was rough!' wailed Corporal Denham, as the weight of the limber finally began to be dragged from his own shoulders and make its way up the slope under the horses.

'*Lang-uage,* all of you!" bellowed the hysterical Friday.

'Sorry, Sarn't!' chorused about twenty-three sappers who, having been cursing and blinding their way up the bank, were now slithering forlornly back down in a confused pile of bruised bodies, sweat, and horse manure.

Coleman looked at Bond, as the two of them braced themselves for a final effort. Then, straining every muscle in their bodies, they finally succeeded in dislodging the last few inches of wagon wheel from the murderous clay. For a second their eyes met, and Jack even managed to squeeze out yet another tight smile for his officer as they fought the final few yards together. Then, such was the relief as the huge grey gun finally churned, ground and grappled its way over the ridge, that the two of them simply slid back down through all the mud and manure, like two sacks of malt in a Kentish loft.

Their faces were a mixture of blood, sweat, mud and grime. Their throats were swollen and parched from a frantic thirst that gripped the glands like rusty irons, and their eyes were sore and reddened from squinting so long in the cruel sunlight.

It was strange, they thought, to be so wet and sodden outside, and yet so dry and parched within. Mind you, that was not to say that the strains of their physical exertions had merely been confined to their internal organs, either. Coleman's hands were lacerated from struggling with the steel-rimmed wheels of the gun carriage, while Bond's right shoulder was bruised, blackened, and throbbing with pain from the weight of the limber. Both men were sorely cut and bedraggled, beaten about by the rough and tumble of their struggle, and bruised and battered by the slips and stumbles of the inanimate equipment with which they had been fighting so hard. Several sappers had been kicked or trampled on by the frenzied horses, and one or two of them lay in a heap amid the mud and chaos of the embankment, groaning and rolling in pain, moaning for a doctor, rum, or both.

For a moment longer, officer and man just lay there silently looking at one another; Coleman with his flushed face, and his soaking wet blond hair flopped in oily brown strands over his screwed up blue eyes, and Bond with his own hair caked in mud, great smears of which covered his face and clung to the saturated velvet of his filthy blue patrol jacket.

Captain Collingwood was by no means so reticent. With a nimble bound, his supple mount successfully traversed in a matter of seconds that dreadful slope that the sappers had taken so many valuable minutes to overcome. Then, without pause for thanks beyond a quick nod of his noble head, Snooker spurred his horse to the gallop and gestured for the two carriages to follow him post haste.

'A pleasure, I'm sure!' quipped the ever sardonic Corporal Denham.

'Burgh!' and a spit ball of mucus was all that the exhausted Friday could emit in response.

'I'll never walk again!' groaned Coleman as he closed his eyes and furiously tried to get re-aquatinted with the deadened limbs of his normally supple body.

'I think I've died,' Bond retorted, agonised still more as the strain of his efforts caught up with him, and he took in for the first time the soaking wet of his hair and clothes, and the reeking stench of his dirty, wounded body. 'Jack.'

'Yes, Mr Albert?'

'What would you give right now for a long hot bath?'

Coleman sighed. A cloud of fine spray shot out from between his teeth, and he sank back ever more wearily into the mud. 'Never had one,' he replied truthfully. 'Anyways, there's nothing like a standpipe in the backyard to freshen you up!'

The British lines, having been under fire from the best part of the entire mountain range, had suddenly commenced volley firing on both the left and right flanks simultaneously. It was placing a heavy strain, not only on the exhausted buglers and stretcher-bearers, but also the smooth flow of ammunition supplies from the nearby wagons.

Somewhere behind his beard, the battalion quartermaster of the Second Battalion of the West Rutlands was quietly cursing the heavy volume of his own side's firepower.

Another rocket screeched and squiggled to its target on the hillside, sending countless Zulus flying amid a massive explosion and clouds of white smoke and red earth, which flew in all directions.

More fire from Arthur McEnry's men cut yet another sizable hole in the advancing Zulu left horn, while the persistent salvos from Will Glazebrook's battery seemed both to destroy and demoralise the force of the enemy attack.

Highly delighted with the way in which the day was turning, Colonel Roystone pragmatically turned his attention to the massing warriors of the Zulu right horn. This small impi, having been clearly visible and chanting and humming for quite some time, now suddenly broke into a charge.

It was impossible to judge entirely what the opposing induna was planning to achieve in his tactics, although he fancied from the pattern of the attacks so far that his adversary was aiming to push his forces further up the road between the mountain tops. 'That's it! The bastards will come at us from the dongas on either side!' he exclaimed aloud. 'Bugler, sound an order. I want the mounted infantry and the men of

Flambard's Horse under Colonel Henderson to advance and counterattack the Zulu right. They are to take the irregulars and cut off anything that tries to outflank the firing lines.'

As the discouragingly overwhelming numbers of Zulu warriors came bounding down the almost vertical camber towards them, Lieutenant Glazebrook's rocket battery was beginning to look decidedly vulnerable on their little summit, just a few hundred yards away from the infantry's main firing line.

The virtually ceaseless salvos, which had previously been projected so successfully against the rocks and boulders sheltering snipers on the nek, had suddenly to be repositioned to provide an adequate barrage that might stall the swarming Zulu left. As it was, the courageous young officer had only time to fire off a further two of the seven-pound Hale rockets before a messenger came belting down from the line to order him to withdraw and seek cover. Had not the message been received, the mere proximity of the Zulu impi would have compelled him to retire sooner or later, but it looked better to wait for the order. With a calm and presence of mind that the truly terrified young man found impossible to account for, Glazebrook meditatively sat on his horse and watched as the hordes of feathers, shields and, most of all, the vicious stabbing assegais came thundering down in row upon row towards him.

Only when both troughs had been dismantled and gathered up, and his dismounted troops had made their way back to the relative protection of the withering fire from their own lines, did the heroic lieutenant finally and gratefully turn his horse and retreat, pausing briefly to fire his revolver.

As soon as the rocket battery had retreated from their position to the north-east of Colonel Roystone's view, they were instantly redeployed on the opposite side, with their salvos trained on the sudden swell of warriors massing on the nek. Once a couple of well-aimed rockets had been hurled in to break up the closed ranks of the Zulu right, two companies of infantry and Major Westgate's sappers under the irrepressibly charged Gideon Knight opened fire with a tremendous roar. Streaks of white smoke and orange flame felled the first three ranks of the Zulu attack completely, driving those who came behind them into broken and bewildered pockets of confusion, stalled from advancing and too far from cover to retire.

A little further down the line, and to the great relief of the colonel, Snooker Collingwood's battery came to a halt on a grassy plateau, just to the left of Colonel Roystone's right flank firing line. The guns were hurriedly unlimbered, and Snooker was just about to send to the colonel for his instructions, when yet another screen of warriors began to deploy, this time on completely the other side of the road.

'Damn it, Matthew,' Collingwood remarked nervously to Bombardier Smith. 'Let's hope they don't all stream down at once, or they'll flood the dongas and be up here in no time at all.'

'I don't like it at all, sir,' Smith replied. 'We can't train the guns that low if they do, even for case shot!'

Gideon Knight's section put down an impressive fire on the now severely depleted Zulu right horn, cutting down the warriors as soon as they came within five hundred yards, and consequently freeing up Will Glazebrook's rocket battery for use against the sudden threat to the opposite side of the column. The hill to the left of their position rose from the nek, connected to a high rocky shoulder that climbed with the shape of the mountain itself to form part of the foothill. The grassy, boulder-strewn ground fell away almost immediately into a deep donga at the base of the escarpment that in turn ran for some considerable distance before dropping away at the point where it emptied into the river itself... just above the steep embankment.

It was at the base of this very slope that Bond and his sappers had fought so hard with the massive bulk and torturous dead weight of Snooker's guns, and where they were now beginning to recover from the shock of their labour.

As a result, any Zulus who might at any point be forced to break off from the main body of a left flank assault could well have ended up siphoning into the donga itself, directly threatening the engineer's position. Indeed, the massive boulders at the base of the hill could quite easily afford excellent cover for the agile Zulu snipers, many of whom were armed with old and obsolete muskets, most of which required a closer range of use, were any notion of accuracy to be achieved.

Westgate himself had not failed to spot this potential threat. Consequently, as Glazebrook's first rocket salvo ripped through the air and hit home and exploded with a mighty crash in the centre of the warrior's manic descent, the worried brevet major wasted no time in summoning little Lieutenant Penfold to his side.

'Earnest,' he barked. 'I need you to ride to Albert. Tell him to form his men into a firing line, and to hold his position until I can free up some support for him. He is now our extremity and is exposed. Do you understand me?'

Penfold, transfixed with horror as another stream of furiously screaming warriors began to plummet down the hill in overwhelming numbers, merely nodded his response. Then, as the gallant little officer turned his horse, he dug his spurs into the animal's flanks with exasperated ferocity and thundered off down the road on his errand.

This was the moment he had feared, and looked forward to, for so long. This was the time when, if all his fears had been true, the Almighty would sweep him from the face of the earth and take him from his place among the living. With a gulp of terror, he clung to the horse's reigns and clenched his teeth. Penfold had not got halfway down the track, before he came upon Snooker Collingwood, who having been ordered to move his artillery up to a better position, came charging up the line with a speed that was not to be challenged. Lurching his animal over to the side, Penfold could only watch, wracked with frustration as the gun carriages, limbers, and the guns themselves rattled past him in a confused deafening clatter of wheels and a jangling of tack, at entirely their own speed. As soon as they were clear, however, he was off again.

Chapter Twenty-Five

When first he saw the danger, Lieutenant Bond was once again stripped to the waist while he, Coleman, Friday, and the others did what they could to remove the foul-smelling dung from their clothes, beards and bodies.

The sappers suddenly became aware of a large darkness beginning to fall on the crest of the hill directly above the donga. When the first companies of the Zulu impi began to mass on the north-western face of the rocky slope, a sudden calming chill fell on each of them. The sky began to grow inexplicably dark and appeared to all to be further away than it had before. A strange buzz coupled with the rhythmical dense and magnified boom of spear upon shield, began to vibrate up and down, both far and near.

Pausing, and allowing the handful of rag to drop from his trembling grasp, Bond watched in horror as the strange gathering of black, white, brown, and tan hide shields began to move in one regimented mass, seemingly fanning out from one end of the world to the other.

'My matchsticks again,' Coleman breathed in a dreamy monotone.

'Look at 'em shields, like little black and brown ants in the distance,' Corporal Denham murmured quietly to the transfixed Sergeant Friday, who seemed to be focusing on something a million miles away from where they were.

'What about that, then?' Coleman gasped, fear and realisation suddenly pouring like a fog through the troubled canyons of his racing mind. He suddenly looked terribly young, standing there in his grey flannelette shirt, blond hair hanging over his soft face, mouth wide open in a kind of passive terror that only comes of a hard slap in the face by grim reality.

Bond, on the other hand, was starting to look terribly old. *I'm so scared*, he thought. *We might all be killed, and all I can think of is you...*

The banging seemed to intensify, and the sweat running down the faces of the paralysed sappers ran from their soaking wet foreheads to the tops of their boots. A cold, passive, and hitherto utterly unheard of terror began to sweep like a nauseous wave across the whitening faces of the static soldiers. Here a man gulped, gasped, or grunted. A few feet away, a spade fell to earth with a wet slap, showering the legs of the men about it with thick red mud. Nobody noticed.

Then, as if in a dream, small groups of the shadow on the hillside began hurriedly to descend, creeping like huge spiders in great hordes of arms and legs, before vanishing among the rocks and stones. The long grasses seemed simply to swallow them up, and the dreadful banging noise began to drown out even the constant volley fire going on all around the valley.

To their deadened nerves and disbelieving eyes, all that occurred to the sappers of Lieutenant Bond's troop was the terrible rattle of feet pummelling the earth, and the stunning reality that there was nowhere else to go. In truth, the sudden apathy can only have lasted a matter of seconds, for no sooner had the first of the small bursts of ill-directed fire begun to crackle from the rifles of the snipers on the hillside, Sergeant Friday snapped into action. In a voice a little higher pitched, even than usual, he ordered stand-to, precipitating the command on Bond's silent lips.

A sudden tremor went running through the icy veins of the sapper company, and with a pang of alarm, they realised that the attack was for real. In an ecstasy of bewilderment and uncoordinated shuffling around, the men somehow managed to squash together into a line, fingers scrabbling to locate lost rounds of ammunition, or fumbling with the virgin breech blocks on their hitherto unused Martini-Henry's.

Coleman, with a strange sensation of someone watching from without, haphazardly succeeded in scrambling about a foot up the grassy bank of the donga to take up his position behind a hummock.

The sappers deployed in two rows, all taking advantage of whatever cover was available to them as they sprang suddenly into order, as if the devil himself had suddenly become their sergeant. The noise they had first heard – the banging of the spears on the shields – had now been replaced by the altogether more deafening and horrific sound of hundreds of bare feet thundering down the hill towards them, together with the protracted screams of their officer and Sergeant Friday.

They seemed to be all around now, and all that could be seen for miles around were Zulu warriors. They began to chant, or pant, as they ran down the punishing slope, and Coleman felt himself let out a little whimper as the enemy swarmed down the hillside towards them.

For a second, Bond's fingers froze on his revolver holster. 'What do I do now?' he gasped in terror. 'Friday, I'm stuck, I can't move!'

Fortunately, Sergeant Friday had been there before. True, this was also his own first experience of a combat situation, but he had met officers who suddenly went blank on a parade square or during an exercise. This one was simply a case of paralysis, and the quick-thinking sergeant's action of unfastening the holster worked the necessary magic on Lieutenant Bond. With a bound, he was up the bank with the others. Someone handed him a rifle, and he even managed to insert the brass-cased Boxer slug in the breech, before snapping shut the hinged rear of the mechanism and cocking the weapon to fire.

They were nearer now, and the massive explosion as yet another rocket found its mark sent hordes of disorientated warriors streaming down through the donga. They soon recovered their wits, however, and with a cry of 'uSuthu!' began to eat up the ground between them and Bond's thin red line of riflemen.

The sappers spread out up either bank of the donga in a sort of V shape, with their officer on the one side and Sergeant Friday positioned at the opposite point. The ground shook beneath them, and Sergeant Friday could not have denied a fluttering in the stomach as he gave the order to mark targets and present.

All Coleman wanted to do now was fire and check the advance, so when the order did come at last, he pulled the rifle tight in on his shoulder muscles and, sparing only a second to look through the erected sight, fired at the first man he saw. He was a big Zulu, an officer, dressed in white feathers and carrying a large black and white shield. As he fell, the black head ring flew from his head, and the polished knobkerri that he carried shot way up above his head. All that Coleman saw was the blood as it sprayed from the warrior's mortally wounded body when he fired. The lad was trembling now, and his paroxysm might well have disabled him were it not for a steady hand being placed on his shoulder by a chillingly calm, somehow absent Sergeant Friday.

Closer, closer, and yet closer still they came into the sights of the rifles and well within their range. They fired again, and yet another wave of shields and spear tips fell amid the stones and brambles of the dried up watercourse. The whole bed of the donga seemed to the men to be a confused tangle of warrior's limbs; arms, legs, spears, and assegais, twisted into unnatural contortions by the nature of their landing, shrouded in a funeral pall of strangely pure white smoke.

Coleman was intense, electrified, animated. He felt he was on a high, and he knew that he must just keep on doing it if he and the others were to stay alive.

The whole of the line exploded in a flash of yellow and great clouds of white smoke. They choked, spat, and barked as the volume of fire became thicker, and the spent cartridges flew in a red-hot shower all around them, rattling and chinking as they bounced off stones, while their shots occasionally ricocheted off the larger boulders beyond their field of vision. The rifles kicked back as they fired, the recoil ripping into their many jacketless shoulders as they did so, each round bursting from the muzzle, each placed to kill. They fired and fired and fired. They fired until the stocks of the guns were red-hot, and the smoke was so thick and so heavy that it choked, blinded, and asphyxiated them, volley after volley, cutting back wave after wave of warriors. Yet still they came on.

Thanking God that he still had his revolver, Bond sprang up onto a rock and, regardless of the heavy fire being put down on them from the hillside beyond, pumped the bullets out of all six chambers into the mass of fog of smoke and confusion. The smell was sickening.

Coleman continued to fire, snatching up rounds from his pouches like they were pennies from Heaven, punching them into the breech and firing at his targets. The pain and the burns had almost gone now, paled into nothing by his desperate lust for survival. He fired again and was beginning to wonder if the force of his shots would throw him over backwards, when finally, the attack faltered.

Bond, who had soon realised the folly of standing on an open slope under fire, soon ducked back down behind his rock, and was just reloading his revolver when the sound of horses' hooves broke upon his ears.

Scrambling about a hundred yards back from the line, he recognised the mounted figure of little Earnest Penfold, grappling with the slippery slope and clinging to the horse's reigns for dear life. 'Earnest, ride to Warren Westgate!' Bond called up in alarm. 'Tell him we need some help. We've broken the first wave, but they keep coming down the donga. We have no bayonets, and finite ammunition. If we run low, it's picks and shovels against assegai. Get us help, Earnest, please!'

Numb with disbelief and rendered speechless by his fearful ride, Penfold could only mouth a silent response through his cloudy blond beard, before turning his horse and riding back for the second time.

'Hole them, boys!' cried Friday, as a bullet whizzed past him and embedded itself in a young sapper to the left of him, sending its victim reeling lifelessly backwards as the side of his head came off.

He was conscious of the need to keep the men focused. All fear had left him now and, as he glanced up at Coleman firing away for all he was worth, a pang of guilt swept over the bald sergeant. It had been he who had talked the lad into attesting after all, and if he were to die, it would be Friday who bore the moral responsibility. He had done it all a million times before, but for some reason he knew this boy was different.

'Still the bastards are coming, sir!' Coleman called back to Bond, who immediately resumed his position and reloaded his rifle for the hundredth time.

Frenzied, manic and wound up to the tension of a bowstring by the speed, the heat, and the scale of events before him, Friday let out a shrieked exhortation to keep on firing. He even forgot to pull Coleman up for swearing.

The bodies began to pile up in the donga. Yet still they fired, until the back of the assault had been broken, and the whole game was turning into a contest as to how hard a blow they could inflict before their enemy gave up and retired defeated.

They blazed away for a further twenty rounds, the deafening noise and the repetitive volleys working them up into an orgy of violent emotion, driving them back with wave after wave of smoke, flame, and bile, cutting through their ranks and smiting them to nothing.

Just as the attack on Bond's position was beginning to burn itself out, Colonel Roystone had seen the last valiant efforts of the courageous Zulu left shattered into pieces by the relentless fire of Arthur McEnry's battalion.

A flash and a roar heralded yet another salvo from number one gun, and a large boom soon scattered yet another cluster of demoralised warriors at the foot of the mountain to the right. The glittering of spear tips and assegai blades was becoming less and less apparent in the cruel glare of the mid-morning sunlight, and the dull thud of fresh corpses falling on the dry grass and amid the aloes seemed to have replaced the heavy thunder of running feet. A steady stream of fire wiped out the remaining Zulus on the hillside, and a large plume of white smoke indicated to the deafened colonel that yet another well placed shell had finally broken up the attack of the right horn.

Down in their donga, the men of Bond's troop continued to let go clusters of sporadic independent fire, broken only occasionally by a massive explosion as one of Snooker's shells exploded further up the bed.

'Fire!' came Bond's strained order. By now he was almost deaf and mute from shouting so loud and so long amid the crash of the guns and the din from the relentless shooting.

Another massive roar ripped the air as the line once more lit up with regimented flashes of volley fire, utterly decimating any who might be left either standing or walking. Certainly, none were advancing, but as the heavy clouds of thick smoke began to lift a little, an order went up for the mounted men to go forth and wipe up the survivors.

As the smoke cleared and a gentle breeze blew what was left away from their position below the level of the road, Bond and his men could only kneel or lay there in stunned silence. Here and there feeble groans or cries went up from the masses of fallen warriors . Some writhed in agony from their wounds, while others merely lay there panting, waiting for the merciless dispatch of the African contingent as they patrolled the field, stabbing with their spears at their fallen ancestral enemy. *There is nothing noble about* this *savagery*, Bond thought grimly.

Their faces blackened, and their clothes wasted by the recoil of their vicious carbines, the men of Number Six Column merely looked on in grim amazement at the biblical proportions of the slaughter before them. The long yellow grass was thick with blood, flattened down by the trampling of feet and the volume of falling bodies. The ferocious lead bullets had cruelly wounded many before death, and their limbs were rent and broken in all sorts of ghastly places. The once proud, colour-coded regimental shields lay holed and tattered amid the hailstorm of bullets, and the entire length and breadth of the field of battle crunched and rattled with the sound of expended brass cartridges, barely audible over their fearful ringing ears.

'L-look how many we've killed, Mr Albert,' Coleman stammered in a macabre state of wonder.

Friday was wretched. It was not for a boy to see the likes of this carnage.

'I never thought that I could feel so wrong to have survived this,' Bond announced in a dull monotone. 'Did you see their eyes as they went down?'

'All right, Mr Albert, sir,' Friday mumbled tactfully. 'It don't do to dwell.'

Bond was still silent, punch drunk on the appalling scene of slaughter, death, and madness. Many of his own men had been hit during the fighting, and several had been killed in depressing and demoralising circumstances.

Coleman must have seen something of what was passing through his mind, for he gently placed his hand over Bond's. The touch was over in a second, too fast for the eye to see, but warm and sincere nonetheless. Catching his breath, Bond looked up at the reddened, squinting, yet still sparkling blue eyes of his young batman. Then the lad smiled. Bond smiled back, but only for a second, for he vomited shortly after.

Considering the volume of men who had been involved in the Zulu attacks, it was perhaps not surprising that many of the greener troops managed – for the most part quite successfully – to view an individual Zulu warrior as being the same as the last. This held some advantage for their states of mind, especially for Bond's initiates who had previously never seen a shot fired in anger. Even so, many were still in a state of some shock over the appalling carnage and scenes of brutal devastation they themselves had inflicted.

'What have we done, Sarn't?' Corporal Denham murmured gravely.

'Done our duty, that's what we done, Corp,' Friday replied mechanically, and without sympathy or tact. 'Soldiers, after all. Hand of God smote them, not us.'

'D'you reckon they see us like we see them,' Denham continued, 'one red-faced man in a red coat, just the same as the next or the last?'

'Yes,' put in a passing black African irregular, unbidden. 'So do we, Seargent!'

Friday looked thunderstruck, but the pitch of his reply rendered it inaudible. Only when he was out of sight did he too surrender to the nausea and vomited.

The African contingent, on the other hand, had no such qualms. They ran about the field, mercilessly stabbing their wounded foe and dispatching many with a swift blow of a rifle butt to the back of the head. Enmity ran deep and long among the border tribes.

Colonel Henderson, who had been wounded during the counterattack on the Zulu right horn, clearly derived grim satisfaction from the pursuit of the retiring warriors with singular and unparalleled ruthlessness. 'For Turnpenny, you bastards!' he cried, watching as the angry volunteers fell upon the pitifully wounded Zulu warriors with a sickening rip of steel on flesh, and the *crack-crack* of the dispatching revolver bullet. 'Take parties of bayonet men,' he told Lieutenant Masters. 'Use the mounted locals to flush out any that are left straggling in groups or hiding out in those hills. We don't want to be subjected to enfilading and pot shots when the column moves off again.'

'Certainly, Colonel,' Masters replied. 'We've lost too many good fellows today.'

That was true, for as well as the tragic and agonising spectacle, several notable casualties had been incurred during the battle. Among those were Colonel McEnry, who sustained a bullet in the calf, and Captain Fenton whom, as well as his bullet in the arm, had been hit in the foot by a deflected musket ball. His foot ached, and a dull numbness seemed to be creeping up his leg and freezing the bruised limb shut when he walked, while the wound in his arm was made even more painful by the fact that he had not yet had the bullet removed.

Another casualty had been poor little Earnest Penfold. As Bond wandered numbly past the surgeon's wagon, now on the road rather than halfway across the river, Penfold called out to him. 'Albert! What happened? Are you hurt?'

'Not remotely,' Bond replied, suddenly regaining his composure as he was brought down to earth once again. 'Why, what happened to you then, Earnest?'

'Well, it was when I turned the horse to take your message back to Warren,' Penfold replied, slightly crestfallen. 'It just came whizzing out of nowhere, and before I knew where I was, there was the ground below me, and my arm pumping blood all over the place.'

Bond winced. 'Oh, that looks nasty. I'm sorry for you, old chap.'

'The wound might have been dealt with quicker, Lieutenant,' Surgeon Major Lamb cut in acidly, 'if certain medical supplies had been given priority when it came to crossing the river earlier today.'

'Yes, and had my men and I spent the whole time getting you across the river, Major,' Westgate interrupted from the safety of the saddle, 'we *might* not be here now discussing the whys and wherefores, and you wouldn't have any wounded to attend to at all.'

'That's all very well, Major,' Lamb replied grumpily, 'but I cannot be expected to see to your officers with no supplies, now can I? Take this poor devil for instance. What is he going to do now?'

'You'll be all right won't you, Earnest?' Bond asked lightly, nudging Penfold's good arm as he teased the little officer.

'Well, I hope so,' Penfold replied with martyrdom. 'I don't know who else is going to run to and fro with your messages, otherwise,' he added mischievously, looking pointedly at both Bond and Westgate.

'Well done, Earnest,' Westgate beamed approvingly. 'And good show, Albert,' he added with a note of great triumph evident in his voice. 'You've done the Corps proud by what you did this morning. But tell me, did any of the lads distinguish themselves beyond their promise?'

'Not beyond their promise at all, Warren,' Bond replied mysteriously, 'for I had absolute faith in them to begin with. Even so,' he added quickly, keen not to lose the ear of his company commander while he had it, 'Sergeant Friday's was the main disciplinary influence during the assault, but young Coleman was arguably the bravest, considering his youth.'

'In what way?' Westgate queried.

'In lots of ways,' Bond replied haltingly and suddenly unsure of his ground.

'Well, what exactly did he do that was so meritorious?' Westgate persisted.

'Come on, Albert! If the boy's done well, he deserves recognition,' put in Penfold.

Bond shot him one of those withering glances that told one to shut up, before stammering that it had been more of a morale effect than a temporal one.

'Did he shoot many?' Westgate continued.

'Several,' Bond replied truthfully. 'Although it is true to say that Sergeant Friday was commanding his section during the melee, I did note his bravery on more than one occasion.'

'How so?'

'Well, you know...' Bond continued awkwardly. He could not maintain this duel of suggestion for too much longer and was struggling in his mind to come to terms with exactly what it was that young Jack had done above the rest, apart from simply *be there*. The truth was of course that had the beautiful smile not fixed so steadily in his mind during the fight, and those beautiful sapphire eyes pacified his hammering heart and stilled him for action, Bond might well have lost his nerve all together.

How the hell could he tell *that* to Westgate?

Relief came in the form of Gideon Knight, who marched straight up to the surgeon's wagon and, taking Bond's hand and pumping it vigorously, proceeded to pat him hard on the back and escorted him off around the field in a bemused, yet triumphal parade.

'Somebody's certainly scored a hit,' Corporal Denham observed to Sergeant Friday.

'Hmm. Worries Friday, mind. Not proper,' Friday muttered back quietly, having only just had to embellish Bond's glowing appraisal of young Coleman with a more or less accurate report. If the truth were told he, Friday, had been too busy firing away for his life to notice the success or accuracy of any one sapper. Even so, he genuinely did begin to wonder exactly what it was that Bond saw in Coleman, above and beyond the regard in which both officers and men held him already. 'Hit indeed, Corp,' he repeated, as Denham moved off to find his water bottle. 'Don't do to favour. Spoils a man, makes him less humble. Soft...'

In the meantime, Captain Horace Fenton was falling to bits. The shot in his arm had yet to be removed, and the deadening numbness of the bullet that had landed on his right foot was frustrating movements far worse than any amputation. Every time he so much as flinched, some part of his body or the other seemed destined to twinge on him, and the intense firing had left him both deafened, hoarse, and unable to see without blinking. 'It's too bad I can't join old Henderson's boys,' he opined miserably to Surgeon Major Lamb. 'I really fancied giving them Zulus a chivvy into the hills after what they put my company through today.'

'Now then, old man,' Lamb remonstrated lightly with him. 'Your men gave them a raw drubbing earlier, so it's not as if you've been denied any of the glory – now, is it?'

'No, not at all,' Fenton replied as the stinging sensation of the bandage being removed from his arm began to pale into insignificance at the sight of the gruesome bullet forceps, which the surgeon used for extracting the lead from the flesh. He screamed in agony as the vicious pincers closed around the slug, and the surgeon deftly tugged it from its deep position in the officer's bicep.

Under Colonel Henderson's ministry, the pursuit of Zulu stragglers had been as ruthless as the battle had been short and bloody. He tolerated no excuses and held firm that the only use for the equally barbaric savages in the African contingent was in hunting down their "own kind", upon whom they could subsequently dispense their justice. He had not been in favour of arresting Captain Toteaux and, unlike Flambard, firmly believed that suppression by force alone would carry the day in Africa. The extent of such comprehensive butchery and the epic scale of the casualties sustained by the Zulu forces was in evidence all around. As far as the eye could see, the ground was littered with the vile remains of a morning's relentless slaughter. So much so in fact that Colonel Roystone, who could never be judged as a hasty commander, begun to believe that the battle had been resultant in wiping out the entire Zulu opposition in the region. Indeed, such were the numbers of different coloured regimental war shields being gathered up and brought in as booty that it seemed almost undeniable that an entire army had met its destruction.

Encouraged almost to excess by this startling victory, Roystone issued immediate orders that the column was to move through the pass and make camp in the open veldt beyond before midday. The camp would be surrounded by a wagon laager, naturally, but such was the relief felt by all in a position to estimate the scale of the British success that it was imagined to be impossible that any groups of warriors could exist above the number of a mere handful.

Chapter Twenty-Six

Further cheer was added to the spirits of the already greatly heartened men of Number Six Column when, at around 10:30 a.m., Commandant Flambard's mounted militia rode into the camp. The burley magistrate's euphoric greeting was tempered, however, by the sullen grumbles and downright rebukes that met his constant demands for a graphic description of the battle he had missed.

'It's too bad you weren't here, Gillespie,' McEnry told him wearily. 'If you had been here when you were expected, you might just have got a chance to give the Zulu a taste of your famous spirit.'

'Believe me, Arthur, I don't ask out of simple curiosity,' Flambard persisted doggedly. 'I've heard five different accounts of this battle so far, not including yours and Harry's, and I've still not heard any of you mentioning what happened to the chest section of the assault.'

'Chest? Whose chest?'

They had now been joined by a rather irritable Colonel Henderson who, having finally quit his observation of the gory battlefield, had returned to the officers' mess tent in search of liquid libations to soothe the pain of his wound. He scoffed at what he perceived to be Flambard's preoccupation with "inferior" African tactics and regarded his interest as armchair curiosity. Scathingly dismissive of any hint that the Zulus might have posed any threat to the safety of the column on the road, he proceeded to lock horns with the already ill-tempered magistrate on the general topics of confederation, missionary conversions, and the use of African troops in colonial warfare.

Leaving the two men to snipe at each other across the table, Arthur McEnry picked up his glass and limped timidly off to Colonel Roystone, whom he found busily overseeing the packing up of his own tent and equipment in preparation for camp's removal.

'Arthur, should you be walking on that leg?' Roystone grunted sourly.

'It's no worse than Abyssinia, Harry,' McEnry responded quietly.

'In Abyssinia, my dear chap, you twisted your ankle.'

'One of Horace Fenton's boys lost a leg completely. Old Lamb-cutlet had to take it off for him, so I hardly think I'm in any position to complain,' McEnry continued, apparently reluctant to dignify the colonel's remark with a suitable response. 'Besides,' he added, looking somewhat sideways at the less than cordial colonel, 'what's got you in such a sore head? I thought we pulled a coup today, didn't we?'

'Yes, yes, it's not that at all,' Roystone sighed, throwing down his cigar and promptly lighting another one in its place. 'You know how it is, Arthur. The men are shattered. Some of them had some very close calls today, and quite a number lost their officers, so it doesn't do for chaps like them,' he gestured towards the mess tent, wherein Henderson and the commandant were still going hell for leather, 'to go upsetting morale with their wild ideas.'

'Nobody takes any notice of that murderous, jumped-up major,' McEnry muttered.

'I'm not talking about Henderson, as well you know, Arthur' Roystone denounced gravely. 'Commandant Flambard may be the celebrity of the colonial order, but he's not been a regular for a good many years. Things have moved on since we all fought Emperor Theodore together in Abyssinia.'

'He served in the African wars,' McEnry countered swiftly.

'That may be so,' Roystone replied firmly. 'But he has no business spreading unfounded terrors about the non-emergence of front chests, or this balderdash about any local impi being held in reserve until we move off. He is an African now, a militiaman, and must give his mind to domestic peacekeeping duties.'

'I don't think Gillespie Flambard is prone to fancies, Harry,' McEnry replied, a note of warning evident about his tone. 'You might just mark my words for a change, instead of taking that fool Henderson for everything he says.'

'Very well, Arthur,' Roystone said at last. 'You were always right in India, so I'll respect your petition now. I'll send out some of Gillespie's men off under that Flounce what's-his-name, and you and he can rest assured tonight.'

'Thank you, Colonel,' McEnry smiled in acknowledgment.

'Although I still can't imagine why,' Roystone could not help adding by way of qualification. 'With the losses today, I doubt whether the old induna has enough men left to count the bodies, let alone mount a second attack.'

The concerns of those below field rank, namely those subalterns and below who had been charged by Major Westgate to prepare the column for an immediate departure, were somewhat closer to ground level.

As far as Coleman, Denham, Friday and even their young officers were concerned, the threat of an attack was over, and the serious business of establishing a steady line of communication from Fort Penfold was now a task of paramount importance to the invasion. The task was made even more poignant by the fact that they were to be left not only in sole charge of the fort and the crossing, but because for the first time Warren Westgate would not be with them. That was a daunting prospect indeed, not least for Lieutenant Gideon Knight who, as senior subaltern and the oldest of the three officers, was to be left in overall command of both the post and the task of acting as quartermaster to all incoming stores from Natal.

Even so, the state of the ground and the condition of the wheeled transport necessary to continue the journey kept the three of them far too busy to brood on their impending desertion by the main column. Wheels of wagon and carriage had become hopelessly choked up with mud and had to be levered by several men at once, while the remaining complement of sappers gave their shoulders to hauling the static burdens up on ropes.

Several oxen had died during the early stages of the battle, and the shock of being suddenly pushed and pulled about again had resulted in whole teams having to be replaced. Carcasses lay here and there; the mid-morning sun speedily precipitating the early stages of decomposition and causing the flies to gather around the bodies in swarms. This resulted in a particularly evil smell, which when added to the fearful stink from the bloody battle itself, was beginning to leave many of the soldiers feeling decidedly sick, and several were unable to go on. At some points, teams of oxen had to be swapped around from cart to cart, depending on the urgency of the loads they were carrying. Picks, shovels and long wooden stakes were all usefully employed as levers, props and general articles of necessity in prising the static wagons from their stopping places in the muddy riverbanks on either side. The column had halted quite abruptly when the first shots of battle were fired, and many had quite simply stopped where they were and sunk.

The constant swing and chop of pick and shovel was soon joined by the strain and crack as timbers gave way beneath the wheels of the stranded carts, and the seemingly endless creak and groan of Warren Westgate's beleaguered sappers. Such labour, especially after more than two hours of hard and bitter fighting, was made even more challenging by the heavy burden of responsibility that the three young sapper officers knew was soon to be placed upon them.

Sergeant Friday was a stalwart nonetheless, and the subalterns soon found that their work was, by and large, completed by the time the senior officers had moved to the rear of the column to inspect their progress.

'Look out, chaps, here comes Warren with the brass hats!' Knight hissed in warning. He needn't have worried, for no sooner had Colonel Roystone's ample form appeared over the crest of the hill above the campsite, Sergeant Friday had the men standing to attention in two ranks, flanking the road on either side.

As the headquarters' staff rode down towards the river, they were saluted on either side by two long rows of grubby, bedraggled, and yet somehow well-presented sappers.

Warren Westgate beamed approval as the three colonels halted to receive the engineers' salute and inspect the work that the men had been so hard at prior to their own arrival. When Colonel Roystone chose to pass a few words with Lieutenant Bond, Westgate was simply ecstatic.

'We owe you our gratitude, or so I am told, Lieutenant,' Roystone smiled warmly down on Bond. 'Apparently, you and your sappers successfully plugged and held what could quite easily have represented a major flaw in our line earlier today. I must confess that the engineers have always held my sincerest admiration, but after today, you go up even further in my regard.'

'Thank you, sir,' Bond replied proudly, and saluting with the flabbergasted pride of his first commendation. His face fell, however, when Roystone suddenly turned his attention to the muddy row of ordinary sappers behind him.

Please don't swear, curse, or break wind, Friday thought bleakly, as he stood poised to hit any member of the troop who looked like stepping so much as an inch out of line. To his combination of surprise, delight and yet to his horror, Friday watched as the colonel's sharp black eye fell on the solid, youthful form of Sapper Coleman.

'My, you're a fine lad, aren't you?' he laughed approvingly. 'What's your name, boy?'

'Charmin'.' Corporal Denham muttered disgustedly as soon as the colonel was out of earshot. 'All of us lot, and he goes and picks on the pretty boy.'

'Lad says what he feels,' Friday squeaked in alarm. 'Can't stop him now, Corp.'

In the event, however, Coleman was polite, upright, and monosyllabic, and failed to upset either of his critical NCOs when asked questions relating to his health, comfort, and general conditions of service in the Royal Engineers.

When asked whether the hot sun was making him suffer from so much hard labour, he smiled, stood smartly to attention, and told the colonel that he was simply proud to be serving in the Corps. Blushing with pride, Bond interjected that Coleman was only eighteen, and that he had acquitted himself admirably, if not to say heroically, during the battle. This pleased Roystone even more and he seemed to have greatly taken to the young sapper's spirit, attitude and bearing.

Thus, did he reward young Coleman with a gold sovereign and a warm, paternal handshake, to great applause from the rest of the company, and smiles of encouragement from a delighted Warren Westgate.

It would have been hard at that moment to say which was the happier: Coleman for his own reward, Bond for the bestowing of such honour on Coleman, or Westgate for the reflected glory that this action had brought him. For himself, Bond was only glad that Jack had finally received, albeit indirectly, the credit that he thought the boy had so long deserved for simply getting him through the long hot days, wet and miserable evenings, and the arduous marches that they had endured. Just thinking about the young sapper had sustained him through cold rainy nights. Now all he could do was look as with his blond head bowed and his hair hanging over his eyes, Jack modestly accepted his commendation. As soon as the staff contingent were out of earshot, however, Friday proceeded to reprove Coleman for being too grandiose in reply to the colonel's question. Anxious to appear disinterested, Bond turned instead to return a congratulatory grin from Lieutenant Penfold.

While all this was taking place, Warren Westgate looked as pleased as a proud father might on his son's first day at school. He would have liked to stop and pass a few words of advice and congratulation with his young subalterns, especially Gideon Knight for whom he was frightfully anxious about being left to his own devices until supplies arrived from Oscaarsberg. Still, he decided, Knight was much older and a far more experienced engineer than the other two; he had a good, solid sergeant in Ludo Friday, and in any case nearly half of the sappers from his own company were remaining behind to help guard the depot. Albert and Earnest were keen, well qualified young men, who liked Gideon and would do everything they could to assist him in his task. Besides which, he reasoned, this was exactly the sort of thing for which he had so long been preparing the ambitious lieutenant – the real beginning of the career of Gideon Knight. As for himself, Westgate decided he must now turn his full attention to securing his majority by and with every means and opportunity that made itself available during the campaign. The colonel seemed pleased enough with his progress to have almost adopted the Irish sapper onto his own staff, and he knew that Annie would be so proud if he went home with a pair of stars for her to sew on his tunic instead of giving them to his tailor. For this reason, when the time came for the parting of the ways, Westgate merely looked back at the three lieutenants on the road and winked his approval at them. Then, with a swift wave of his right hand and without so much as a backward glance, he set off up the road with the three colonels.

'The luck of the Irish, Gideon,' he murmured. 'Colonel at forty, general at fifty.'

'Goodbye, Warren,' Knight muttered sadly to himself. 'God protect you till I'm a captain and you're confirmed a major.'

Even as they watched him go, Bond and Penfold were seized with pangs of conflicting emotion. Warren Westgate had been both father, brother, and mentor to them during their first fretful few weeks at Brompton Barracks, offering advice, giving them guidance, and sometimes lending them money or helping to manage their meagre allowances while they adjusted to army life. Now it was as if the big brother that the two of them saw in Gideon was suddenly being promoted above them. No longer was he simply one of their numbers, but their superior, charged with the burden of command and the ultimate responsibility for the final say, possibly over life and death. It was indeed a pang of melancholy felt by Albert Bond and little Earnest Penfold as their company commander rode off into the distance, but for Gideon Knight it was the role itself that remained with him. For so long, Westgate had been their guiding light, their source of inspiration, there for each of them on an individual basis. Now, with the stability of command and the expectant glances from his two close friends, Lieutenant Knight felt the mounting demand upon him to succeed for all of them.

In the event, it was Penfold who finally broke the pervading silence. 'That's it then, I suppose,' he remarked causally, as the long and mighty column tramped off across the mountains once more.

'Glad we're staying behind?' Bond asked monotonically, as they gloomily watched the heavily burdened soldiers of the West Rutlands trail arms and lumber up the slopes they had climbed once already under that torturous sun.

It was strange, they thought, how long and proud and mighty it looked, now that it was moving away from them, and the insecurities began to swamp them once again. Penfold made no reply as they watched the passing infantry, some looking utterly wretched. Many of the young recruits were just about making it, bent miserably under the weight of their heavy equipment, tired from fighting and still blackened and bloodied by their baptism of fire. Many raw recruits had tears in their eyes as the straps cut deep into their shoulders, dragging their aching limbs along through the stinking mud as it dried on their uniforms, trying desperately not to think of home.

Just at that moment, Bond found his eyes instinctively draw across to Coleman. He too was grubby, wet, and weary looking with bloody hands from digging, firing, and then digging again so hard, but the smile on his face at the shiny gold coin in his hand alone was worth a hot bath and a change of clothes. *When I get you home*, Bond thought longingly, *you'd have enough of those gold sovereigns to fill a coal scuttle*. Then he thought again about his reason for being there in the first place, and his heart began to sink once more.

Knight saw his friend's preoccupation and decided to take his mind off the departing column. 'What's our strength, Albert?' he enquired airily, even though he knew perfectly well already. It seemed like a facile question, but at least it broke the silence.

'Let me see,' Bond began slowly. 'We've roughly ninety-odd men, although it's more like about seventy because half the infantry is sick or wounded.'

'Walking?'

'Hardly.'

'Capable of walking, then?' Knight persisted.

'Oh, about half that number again,' Bond replied, scratching his beard as a nervous reaction to so reactionary an application of mathematics.

'Not so much an embarrassment of riches as simply an embarrassment, some might think,' Penfold interjected unhelpfully.

'Never mind, Earnest,' Bond retorted. 'If the Zulus do decide to attack us again, we can all hit out at them with crutches, or trip them up with lengths of bandage.'

'You'll have to excuse me,' Penfold added, pointedly directing his remarks to Gideon. 'I must check a few details with Friday on the defences.'

'Ah yes, and therein lies another point,' Knight suddenly observed, snapping out of his reverie and turning to Bond with a brisk smile. 'We need to run in those few wagons we were left with by the column. Will you help me see to it then, Albert?'

'Certainly, Gideon,' Bond replied obligingly. 'In fact,' he added, 'why don't I put Sergeant Friday on to that right now while you go off and put pen to paper for Flora? You haven't written anything down in that journal of yours for ages, and she's bound to worry if there are gaps.'

Knight thought for a moment, then smiled. 'Thanks, Albert,' he replied, patting Bond on the arm. 'You're a brick, do you know that? But I really must see to entrenching the position before we even think about anything else.'

With a muffled sigh, Bond nodded obediently and trailed off in search of an NCO.

By midday, the heat they had to work in became unbearable, reducing muscular efforts to a useless gesture of mud scratching. The shovels hardly broke the dry crust of the now hard, baked red earth, and the flies around the glistening, sweaty bodies of the weary sappers made the job even less pleasurable than usual. More than once, an exhausted young sapper would unearth some beastly scorpion, and jump back in terror of his life. Ant hills became disturbed, and for the rest of the day the men had to put up with hundreds of them, crawling in and out of their boots and biting their legs unmercifully. Yet the work had to be done, nonetheless. Protection was everything, and Gideon Knight understood a well-prepared defensive position. Range on all sides and adequate protection from a Zulu onslaught was far more pressing a concern than meat, bread, or the short-term comfort of his troops.

All this he watched from beneath the brim of his grubby brown topi, as the harsh sun reduced a gaze to a squint, and the heat began to boil and swelter his sweaty body as the temperature inside the serge cloth of his red undress frock grew ever greater. How Gideon envied Bert Bond, and those ever more tanning muscles flexing as he dug and scraped and worked with his men, and the navy patrol jacket cast idly into one of the wagons behind him. He knew he really ought to off-kit and set to with the men – it was the first principle that set a sapper officer apart from his contemporaries – but he also realised that an hour in the sun would just about finish him, and there was so much more work to be done before the evening, and so many more decisions had to be made.

By the time the cooks had set up their tables and stirred up the fires under the two huge cauldrons of mealy porridge, the three flatbed wagons had been run in on the sandbag walls of the fort, and a five-foot ditch had successfully been dug. All seemed to be going along quite well, until little Earnest Penfold pointed out to Lieutenant Knight that, owing to the size of the defences, it would be quite impossible for the soldiers' bell tents to be erected within the fortified perimeter.

Consequently, and much to the chagrin of Bond, yet another working party was assembled shortly after the men had eaten their lunch, and the work on yet another trench was commenced, this time just beyond the line of the original, and designed to accommodate a rather grim, if necessary, latrine. When they finally pitched camp that night, there was only just enough light left to build the fires and get some dinner on the go for those who were not so misfortunate as to end up on piquet duty.

All were utterly wasted; many had fallen during the long hard toil of the day, and some had even passed out through heat exhaustion.

Further insult was added to injury when, having prised open a box that had been thought to contain sardines, two privates of the West Rutlands discovered instead that they had been left with about half their quota of actual food rations, and rather a lot of superfluous ammunition supplies.

'We can't really complain too much, I suppose,' Penfold observed gravely to his two colleagues, as they stood and stared in bewilderment as box after box of .45 calibre rounds were opened out before them. 'I heard of some engineer companies not getting enough rounds to properly equip one sapper, let alone an entire field company.'

'No danger of that,' Bond replied grimly. 'At this rate, we're all going to have to start eating munitions and save the sardines for the Zulus.'

'How much longer did you say we would have to wait for the supplies, Gideon?' Penfold asked innocently.

'That depends,' Knight replied shortly.

'On what?' asked Bond.

'Who's bringing them.'

'Well,' Bond persisted, rather peeved at being played games with, 'tell us who it is, Gideon. Oh no!' he added suddenly. 'You surely don't mean—'

'That's right,' Knight sighed resignedly. 'So, unless you have some way of second guessing your uncle, Albert, we shall still be none the wiser as to the progress of AW McGonagle. Either way, you can all stop asking me because I'm sure I'm damned if I know!'

'What do you suppose is the matter with him now?' Penfold asked in alarm, as Gideon stalked off in the direction of his own tent.

'Power, I expect,' Bond sniffed back haughtily. 'He's so taken up with running things book fashion that he's forgotten who we are.'

'I suppose he just wants to make captain,' Penfold replied in his friend's defence.

'Oh, he's already made captain,' Bond added wryly. 'He just needs it ratified.'

For a moment, Penfold looked utterly disgusted. His nose twitched, and his lip curled under his shaggy blond beard. 'You know, sometimes I wonder about you, Albert,' he sighed irritably. 'What exactly is eating at you suddenly?'

'I'm not sleeping in here and listening to you go on like this,' Bond snorted, as he and Penfold arrived outside the flaps of the already erected two-man canopy. 'You can have this awning to yourself tonight. I'm off to take the watch with my boys.'

'Fine by me,' Penfold grunted as yet another of his friends marched into the dark under a cloud, and he was left by himself to awkwardly to remove his red jacket and the shoulder belt that held his wounded arm in place. 'You probably still snore, anyway,' he added grumpily as he extinguished the lamp. Only when it was truly dark did he realise just how much he missed Henerietta.

Chapter Twenty-Seven

As he paced around the perimeter of the improvised wagon laager, listening to the shrill bleep of the crickets, and the crackle and burst of the embers as they died under the cooking pots, Bond smoked a cigar and pondered on the events of the day. He was not awfully worried about the falling out, either with Gideon or Earnest. They had had set-tos before, and always come back laughing together.

Thinking back to the days when the three of them used to drink at the Bull Hotel in Rochester, also known as The Royal Victoria after a visit from the queen, he wandered idly around behind one on the wagons, to a point where the sandbag wall was highest. The fire spat and gutted a few yards away from him, and somewhere just on the other side of the parapet a sentry's boots dragged and stamped through the dry grass of the dusty veldt.

If only the rain holds off, he thought, *I should be able to start work on a pont to cross the river tomorrow*. In fact, he was just beginning to drift off into that sort of waking trance that thinking too deeply about a project or venture, yet undone, can induce, when a thin little cough caught his attention, somewhere off to the left.

It was one of the few dry nights they had had so far, and the stars twinkled in the dark sky like thousands of little diamonds on a piece of blue velvet. The smell of the campfires was beginning to die away, and a gentle breeze had begun to blow across the open countryside, gently caressing the long yellow grasses, and tossing the bronze locks on either side of his forehead. In the clear pale light of the moon he could plainly see the youthful, glowing form of a slumbering Coleman, snuggling up as best he might against the piles of sacking and a discarded greatcoat on the sandbag perimeter.

Turning up the collar of his own coat, Bond felt the night chill suddenly grow colder. Dreamily smoothing the tumbling locks off his forehead, the officer replaced his muddy helmet and looked searchingly out into the night. He was just about to light another cigar when he suddenly felt a hand tugging at the hem of his cuff. Whipping round, he tried desperately to locate the handle of his revolver, before exhaling with relief and groaning inwardly as he beheld the smiling face of Coleman, looking simultaneously impassive and yet somehow knowing.

'Share my blanket, sir?' he whispered, so faintly that it was a moment before Bond was able to comprehend either the words or the nuance.

He glanced nervously around for a few seconds, before carefully removing his helmet and quietly subsiding amid the sackcloth and debris of mealie bags, oilskins, and sacking. Jack had dug himself in on a sort of bend in the barricade, apparently making full use of the concealment and proximity of a nearby supply tent.

'Can't you sleep?' Bond murmured. He was a little awkward at first and did not know exactly where to place himself, far less what to say or how to behave in this new and frightening situation. Yet still the smile radiated from the soft features of the young sapper's face, the creases around his eyes narrowing them to slits, and the blond fringe ashen in the ghostly moonlight.

'I hoped you'd come, sir,' he whispered tenderly, deliberately ignoring the question as the dazed officer slid a little further under the soft woollen blanket. 'I haven't slept in the tent with the others since you gave me this. I've been warm enough by myself.'

'Y-you shouldn't really be out here, you know,' Bond stammered clumsily. 'I mean, you don't want to be stuck out here if, well... anything... happened.' Then, even as he spoke, Bond found his hand reaching up from under the blanket.

Gently, the fingers of one hand caressed the boy's face, while the other found the nape of his neck, just below where the mop of thick hair had been cropped close to stubble.

Jack said nothing, merely smiled, closed his eyes, and allowed his hair to be stroked, played with, and smoothed back into place again until, eyes still closed, he leaned forward and pressed his nose even closer to that of his officer. Bond breathed a deep sigh as the soft pink lips parted in front of him and finally, letting his inhibitions go, he leaned forward and tenderly kissed them. For a second, Coleman's whole body seemed to go tense. Then, as they gradually warmed more and more to each other's responsive touches and deep breaths, he reached up with both hands and ran his fingers through Bond's glistening hair.

The atmosphere seemed static, heady with the tang of twilight, thick with the smell of wood smoke. Somewhere, here, or there, a spark leapt in the darkness from the glowing embers of a dying campfire. Sounds echoed, sensations heightened, and emotions seemed stronger than either one had known. All became dark, thick, and inky, but for the leaping red and orange, the golden glow from the crackling twigs, and the softly lit images of their flushed faces. A dusky, dull feeling of oppressive closeness began to fall heavily upon them, freezing out all other things and drawing them together in silence.

They could feel the coming of something almost supernatural, as finally the tensions between their sweat-tormented bodies tantalised their awareness to its furthest degree and finally drew them together as the electric vibration pressed home its offensive. A Zulu attack would pale in comparison to the anticipation, the tantalising thrill of that ultimate conjunction. When they came together, there was an air of the unstoppable, of final release from the turmoil of those emotional bonds that had held them apart for so unbearably long. Reaching out, clammy hands contorted, smoke pervading their very sensation, the two young soldiers finally found each other in the night.

Tenderly, carefully and with delectable tactility, they explored each other's equally well-proportioned, well-matched physiques. Madly, deftly, nearer and nearer they came.

With profuse sweat-flushed faces, caressing fingers delicately slipped along the strong, golden limbs, stroking cheeks with the backs of hands, tenderly drawing up and down the smooth contours of the other's muscular body, finally clasping buttocks, hands upon the smooth golden back. Firm yet tender soft, pink lips met the other; the perspiration trickled down chest, hair, legs and torsos, a rich amber light bathed their naked bodies and, eventually, the stars came out to shine. They didn't know what would happen come the morning. Neither did they know what either of them would do if they were discovered. All they knew was that this time was their time, and that finally each of them was at last where he was truly supposed to be.

Chapter Twenty-Eight

As the dawn began to creep slowly across the veldt, and the endless noises of insect life were gradually joined by the squawking of birds and the distant call of the hyena, Bond's eyes opened to find Jack crouched beside him, looking lovingly and sorrowfully down. Convinced that he had half imagined the happenings of the previous night, Bond reached up for further reassurance. Jack smiled, looked at his boots, looked back at Bond and then looked away again.

'Don't go now,' Bond whispered earnestly. 'Come here, let me hold you again.'

'Better not, sir,' Jack smiled sadly. 'Sarn't Fridays up already, wants us out digging again.'

'I'm the officer, I'll give the orders,' Bond muttered, aghast at what he thought the young lad had been about to say. 'Where is Friday now, anyway?'

Again, Jack shook his head and smiled. 'Best be off, sir. Don't want to get you into trouble. Mr Knight wants another latrine dug for the hospital tent just in case, sir.'

Before he could utter further protest, Bond found himself alone beneath the blanket, listening to the world waking up around him. It was only after about five minutes that he realised he had not had a wash in three days, nor had he changed his shirt, and the velvet on the collar of his grubby patrol jacket was utterly black from not having washed his oily hair.

When Bond found him, Gideon Knight was up, dressed and already in deep confabulation with Earnest Penfold about the structure and dimensions of the fortification. 'I don't like these sandbags, Earnest,' he was saying. 'They're far too high up off the ground, and they stand out like white pillows against the red colour of this blazed earth.'

'Surely you don't want the whole thing lowered further, Gideon? Why, that would take ages, and the men would have no cover whatsoever tonight.'

'No, perhaps you're right, after all,' Knight replied, rubbing his brow with his hand as he brooded over Penfold's sketch. 'Look, here's Albert. Perhaps we'd better ask his opinion.'

'About what?' Bond retorted, perhaps a little more irritably than usual, for he held his brother officers singularly responsible for his premature removal from bed, and all the depravations that came with it.

'What you think of our position,' Gideon began seriously.

'He's brooding again,' Penfold remarked, to provoke a debate.

'Oh, Gideon, there are only so many ways to dig the perfect trench,' Bond rejoined, acidity getting the better of tact at the prospect of digging yet more holes.

'It's all very well you two taking it all so lightly, but don't forget that the Zulu have rifles, with which, need I remind you, they are far from ineffective. If the trenches are all banked on one side, and nothing whatsoever on the other, we could well be cut to pieces by fire put down on us from that damnable mountain. For a post this size, there are no such things as flanks and a front. We come under threat from all sides.'

'Well, I think you're giving the Zulus too much credit, quite frankly,' Penfold replied with an uncharacteristic note of bile. 'Take my "earners". They were hopeless at loading and reloading. I'm almost glad they stayed behind now.'

'He's right, you know, Gid,' Bond told the officer soothingly. 'If they do come down on us, and God alone knows why they should, they'll do it the way they did last time: run in from three sides and dash themselves to pieces on volley fire or, if it came to it, bayonet points. I'd be more worried about the men having enough room to sleep in if I were you.'

'That's a point,' Penfold muttered reflectively. 'Where did you get to last night, Albert?'

'Oh, I must have dozed off in the laager somewhere,' Bond replied quickly, although he was sure that the colour of his skin was beginning to give away his guilty secret. Hurriedly, he changed the subject. 'Gideon, I've been thinking – the drift is an important position, in as much as it's the only place for several miles for any wheeled transport to cross in comparative safety, correct?'

'Quite correct, old man,' Knight affirmed with a nod.

'Well then, suppose those supply wagons left Oscaarsberg a little after we did. Wouldn't they be here in something like a couple of days?'

'Only if they've followed the right path,' Knight replied. 'And from what I could cop off old Flambard before the column moved, it looks as if McGonagle's got himself and his company well and truly adrift, so we shall just have to wait until supplies are sent as a matter of routine.'

'Well, we shan't run out of bullets,' Penfold quipped. 'But as to the food situation, I just don't want to imagine.'

It was true to say that the sudden and totally unexpected change in the number of supplies left for the defenders of the depot would, in a matter of days, begin to prove something of a headache for the officer in charge. This worried Lieutenant Knight to no small degree and, consequently, when people came to him with either request for something, or permission for something else, he was likely to be found in a negative frame of mind. The issue of their security worried him greatly, not least since the place seemed designed for a stealthy, light infantry foe like the Zulus to attack as they pleased. The nearby ground was strewn far and wide with large anthills and boulders, and the base of the nearby mountains was peppered with cracks and crevices wherein a sniper could happily take up his position unseen. Much of the riverbed on both sides of the drift was tangled and matted with a dense carpet of coarse thorn and bramble, and even though the post was some distance from the river itself, the near side of the bank was all dead ground. The banks themselves were heavily eroded from the heavy rainfall, and a donga tributary to the one in which Bond and his men had such a stiff fight ran along parallel to their outermost trench. Even so, the ground between them and the mountains spanned some thousand or so yards of open grassland and was largely exposed to view from both their own command position, and that of the lookout on the hill. 'I wish I knew what to do for the best, Sergeant,' he sighed wearily.

'Not my place to say, sir,' Friday opened, with characteristic reticence. 'Senior officer didn't ought to take no notice of nobody else, if sir will pardon my saying so.'

'No, no, you're quite right, Friday,' Knight replied. 'These are decisions that I must take, after all. I just hope it all lends itself better to practice than theory, that's all.' Knight himself had not had the best repose, either. He had lain awake half the night worrying about Flora, and the other half worrying about their exposed position in the geographic scheme of things.

In the small hours, it suddenly occurred to him that he was breaking one of the most obvious laws in the military book by sleeping out in the open. Fire from without their position would undoubtedly rip straight through the tents. What good were sentries and abatis if the officer commanding was shot in his bed?

Miserably and in frustration, he scrambled out from under his blanket and greatcoat, and quit his tent for the cover of Penfold's sandbag redoubt. It was a mean structure of about six-foot in height, and about five-foot wide. A bracket-shaped partition meant that, while the entrance to the redoubt was theoretically protected from enemy sniper fire, the space within its walls was further reduced, and thereby reduced the comfort of the occupants. The position of the fort and the nature of the African weather meant that the place was cold by night, swelteringly hot during the day, and damp all the time.

'Outside you burn, inside you boil,' Knight muttered miserably as he scribbled a few lines in his journal. 'At least the ants have room to move around in here.'

Chapter Twenty-Nine

While the first twenty-four hours of the sapper's stint in Fort Penfold had elapsed, Captain AW McGonagle's dangerously small column had begun to make its steady progress across country, and was now making straight for the river, and the site of the column's first confrontation.

In the time it had taken McGonagle, first to cross the river, and then to traverse the more minor drifts, rivers, dongas and watercourses that bisected their route, Commandant Flambard's search party had not even seen so much as the smoke from their fires.

'Confound the man!' Flambard had remarked to the officer in charge of the Lyndhurst Rifles, at about the same time as Colonel McEnry's battalion had just encountered the first reports of fire from the mountain. 'He's probably wandered so far off course that none of us shall ever see him again.'

'Not all bad then, Colonel,' Faunce-Whittington quipped uncharitably.

'What really grates with me is that we can't find the fellow,' Flambard had persisted, ignoring the barb. 'Good Lord, Faunce, you and I should know this country better than anyone in either army, and if we can't track down a company of Scottish Highlanders – pipers and all – we really ought not to be here to begin with.'

Flambard's assertions had, as it turned out, owed more to

the truth than any of them might well have imagined at the time.

McGonagle had, he claimed, as a result of his long time in India, developed an inexplicable mistrust of maps and mapmakers. He further claimed that he had never quite entirely forgiven the Royal Engineers for the last minute disappearance of the explosive charges required to blow the gates of Magdala in Abyssinia. The fact that he had neither been there, nor suffered any direct loss or consequence due to this error was scarcely worth remarking upon. Lieutenant Simonides, whatever he was, had learned the hard way that McGonagle was not be argued with.

'Cartographers are fools and maps are irrelevant,' the captain informed his men. 'If you can see the sky, you can find your way about... just like the Ancients! Ancient Pistol... "*Iago, my ancient...*"' quoted McGonagle, as they tramped and stomped across the open sun-blanched grassland of the river valley 'Lieutenant... Acolyte!' McGonagle muttered audibly, while Simonides boiled. 'Commissioned by virtue of the books you've read and the maps you've studied. So, schoolroom Second Lieutenant, you can take charge of the navigation!'

At this, Lieutenant Simonides merely glared and cursed below his breath. Something about Dogberry, Verges and one man riding behind the other sprang to mind. There was no point arguing with the old fool; that had been tried before. When he did, however, consult the maps and compasses, the subaltern discovered to his horror that they had, for the last three days, been going round in a forty-five-degree detour, and virtually circumnavigating the place where they needed to cross the river.

'We'll get there in time, don't you fret yourself,' McGonagle rebuffed him lightly. 'Company to a halt, Sarn't Andrews,' he instructed, raising his right hand, and indicating that the line was to make a stop in the shallow depression that they had just entered. 'There should be some fowl around and about the banks,' he remarked casually to Simonides. 'I'll see if I can bag us some supper, you miserable wee man, you.'

Simonides, for all his hostility and mean spirit, had to be pitied in his arranged marriage to McGonagle's company. Few warmed to Simonides and, although this was arguably not entirely his own fault, his resulting introspection and deep-seated mistrust of everyone around him was to be responsible in no small measure for his lack of popularity. Thin, bony, with the unfortunate gifts of a protruding forehead, an unattractively rectangular jaw, and a jutting chin, he was also disadvantaged by a toothy grin which, when manifested, gave the distinct impression of a debauchery, Simonides's "gifts" conspired with his temper to keep him alone. In fact, quite how he had survived school, officer training and regimental life as a subaltern might have been something of a mystery, had anyone cared sufficiently to reflect upon it.

Grimly, gloomily and with that same simmering bitterness that he had so often felt at home, Simonides listened numbly to the ramblings of McGonagle as they sat before the crackling fire. *How likely was it,* he wondered, *that someone such as me should spend so long struggling to escape one drunken, frustrated old captain in his father and almost immediately be lumbered with another? If you would only treat me with the respect I deserve as your only officer,* he thought bitterly, *I might almost be able to like you.*

'*In Africa there are no trees*,' McGonagle rambled. '*So, search I for the green of me...*'

'There's nae many in Egypt,' one soldier murmured. 'Ye can gie the cap'n that!'

'Nah, nair the Soodan,' observed another in response.

'Look over there!' Simonides hissed in impatience.

'What?' McGonagle demanded, peering through the gathering gloom of the evening at the faint outline of a small sapling set against the craggy backdrop of the riverbank.

For a second, the old officer looked on in frustrated bewilderment. Then, as he slowly took Simonides's point, his tangled black eyebrows began to curl in distaste. 'Pedant,' he grumbled in retaliation. The thing just didn't seem worth explaining. Even so, McGonagle was not one to remain silent for too long. 'Did they not teach you anything at that ridiculous academy?' he demanded.

'They certainly didn't teach poetry,' Simonides muttered subversively. 'Just the odd thing – tactics, fortification, philosophy... history, which fits one well for serving under you, I suppose.'

'I never went to school,' McGonagle resumed, sighing long and hard.

Several eyebrows were raised to Heaven, and the men began gradually to slip away under cover of the shadows in search of less tedious diversions.

'They never taught me a thing about poetry. Some are poetic, others are not!'

'Quite,' Simonides retorted.

McGonagle stiffened, and his subaltern realised that perhaps he had overstepped.

Up until that point, they had had an uneasy relationship, based on a grudging respect for one another's position and complete characteristic difference. McGonagle had initially not known enough about his new lieutenant to like or dislike him, and Simonides had naturally submitted to the authority and direct superiority of a captain over a subaltern. From then on, McGonagle's resolute dislike of Simonides was established, and their hitherto tenuous relationship as the only two commissioned officers in the tiny company simply dissolved into nothing.

'I have loved!' McGonagle lamented loudly, as drink assumed command of his oratory.

More men peeled off to find jobs to do, or to stomp off into the darkness for a smoke.

'All my life I have dedicated to the written word, the iambic pentameter, the rhyming couplet! All these years... given to a homage of digestion of language, prose!'

The audience dwindled. Still, the distilled, malted oration continued:

'The passion must be there! For passion it must be... Oh, how I have fought!'

'With the army,' Simonides remarked bitterly. He had also been drinking and was fairly convinced that anything he might say would just as likely be lost amid a fog of other things by the time the morning caught up with them. 'Senior officers, junior ones...'

'Just you listen, laddie!' McGonagle cried, changing direction as swiftly as an airborne bird in a gale. 'Thirty years I spent in India. I learned to live as they do; I wore a turban and lived as any high caste would be proud of. I knew my men, and for all your books and your learning, that is something you will never understand, my boy! The sepoy was a wolf in sheep's clothing, and they,' he gestured accusingly towards the sullen clumps of African troops dotted around the camp, 'will just as likely rise and kill the lot of us as the Pandies did. We do not share this country as we did India in my day – we invade it!'

'Modern opinion favours soldiers who know their own terrain,' Simonides muttered in response. He knew what to expect now that the subject of India was on the go, and there was nothing else to do but listen to it roll on and on until, with any luck, the old fool would pass out under the influence or simply fall asleep.

'The sepoy was an ally, a loyal solider!' McGonagle announced loudly. 'We gave him a rifle, and taught him our ways of discipline and fairness, and he was happy enough. Simple, obedient fellows they were... until we changed their rifles.'

Here we go, cartridges greased in pig fat again, Simonides mouthed. 'Go on!'

McGonagle carried on, unperturbed.

It is debatable, thought Simonides, *whether he really is so deaf that he can't hear anything said to him, or whether it's just because he doesn't want to listen*.

'You know what we did?' the captain continued. 'We ignored his religious sensibilities and gave him cartridges greased in pig's fat.'

'"And we sent him overseas",' quoted Simonides. 'Go on, McGonagle.'

'Until that time, and mark my words, laddie, I knew well enough,' he continued. 'The sepoy was a happy, obedient ally. He didn't lack for intelligence, but he was happy enough with his lot. He obeyed his orders and had pride. "*Not so happy, yet much happier*",' he quoted wistfully.

A consolatory hum of obliging assent stirred amid the remaining prostrate soldiers, probably in the hope that it might end sooner if they went along with it. Not so, it seemed, for McGonagle was just warming up.

'There is with the African solider,' he told them, 'no amiability, and no real willingness to work or aspiration to be a British solider. There exists within the African man a sullen, aggressive, and troublesome private. He has no concept of regimental pride, no achievement, and he cannot be relied upon above anything but the basic actions necessary to his own animal instinct of survival. He is not like the Indian sepoy, no!'

'I hope them lot don't speak English,' remarked one soldier to another, upon seeing the simmering expressions on the faces of their African comrades. They had not yet eaten, there were no provisions for their shelter within the encampment, and McGonagle had instructed that all but one in ten of their rifles were to be removed from them as soon as the column was halted. Nevertheless, the elderly captain continued undaunted:

'Those hands require toil to keep the minds focussed on duty. If left unemployed, or allowed to remain too long at leisure, he will simply become a mischief to himself and his masters. Complacency breeds contempt,' he added, as he felt his eyelids closing involuntarily, and a great yawn began to gather in his mouth. 'And mark my words, this will inevitably lead to insurrection!'

'Sounds like a Glaswegian private te me, nae mind an African!' remarked a sergeant.

'Do you think they'll have us ba night, Sarn't?' asked a nervous young soldier nearby.

'Unlikely, wee boy, but who can tell?' replied the sergeant. 'They've their own beliefs, own gods, own ways about them. I sure as hell know one thing, lad.'

'What's that, Sarn't?'

'That it's a toss-up between who kills the old man first: them there African allies o' ours over yonder, or wee Mr Simonides hi'self!'

Chapter Thirty

The following day saw no real change in life at Fort Penfold. The men were roused from bed at 4:30 a.m. by their NCOs and breakfasted before parade. That ritual was necessarily conducted daily, not just for the sake of discipline and keeping the men to a system of routine, but also as a safeguard. By keeping up with the garrison's immediate strength, their three officers were able to ascertain with a degree of immediacy how many, if any, had fallen sick during the night, if any were missing or generally, in the parlance of their naval brethren, "swinging the lead."

Bond, who had been up since daybreak and so had already eaten, wandered around the perimeter of the camp with his notebook and pencil, idly sketching things and keeping an eye on the movements of his troop. The air was still a little chilled by the mists of the early morning, but a dull closeness and humidity had begun to overcome the cold, damp sensation, and every so often a ray of penetrating sunlight would burst through the canopy of silver. At length, he came across Coleman. He was sitting down, cross-legged on the ground, still in his greatcoat and gobbling down his hot porridge indigestibly. Sensing a looming subaltern, the two sappers who had previously sat with Jack bade him farewell, saluted the officer and gradually filtered off on one spurious assignment or another. Looking meditatively at him for a moment, Bond gloomily lamented the fact that his labours the previous day had caused him to drop virtually to sleep on the spot that night and had consequently robbed him of a few hours under Coleman's blanket.

At this, Jack seemed to sense that his officer was reflecting upon him and looked shyly upwards. As their eyes met, Bond broke into a smile. Coleman returned a broad grin and looked up at his officer affectionately, but still carried on with his grub. There was something almost bizarrely endearing in the freedom with which the young sapper gazed so tentatively at him, while the spoon in his hand still shovelled away at an uncouth pace. Bond smiled again but said nothing.

All soldiers liked their food, and sappers were no exception. If not so much because they were often desperately hungry, but because it gave them something to do that was entirely their own. It kept them warm, gave them something to look forward to at least twice daily and, even though there was not much variety to be had – especially in the field – it occasionally turned out to be a pleasing distraction, and even a comfort. All this added something of a little colour to the drudgery of an otherwise toilsome and monotonous daily routine, and Bond as a young officer was by no means oblivious to the value of such an activity when boredom was almost as fierce an enemy as their still mysterious, even ethereal, foe.

He also knew how hard most of his sappers worked for the seemingly little food that went into them. By being with Jack, sometimes day and night, he had begun to gain a singular insight, quite peculiar to himself and utterly unprecedented for an officer, into the types of men who served under him in the troop. For once, and without the conformist conservatism of Sergeant Friday to dilute and interpret the other ranks' viewpoint, he was beginning to build up a picture straight, as it were, from the horses' mouth. Gradually, as this learning process continued, Bond began to hanker as much after understanding the needs, hopes and ambitions of his men as much as the tricks and dodges that might be practiced in the singular avoidance of the execution of his orders.

He began to understand for the first time why men were prepared to risk punishment by going behind the backs of their superiors to obtain those few small advantages that meant so much to their comfort and sustenance. At last, he thought he had begun to imagine what it was like to be the lowest of the low, deferring to everyone. To himself, the ordinary sapper was subordinate to a corporal, scarcely regarded and indistinguishable from the next man to virtually anyone of field rank. In fact, he was utterly reliant on the protection and solidarity of his mates.

For Coleman too, Bond came at last to realise that the position of being a new young recruit placed him so very low on the barrack room pecking order. Although he was well liked by all his contemporaries, many had to do without the protection and guidance of the old sweats, and the fraternity of his fellow recruits. *At least he hasn't suffered too much from being Friday's pet as well as mine*, Bond thought wryly, as he and Earnest Penfold watched the NCOs take a rollcall some twenty minutes later.

'It's funny,' he remarked to Penfold, 'but I never realised exactly why the rankers became soldiers before. Oh, I can see why the likes of you or I might take a commission, but appeal of enlisting never really explained itself.'

'Something to do, money and such like, I suppose,' Penfold replied. 'I can't say that it's ever been made apparent to me in the time I've been with the Corps.'

'You see, that's what I thought, to begin with at any rate,' Bond continued, clearly warming to his role as the voice of the unheard.

'Go on, then,' Penfold smiled with characteristic generosity. 'Enlighten me.'

'Well, many join to save themselves from poverty and such, it's true to say. But then again, a good few fellows do it because they want something more, to see something of the world and all that it has to offer. Adventure, promotion, and a chance to serve the Empire must be better than bashing out horseshoes for thruppence ha'penny a month.'

Penfold looked at Bond, quite seriously for a moment. There was a light in his blue eyes that had never quite shone there before, and the striking pose of the man in his blue patrol, with his bronze locks and his beard as he looked imperiously out across the veldt seemed most fitting. 'You really do care, don't you, Albert,' Penfold observed.

Bond thought for a moment, then he nodded.

'I can see what it is, too,' Penfold opined.

'Oh?' Bond replied cautiously.

'Yes, it's young Coleman. He's been good for you, Albert.'

'What?' Bond demanded, colouring in alarm. 'What on earth has Coleman got to do with this? Really, Earnest, you do have a grasshopper's mind, you know.'

'W-well, you do seem to have struck up a certain rapport with the boy,' Penfold stammered, somewhat taken aback by the sudden violence of Bond's swing.

'Yes, well... I suppose I have,' Bond murmured awkwardly. *That was tactless*, he thought. *The chap's only saying what's true, after all.*

'I mean, I know there's the rank issue,' poor Penfold continued nervously. If there was one thing a sapper officer knew how to do when down a hole, it was to dig it even deeper. 'But types like you and me really ought to know something of the men we command. After all, it's what sets us apart as leaders.'

'I quite agree,' Bond assented in embarrassment. 'Earnest, don't take my overreaction to heart, old man, it's the heat, you know?'

Penfold nodded, but his attention was necessarily distracted elsewhere.

Sergeant Friday was apparently engaged in issuing orders, and the men were running around in hasty obedience, snatching up picks, shovels, spades, and tools.

'Another attack of a certain subaltern's paranoia?' Penfold suggested wearily.

'Looks like it, Earnest,' Bond responded. 'Come on, then,' he added gloomily as he set about removing his jacket, shoulder strap and accoutrements. 'If you can't work with that arm, you can at least tell your lads to keep mine company in the digging.'

At first, Gideon Knight had been very much on a textbook defensive, throwing out piquets on the top of nearby hills, knolls, and kopjes. Conscious that this was his first and, if all fell horribly flat, potentially his last independent command, the beleaguered senior lieutenant took no precaution too lightly.

Bond and his sappers spent the day busily engaged upon marking out and clearing the thorn bush and scrub from around the edges of the old traders' track, with the intention of excavating a proper supply route back to the drift. The work was toilsome, the weather hot and barbarous by day, and the atmosphere humid, still, and oppressive as evening wore on. Once the work had been completed to a standard Lieutenant Knight deemed satisfactory, neither Bond nor his men were fit to undertake anything but a sombre meal, followed by immediate repose.

By the time the sun went down, the gallant officer was utterly exhausted. His arms ached, his eyelids were heavy, and his muscle strength had turned completely to water. He was lethargic, with that feeling of after-dinner drowsiness so peculiar to a heavy dessert and a lot of wine. On top of that, Bond's earlier conversation with Lieutenant Penfold had left him anything less than comfortable with his position. Indeed, he seemed to have spent half the day and expended much of his energy in studiously avoiding those little, endearing looks from young Coleman which had, up until then, been the only thing to get him through the long day. This was undoubtedly painful to both parties; the feeling of rejection on the one had married so tragically with the fact that, more so than anything else, all he wanted to do was gather the brave lad in his arms and soothe away the pain of their weary labour. All those things ran through the subaltern's mind as he chewed without pleasure on a piece of tough meat, and watched the glow of the campfire as it projected orange flames across the tents of the wagons and played with mischievous impunity against the backdrop of the lengthening day.

The light that it gave was dim, low, and moody, and somewhere far off in the darkening sky, the vaguest hint of a silver twinkle could be seen amid the hazy shades of lilac and grey. Just as he began to feel lonely, a familiar voice coughed pointedly from somewhere up above him.

'Mr Knight sends his regards, sir.'

'Oh, hello, Sergeant Friday. I didn't realise you were there,' Bond sighed.

Friday reached out, proffering a mug of something or other. 'Don't hold with liquor, as you well know, sir,' the sergeant began awkwardly. 'But Mr Knight thinks it will do you some good, Mr Albert, sir.' Again, he pressed the libation on the officer, and Bond reluctantly accepted it after a pause of some several seconds.

'What is it? Brandy?'

'Rum, sir,' Friday replied hastily, turning a little red as he spoke. 'Surgeon's surplus.'

'Oh well, if the surgeons are having to make do with rum, I suppose I shall just have to do so also. Thank you,' Bond answered grudgingly. 'Was there anything else, Sergeant?'

'No, sir,' the NCO replied but seemed to be making no effort to go.

'I wonder where the column is now,' Bond sighed, resolving to make some use of his audience if he wasn't to be left voluntarily to his own devices.

Friday looked blank.

'I suppose Major Westgate will see some action,' the officer continued, oblivious to the darkness that was beginning to envelop their position. 'I should think that's the last we are to see of this war,' he added, this time looking searchingly up at the bald, impassive sergeant in the hope of securing some sort of response.

'Permission to dismiss, sir,' Friday requested at last.

'You for bed?' Bond enquired.

Friday nodded.

'Well, sleep soundly, Sergeant. Good night.'

'Good night, Mr Albert,' Friday replied, but his was not the voice that the officer was hearing. Suddenly, it did feel decidedly lonely out there in the dark.

Bond couldn't possibly go back to the tent. The rum was making him feel almost giddy after so long without alcohol, and he knew there was the danger that all men were exposed to if they talked in their sleep. With a sigh of gloom and depravation, Bond lay his head on a mealie sack, did his best to snuggle down amid his greatcoat, two blankets and a tarpaulin, and made the best of his rough accommodation.

The sun was beginning to set below the distant horizon and stood out like a big red ball of fire against the broken and craggy black lines of the mountains. The mist was beginning to gather amid the distant slopes, and somewhere within the confines of the defensive position a cricket chirped rhythmically, as it tortured his already worried mind with yet more guilt and uncertainty for what the future held in store.

Bitterly, desperately, hopelessly, he caressed the hessian between thumb and forefinger, longing for sleep to come and take him away from the rum-induced state of terminal melancholia. There, in that lonely state of darkness, cold and alone with nothing and nobody to lean on, he knew at last what he really wanted: he wanted someone to hold on to, someone to give him back all the warmth and love that he himself could give, right then, at that moment, when he was no longer up to the challenge of pretending, of fighting back the desire within him, and it simply wasn't there. Burning, aching, with more fire in his belly from the drink than any pointed assegai, the tears of frustration and desolation finally broke forth and ran down his cheeks. He sobbed, silently, so as not to allow any other to hear but the one for whom he knew himself to be crying. He did his best to ignore the gathering cloud of midges above and tried to shut out the increasing din of the African wildlife as it gradually awoke outside. Angry, sullen, and bitterly resentful, with feelings of utter worthlessness and doom crowding in upon his troubled mind and his thumping heart, Bond kicked out his legs under the protective cover of his greatcoat and did his best to wriggle into a more comfortable position.

He seemed to be sleeping and waking fitfully, and always when he woke the stars seemed to be getting brighter and brighter. Aching inwardly, partly from the drink and partly from an agony of longing for those beloved blue eyes to look tenderly into his once more, he groaned miserably. A log on the nearby fire popped, the fire gutted and somewhere a sentry stopped to strike a match on the other side of the sandbag rampart.

Throwing open his eyes and rolling from his side to lay flat on his back, Bond drew a deep, helpless, plaintive sigh and closed his eyes in the hope of sleep.

When he dreamed, it was of London. A fog of rain hung over the dark, gloomy streets, freezing cold and soaking wet without, as he strode manfully down Bond Street to his club. Then, even as he dreamed of knocking at the door and waiting on the steward to be admitted, the scene changed to the grimy brickwork and blackened railings of the wintry Medway town, and he was plodding half-shod through freezing cold water, just like Jack. Then, as he moaned and groaned in his sleep for someone to bring back his shoes, the scene suddenly changed to that of the panoramic African veldt, with herds of springbok and the hot, sunlit grasses of the grazing land, dotted here and there with a tree or bush. The whole of the land seemed rich, bright colourful and animated, hotter than he could ever have imagined and free as the breeze on which the sounds of running water carried on his ears. Once more the spectacle was altered to one of wet, dirty stonework and the running slime of the back of the washhouse in Brompton Barracks. Rancid potato peel that clogged the drains; the rank smell of damp and decomposition, intermingled with the smell of the stables and the stench of leather and polish. Soot and grime smeared the window opposite his tiny cramped little office, while the black steps and low stone arches seemed to lead him to a basement world of darkness and discomfort, a nightmarish cell of some long-forgotten town prison.

He dreamed too of the heavily decorated drawing room of his father's house in Leeds: the dark purple velvet that covered the long dusty sideboard, the tarnished silver and brassware, too numerous to polish and to maintain after the death of his mother and the dismissal of servants. He dreamed too of her proud, glossy green houseplants and how they died when she fell ill, the gradual destruction and profusion of brown specks on their leaves so aptly reflecting her own physical decline. The home that had once seemed so big and warm and welcoming to him as a boy had now turned into a grim, gothic nightmare. The vision became oppressive, with no light or life, hidden behind layers of blinds, drapes and calico, cut off from the world in a gas-lit gloom of discolouration and decay, as lost to him as a home as the loving family who had once made it so. A cloud began to sweep across the sky of his imagination and a crack of thunder shook the tearless crystal of the great chandeliers so caked in dust and cobwebs that they no longer sparkled, and the big old oil paintings in their huge gold frames. What would his mother have said if she had left her room and walked around that house for one last time?

Suddenly, with as loud a gasp as a diver coming up for air, he awoke. The iron-railed cellar steps, the coal scuttles, dust, and smoke of the England of his dreams suddenly morphed into the dew-laden, misty valley of the Zulu river, and he knew at once from the aching in his bones that he had lain all night in the open.

With yet another gasp, this time of abject agony, Bond realised that he had spent the whole night with his head on his elbow. Once the feeling had returned, the pain of the pins and needles was unimaginable, and he felt so stiff that he was sure his jaw would drop off all together if he opened it to yawn. With a groan, a moan and a slight shift to the right, Bond's sore and tired eyes gradually began to focus on something before them. A quantity of steam seemed to be rising from something or other, perhaps a bowl or receptacle before him, and he could tell from the smell of coffee that the bearer be of a benign spirit.

For a moment, Coleman looked at his officer, his head resting on a mealie sack and his face all creased like a ball of newspaper. His hair hung in glossy bronze tendrils on either side of his screwed-up features, and his sore blue eyes blinked and struggled to focus as he gently knelt beside the crumpled mass of coat and blanket, proffering the beverage like the elixir of some steamy miracle. Bond's face bore a placid, docile expression, and every so often he would sniff, or swallow hard like one still deep in slumber. Coleman's initial inner urge was to kiss him and wake him up, but propriety dictated that he remain in character, even with one to whom he was so close, lest eyes be upon them. Even so, the mere thought of it made him smile mischievously.

As the sun began to rise and the light began to filter through in places, Bond properly awoke to see before him the face that had so preoccupied him the whole night through. Breathing a sigh of blissful contentment, and yet without allowing as much as a word to pass his lips, he reached out and gratefully accepted the mug.

'Have you had anything?' he asked, when at last the steaming libation had lifted his spirits sufficiently to speak.

Jack, still smiling, merely shook his head. Bond took another sip and held out the mug by way of invitation. Instinctively, he moved to wipe the rim with his sleeve, but Jack, anticipating the move, simply shook his head and took the cup from him and, with defined slowness and deliberate action, closed his mouth around the rim and drank from the same spot.

'I dreamed last night,' Bond began slowly.

'I know that,' Coleman smiled, interrupting the officer's speech with a look of such tender adoration that Bond felt his heart come into his mouth.

'How... long were you there?' he asked in slow surprise.

'Since I saw you were fitful,' Jack replied truthfully. 'I saw you were fretting about something, so I came over and sat with you. Sometimes,' he added in a lower tone, 'when you were really bad, and grasping about,' he gestured with his own hands as he spoke, 'I held your hand for you, and you seemed to settle.'

'No one—'

'Saw me? No, sir, I was ever so careful,' he smiled.

'You are a sweet boy,' Bond sighed in wonderment, but before he was able to qualify the sentiment with any physical manifestation, the deafening sound of reveille sounded across the open landscape, and they knew the camp to be stirring.

Epilogue

Lieutenant Penfold was not in good spirits. He hadn't slept well, his arm was hurting, Lieutenant Bond was nowhere to be seen and Lieutenant Knight seemed to be badgering him doubly with tasks, chores, and fatigues, not seeming to care overmuch that Penfold was bearing the burdens of two officers.

To crown it, he had been further exasperated by overhearing a conversation between some younger sappers, lollygagging and expatiating upon Bond's patronage of Coleman.

Penfold himself was benignly envious of the loyalty between his brother officer and able young batman, and not a little covetous of enjoying such a relationship of his own, if one such might be procured. For all too long he had endured his family's conceit over his marriage and their pretentions over Henrietta's kinsfolk falling beneath them in the lower draws of the middle-class chest.

Of course, he understood the constraints of status, especially in the army, and after all there could be no question of Bond and Coleman being friends in the ordinary sense, that much was a given fact.

Yet the idea that a young and relatively junior officer such as himself, and not a lot better off by Penfold's reckoning, might enjoy the manly and sacred confidence of a loyal manservant, amplified by service in a theatre of war and as master and man, felt almost reassuring to think of.

He had given short shrift to the sappers in question and had betaken himself for a walk along the outer defences to check the abattis and clear his mind, when he suddenly spotted movement outside the camp confines.

'What the blazes?' he remarked to himself, wresting his field glasses from their velvet lined lodgings in the leather case suspended between his slung shoulder and his right hip. 'What on earth do you think you're about then, my man? By damn, if that dark blue coat doesn't look to me like an officer...'

Out in the veldt, the lost supply company rested uneasily under the command of a slumbering Captain McGonagle. Periodic inspections of the sentries were, naturally, required and, as the only conscious, sober officer, the task befell Lieutenant Simonides.

He carried out his duties in cold silence, unless there was something to be said by way of critique. His introspection bred ill will. The skeletal pallor of their English officer's face appearing out of the gloom, clad as Simonides was in dark navy and black braid, did little to enhance the Highlanders feelings for a man who was, after all, the only buffer between themselves and their erratic elderly commander's whims and fancies. Inconsistent he may have been, senile even, some said. Yet McGonagle was their captain, and a Scot to boot, not some young sassenach from an English regiment on sabbatical.

Thus Simonides avoided intercourse altogether, walking the extremities of the camp like some sinister, monastic wraith amid the cloisters of the tented wagons, floating out of the dark and surprising the sentries on their beats like an assassin, risking getting shot in the process.

He watched the moon wax, then wain as the clouds parted and the stars twinkled, thinking back to the early days with McGonagle. He had appeared to Simonides as the paternal substitute he had been lacking since childhood, after he had robbed his father of his mother during childbirth, and thereafter further disappointed the drunken Captain Simonides senior by simply being himself.

Yet the moments of commonality had grown fewer between the two of them, especially since the march into Zululand, and the presumed cohesion engendered by being the only two officers in a small unit on the front line, far from bonding them in adversity, seemed to have stripped McGonagle of any remaining cordiality, especially, it seemed, toward Simonides.

One night on the border, some time prior, when McGonagle's poetry readings had emptied the officers' mess of all but himself and Simonides, and when both were well into their cups, the lieutenant had gone so far as to confide the tragedy of his bereavements to his captain. Whether to elicit sympathy, empathy or even because of some deep-seated instinct about McGonagle's own past, Simonides might well have been too drunk to articulate.

As it was, McGonagle had fallen uncharacteristically quiet, poured another drink and remarked 'our private griefs are our own affair, laddie, and are best not brought along on campaign,' before quitting the mess and leaving Simonides alone, rebuffed, and sullen.

From there on out, McGonagle seemed only to tolerate the input of his sergeants, to take council with no one save the bottom of a hipflask, the pages of a book or the blank leaves of his appalling poetry journals. It almost seemed to Simonides that McGonagle resented him, somehow, for being the only other officer, thereby usurping his own tenuous authority and credibility, for all that commodity that remained.

Stalking across the encampment through the thick blanket of morning mist, he paused only to bark orders at Sergeant Andrews to make ready the camp and stand fast until he returned, or until Captain McGonagle had emerged from his intoxicated slumbers.

'Assuming, of course, that he hasn't died overnight,' he caught himself adding, as he stomped back towards the kraal, wherein one of the African troopers had been told to saddle his horse.

The habitual lumbering slowness of the column's progress meant that the occasional opportunity to ride at a trot or even a gallop, when presented, was not to be missed.

With the sun rising, mist lifting and the wind in his face, Simonides spurred his dark horse and scattered the damp red sods and tufts of yellowing ochre grass in his wake, and he thundered across the open veldt.

Cresting a ridge and cutting along the escarpment in the direction of the river valley, he suddenly became dimly aware of a wispy veil or two of bluey grey woodsmoke, rising in columns above the dissipating blanket of damp laden whiteness below.

Reaching down, his black gloved hand snapped open the fastening on his binocular case and withdrew his field glasses, a surreptitious keepsake of a long-lost friend at the Royal Military College.

In the distance, he was just able to discern the long, low cantonments of an earthwork, the russet brown earth topped off with buff-coloured sandbags and tea-coloured box barricades. Lower down he observed the dark, cavernous sockets of the loopholes and, in the foreground, picked out against the emerging olive of the grassland, the wooden abattis and white painted raised markers of Fort Penfold.

I must have ridden out further than I anticipated, he thought.

Scanning the defences as the sun burnt through the canopy and the image clarified, he could see last night's grey coated sentries rotating with their red coated reliefs, the glimmer and glint of metal and the billowing, sail like pinnacles of the bell tents and wagon canvass within the camp itself.

Curious, and oddly comforted by the sight of a model, cohesive and, from that distance at least, professionally functioning garrison, he began to search for sight of an officer.

Up and down the ramparts his penetrating gaze travelled, yet no one of rank could he discern, beyond the suggestive white blazes of some junior NCOs stripes on the red sleeves above the yellow worsted and blue serge of the cuffs.

All abed still, I suppose. Amateurs all, these sappers. No wonder McGonagle calls them navies commanded by civil engineers and led by clerks of works— his internal condemnation halted.

'What do we have here, then...?'

He shifted the scope of his lens view to stray beyond the camp confines. His eye had fallen on an area of rising ground, some distance from the camp and within the range of their fire, yet beyond some smaller streams and rivulets past the outer perimeter. While the top of the escarpment fell almost level, at a distance, with the top of the earthworks yet below the upper stories of sandbag and biscuit box defences, the farther side dropped away into effective dead ground beyond the sight and scope of the defender's fire.

Someone must have overlooked the blind spot, Simonides remarked smugly to himself, *silly little sappers in their mud huts, all the while pretending to be soldiers!*

Yet as he ruminated on this apparent oversight by the garrison's architect, and doubtless what pleasure he might derive from pointing this out to whoever was their senior officer, a trace of movement in the dead ground arrested his attention.

Two figures, one in red with blond hair and one in a dark uniform, possibly navy, with darker hair, appeared to be creeping along the leeward side, almost as if they were seeking to invest the camp... or evade the gaze of the sentries.

Eyes narrowing, Simonides adjusted the scope of his glasses and squinted, hard.

The two soldiers, for such they clearly were, appeared to be moving in such close formation as to almost be... *no... yes! Surely, holding hands together?* The harder he looked, the less he was able to doubt it. Indeed, the taller one in the darker uniform was unmistakably leading by the hand the shorter, blond haired one in the red tunic. For a moment or two he fell to contemplating whether some wily officer had somehow managed to smuggle a trader's daughter or settler girl away on campaign. Certainly, the blond one was pretty enough, though the hair was short and the back broad. He had seen similar antics at the academy, and even more frequently at the barracks in England for that matter, as men of all ranks had tried to smuggle in females in defiance of form and protocol.

Yet here were two male soldiers, that much could not be mistaken, one leading the other by the hand as though they were trying to walk in the dark.

Puzzling, musing, he suddenly became aware of a slight coolness pervading the breeze and noted to his irritation that a bank of cloud had begun to form, darkening the sky, and tossing ripples across the grasses as if in prelude to a storm.

Dismounting, he moved forward a few paces and even mounted an anthill for a better look at the anomalous pair, determined to establish who they were and, even more significantly, what they were doing out there, together, apparently surreptitiously.

Just a few feet away from Simonides' anthill dais, a young, muscular Zulu scout of some twenty summers crouched impatiently, assegai in hand. Flat on the grass beside him lay his shield and throwing darts, and slung across his broad, glistening back was an antiquated but relatively well-maintained, rifled musket, powder horn and a bag of round lead balls.

However, even as his dark eyes darted avariciously between the horse and the thin, pale faced British induna, a steadying hand was placed over his, and a bearded warrior shook his ringed head, gesturing for the young scout to withdraw and not to engage. Reluctantly, sullenly, the younger Zulu accepted his orders and relinquished his prizes, retiring slowly, quietly, but by no means finally...

Oblivious of the proximity of his peril, Simonides remounted his horse for a return to McGonagle's column.

If the old buffer was up and grumbled about his absence, he might triumphantly announce that he, Simonides, had successfully located the route to Fort Penfold. Then again, such disclosure might just provoke the belligerent, contrary old buzzard into turning about and driving the column in the wrong direction out of spite. Yet again he would just have to keep his powder dry and lead from beneath.

Something told Simonides that, whatever the outcome, McGonagle's actions or inactions would cast an unavoidable shadow over his own career and that, whatever was to come, he was entwined with the old man, whose fortunes were now his own. Yet something new and unexpected had piqued his interest within Fort Penfold and, for a strike of fortune, might afford him some ascendancy over those smug, supercilious sappers for whom he had developed a distinct dislike.

Glossary of Military Ranks

Below are most of the ranks referenced in this story in ascending order, starting with the most junior (not exhaustive).

Enlisted or "other" ranks

ordinary soldiers, usually (but not always) from less advantaged social backgrounds.

Private: an ordinary enlisted soldier of any colour, usually infantry

Trooper: as above, though usually part of a mounted unit

Piper/Drummer: an army musician of enlisted rank

Gunner: an enlisted man in the Royal Artillery, a specialist

Sapper: an enlisted man in the Royal Engineers, from a labourer to a specialist such as a blacksmith, carpenter, wheelwright, and many other trades and professions besides

Non-Commissioned Officers (NCOs)

ordinary soldiers who had served longer and attained supervisory rank through experience, vocational training, and education.

Lance Corporal/Second Corporal/Lance Bombardier: the most junior enlisted Non-Comissioned Officer or NCO, denoted by one white stripe or chevron on the upper arm

Corporal/Bombardier: a more senior enlisted, junior NCO denoted by two stripes

Lance Sergeant: an enlisted, more senior NCO denoted by three white stripes

Sergeant: A senior enlisted NCO denoted by three yellow or gold stripes

Quartermaster Sergeant/Sergeant-Major: a senior enlisted man above NCO but below commissioned officer rank. Usually long serving and highly respected. A warrant officer, with rank denoted either by four gold chevrons worn on the lower forearm or by the wearing of an officer's undress uniform

Officers

awarded a "Queen's Commission" based on education, examination and often social status, these men have entered the army young and automatically hold seniority over even the long serving enlisted men of the other ranks. Many officers serving before the 1870s purchased their commissions and even their subsequent promotions before the practice was abolished. In this story the younger, more junior officers are educated, qualified men. However, some of the older, more senior officers above them would have obtained their ranks under the old purchase system.

Second-Lieutenant: a junior commissioned officer, a subaltern, also known as an ensign (infantry) or cornet (cavalry) at different times during the same era. Denoted by one pip on dress uniform collar only

Lieutenant: a junior commissioned officer, also a subaltern, commanding a platoon, troop and in some cases even a company, subject to seniority, establishment, or assignment. Sapper officers were commissioned directly to a first or full lieutenancy due to their extended military studies. Denoted by a crown on dress uniform collar only

Captain: a commissioned officer senior to a subaltern, often commanding a company. Denoted by a crown and star on dress uniform only

Major: a commissioned officer of seniority often commanding a company/above. Field officers wear their rank on both dress and undress uniforms, in this case a silver or gold pip on the collar.

Lieutenant-Colonel: a senior field officer commanding a battalion or equivalent. Denoted by a crown on both dress and undress uniforms, also worn on the collar.

Colonel/Commandant: a senior field officer commanding a regiment or a unit such as an invading column, as in this story. A colonel was denoted by a crown and pip on the collar, whereas a commandant may have worn different insignia, subject to substantive rank.

About the Author

Having spent many years in uniform, both military and civil, DJG Palmer now divides his time between writing and the heritage and charitable sectors, working in governance and supporting both homelessness and LGBTQ+ veterans' causes. His pronouns are "he/him".

Acknowledgements

When I began Babanango in the dying days of winter 1999, I could never have imagined that an uneducated, unworldly, untrained rookie with nothing more than the notion to tell a story could have ended up finding so much credible help from so many distinguished people and institutions.

On historical and military research, I must thank David Bryant, the Assistant Curator of the Royal Engineers Museum in Medway back in 1999, firstly for taking me seriously, subsequently for all the other information he took the time, trouble, and patience to provide to an absolute nobody. The late Colonel H.B.H. 'Blick' Waring, OBE, of the Queens' Own Royal West Kent Regiment Museum, Maidstone, must be similarly credited for his help back in 2000... (and I'm sorry Sir, it turns out that you were right about the blue cuff/collar velvet!). The curatorial and administrative staff of the former Buffs Museum, back then housed within the Beany Institute in Canterbury, for allowing me access to the secondary source material and the diaries of Eshowe, which provided invaluable insight into the rain-soaked encampments of Zululand, year 2000. To John Iverson of Dover Museum and the (then) Old Town Gaol in Dover, 2000, thanks, and to M.I. Moad and the staff at the Guildhall Museum, Rochester, and to dear, dear departed and still loved Captain Alan Florence, BA, for that copy of the folio society's edition of William Howard

Russell's journals and for the shotgun intel, points on social history and countless other gems of wisdom up to and beyond completion of this tale. Thanks also to Anne Man-Cheung for recommending the resources of the Centre for Chinese and African Studies.

Literary acknowledgements 1999-2001 include (not exhaustively, nor with any pretence at chronology) *The Defence of Duffer's Drift* by Major-General Sir Earnest Swinton K.B.E C.B., D.S.O. (1948 ed); *Weapons and Equipment of the Victorian Solider* by Donald Featherstone (1978); *Red Earth, The Royal Engineers and the Zulu War 1879* courtesy of the RE Museum (1999); *Diaries of William Howard Russell* (1995 edition); *Heroes for Victoria* by John Walton and John Duncan (1991); *Brave Men's Blood* (1990) and *Zulu* (1994) by the revered authority Ian Knight FRGS.; *A Widow Making War, The Life and Death of a British Officer in Zululand, the diaries of Captain W.R.C. Wynne RE, edited by Howard Whitehouse* (1995); *Victorian Imperialism* by C.C Eldridge (1978); *The Victorian Town Child* by Pamela Horn (1997) and the journals and periodicals of the Anglo-Zulu War Historical Society with their various scholarly articles, records and expert contributions, all of which helped to build whatever realism might be found amid the fiction, particularly Lieutenant Colonel Alan Spicer R.A.M.C and his publications on the writings of Surgeon Blair Brown FRCS, a noted military medical practitioner of the Anglo-Zulu War.

On the significant battles of the trilogy, I have of course drawn from real life contacts in Zululand such as Captain Moriarty's defeat by the Zulus at Ntombe River and, naturally, the well-trodden battlefield of Isandlwana. I would challenge anyone to write a credible fiction based on fact without recourse to these events and representations of the tactics and mistakes which led to their outcomes. The admittedly triumphal defence of Rorke's Drift and association with the celebratory jingoism of the feature film *ZULU*, I have sought to avoid at all costs, both in parody and in testament. I make no apology for that. In creating my characters, I have sought to portray plausible Victorian soldiers who also evoke some sense of empathy and relatability to a modern readership averse to justifications of imperialism, racism, and homophobia. For any among my readership who do not reject such prejudices, please return this book, and request a refund with my grateful thanks for doing so. If you believe in white supremacy, colonisation, glorified militarism, or heteronormative purity of any kind, I don't want your money. Please spend as much time as you can indoors and offline.

Personal acknowledgements are due to my aunt, Irene, who always believed in me and in the book, to my late parents, and to my darling husband, who has lived through every second of every stage of the process, from vacillation to publication, during the last nineteen years and the next. To Vicky and her amazing, expert team at Cranthorpe Millner for recognising something in this offering, and for helping me to subdivide my epic tome into a trilogy, while apologies are due to the editors for my reactionary, drill sergeant rollockings on each occasion they sought to temper army lingo in favour of marketable romanticism, for their patient revisions, recommendations and good humour when mine has been bad.

Lastly, to one special pair of blue eyes, to the person to whom they belonged, and for everything you never knew you did for me thirty-something years ago. Thank you.

DJG Palmer, 'Englewood', 2024